VICKI LEWIS THOMPSON'S NERD BOOKS ARE:

"Sexually charged...
funny!"
—*Publishers Weekly*

"Laugh-out-loud...
exceptional
characters and lots
of racy dialogue."
—*Romance Reviews Today*

More . . .

THE NERD WHO LOVED ME

"A winner . . . Thompson has written a laugh-out-loud, sexy romp that will capture readers from page one."
—*The Best Reviews*

"This extremely sexy and humorous book is over the top . . . her characters are so visual with their sparkling dialogue . . . another bright, shining star for Vicki Lewis Thompson." —*Rendezvous*

"Smart, spunky, and delightfully over the top, Thompson's newest Nerd romance possesses all the sparkle and vibrancy of a Vegas show, and it's just as sexy." —*Publishers Weekly*

NERD IN SHINING ARMOR

"A sharp, sassy, sexy read. Stranded on a desert island? I hope you've got this book in your beach bag."
—*Jayne Ann Krentz*

"Ms. Thompson continues to set the romance world on fire and keep it burning." —*WritersUnlimited.com*

Also by Vicki Lewis Thompson

Talk
Nerdy
to Me

Vicki Lewis Thompson

St. Martin's Paperbacks

To the real Eve,
who happens to be my
extremely glamorous, black office cat;

and to the real David and Jill Henkel,
who happen to be married and living happily ever after.

Acknowledgments

Many thanks to my engineering persona consultants. What would I have done without you? Kudos to Patty Anderson, Barb Betke, Lynn Bielin, Benjamin Foresta, Nicole Hulst, Ericka and Don Poletti, Julie Wang, and Gina Watson-Haley for sending me advice, jokes, and encouragement on the subject of engineering nerds. If I screwed this up, it's my fault, not yours!

And as always, I'm grateful for the unwavering support of my editor, Jennifer Enderlin, and all the folks at St. Martin's Press; my agent, Maureen Walters; my husband Larry; and my daughter and assistant, Audrey Sharpe.

Chapter One

The explosion caught Charlie by surprise. People didn't usually blow things up in Middlesex, Connecticut, especially at four in the afternoon. But as Charlie rode his Harley down Elm Street, something exploded behind the metal door of an ordinary two-car garage.

The door was still rattling as he made a U-turn and swerved his bike into the drive, skidding on layers of snow and ice. He damned near hit the Civic Hybrid parked there.

Leaping from his bike, he ran toward the garage. "Don't panic! I'm here!" He banged on the door. "Can you hear me? Are you okay?"

"Yes!" The voice was muffled and female. And she was coughing.

"I'm calling 911!" He reached for the cell phone clipped to his jeans pocket.

"No! Don't do that!" More coughing.

He paused, his finger over the send button. "Why not?"

"Because I'm fine!"

Charlie needed more information. There had been an explosion, for God's sake. And there was this funny smell seeping out of the cracks around the garage door molding. "Can you open the door? You could be in shock or something."

"Honestly." She coughed again. "I'm okay."

"Are you sure?" Charlie tried to picture himself climbing back on his bike and riding away without knowing what had caused the explosion and whether the woman in the garage was as fine as she claimed. Nope, couldn't do it. "Open the door. I need to know you're okay."

After a moment of silence, the door started up. Then it quickly stopped, leaving a gap of six inches. The funny smell grew stronger.

"See there?" Charlie breathed in the fumes and the back of his throat tickled. He cleared his throat. "Now your door's jammed."

"No, it's . . . uh, yeah! It must be jammed! But I'm fine, really." She coughed twice. "Here's my hand, in one piece."

Charlie stared at the hand she stuck through the six-inch opening. He thought of Thing from *The Addams Family,* except her hand was a lot prettier than Thing. She was wearing a pink sweater with the cuff turned back over a very delicate wrist.

She wiggled her fingers. "See? Everything works." Her nails looked manicured, although she wasn't wearing polish. No rings, either. She'd have to be lying on her back on the garage floor in order to stick her hand out like that. Maybe she'd landed on the floor after the explosion.

But that made no sense, because she'd just activated the garage door opener. Sure, she could have been holding the opener at the time of the blast, but that was highly improbable, which meant she was lying there specifically to stick her hand out and convince him she wasn't maimed. She was hiding something in that garage.

Just his luck, that kind of behavior intrigued him. Not too many women he knew caused explosions and then tried to pretend nothing had happened. None, in fact. He dropped to one knee and took off his helmet so he could peek under the door, but the warm air coming out made his glasses fog so he couldn't see much of anything. "What's that smell?" Now he'd started coughing, too.

She pulled her hand back inside. "I'm . . . um . . . making something."

"Moonshine?" Charlie had never smelled moonshine, but he'd tasted his share of cheap whiskey in his under-grad days. This garage had distillery written all over it, not that he cared, philosophically speaking. He was just damned curious.

Her laughter was interspersed with more coughing. "Are you a revenuer?"

"No, I'm an engineer." His knee was getting cold where it rested on the icy cement. His leather chaps helped, but he decided to shift to the other knee to balance out the chill factor.

"An engineer? The choo-choo kind or the brainy kind?"

"The electrical kind." He tried not to breathe the fumes. "I work at Middlesex Light and Power." At least for now. Before the end of the month he'd have his new position nailed down at Hoover Dam. At that point the ML & P would have to survive without him.

"Interesting." Her coughing fit seemed to have ended. "Are you out reading meters?"

"No. I have a desk job." He shifted knees again.

"Then why aren't you there? At your desk?"

"In winter I come in an hour early so I can knock off at

four. Look, we're straying from the topic here. Are you sure you're okay? Some injuries have a delayed reaction. You can bleed to death without really knowing you're hurt."

"I'm not bleeding."

"It could be internal. I've heard of people who had no idea they were wounded and then bam! They keel over dead."

"That would be bad." She didn't sound as if she were taking this seriously at all. "Are you qualified to assess internal bleeding?"

"Well, no. But I'll bet I could tell if you were mortally wounded or not." Besides, he wanted to know what she was hiding in there. "If this door's jammed, you could come to the front door." And after he'd made sure she was fine, he'd talk her into letting him into the garage.

"What happens at four that you take off from work early?"

"I like to shoot pool at the Rack and Balls before dinner. I was on my way there when I heard the explosion. Naturally I stopped." He could still smell the noxious odor, but it was much fainter.

"I appreciate your concern. I really do."

"Anyone would have done the same. And speaking as an engineer, I'm not sure you should be breathing those fumes."

"The Rack and Balls has a pool table?"

"Yeah." It was common knowledge. "You must be new here."

"I bought the house in October. I guess that's new."

With that, Charlie's brain processed the data and came up with an ID. She was the New York model who'd moved to Middlesex last fall. Both his mother and his aunt Myrtle had mentioned that a model had bought a house on Elm Street and she sometimes came into the bakery. But she'd only allow herself one cinnamon roll and then she'd make it last several days.

And what was her name, anyway? Erin? Elise? He couldn't remember. But now he was really confused about the explosion. Fashion models and explosions only coexisted in James Bond movies.

Curiosity made him ignore the cold cement. Leaning down, he balanced on his forearm and took off his glasses so they wouldn't fog up while he tried to get another look inside the garage. He ended up with a fuzzy view of denim overalls and lots of brown wavy hair. He couldn't see her face and he definitely couldn't see what was going on in the garage.

Obviously she wasn't planning to open the door all the way. He might never find out what had caused the explosion, but at the very least he needed to make sure that she wasn't in shock and therefore numbed to the pain of something like a piece of metal sticking in the back of her skull.

"About the pool table," she said. "Is it full-sized or bar-sized?"

"It's an Olhausen eight-footer."

"Really?" She sounded more than a little interested.

He knew she could be faking that interest to distract him, but somehow he didn't think so. It seemed as if she recognized the make of the pool table. He acted on impulse. "Want to come with me and try it out?"

In the resulting silence, he could almost see wisps of indecision curling out from under the door along with the noxious fumes. Of course she was hesitating. A New York model might not see herself playing pool with just any schmuck who happened along after an unscheduled explosion.

In point of fact, he'd never envisioned himself playing pool with a New York model, either, regardless of whether an explosion had preceded the game or not. But pool required such concentration and coordination that even one game would probably be enough to convince him that she was okay.

If she was new in town she might not have any close friends who would check on her tonight. She could lapse into unconsciousness and lie on the garage floor for hours, maybe even days, before anyone noticed. She could die in there and not be discovered until she failed to show up on some runway or another.

Time to get tough. "Here's the deal," he said. "If you'll come down to the Rack and Balls and play a game of pool with me, I'll be able to see for myself that you're not hurt. If you won't, I'm going to call 911 right now."

"I'd rather you didn't call 911."

"That's pretty clear. Obviously, whatever you're building is top secret, but I can't let myself leave you lying on your garage floor, when something could be seriously wrong with you."

"I see. Well, come to think of it, I wouldn't mind a game of pool."

He smiled with relief. "Great! We can ride over on my motorcycle. I always carry an extra helmet."

"Thanks, but I'll meet you there. It's an easy walk. So you go ahead. I'll be there in twenty minutes."

He wished she'd come out right now, but she probably wanted to fix her face. Women always wanted to fix their face, and that had to go double for models. After an explosion it would be even more critical. "Okay, but if you're not there in thirty minutes, a truck full of paramedics will arrive on your doorstep."

She laughed. "All right, all right, I've got it!" Then she stuck her hand through the opening again. "Eve Dupree."

Eve. That was it. He took off his glove, reached down,

and shook her hand. "Charlie Shepherd." She had a soft hand, a firm grip, and warm skin. Not everyone had a really good handshake, the kind that made you think the person was worth knowing. Eve did. Shaking hands through the bottom of a garage door without being able to see her felt sort of kinky and sexy, like making love with masks on. Not that he'd ever done that.

"Well, Charlie Shepherd, I'll see you in twenty minutes at the Rack and Balls."

"But not a minute later."

"I'll be there." She pulled her hand back inside. "And bring your A game."

"You bet." Charlie's A game was pretty good. He didn't expect to need to perform at that level, but you never knew. A fashion model who exploded stuff in her garage might be closer to a James Bond heroine than he thought. She might be a pool shark.

As Charlie stood up and walked back to his bike, Eve scooted toward the opening in the garage door. Turning on her side, she pushed her prescription goggles tight against her face so she could get a good look at the guy she'd just agreed to play pool with, a guy with an electrical engineering degree. She couldn't decide which was more exciting, the chance to play pool or the chance to play pool with an electrical engineer.

Much as she hated to admit it, she could really use an engineer right now. But she had to evaluate this guy's character before saying anything about her project. She wasn't spilling the beans to just anybody who happened along.

Then she caught her first glimpse of Charlie's jeans-covered ass framed in black motorcycle chaps and character became a secondary issue. Her reaction to seeing that great butt was a shock. Ever since she'd run screaming from Lyle's proposal in September, her libido had been in time-out.

No longer, apparently. Maybe Charlie's white-knight rescue attempt had started the sap flowing through her dormant sexual equipment. Whatever the cause, she found herself getting turned on by those excellent buns. Then there was the added attraction of his black leather jacket. Nothing made a guy's shoulders look broader or his hips leaner than a black motorcycle jacket. She'd fallen for the Fonz as a kid and had never gotten over that crush.

But Fonzie hadn't been much of a student. Charlie was a brainy guy decked out in a Fonzie outfit. Eve couldn't imagine a better combination than that. Fortunately, Charlie didn't have Fonzie hair, either. Brown and un-gelled, it looked thick enough for a girl to bury her fingers in and wavy enough to make that experience sensual.

She wondered if he had a girlfriend. Not likely. A guy who had a girlfriend wouldn't be so quick to invite a woman to play pool with him.

Okay, so she was interested. Still, she might have a hard time flirting with him unless she told him what she was inventing in her garage. He obviously wanted to know about that.

When he turned around so he could sling one of his long legs over his macho motorcycle, she pushed back from the door. No point in taking a chance that he'd glance down and see her face wedged in the opening as she checked him out. Besides, she needed to get going if she expected to make herself presentable so she could ar-rive at the Rack and Balls before Charlie sent the para-medics to her door.

Getting to her feet, she assessed the damage in the garage. The rotary engine on her workbench was trashed, as was a chunk of the bench itself. The veggie fuel was way more volatile than she'd expected. Maybe she'd added too much broccoli.

She'd hit the deck fast enough to avoid flying metal, but she'd singed her hair. That wouldn't be popular when she went into the city tomorrow to shoot the toothpaste ad, but they could airbrush the frizzy parts. She probably should have waited to test her newest version of the fuel, but now that she had space for her experiments, she hated putting things off. Thanks to her impatience, she'd have to buy a new engine.

At least the hovercraft was okay. She glanced at the purple disc-shaped object that took up more than half the garage. Thank goodness no metal fragments had lodged in the fiberglass hull of the hovercraft. The day she'd found the flying saucer mock-up on eBay had been a glorious one, indeed. She'd never get that lucky again, and she loved how her purple paint job made the hovercraft stand out.

But there would be no more progress on the project tonight, so she might as well find out how Charlie Shepherd handled a cue stick and whether he had a decent screw shot. You could tell a lot about a guy from the way he played pool.

Charlie fought the urge to wait outside the Rack and Balls for Eve to show up. But hanging around outside the tavern wouldn't get her there any faster and it would make him look dorky. So he pushed open the heavy oak door and walked in. If she didn't arrive in fifteen minutes, he'd retrace his path to her house, in case she'd collapsed on the way.

The interior of the Rack and Balls smelled comfortingly familiar—a combination of cedar smoke from the log-burning fireplace in the corner, the aroma of clam chowder on the stove in the back, and the acrid scent of beer on tap at the bar.

A huge set of elk antlers hung on the wall behind the bar. On one side a basketball autographed by Michael Jordan hung suspended by a piece of basketball netting, and on the other side hung a football signed by every member of Middlesex High's 1992 state championship team.

The antlers and sports memorabilia were one socially acceptable explanation for the tavern's name. The pool table that took center stage was another. Either explanation could be used when kids were around.

But everyone in town knew that the tavern's owner, Archie Townsend, appreciated stacked women and good sex, so he'd most likely named the Rack and Balls with no thought to sports or pool equipment. A burly guy with a thick black beard, Archie had tried monogamy and had found it too confining.

He was behind the bar washing glasses when Charlie walked in. "Hey, Charlie, how're they hanging?"

"Just fine, Archie." Charlie took off his jacket and chaps and left them on a peg by the door before taking a seat on one of the vinyl-cushioned bar stools.

"Sam Adams?"

"Not yet, thanks."

Archie gazed at him with the kind of scrutiny that time and mutual affection allowed. "Expecting somebody?"

"Uh . . . yeah."

"A woman, judging from the look in your eye." Archie flipped his towel over his shoulder and leaned against the scarred oak bar. "Not Mariah, I hope."

"No." Charlie noticed he felt no twinge of regret when Mariah was mentioned. It had taken a few months, but he was definitely over her.

"That's good. She wasn't right for you."

Charlie didn't think so, either, mostly because Mariah had labeled his proposed relocation to Nevada a stupid idea. "Maybe I wasn't right for her. Did you ever think of it that way, Archie?"

"Well, no, on account of any woman would be lucky to hook up with you." Archie used the towel to polish a section of the bar. "If I had a daughter, I'd advise her to chase your ass all the way to Hoover Dam."

Charlie laughed. "Thanks for the vote of confidence." Good old Archie. He'd come to mean even more to Charlie now that his dad was gone. Hard to believe it had been fourteen months since the funeral. Fortunately, his mom had perked up in the past couple of months. Helping Aunt Myrtle in the bakery was taking her mind off widowhood.

"You get that interview set up yet?" Archie asked.

"I heard from them this morning. I fly out to Vegas a week from next Wednesday." Thanks to Aunt Myrtle and the bakery, Charlie didn't feel so guilty about the new job prospect.

"Good." Archie nodded. "That's good. I was afraid you'd hang around here forever, thinking you could bring the ML and P into the new millennium."

"I tried."

"God knows you tried. Those old fossils in charge have shit for brains."

Privately, Charlie thought so too but he'd never say so out loud. No point in creating bad feelings. "Ah, you can't blame them. They still think of me as Rose and Henry's nerdy little kid, the one who flooded the cafeteria with his science experiment. Nobody's a hero in his own hometown."

"Like I said, shit for brains. Anyway, their loss."

"I might not get the job."

"You'll get it." Archie flipped the towel back over his shoulder. "So who's the lucky lady who's causing you to delay your Sam Adams purchase?"

Charlie glanced at his watch. Three minutes to go. "This isn't exactly a date."

"She's meeting you here, right?"

"Right."

"Then *voilà*, it's a date. Two people happen to run into each other somewhere, that's not a date. Two people *agree* to run into each other somewhere at a stated time, then it's a date. And from the way you keep looking at your watch, you absolutely have a stated time."

"Archie, that's faulty logic. Two people could have a business meeting at a stated time. That's not a date."

"Is this a business meeting?"

"Not exactly." Charlie had already decided not to tell anybody about the explosion, provided Eve showed up and he didn't have to call 911.

Archie smiled. "Then it's a date."

"Not exactly."

Archie blew out a breath. "You sound like a rental car commercial. Are you going to tell me who it is or what?"

"Eve Dupree."

"Eve Dupree." Archie squinted as if trying to place the name. "Isn't she the New York model who moved here last fall?"

"Yeah. So now you can see why it's not exactly a date."

"Why can I see that?"

"Hey, I'm an engineering geek. You don't catch successful New York models going out with—"

"That's what you say. She just walked in the door."

Adrenaline shot through Charlie's system, but he turned the bar stool seat slowly because he wanted to play this cool. He was aware of Archie watching the proceedings with great delight. Naturally, the seat creaked like the hinges in a horror flick.

"I'm here," she said. "Right on time."

"That's—" He had to stop and clear his throat. "That's good." He'd prepared himself to be knocked out by her glamorous beauty. He'd figured on makeup and some designer outfit.

Instead she stood there in a bulky green jacket and fuzzy white earmuffs. Her mop of brown wavy hair was pulled back into a ponytail, and she had on a pair of large-framed glasses. If she had on makeup, he couldn't see any evidence of it. She might be wearing a little bit of lipstick.

She'd obviously taken no pains with her appearance, so why couldn't he stop looking at her? Critically speaking, her nose was a little too prominent and her forehead a tad bit high. But something kept his attention riveted on her face.

It was her mouth, he decided at last. Her mouth was wide and her lips full in a way that made him think of kissing and . . . yeah, to be completely honest, oral sex.

But surely other women had great mouths and he hadn't been this fixated. Maybe it was her eyes. Even partly obscured by the lenses of her glasses, they were very blue. And besides being beautiful, they shone with a kind of creative intelligence that he found extremely seductive. No telling what was going on in her head, and he loved that. Predictable women drove him nuts. Give him a creative woman anytime.

Apparently the combination of her eyes and her mouth fit his idea of perfection. Or maybe the big draw was the secret she had refused to tell him. He'd always loved puzzles, and she'd presented him with one by having a mysterious explosion in her garage. No matter what the reason, he wanted her. He wanted her bad.

And what an idiot he was! As he'd taken great care to assure Archie, this wasn't a date. She'd come because he'd threatened to call 911 and expose her garage accident. She wasn't here because she thought he was wonderful, so the fact that he found her wildly attractive made no difference. Besides, he was leaving town.

He swallowed and attempted to curb his lust. "Want a beer?"

"Sure." She took off her coat and hat.

"What kind?"

"Sam Adams would be great."

Charlie almost groaned out loud. She was sexy, she was smart, and she drank his brand of beer. Just his luck, he was not in the market.

Chapter Two

*T*wenty minutes, which had to include the walk to the tavern, hadn't given Eve time for more than washing her hands, putting her hair in a ponytail, and swiping on her favorite mocha lipstick. Just as well, she'd thought. From now on, any guy she took a shine to would start out with the real Eve Dupree, not the airbrushed version. That way she'd never be worried that they were attracted to glitz. In spite of her career, glitz was so not her.

Charlie might have expected some glitz, though, because he was staring at her as if he'd never seen a woman without makeup before. Or even one wearing glasses. Oh, well. Great tush or not, he might not work out.

Too bad, too. She certainly admired what she saw—sexy brown eyes, nicely squared-off jaw. She also liked the thin-framed, black-rimmed glasses. The guys she'd dated in the city were into contacts. Personally she didn't care for them and only used them when she had to on the job. There was something honest and refreshing about just wearing the glasses.

His black leather jacket was gone, revealing a white

dress shirt with no tie and the sleeves rolled back. When paired with the jeans, it gave him a casual, almost wholesome look. But she'd seen how the black leather chaps outlined his butt and his package. She didn't think Charlie was all *that* wholesome.

As she approached the bar, Charlie stood and introduced her to the tavern owner, Archie Shepherd. As if Eve needed another reason to be attracted, she discovered that Charlie was a good five inches taller than she was. Although she would have loved to be evolved enough to date shorter guys, she wasn't there yet.

She exchanged niceties with Archie, but all the while she was aware of Charlie's intensity of focus. There was definitely energy pulsing between them. Whether it was sexual energy or not, she wasn't sure.

Maybe his stare had been complimentary. He might like his women nerdy. If so, that boded well for the future, because she was and always had been a nerd in a model's body. No one ever believed that of her, but here was a guy who might.

Finally she picked up her beer, which she'd asked Archie to leave in the bottle, and turned to Charlie. "Ready for that game of pool you promised me?"

"Sure am."

"Whoa, there, Nellie," Archie said. "Did this guy give you a handicap?"

Eve looked Charlie in the eye. Oh, yeah. Sparks. Maybe there *was* sexual chemistry. "Do I need a handicap?" she asked.

He met her gaze, and his was starting to smolder. "I don't know. Do you?"

No doubt about it, now. This connection had potential. "That depends." She paused for emphasis. "How good are you?"

"Nobody in town can beat him," Archie said.

Eve lifted her eyebrows. "Is that true, Charlie?"

"Mostly."

"Well, then." She brought the bottle to her lips and tipped it slightly to take a sip. "Let's see if it's still true, shall we?" Then she winked and walked over to the cue rack. She used her runway walk on purpose.

"Let's make it interesting," Charlie called after her.

She already thought it was plenty interesting, but she glanced over her shoulder as she reached the rack. "By doing what?"

Instead of answering right away, he walked up beside her and lowered his voice. "If I win, you'll tell me what happened in your garage today."

His manner indicated that he hadn't told Archie about the incident. She appreciated that. "And if I win?"

He smiled, which had quite an effect on her already supercharged libido. "You can tell me whatever you feel is appropriate, given my efforts to make sure you came through it safe and sound."

Standing almost near enough to touch him while they had their own private conversation felt delicious. Now she was certain he didn't have a girlfriend. Either that, or he was a louse, and she didn't want to believe that.

"Fair enough." She studied the cue sticks and reached for one that was quite obviously better quality than the rest. The shaft looked straight and the handle was inlaid with onyx and mother-of-pearl in an intricate diamond pattern.

"That's mine."

She paused, her hand on the smooth shaft. Unconsciously she stroked it. The wood was incredible. She glanced over at him. "Yours? Really?"

"Yeah. I keep it here instead of carting it back and forth on my bike." He paused. "But you can use it."

"I'd be honored." She really should buy herself a pool cue. She'd considered it, but she'd never owned a table, and walking into a pool hall with your own stick advertised either your ability, your arrogance, or both. During her years of playing in the city, she hadn't wanted to broadcast anything. But this cue of Charlie's was a pleasure to hold and inspired all varieties of lust, including the sexual kind.

Setting her beer on a nearby table, she wiped her hand on her overalls so she wouldn't get any moisture from the bottle on Charlie's stick. Then she sighted down the shaft. Perfectly straight. She didn't want to read too much into a guy's choice of pool cue, but so far, she was impressed with everything related to Charlie Shepherd.

If he played a clean game of pool and didn't throw a tantrum when he missed a shot or happened to lose, then she thought she should tell him about her invention. Fate seemed to have thrown him in her path. He could be just the guy she needed, in more ways than one.

Charlie had never let anyone use his thousand-dollar pool cue. The locals knew it was his and avoided it. During tourist season Archie put it in the back. But this wasn't tourist season, so Archie had left it on the rack, easily accessible when Charlie came in to practice.

When Eve had wrapped her fingers around it, he'd felt a sexual charge as if she'd taken hold of his dick. Then, to compound matters, she'd started stroking the shaft. Charlie had never seen pool as a sexual game, but he was seeing it now. And Eve could hold his cue stick for as long as she wanted.

Meanwhile his brain, what few cells he still had working, kept repeating a message like a blinking traffic sign: *You're leaving. Don't get started.* But he was already started and didn't know how to stop. She hadn't even told him what the explosion was all about, but he had a gut feeling that would only enslave him more.

He studied the remaining cues, reaching for and rejecting three before he finally settled on one. Sheesh. It was just a game, for chrissake, not the national billiards championship. But he didn't want to look like an idiot in front of her and he would love to win and have her tell him about the explosion.

Finally he settled for the best of Archie's house cues and turned to discover Eve had picked up a tray of balls and was racking them. She knew how to handle balls, too, cupping them gently in each hand as she positioned them in the wooden triangle.

Charlie broke out in a fine sweat. He'd played tired, he'd played sick, and he'd played drunk, and he'd still been able to make the shots. But he'd never played aroused, and he had a feeling that could destroy his game.

She positioned the balls precisely, sliding her fingers between the bottom row of balls and the rack to keep the triangle tight. She had the sexiest fingers he'd ever seen in his life. He wanted to suck on them.

Lifting the rack, she glanced at him. "Got a quarter?"

"Yeah, but there's no jukebox here. Archie decided that—"

"We need a quarter to toss so we can see who breaks."

"Oh." He was losing it fast. He'd been worried that she'd been affected by the explosion, but obviously she was functioning just fine. He was the one acting as if he'd taken a blow to the head. At this rate he'd be lucky to remember which end of the cue stick to use.

"Yeah, I have a quarter," he said. Digging in his pocket, he produced one and held it over the table as he bounced it in his palm. With the way his reflexes felt, he didn't trust himself to catch it, so he'd let it land on the table. "Your call."

"Tails."

The quarter dropped tail side up on the green felt. "Tails. Your break."

"Okey-doke." She leaned his stick carefully against the cue rack and pulled out a house cue for the break.

Could this woman be any more perfect? On top of her X-rated mouth, intelligent eyes, and sexy fingers, she understood that you didn't use a custom cue for the break. He had to hope that she wasn't interested in him, because if she had even a smidgen of attraction going on, his plan to move to Nevada was in serious jeopardy.

As she lined up for the break, he stood at the opposite end of the table staring like a love-struck fool. She handled that stick like a pro, but it was the wiggle in her butt as she concentrated on the cue ball that made his equipment twitch. The break came fast and furious, scattering balls to every corner of the table and dropping two solids.

"Nice break," he said. He would call it a spectacular break, but she might think he was patronizing her.

"Thanks." She retrieved his cue, adjusted her glasses, and lined up for another shot.

It was a fairly easy one, so he wasn't too worried when she made it. But when she executed a complicated combination, he began to wonder if he'd fall without firing a shot. She could run the table.

If he'd thought he'd beat her and get the answer to his explosion question, he had another think coming. He was more likely to get his ass whipped. Reaching for his beer, he took a couple of fortifying swallows. In the process he happened to glance over at the bar and noticed Archie leaning on it watching with a big smile on his face.

Suddenly Charlie had a horrible thought. Archie was old enough to be Eve's father, but he'd never let little details like that stop him. As much as Charlie loved Archie, he didn't love the idea of Archie putting the moves on

Eve. Charlie had seen her first, dammit. But Charlie was going to Nevada. Wasn't he?

He became so absorbed in thinking about leaving town right when he'd discovered the perfect woman that he didn't notice that Eve had stopped shooting. And wonder of wonders, she still had one ball on the table. It wasn't all over.

"Your turn," she said, walking over to retrieve her beer.

Brushing away the unwelcome thought that she might have missed on purpose to make him feel better, he put down his beer and evaluated the situation to see if he could still save himself. He might have a chance if he planned his shots carefully and didn't look at her while she sipped from that Sam Adams bottle.

Her mouth should come with a warning label. One glance and several suggestive thoughts popped into his head. Worse yet, those knowing eyes of hers seemed to be reading his mind. No doubt she could easily spot the lust in his expression after years of having men drool over her.

But because he was interested in her brain, not to mention her ability to play pool, he liked to think his interest was different, more intellectual, more discerning. Yeah, right. That's why he was gazing at her mouth and dreaming about blow jobs. He was the soul of subtle.

With great effort he focused on the balls on the table and told the ones in his pants to cool down so he could concentrate. Nothing good could come from muffing his first shot. A guy with his own pool cue and a habit of practicing every afternoon after work had better come up with the goods.

Fortunately he managed to knock something in, and the technique wasn't half-bad, either. He'd put a satisfying amount of backspin on the cue ball so that it lined up perfectly for his next move.

"Nice screw shot," she said.

"Thanks." He should have guessed she'd know what to call it. Now if only that particular word coming out of her mouth hadn't given him a boner, everything would be ducky.

"You're good," she said. "You have a nice steady rhythm."

Oh, *man*. Since when had everything turned into a sexual reference? "Thanks," he said again, and swallowed a groan of frustration.

"I can see why Archie thought I should get a handicap."

"I'm the one who needs the handicap." And he had a doozy pressing against the fly of his jeans.

"Nah. You're doing great."

"I will be if I don't give you any more shots." He pictured how deflated he'd feel if he lost, and that helped his buddy deflate some, too. He knocked in one ball, then managed to sink another. Finally he had à groove going, until he hit a ball too hard because he was showing off. Instead of sliding into the pocket, the ball bounced off the rail. Well, at least he'd blocked her shot.

She put down her beer and wiped her hands on her overalls before she picked up his cue stick. He really liked that she was so careful with it. Then she did the stroking thing, caressing the shaft of his stick, and he was in trouble again.

"I really love your stick," she said.

He almost choked. He managed to say thanks, although he sounded like the Godfather.

"However, I'm not going to use your stick for this one." She walked over to the wall rack and leaned his pool cue carefully against one of the prongs.

Her walk was getting to him too, he realized. Made sense. She walked for a living, prowling down runways while wearing the latest fashion. She was paid to look sexy doing it, and by now her walk was probably ingrained and unconscious. But he was extremely conscious . . . of every sway of her hips, every nonchalant shrug of her shoulders.

She wasn't particularly chesty, or at least she didn't seem to be. Hard to tell in the bulky pink sweater and overalls. But chances were she wasn't hugely endowed because most models weren't. That should mean Archie wasn't interested, yet he was still leaning on the bar looking quite interested.

As for Charlie, he didn't care whether a woman was stacked or not. He was intrigued with how they moved, which might have something to do with his engineering background. Eve moved with smooth precision, all parts synchronized. That worked for Charlie.

"I'll try this one." Eve took down the jump cue.

Charlie's eyes widened. Was she seriously expecting to go over or around his ball? He'd practiced both the swerve and the jump, but he didn't feel confident about either of those shots. If she did . . . then she was way out of his league.

Sure enough, she lifted the butt end of that jump cue and came down on the cue ball with the stroke of an expert.

Charlie let out a low whistle as the cue ball traced a semicircle around his ball, hit her ball, and drove it into the side pocket. "Where the hell did you learn how to play pool like that?"

"From my dad. He was a hotshot bar player back in the seventies."

"I'll just bet he was." Charlie watched as the inevitable happened and Eve dropped the eight ball neatly into the corner pocket. He didn't like losing, but at least he'd lost to a worthy opponent. "Congratulations."

She smiled at him as she returned his custom cue to the rack. "Thanks."

He hung on to the house stick. "So much for me getting

that explanation, though. How about best two out of three?"

"I might beat you again."

He certainly believed that. "Then we can move on to best three out of five. Who knows, I could get lucky." Then he heard himself. "At pool. Lucky at pool."

"I knew that's what you meant." She gazed at him. "But it might not work, you know."

His hopes faded. "And you don't feel like hanging around."

"Well, yes, I do. But you don't have to beat me at pool to get an explanation. I—"

The front door of the tavern opened with a loud bang and three men came in, laughing and joking as they stomped snow off their shoes.

At first Charlie was irritated by the intrusion. Talk about your lousy timing. Then he took a closer look at the men. No. Couldn't be. But it was. In the lead was none other than his cousin Rick, who was supposed to be in L.A.

Charlie hadn't seen Rick in more than a year, but he hadn't changed much. He was still tanned and fit, his brown hair streaked either by the sun or a hairdresser. Rick would never say which. In any case, the sun was beginning to trace crow's-feet around Rick's lady-killer brown eyes. Still, the guy looked good. He always had.

"Surprise!" Rick grabbed Charlie's hand, pulled him into a quick hug and turned him loose. "Bet you didn't expect to see me walk through that door, today, cuz!"

"Nope, sure didn't. I pictured you lying on the beach at Malibu next to Heidi Klum." Charlie battled the conflicting emotions he always felt when Rick was around. Charlie was only two months older, so they'd grown up like brothers, alternating between loyal friendship and bitter rivalry. Back when they were teenagers, Rick always got the girls and Charlie always got the grades.

"Lying on the beach?" Rick laughed. "Don't I wish! Instead I have to scout out a location for a winter fashion spread."

"Does anyone know you're in town?" Charlie was aware of Eve standing back by the pool table. Soon common courtesy would dictate that he bring her into the conversation, and he didn't want to. Rick would change the dynamic.

"I stopped at the bakery," Rick said. "Mom and Aunt Rose told me you'd be over here. Listen, we have to talk about that bakery, man. But first, let me introduce you to my assistants. This here's Manny Flores and the short dude is Kyle Harrington."

Charlie shook hands with each of them. Manny was tall and rangy, a mix of Hispanic and Anglo, while Kyle was short and compact, a Doug Flutie type who looked as if he would be quick on his feet. Rick must be doing well if he had two assistants trailing him around.

And now Charlie was obliged to introduce Eve. "This is Eve Dupree," he said. "Eve, this is my cousin Rick Bannister."

As Eve came forward, Rick flashed his very white smile. "Eve? I thought it looked like you! We did that Chico's shoot together at Dana Point about four, maybe five years ago. Yeah, I think it was five, come to think of it. Time flies, and all that."

Charlie sighed. It figured that Rick would know her, which gave him an even bigger advantage. Charlie took some comfort in the fact that Eve's face didn't light up right away, though.

Instead she gazed thoughtfully at Rick as if trying to pin down the occasion. "Was that the time we got rained out and all ended up in a little bar drinking wine for two hours?"

"That's it." Rick stepped forward and held out his hand. "It's great to see you again. Small world, huh?"

"Sure is." Eve shook his hand. Then Rick repeated the introduction of his two assistants, and Eve shook their hands, too.

Obviously Rick was damned proud of those assistants, since he kept introducing them every five minutes. Charlie had to admit it was impressive, traveling with a retinue. Strangely enough, Eve didn't seem all that impressed. She acted hesitant, almost wary of Rick.

Charlie hoped that wasn't because they'd had a thing going on during that Dana Point shoot. Rick was famous for getting horizontal with the models. Charlie didn't want to believe Eve had been one of Rick's conquests.

"You know what I remember from that time we spent in the bar?" Rick said.

Charlie didn't think he wanted to hear this.

"Heaven knows." Eve laughed nervously. "After two glasses of wine, no telling what I might have said."

Now Charlie *really* didn't want to hear it.

"You got very serious," Rick said. "And then you told me that you felt as if modeling were a waste of your life. You said if you ever had the time and the space, you'd create a laboratory and invent a manned hovercraft that ran on veggie scraps. I never forgot that. What a concept."

Charlie stared at Eve. Judging from her red face, he knew what had caused the explosion in her garage. So Rick had heard all about it five years ago. Charlie's jaw clenched. Some things never changed. When it came to women, Rick was ahead of the game every damned time. And Charlie was sick of playing second fiddle.

Chapter Three

Well, shit. The minute Eve had figured out who Rick was, she'd remembered that conversation they'd had over wine all those years ago. She wasn't in the habit of talking about her dreams and schemes, but that day she'd been frustrated by the delays in the shooting schedule and had seriously begun to question whether she was throwing her life away just because the money was good.

Somewhere into the second glass of wine she'd started talking to Rick about her idea for a hovercraft. She'd thought about that conversation several times in the years since. Turned out it had germinated and flowered into a viable life plan. Breaking up with Lyle had been the first step in getting back to something she loved.

She didn't regret that talk with Rick because it had started her thinking again after several years of being mentally asleep. At the time he'd seemed like a safe person to confide in, someone who lived on the other side of the country, someone who didn't know she'd flunked out of high school and wasn't considered particularly bright by her family. He hadn't laughed when she'd suggested that powering the hovercraft with veggie fuel could make a real contribution toward solving the world's oil crisis.

But she wished Rick hadn't shown up and exposed her secret just now. Charlie, a guy she was becoming increasingly fond of, didn't look happy about that, not happy at all. She didn't blame him. She should have told him sooner, before he'd had to find out this way.

She'd also rather not discuss it while they all stood in the middle of this very public tavern. A quick glance at the bar told her that Archie had gone in the back and probably hadn't heard Rick mention the hovercraft. But Manny and Kyle were all ears.

"It's strictly experimental." She lowered her voice. "It may never get out of my garage. I'm just—"

"So you *are* building it!" Rick turned to Charlie. "I'll bet you're helping her, aren't you?"

Charlie looked at Eve, his expression stormy. "Well, you see, I didn't—"

"I would love some help, Charlie," Eve said. "There are definite gaps in my knowledge when it comes to the electrical system. I'm pretty much self-taught, and it would mean a lot if you'd check out my wiring."

"I'd be glad to."

He said it so quickly that she had no doubt he was thrilled to be asked. Being asked to help might make up for not being told about the hovercraft earlier. She let out a breath. Maybe this wouldn't turn into a complete disaster.

But she needed to move this party elsewhere. The workday was over in Middlesex, so happy hour could begin any time. A couple of guys in jeans and flannel shirts had just come through the door and were headed over to the bar. She thought Charlie had noticed them, but Rick seemed oblivious.

"I'd like to get a look at that thing, myself," Rick said.

She edged closer to the door. "I'm trying to keep the project under wraps. Until now, I haven't told anybody about it except my neighbor Eunice, and she's sworn to keep it secret. It may never work, so there's no point in making a laughingstock of myself, right?"

"I doubt that's going to happen," Rick said. "You're one smart woman. If you're building a hovercraft, then I'll bet good money that it'll work."

Eve winced and hoped the two guys at the bar hadn't heard that. Maybe she'd better take steps to contain the information within the circle of people who already knew. "Tell you what. I only live three blocks away. Why don't we head over to my place and I'll show you what I have so far?"

"Sounds good," Rick said. "I rented a Subaru, so we can all ride over in that. Unless Charlie wants to follow on his bike."

"I'll ride with you," Charlie said quickly, as if unwilling to be odd man out.

After Charlie and Eve grabbed their coats, everyone left the tavern. Eve gave Rick the address as she climbed into the passenger seat. That left Charlie, Manny, and Kyle crammed into the backseat. Good thing it was only three blocks, because nobody looked comfy back there.

As the shortest, Kyle got the middle, and Charlie ended up behind Eve. He helped the crush of broad shoulders by leaning forward and talking to her through the little space between the seat and the door panel.

"What kind of silhouette did you go with?" he asked.

"Round," she said. "I wanted it to be multidirectional and aerodynamic."

"I'm picturing a Frisbee," Rick said.

Charlie ignored him, leaning closer so he could talk more directly with Eve. "So I'm assuming you decided on fiberglass?"

"Right." She twisted her body and talked as best she could through the narrow opening. "Although the choice was made for me, in a way. I found a flying-saucer proto-type on eBay, and the hull was fiberglass."

From the driver's seat came a chuckle. "A fiberglass Frisbee," Rick said. "Catchy. You could call it that."

"With fiberglass you wouldn't need as much thrusting power to give it forward momentum," Charlie said.

Eve nodded. "Fiberglass is great, but I'm still dealing with the safety angle. Right now it's too fragile to with-stand much of an impact. When the engine on my work-bench exploded this afternoon, I was lucky that no pieces hit the frame."

Rick braked at a four-way stop. "You exploded some-thing?" He sounded worried.

"A little glitch with the biofuel," Eve said. "Listen, Charlie, before you agree to help me, you might as well hear about the fuel situation. You're liable to think I'm completely bonkers to consider it."

"I'll help," Rick said as he pulled through the intersec-tion. "Even before I hear about the fuel situation. Unless you're running gerbils around in a wire cage. I'm against that as a fuel source. So's the ASPCA. I—"

"I'm making the fuel myself," Eve said.

"Excellent." Charlie's tone conveyed total approval.

Eve had expected doubt and disbelief. Instead she was getting praise. It was a heady experience. "I also have a tank of hydrogen that I may end up using, but—"

"Isn't that what they had in that blimp that exploded a long time ago?" Rick said. "The photos of that were awesome."

"I don't want to use hydrogen if I can help it," Eve said. "I'm . . . exploring the option of using biomass as a feedstock for ethanol. My idea is to use the hovercraft as a fun teaching tool, to show people we don't have to depend on oil as a fuel source."

"Cool." Charlie sounded excited.

"If biomass has something to do with the Catholic church, I'm in trouble." Rick said. "I am so lapsed."

Eve decided to take her cue from Charlie and ignore Rick's comments. "I'm using my own kitchen scraps," she said. "Leftover veggies from the salads I make all the time. I want to make fuel options easily accessible."

"There you go," Rick said. "At last, a legitimate use for broccoli stalks."

Then it came to her—Rick wasn't used to being left out of a conversation, especially one that included a woman. Well, too bad. Charlie was the man of the moment, and she intended to concentrate on him.

"So what are you doing for a converter?" Charlie asked.

"I designed my own."

"Wow." Charlie blew out a breath. "That's amazing. Good for you."

"But the mixture I'm getting may be too rich for the engine I bought. I have a small rotary. Or had, past tense. It's destined for the landfill, now."

"I love rotary engines," Charlie said. "Inspired choice."

"Thank you." Good thing she was flexible, because she had to twist around to carry on this conversation properly. She leaned her cheek against the headrest. "I was so afraid you'd laugh at the whole thing. I've read tons of books and taken a bunch of online courses, but I don't have an engineering degree like you, so there may be some structural—"

"We're here," Rick said. "All out for the incredible hovercraft show."

"I'm sure it's going to be great," Charlie murmured

through the opening, before he unsnapped his seat belt. "Absolutely great."

"Thanks. That means a lot to me." As she climbed out of the Subaru, Eve realized she was very turned on. She hadn't known how much she'd craved this kind of enthusiastic endorsement. She'd thought that inventing something all by herself had given her more creative freedom.

Maybe it had, but she'd also had to battle her doubts alone, and many times she'd wondered if she was totally crazy. Or maybe she was just plain arrogant to believe that her little toy had the power to revolutionize the fuel economy.

Yet in her heart of hearts, she did believe that. For a concept to take hold, it needed a fun factor. The hovercraft, running on alternative fuel, would be that fun factor.

Finally having someone validate her decisions meant the world to her. She liked that the someone had turned out to be Charlie, who was getting hotter by the minute. Brains could be so damned sexy.

As she ushered everyone inside, she thought briefly of her lack of housekeeping skills and then decided not to worry about it. These were bachelors. Bachelors weren't neat. Well, maybe Charlie was. She'd turn on only necessary lights as she took them from the front door through the kitchen to the garage.

"Don't mind the mess." She said that mostly for Charlie's benefit, in case he was a neat freak. "The cleaning lady comes tomorrow." That wasn't precisely true. She hadn't hired a cleaning lady yet because she didn't want someone from Middlesex gossiping about the fuel converter in her kitchen or the purple spacecraft in her garage.

On Mondays she usually shoveled out the worst of the

clutter and ran a vacuum around, but today she'd been too involved with testing her fuel to think of it. Leading the way through the dark hall to the kitchen, she flipped on a light so they wouldn't bang against things on their way to the garage.

Whoops. She'd completely forgotten about her Victoria's Secret underwear. Because her washing machine was on the fritz, she'd handwashed her bras and panties in the kitchen sink last night. Then she'd draped them over the kitchen chairs.

Most models she knew wouldn't have cared a bit if a bunch of guys caught sight of their underwear drying in the kitchen. But Eve was shy. Always had been and probably always would be.

She didn't do lingerie ads for that very reason. Still, she loved fancy undies, especially in vibrant colors like red, purple, and jade, all of which were represented in her kitchen right now. And she was blushing. Damn it.

She paused, trying desperately to think of something clever and sophisticated to say. Meanwhile all four men stood staring at the colorful and intimate display. No witty words came to her.

Charlie was the first to speak. "Oh, wow."

She gulped. If Charlie, the man she most wanted to impress, made some comment about her lingerie lying around, she might die of embarrassment.

He cleared his throat. "I've seen something similar, but never quite like that."

Rick laughed. "Cuz, you really need to get out more."

"I'd like a closer look." Charlie started toward the table.

Yes, she would definitely die of embarrassment. Charlie wasn't content to gaze on her underwear from a distance. He wanted to scrutinize it up close, probably analyze the structural capability of the elastic and underwire.

She searched for a way to end this excruciating moment. "Hey, let's not forget about the hovercraft." She forced a smile. "Isn't that what you guys came to see? Let's go on out to the garage and check it out!"

"In a minute," Charlie said. "First I want to examine . . ."

"*Charlie.*" She couldn't bear this another second.

". . . your converter." He brushed past a purple bra as if he hadn't even seen it. Then he crouched down beside the large stainless steel contraption she'd rigged up—thanks to more finds on eBay—to distill her fuel. "This is wild, Eve. Absolutely wild."

Rick shook his head. "Charlie, you are such a nerd."

And that, Eve realized, was why she found Charlie irresistible.

The discussion with Eve in the car had stimulated every one of Charlie's nerve endings, including the ones connected to the playground equipment below his belt. Some guys got excited when a woman talked dirty. Charlie got excited when a woman talked nerdy.

Discovering this side of Eve was like opening up the wall of a cute little cottage and finding it wired to support NASA's flight center. It got him hot.

Now this underwear display had added jet fuel to the blaze. Surrounded by Eve's lingerie, he couldn't help but imagine her wearing those jewellike pieces of silk and lace, and his brain was on tilt. Or maybe it was the blood draining south that made him so fuzzy that all he could think about was hot, sweaty sex. With Eve.

He hadn't come over to her house so he could imagine having sex with her. Why had he come? Oh, yeah. The hovercraft. Just in time, he'd remembered. The fog had cleared from his brain long enough for him to notice something besides the touchable silk all around him. In the corner stood her converter. The converter had become his life preserver in a sea of sexual currents.

"Reminds me of a smaller version of what I've seen in a microbrewery," Rick said.

"That's actually where I got the idea," Eve said. "But don't try to drink anything that comes out of there. It'll corrode your insides."

Charlie studied the dials on the converter. They were fascinating, but not as fascinating as the purple bra dangling six inches from his face. The tag was right there, available for him to read her specs. He should ignore it. Nothing good could come from reading that tag.

But he was an engineer, and engineers focused on measurements. She wore a 36B underwire. Despite claiming not to care about the size of a woman's breasts, he'd always been partial to the elegant proportions of a 36B.

The converter. He needed to say something about it. "You could patent this, to go along with the hovercraft. They could come as a package." And speaking of packages, his was growing exponentially as he contemplated the structural wonder of that underwire gently lifting Eve's breasts, thereby producing nuzzle-worthy cleavage.

"I'd like that," Eve said. "In fact, that would be part of my ultimate goal, so that people would see how easy alternative fuel could be. And I'd *really* hate to see anyone using petrochemicals to operate something that's just for fun."

"You mean gas?" Rick said.

"She means gas." Charlie remembered having to coach Rick through chemistry, and even at that he'd only pulled a D. Rick wasn't dumb, but no one would ever accuse him of being a scholar.

"I get it," Rick said. "A green toy to promote green

living. I can see it catching on in Southern California, no problem."

Manny shifted his weight impatiently. "Is the garage through that door?"

"Yes," Eve said, "but I'd rather wait until we're all ready to—"

"Let's take a look at that hovercraft." As Charlie stood, he hoped his erection had subsided sufficiently to make it unnoticeable.

He needed to get out of this kitchen full of Eve's underwear, and she obviously didn't want to let two guys she didn't know wander around in the garage without her. Charlie was beginning to feel rather protective of this project himself.

Because he'd been over in the corner, everyone else filed through the door ahead of him. That gave him one precious opportunity to test the silky fabric of the bra between his thumb and forefinger. Pure tactile pleasure.

Out in the garage, Rick whistled in surprise, and Charlie reluctantly let go of the bra. Manny and Kyle had said nothing, but maybe they'd been struck dumb by the sight of the hovercraft. Probably not, though. Charlie had an idea nothing fazed these two, not even dainty purple underwear.

Compared with Rick's out-there personality they seemed almost stoic. Maybe he'd hired them to balance his carefree attitude. That was the only explanation Charlie could come up with, because they sure didn't seem to fit into Rick's happy-go-lucky lifestyle.

Then Charlie caught his first glimpse of Eve's hovercraft, and his jaw dropped. He'd expected it to be interesting. He hadn't expected it to be the same gorgeous shade of purple as her bra and panties.

It sat on the floor of her garage like something right out of *The Jetsons*. He half expected George Jetson to open the Plexiglas dome covering the cockpit and climb out wearing his space suit. Charlie was vaguely aware that the workspace was a mess, but after all, she'd just had an engine explode. Her workbench had a big hole in the center of it and there was debris everywhere.

He itched to clean it up and get this project back on track, but that wasn't his place. So instead he stepped over pieces of metal as he circled the craft and took note of the design elements she'd incorporated to give the necessary lift to the fuselage. When he was finished, he sent Eve a glance of silent admiration.

She stopped chewing on her fingernail and took a deep breath. "So, Charlie, what do you think?"

Apparently his opinion on this subject meant a lot. That thought warmed him. "It's brilliant."

Her shoulders relaxed and a wavering smile appeared. "I wouldn't go that far."

"I would," Rick said. "How about it, Manny? Kyle? Can't you see these cruising up and down the beach at Malibu?"

Manny nodded. "I can already think of a couple of guys who would love one of these. Maybe not in purple."

"It's my favorite color," Eve said. "But you could have one in any color."

"I was thinking camouflage," Manny said.

Kyle rubbed his chin. "That would be cool. But you'd need a name for it. Gotta have a name so people know what to call it."

"I, um, call it the Skimmer." Eve offered the name tentatively.

Charlie was ready to support whatever she suggested, just because she looked so unsure of herself. She'd done something amazing with this hovercraft, but she didn't seem to have great confidence in her creative abilities.

"That works," he said. And the more he thought about

it, the better he liked the name. "It's simple, easy to spell, and describes exactly what this does."

"Or what I hope it will do."

Rick stepped forward. "If you need a test pilot, you're looking at him."

"Thank you, Rick," Eve said. "That's brave of you, but I wouldn't consider letting anyone ride in it the first time except me."

That scared the shit out of Charlie. She definitely needed him as her consultant. For one thing, he had a private pilot's license. For another, he could get a few tips from some aerospace types he knew. He'd cover his tracks by telling them he was building a remote-controlled model.

"Hello, out there!" A woman's voice drifted from the interior of the house. "Eve, I saw your light on and your front door was unlocked." A short, curvy blonde came into the garage. "Oh, hello." Her gaze traveled around the group.

"What can I do for you, Eunice?"

Eunice's gaze made another circuit as she talked. "I'm cooking up the most sinful fudge. It tastes almost as good as sex feels. But I need to borrow a cup of sugar."

The sudden intrusion startled Charlie, but Eve seemed to take it in stride.

"Sure, help yourself," she said. "But first let me introduce you. Everyone, this is Eunice Piven, my next-door neighbor."

"I thought you had visitors when I saw the Subaru parked outside." Eunice wore a tight black jumpsuit and carried her parka over one arm.

The jumpsuit didn't look like the kind of thing Charlie's mother baked in. He also thought Eunice had deliberately removed the parka once she got in the door so she could show off her figure. He pictured her at her window watching four men traipsing into Eve's house and being consumed by curiosity.

Eunice Piven was legendary in Middlesex, although Charlie hadn't realized that she lived on Elm Street, right next door to Eve, it turned out. But he definitely knew all the stories about Eunice.

Not many people believed that she'd been carried off by aliens and taught unusual sexual techniques, but something must have happened to her. She'd come to town about five years ago as a conservative, churchgoing woman, sort of on the frumpy side. Then she'd disappeared for a couple of weeks, and on her return she'd been mysteriously transformed into one hot tamale.

Eve introduced the guys, and Eunice gave each man a dazzling smile that hinted at the possibilities she could offer. Except for Charlie, of course.

"Oh, Charlie." She waved a hand in his direction. "Of course I know you. You're the one who keeps this town humming like a Swedish vibrator." She winked at Rick. "Although some people don't need wires and transformers to generate a charge. Tell me, Rick, are you into electricity?"

"I sure know a live wire when I see one," Rick said.

Charlie stifled a groan. Not only was that a corny line, but Eunice grinned as if she thought it was the cutest, most original comment she'd ever heard. Charlie glanced at Eve to get her reaction to this nonsense.

She met his gaze and rolled her eyes. He winked back. And there it was again—the intimate connection that was pulling him deeper into an attraction that was doomed. His goal was to leave town, and soon.

"So, Eve." Eunice swept an arm to encompass the people gathered in the garage. "Does this tempting array of manhood mean you're ready to go public with your spacecraft?"

"Hovercraft," Eve said. "And not quite yet."

"It's my fault," Rick said. "I asked her about it this afternoon, not knowing the project was top secret. Charlie got kind of excited about seeing it, so here we are. Manny and Kyle just came along for the ride."

Eunice frowned. "You asked her about it? Don't tell me you're gorgeous *and* psychic."

"Nope." Rick looked pleased with the compliment. "She talked about this machine years ago, before she'd started building it."

"Rick and I worked together for a week in L.A.," Eve said. "We had a shooting delay so I had some wine and ended up spilling my guts to Rick. I didn't think he'd remember." She shrugged. "He did."

"Oo." Eunice wiggled her shoulders. "Does that mean we're all sworn to secrecy? What happens in this garage stays in this garage? I love intrigue."

Charlie decided to take charge. "I can't speak for Eve, so feel free to contradict me if you want, but I think we're looking at a potentially valuable patent, so we should keep this to ourselves."

"I don't know." Eve looked skeptical. "I just blew up an engine. The biofuel concept is important to me, so I'm afraid I'm not that close to a working model."

"Charlie can fix anything so it works right," Rick said. "I'll help too for that matter."

Charlie didn't think that would be a plus, but he couldn't shoot Rick down in front of his assistants. "Are you going to hang around Middlesex for a while, then?"

"Oh, I hope so." Eunice put her hand to her heart.

"The schedule's fairly loose." Rick glanced at Manny and Kyle. "We haven't booked a return flight yet."

"Not yet." Manny crossed his arms over his chest. "We had to see how things would go first."

"Exactly." Rick cleared his throat. "I need to find the perfect location for this shoot. I dunno. Ten days?"

Manny looked over at Kyle. "You think ten days is okay?"

Kyle shrugged. "It's cutting it close, but if everything works out here, ten days should be okay."

Charlie listened in wonder. Apparently Rick really had turned his calendar over to his assistants. "Then let's see what we can get accomplished. We have the evenings, and next weekend." He decided not to mention that he was leaving for a job interview the week after that.

"I'm taking the train into New York in the morning for a photo shoot," Eve said. "I won't be back until Wednesday about five. But that gives me time to order a new engine and have it express shipped to the house." She looked at Charlie. "If you and Rick would be willing to come over and bring pizza around six, we could get started."

"Sounds good," Charlie said.

Rick turned to Manny and Kyle. "Will you guys be okay if I spend a few nights over here helping out?"

Manny nodded. "Just don't forget to take your cell, in case something comes up."

"I always have my cell," Rick said.

"Then it's settled." Charlie took one last look at the hovercraft. "Wednesday night we'll start getting this baby ready to test."

And the sooner the better. The longer Charlie hung around Middlesex with Eve, the more he was liable to question whether he should leave at all. But he had to leave. He'd dreamed of working at a major hydroelectric plant for years. Eve might be delicious, but he had to pursue his dream or live with regret forever.

Chapter Four

Eunice stayed until the guys left, which didn't surprise Eve. That whole cup of sugar thing had been bogus and they both knew it. Eunice couldn't tell one end of a potholder from the other, just like Eve.

"So that's Charlie Shepherd's cousin." Eunice peered out the peephole in Eve's front door as the men headed toward their car. "He even looks good distorted."

"That excuse about a cup of sugar was lame, Eunice."

"I know, but it's not every day a hunkmobile pulls up in front of your house. I had to quickly finish up my phone-sex client and come over to investigate."

"I hope you didn't leave the poor guy hanging." Eve figured she was the only one in town who knew that Eunice moonlighted as a phone-sex girl. Eunice's day job as the receptionist for Patriots Independent Insurance Agency didn't pay enough to keep her in designer accessories, so she supplemented her income by giving phone sex on nights and weekends. She considered it a stress-free way to make extra money now that she'd been relieved of all sexual inhibitions by her alien abductors.

"Nah, I wouldn't end a call before the guy gets his jollies. I'm not that mean." Eunice pressed her face to the door. "Ah, will you look at the fluid way the Rickster climbs behind the wheel? Yum."

"I can't look. You're hogging the peephole." Eve wouldn't have been interested in watching Rick, though. She only had eyes for Charlie, the guy who liked her hovercraft. His body movement was fine, but she was especially drawn to the fluidity of his mind.

"Well, they're pulling away, so you couldn't see anything, anyway. But if the Subaru designers offered Rick as an optional accessory, they'd sell a ton of cars." With a dramatic sigh she turned back to Eve. "Thank you for introducing me to such a fine specimen of manhood. Even if it doesn't work out, I have someone new to use as my fantasy guy during phone sex."

"You picture a fantasy guy?" Eve hadn't ever thought of it from Eunice's perspective.

"Only if I want to really get into it. Sometimes I fake everything, but sometimes I actually go for it. An image of Rick would definitely inspire me to go for it."

"Yeah, I guess he's pretty cute." But Eve had lost interest in the subject of Rick. She'd even lost interest in the subject of phone sex.

Instead she was remembering that precious moment after Charlie had made his circuit of the hovercraft. He'd looked at her then, his brown eyes shining with admiration. She could live a long time on the memory of that warm gaze.

He'd given her the geek stamp of approval, and that meant more than he could ever know. If someone like Charlie—someone with an engineering degree and smarts coming out his ears—if a person like that admired her invention, then she'd done something special.

"You *guess* he's pretty cute?" Eunice stared at Eve in

the dim light of the hallway. "You *guess*? You need your prescription changed in those glasses, dearie. I'm just praying he's not gay."

"Oh, he's not." Charlie was one hundred percent hetero. Eve had worked with a fair number of gay models, and she'd become good at picking up on the vibes. Acknowledging that Charlie was all-male gave her a sexual thrill, which probably meant she was into him whether that was a good idea or not.

Eunice looked heavenward. "Thank you, God." Then she glanced at Eve. "Are you sure? I mean, what's with the two male assistants?"

Eve blinked, disoriented. Oh, right. She might be daydreaming about Charlie, but Eunice was talking about her crush *du jour*, Rick Bannister. Eve didn't think Rick was gay, though. "A guy can hire another guy without being gay."

"Yeah, but they are all California beach-bum gorgeous. I see three pieces of male eye candy traveling together, I figure either they're headed to a Chippendale's convention or they're gay."

Eve laughed. "You're making unnecessary problems for yourself. Unless Rick's changed his sexual orientation since I last saw him, he's straight. I can't speak for the other two, but I doubt—"

"The other two don't concern me. Rick's my wiggle-the-wiener candidate, and I would hate it if he swings the other way. Or maybe he's bi." Eunice's expression brightened. "I could handle that."

"I'm sure." Eve wished she could treat sex like a pastime, the way Eunice did. Eunice could probably have sex with a guy and stay friends with him if it didn't work out. Eve was sure that if she ever ended up in bed with Charlie—which she might not, but saying she did—if they broke up, then the friendship would go down the drain at the same time.

Eunice reached for the jacket she'd hung on the hooks Eve had installed next to the front door. "Just so I don't have to beat off Manny and Kyle to get a shot. They could have a ménage à trois going for all I know. Don't forget they're from L.A. The rules are lax out there."

"Ugh. I don't even want to think about a male threesome, thank you very much." She just wanted to think about Charlie. Maybe Charlie with her? The concept kept inserting itself in her brain like a new equation begging to be solved.

"I'm just sayin'." Eunice pushed both arms into the sleeves of the coat and hiked it up on her shoulders with a flap of nylon. "L.A. people aren't like Yankees."

"All I can tell you is that when I first met Rick he flirted with all the models like crazy. I'm thinking he got involved with one of them. It sure looked like it from the way they both acted."

"Good news." Eunice zipped her jacket. "Can I come over Wednesday night?"

"Why not?" At first Eve had been excited about the prospect of working with Charlie, but then Rick had become part of the mix. Eve would rather have had Charlie all to herself. With Eunice around to distract Rick, Eve might get that quality time alone with Charlie, after all.

"Cool." Eunice opened the door. "Do you think I should leave my phone off for that night?"

Eve grinned at her. "Maybe you should put it on vibrate."

"Come on, I'm serious. I could leave it off and just forget about the extra income for the evening, but maybe Rick would get turned on by listening to me take 900 calls, so I could accomplish two goals at once. What do you think?"

"I have no idea. You have to decide that one." Eve couldn't even imagine such a scenario. "Tell you what, though. If you bring your phone, take the calls in the house, not in the garage. I don't want to listen to 900 calls while Charlie and I are working on the hovercraft. We're dealing with volatile stuff."

Eunice winked. "Gotcha. The way I look at it, we're both dealing with volatile stuff."

Charlie wished there weren't so many damned people who knew about this hovercraft. Apparently Rick would have found out, regardless, but Charlie didn't like the idea that Manny and Kyle were in on it. What did Charlie know about these two men? Nothing.

He turned toward the backseat. "Are we all agreed that we don't talk about this invention to anyone?"

"Sure thing," Manny said.

"No problem," Kyle added.

Charlie figured that was about the best he could do, short of threatening them with . . . something. Charlie wasn't into that. "And Rick, you're cool with keeping this quiet, right?"

"You betcha, cuz. I have a feeling I'll be too busy with a certain Eunice Piven to care about some purple hovercraft."

Charlie considered mentioning Eunice's alien abduction claim but decided against it. Rick was a big boy. He could take care of himself.

Rick braked the Subaru at the four-way stop. "Speaking of inventions, have you heard what your mom and my mom are up to?"

"Well, I know they were talking about a new sign out front."

"This is way more than a new sign, cuz." Rick accelerated through the intersection. "This is a whole new image.

They're thinking of ditching the old name altogether."

Charlie frowned. "Why? What's wrong with the Pastry Parlor?"

"Too tame, I guess."

"Too *tame*?" Charlie could have sworn he heard a snort from the backseat. "It's a bakery, not a massage parlor."

"Don't give them any ideas," Rick said. "That could be next."

Charlie glanced over at his cousin. "Okay, what's going on?"

"It started with the cinnamon buns."

"Yeah." Charlie could go for one right now. In the excitement of Eve's hovercraft, he'd forgotten all about dinner.

"Here's how they tell it. A couple of days ago they had one of those buns in the case and it had one lone raisin at the top, right in the middle. A customer called it a 'booby bun.' She said if they had any more like that, she'd take them home to her husband as a joke."

"Hm." Charlie had a feeling he wasn't going to like this.

"So they promised to make some more. Turns out the woman spread the word, and for the past two days there's been a run on booby buns. They couldn't bake those things fast enough. When I showed up this afternoon they'd already taken in more in one day than they normally earn in a week."

Now there was no doubt that Kyle and Manny were quietly cracking up in the backseat.

"It's probably just a fad." Charlie sure as hell hoped so. The thought of his mother in the booby buns business wasn't a comfy one.

"Maybe." Rick seemed to be trying not to laugh. "But they're pretty high on the success of those buns. There was some talk of expanding the offerings."

Charlie turned to him in horror. "Like what, for God's sake?"

"Like tonight they're going to create bawdy bread-sticks."

That should give his cousin plenty to think about. Rick was pleased with himself as he dropped Charlie off at the Rack and Balls and drove on over to his mother's house. Bless his mother and Aunt Rose for dabbling in X-rated bakery products. That would help distract Charlie, and right now Rick wanted Charlie to be very distracted. Rick needed to raise some cash.

That would have been simpler if his mother had been able to loan him a couple hundred grand, but she'd said that was impossible. If he'd told her it was life or death, she might have found a way to get the money, maybe put the bakery up as collateral. After all, he was her only kid. But he hadn't wanted to scare her, and now it might not be necessary.

Maybe his luck was finally turning. If Charlie, the family brainiac, thought the hovercraft was a valuable invention, then Rick would make book that it was extremely valuable. Charlie's comments were always on the conservative side.

Rick didn't think it would take much effort to secretly get some pictures of the hovercraft. Then maybe he could temporarily borrow some of the plans he'd noticed sitting on Eve's workbench. All he needed was enough info to sell the concept to the highest bidder. Eve made good money. She really didn't need the income from this thing. But Rick did.

After Rick dropped Charlie off, Manny moved up to the front passenger seat. "So what do you think of that hovercraft?"

"Ah, I think it's bogus," Rick said. "Veggie fuel? Come on! I was just trying to be polite."

"Personally, I think it's very cool," Kyle said from the backseat. "I wouldn't mind owning one of those things. I'd soup up the engine, though. Veggie fuel sounds like a wimpy fuel, if you know what I mean. No chick will be impressed by a guy who's burning broccoli. You gotta have high-octane performance if you wanna get laid."

"Exactly," Rick said. "She's adding in all this environmental crap, and that won't be popular with the crowd who would buy something like that. It'll go nowhere."

Manny shifted in his seat. "You could be right. I think the X-rated bakery is a much more solid concept. Your mom and aunt are smart ladies. Some businesses are undercapitalized, but I don't get that feeling about the bakery."

"They do all right." Rick knew where this was leading.

"Those booby buns are great-tasting, too," Kyle said. "Almost as good as the real thing. Which gives me an idea. I could get a jar of vanilla frosting and maybe some raisins and try putting that on my girlfriend's—"

Manny groaned. "Spare us your adolescent sexual fantasies just this once, okay? What we need to find out here is what happened when Rick had that private little conference with his mother. Can she come up with the money or can't she?"

"I'm sure she can." Rick wasn't about to tell either of these guys that his original plan to get the money from his mother was looking dicey. He had another plan, a brilliant plan, and it wouldn't involve sinking his mother into debt. "It might take a few days for her to get it, but everything's looking good."

"Peterson will be glad to hear that." Manny reached

for the cell phone clipped to his belt. "I need to check in and let him know we're on schedule."

Peterson. Just the mention of his name made Rick want to pee his pants. To look at the guy you'd think he was an alderman at his church and enjoyed reading bedtime stories to the kiddies. There was a chance he even did those things, which made him all the creepier.

Blond and rosy-cheeked, Peterson was the kind of person you'd invite to a family picnic. You might even ask him to bring the volleyball net and the horseshoes. And he'd do it, smiling that casual smile of his. Not even his eyes gave him away. They were an innocent blue with crinkles at the corners.

The average Joe, especially if he happened to be lucky, didn't have to worry about a man like Peterson. But if a guy had a streak of bad luck and had to go to Peterson for some ready cash, and if that streak of bad luck refused to go away no matter what, well, then that guy had to worry about Peterson. Peterson liked loaning money. And he expected to get it back. Or else.

On the early train to New York the next morning, Eve had the urge to call her sister Denise. They hadn't talked in weeks, partly because every time Eve had contact with Denise she ended up feeling stupid. A long time ago their parents had divided up the turf. Eve was designated the pretty one and Denise was labeled the smart one.

Eve wondered if Denise was as unhappy with her role as Eve was with hers. But Eve couldn't argue with the fact that she sucked eggs when it came to school. She loved to learn, but only on her own terms. If she'd been an ugly kid her parents might have insisted she at least graduate from high school, but she'd been cursed with beauty, so they'd guided her relentlessly into a modeling career.

She didn't like it much, but a person had to make

money somehow. And the career gave her periods of down time for reading books on all the subjects she loved, such as alternative fuels and futuristic transportation options. She dreamed of pioneering improvements that would clear the air and slow the drain on fossil fuels.

She'd always hidden those dreams, both from her parents and especially from Denise, for fear everyone would laugh. But if Charlie thought the hovercraft had potential, then Eve finally had something to tell Denise that her brainy sister might find interesting.

Denise wouldn't have left her apartment for her first class yet. Pulling out her cell phone, Eve hit the speed-dial. Sisters should be closer than she and Denise were, but she'd never known how to bridge the gap. The hovercraft might be just the thing.

Halfway through the first ring, Denise picked up. "Hey, glamour girl. You must be on the train."

"Why would you think I'm on the train?"

"You always call me from the train."

"I do not." But it was true. On the train she had time to think about things like why she and Denise didn't have the bond that Hallmark said they were supposed to have. Then she'd drum up some excuse to call and see if that bond had mysteriously developed since the last time they'd talked.

"Yes you do, but that's okay. You have demands on your time."

Eve sighed. Was Denise being sarcastic or did she really mean it? "You have demands, too. We're both busy. I know you have class, so—"

"I have to walk out the door in five minutes. What's up?"

The clock was ticking. Eve pictured her sister standing by the door in all her orderly perfection—short black hair washed and styled, black pantsuit free of all wrinkles, white blouse spotless, briefcase packed with the notes she'd need for the day. Denise was always ahead of schedule, which left time for interruptions like Eve's phone call.

Eve, on the other hand, was usually behind schedule, distracted by the ideas churning in her head like fruit in a blender. But one of those projects might turn into something great. She wanted to tell Denise about the hovercraft, but she thought it would be classier to lead up to it. Unfortunately, with only five minutes . . . less than five minutes, now, she didn't have much time to lead up.

"Eve? You still there?"

"Uh, yeah." She saw the conductor coming down the aisle. "Hold on a sec." After some searching, she found her ticket stuck between the pages of the book on biomass research she'd brought to read on the train. She handed it to the conductor, and before she could reconsider, she blurted out her news. "Denise, I've invented something."

A full second passed before Denise spoke. "Invented something? What do you mean?"

"I've had this idea for a long time, and now that I have a house with a garage, I've been designing it. The bugs aren't worked out yet, but a friend of mine who's an engineer thinks that it has—"

"Back up. You're building something in your *garage*? Eve, I can't even begin to take this in. You're a model, not a . . . a . . . You don't invent things. Period. That's crazy."

Eve should have expected this reaction, but it got to her, anyway. "I guess you forgot the time I tied a rocket to the back of my Barbie and shot her over the neighbors' roof."

Denise gasped. "You've invented a personal rocket system?"

"Not exactly, but—"

"Omigod. It's all coming back to me. The motorized wagon that ran us into the duck pond. The catapult that smashed a two-hundred-year-old stained-glass window at the church. Disaster at every turn."

"Denise, it wasn't that bad." Those things had happened before Eve had learned to keep her inventions a secret.

"Oh yes it was. Barbie's leg ended up in Mrs. Jorgenson's flower bed and one arm was in the apple tree behind the Mastersons' house. We never found her head, except I swear that Edgar Abernathy was using it as a parking lot gizmo for the antenna of his car."

"I'm not building a rocket," Eve said. *That's the next project.*

"I don't care! You could kill yourself, Eve! You're not to work on this anymore, understand?"

Eve's jaw clenched, exactly the way it used to when she was eight and Denise was a very superior twelve. "It's not a rocket. And I will work on it. Once Charlie helps me iron out the problems, I will really have something."

"Are you going into the city or going home?"

"Into the city."

"When are you coming back?"

"Wednesday night. Listen, Denise, this is a perfectly legitimate project."

"Right. I wish I could get there Wednesday night, but I have this awards thing and I'll probably be getting something, so it would look bad if I didn't go. I'll be at your house Thursday morning."

"What?" Eve sat up straight in her seat as panic set in. She'd need two days to clean to Denise's standards. "You can't come. Sorry. Not that I wouldn't love to have you, but I'm having the . . . exterminators on Thursday."

"For what?"

"Bugs. It's truly disgusting. You wouldn't believe the invasion of bugs."

"You're right, I wouldn't believe it." Denise's determined calm was unnerving. "Not in February. Mice, maybe, but not bugs."

"I meant mice! Mice, bugs, who can tell the difference when they move so fast? Things are scurrying around here all the time. You would hate it, Den. Don't come. Save yourself some trouble."

"I'll be there by ten."

"What about your classes? You can't just walk out on your economics classes! Students are depending on you to give them the secrets of Wall Street!"

"I have a TA who can take over for a couple of days. See you on Thursday. Now, I really have to go."

"No! It won't work! The plumbing is stopped up! The TV's broken! The washing machine—" But her sister had already disconnected.

Still clutching the phone, Eve banged her forehead repeatedly against the seat in front of her. She must have fear of success. That was the only explanation for this idiotic phone call to her sister, a phone call that would result in Denise ruining what had promised to be an excellent few days spent with Charlie while they worked on the hovercraft.

Now bossy Denise would be there getting in the way, right when Eve was about to spend some quality time with Charlie. And that was the crux of it. It wasn't only Denise's interference that Eve was worried about.

Eve could hold her own in a beauty contest against Denise, but what about a brainy contest? What if the guy in question was an engineer type who would likely choose mind over measurements? What if Denise swooped in and wowed him with her IQ points?

Eve's reaction to that possibility told her more than she wanted to know about her current state of mind concerning Charlie. She didn't just *like* him. She had *designs* on him.

Suddenly her move to Middlesex took on a whole new meaning. Sure, she'd meant to escape the city and Lyle's proposal. But her motives had been more complicated, apparently. She'd been running away from one thing, but unconsciously running toward something else.

She wanted more than her little house in a cute New England town and more than a place to create her inventions. She wanted a certain kind of man to live in that house with her. A man pretty much like Charlie. Now that she'd found him, Denise couldn't have him.

At least her sister wouldn't show up until Thursday morning. If Eunice could keep Rick busy Wednesday night, then Eve would have time alone with Charlie. Just her, a sexy engineer, and a hovercraft in the garage together—the perfect setup to put some moves on her favorite nerd.

Chapter Five

The next two days moved slower than an overloaded circuit for Charlie, but finally Wednesday night arrived. The pizza was ordered and all he had to do was hop on his bike, run by his aunt Myrtle's house, get Rick, pick up the pizzas, and head on over to Eve's. Charlie had ordered three pizzas because he couldn't decide what kind Eve would like.

He'd ended up with one plain cheese—something just about anybody could eat—one with pepperoni and sausage, which was your classic choice, and the third with all veggies, in honor of Eve's veggie fuel. If she couldn't find something to love in that group, then pizza wasn't her thing.

Two guys and three pizzas on one motorcycle would be tricky, but Charlie was up for it. Still, his life would have been easier if Rick could have picked up the pizzas and met him there. Instead, Rick had loaned his car to Manny and Kyle, who had driven to Hartford on an emergency run for the bakery.

For two days Charlie had tried not to think about the

bakery. He'd gone out of his way to avoid driving past it. So long as he didn't talk to his mother or his aunt, so long as he didn't drive by the bakery and see some titillating sign out front, he could believe that the booby bun craze was over.

Apparently Charlie's mother and Aunt Myrtle were treating Manny and Kyle like family, which meant they got to run errands for the bakery. Rick would have been sent to get them if he hadn't mentioned that he and Charlie were going over to Eve's at six. The evening had been billed as nothing more than a social occasion. Charlie trusted his mother and his aunt, but the fewer people who knew about Eve's project, the better.

Consequently he'd asked Rick to listen for the motorcycle and be ready to leave immediately to forestall any discussion. But when Charlie arrived, his mother's red Volkswagen Beetle was sitting in the drive of Aunt Myrtle's two-story clapboard house. Nobody came to the door when he rang the bell, so he just went in, because his aunt never locked the door.

That's when he heard the kind of laughter and chatter in the kitchen that indicated that Aunt Myrtle and his mother were in old-fashioned mode. Charlie wasn't an old-fashioned fan. The sugar, the cherry, and the orange wedge seemed like a fine way to eliminate the taste of good whiskey. But his mother and Aunt Myrtle thought it was the height of sophistication.

Rather than get sucked into that program, Charlie stayed in the entryway. "Rick?" he called out. "Time to get moving!"

"Come on back here, Charlie!" Rick sounded in no mood to rush off. "You have to get a look at this cookie cutter!"

Knowing it was probably a mistake, Charlie walked into the kitchen and found his mother, Aunt Myrtle, and

Rick at the old oak table at the end of the kitchen with the familiar squatty glasses in their hands and the smell of oranges in the air. Judging from the flushed faces, Charlie estimated Aunt Myrtle had served a couple of rounds already.

Neither of the two sisters had been born with red hair, but they went to the same hairdresser so they both had red hair now. Aunt Myrtle was the tallest and thinnest, and Charlie's mother was the oldest and plumpest. She was forever trying to diet, but she loved to cook, which was her downfall.

Nobody would have guessed Aunt Myrtle was the younger of the two widows. Twenty-seven years of marriage to Jasper Bannister combined with the cigarettes she'd finally given up had taken its toll on poor Aunt Myrtle. Charlie didn't think she'd been all that sorry to see her husband leave this world at the age of forty-eight, but he was absolutely positive she missed the cigarettes.

Rick had a catalog in front of him. "You have to see this stuff," he said. "Who knew?"

Charlie didn't want to know. One quick glance at the catalog was more than enough for him. "It's quarter to six," he said. "We need to go."

"Hold on a minute." Rick held up the open catalog and turned it so Charlie could see. "Check this out."

Charlie could either come off as a prude in front of his much cooler cousin or look at the catalog. The cookie cutter was, as he'd feared, X-rated. The picture wasn't only of the cookie cutter, of course. Included was a decorated vanilla sugar cookie. The frosting filled in every last detail, leaving no doubt what the cookie couple was doing.

"Innovative." Charlie could feel the heat rising from the collar of his flannel shirt.

"We're embarrassing Charlie," Aunt Myrtle said. "He's turning red."

"He'll get over it." Rick flipped the catalog page. "And look at this. In case your couple isn't Caucasian, we have the chocolate version and the gingerbread version. I'm not sure how it works if you have a multicultural couple, though."

"You have to go with dual dough," Charlie's mother said. "But vanilla will work for this couple, which is good because we have a time crunch."

Charlie decided that in this case, ignorance was not bliss. "You say that like you're talking about a specific couple."

"Oh, we are!" Aunt Myrtle said in her deep smoker's voice. "These will be for Jill's bachelorette party Friday night. That's why we sent Manny and Kyle into Hartford. We didn't have time for the cutter to be shipped."

Charlie vaguely remembered that there was a wedding coming up in Middlesex, which meant almost everybody in town would be going to either the bachelor or the bachelorette party. "You're actually going to make these cookies." He battled a sinking sensation. "Did someone ask for them?"

"In a way." Charlie's mother gave him a coy glance. "I haven't had a chance to tell you, Charlie, but the bakery seems to be going in a different direction. A very profitable direction, I might add."

"I told him something about it on Monday night." Rick winked at Charlie. "Right, cuz?"

"Yeah, but I thought . . . well, Middlesex doesn't seem like the place for . . . I'm just surprised that people . . ." He balanced precariously between happiness and embarrassment. On the one hand, he was thrilled to see his mother so excited about something, but on the other, why did it have to be X-rated baked goods?

"Puritan blood, Charlie." His mother looked smug. "Myrtle and I were surprised, too, but then we figured it out. Nobody's more interested in the topic of sex than folks who have Puritan blood in their veins."

"Makes sense to me." Rick studied the cookie picture. "And these cookies should scratch that itch for the Friday night deal. There's a lot of detail in here."

Too much detail, as far as Charlie was concerned. Besides, he didn't want to have his mind on sex when he was about to go over to Eve's. He'd thought this through and had decided that because of the timing, he couldn't get involved with Eve. He could only help her with the hovercraft.

"It's the detail in the frosting that will take us so many hours," Aunt Myrtle said. "We could really use some help."

Charlie backed away, hands out. "I'm not helping frost. My evenings are booked."

His mother laughed. "I wasn't going to ask, but now that you mention it, we might get Manny and Kyle to do it. They're nice boys, and I'll bet they'd help. We need to get most of them done tonight, because we have to start on the wedding cake tomorrow night. Some extra hands would be a lifesaver."

For some reason Rick got a huge charge out of that. "Yeah, ask Manny and Kyle. I'll bet they'd love to."

"We will, then." Charlie's mother looked ten years younger tonight. "We'll have a frosting party."

Charlie decided to comfort himself with his mother's cheerful mood. "And now we really have to go," he said.

"Right." Rick drained his glass and stood. "See you two entrepreneurs later."

"Have a good time!" Charlie's mother called after them as they headed for the front door. "That Eve's a very nice girl!"

Rick lowered his voice as he pulled on his coat. "You do realize she wants to match you up with Eve, right?"

Charlie snorted. "No. Where'd she get a wild idea like that?"

"The word's out that you had a pool date on Monday, and you're going over to her house tonight, so gossip has you engaged by next week."

"I hope this isn't some plan to keep me in Middlesex." Charlie followed Rick out the door and down the steps to the motorcycle parked in the drive.

"Nah. Your mom understands that you're hoping to get that job in Nevada. She just wants grandkids."

"I barely know Eve." Except that didn't seem true. Although they hadn't met until Monday afternoon, he'd felt an instant sexual attraction. On top of that, he'd recognized a kindred spirit. He knew Eve because he knew himself.

"Whatever you say. I'm only reporting the word around the breakfast table is that you're stuck on her."

He handed Rick his spare helmet. "Well, I'm not." *Yet.*

Denise was coming. Eve had been trying not to panic for two days, but her self-talk wasn't working. The minute she hit the front door her tummy started to churn. Denise was so neat, so together, so critical. She would take one look at the clutter that was Eve's life and—

My door is unlocked. She had a moment of panic. She didn't have anything valuable in the house except the hovercraft, but what if vandals had come in?

She almost stumbled over the big box sitting in her entryway, and then remembered that Eunice had taken delivery of the new engine while she was gone.

Although FedEx could have delivered packages to Eunice's house, Eve liked this arrangement better. Then neither of them had to lug heavy boxes across the yard.

Okay, so Eunice had forgotten to lock the door after her. That could happen. And it wasn't like New York where a locked door was critical to life as she knew it. The Middlesex police report might include a stolen bicycle and a speeder or two. That was about it.

And her engine had arrived! Once she'd pried the box open and looked inside at that gorgeous piece of equipment, she could barely make herself close the box. No doubt about it, she was obsessed with making the hovercraft fly using veggie fuel, and this engine was the key component. She resented every moment she had to spend doing something else.

Three months ago she'd searched the Internet for a supplier who would give her what she wanted, an engine small enough to fit into her hovercraft without adding excess weight and large enough to power her invention. Then she'd blown it up. Here was the replacement, and she wasn't about to let history repeat itself.

With great reluctance she closed the flaps on the box. Now was not the time. Instead she had to brainwash herself into full cleaning mode, "cleaning" being a euphemism for shoving everything out of sight.

But first she'd drag the engine box out to the garage and take another look at her beloved purple Skimmer. After all, she hadn't seen it since Tuesday morning. By the time she got the box through the kitchen door into the garage, she was puffing. But her baby sat there in all its magnificence waiting for the new engine. And thanks to some fuel research she'd done on the Internet while she was in New York plus the book she'd read on the train, she had some ideas for that, too.

In fact, she ought to make some notes before she lost track of what she'd read in the hotel room last night. After turning on the space heater to warm up the garage, she crossed to her workbench and looked for the pile of notes she'd left there. For some reason they weren't under the

Darth Vader mask paperweight where she always kept them.

That was irritating. Her workbench wasn't the most orderly place in the world. Nothing in this house was what anyone would call orderly, but she'd always been able to find her notes. She checked everywhere else they might be, even inside the cockpit of the hovercraft. Nothing.

Feeling more disoriented by the minute, she rummaged through the kitchen, looking in drawers and cupboards. Still nothing. And time was running short. Charlie and Rick would be here soon, and she'd hoped to get the house straightened before they arrived. If she didn't, then it wouldn't get done. She knew once Charlie was here she'd be completely absorbed in the hovercraft project.

Maybe she'd come across the notes while she was cleaning up. Now there was a good thought. She'd search for the notes and tackle the mess at the same time.

Her closets were basically stuffed already, but she managed to shift a few things and push some unread fiction books inside, along with the videos she'd bought and never watched and the collection of beads she'd accumulated back when she'd thought it might be an okay hobby.

For years she'd tried to interest herself in a more peaceful pastime, one that wouldn't cause explosions and alarm the neighbors, but all her efforts in that direction had seemed wimpy and dull. Why make a necklace when you could create a hovercraft? But she kept trying to be normal, which was why she also had a rock tumbler and a sack full of rocks that had to go somewhere.

She tucked them under her round bed, although the hand loom and calligraphy set were already taking up most of the space. A rectangular bed would have more storage space underneath. Maybe she ought to consider trading in her round bed for a traditional one.

Because the washing machine wasn't working, anyway, she filled it with whatever she didn't know what else to do with—unread fashion magazines, widgets she'd bought at the Middlesex Hardware Store because they looked interesting, the box of candy she didn't like but couldn't bear to toss because the receptionist at her talent agency had given it to her. And on top of all that went the book she'd bought on how to unclutter your life. She hadn't made it past the first chapter.

Denise would be sleeping in what Eve laughingly called her guest room, a den that opened off the living area. At the moment the daybed was buried under a mound of clothes still in their plastic dry-cleaning bags. Her broken washing machine had forced her to get everything but her underwear professionally cleaned. Scooping the bundle into her arms with a crackle of static electricity, she looked underneath, hoping to see her notes. No such luck.

She was on her way toward her bedroom down the hall when the doorbell rang. A glance at the clock told her it was still too early for Charlie and Rick. "Come in!" she called. "It's open!"

Then she wondered if maybe she was carrying her complacency about unlocked doors too far. The crime rate might be low in this little town, but that didn't mean she should invite someone in without having a clue who they were. A burglar might have recently located in Middlesex.

So she stood there with her arms full of her dry cleaning, unsure what she'd do if the person on the other side of the door had theft in mind. Smother them in cleaning bags? Jab them with a metal hanger?

She was relieved when Eunice walked in, stomping snow from her booted feet. She held up two bottles. "I brought wine!"

"Well, um, thanks." Eve needed wine tonight about

like a battery needed a bow tie. She had two goals—work on the hovercraft and work on Charlie. She wanted a clear head for both projects.

"Not for you and Charlie, of course. You'll be operating machinery and such. But Rick and I could have some." Eunice plunked the bottles down on the floor and started taking off her coat.

"Yes, you certainly could have some." And a bottle apiece should keep them busy while Eve worked her program. "Not that it's any big deal or anything, but is it possible you forgot to lock the front door after the FedEx man was here?"

Eunice frowned. "I don't *think* so. Was it unlocked when you came home?"

"Yeah, but don't worry about it."

"Jeez, if I forgot to lock it I really apologize. Are you missing anything?"

Eve thought of her notes, but they could still turn up somewhere. "No," she said and decided to change the subject. "Did you decide for or against the cell phone?"

"Against." Eunice had piled her blond hair in a fancy arrangement on top of her head, and she wore a slinky red lounging outfit. "I think this should do the trick."

Eve surveyed the generous display of cleavage. "You know, I always wondered exactly what they meant by a plunging neckline. Now I get it."

"This sucker plunges like Niagara Falls, doesn't it? If I move just right you'll get a glimpse of the diamond I have in my belly button. Well, cubic zirconium, to be honest, but if somebody gets close enough to check, they're going to be interested in something besides gem quality." Eunice glanced at Eve's burden. "Sarah down at the Press 'n' Go probably paid off her Toyota after you picked up that load."

"This is an accumulation. My washing machine's broken."

Eunice leaned against the wall and pulled off her boots. "I'm surprised you haven't fixed it yourself." She took a pair of jeweled sandals from her purse and slipped them on her feet. "You being so mechanical and all."

"Fixing broken things is boring. Making something new that didn't exist before—now that I can get into."

"So I've noticed."

Eve shifted the weight of her dry cleaning. "I'd better put these away. Make yourself at home." The comment was superfluous for Eunice, who always did that, anyway. "I'll be right ba—" The doorbell rang, and this time, she figured it would be Charlie and Rick.

In case she had any doubts on that subject, Eunice reacted by racing to the peephole and sucking in her breath.

"It's them?" Eve asked.

"He is so gorgeous that if I were a nun, I'd leave the order for him."

"Fortunately for you and the Catholic church, you're not a nun." Eve was delighted with Eunice's choice of guy. That left Charlie free and clear. "Are you going to open the door?"

"Yes." Eunice stepped back and grabbed her purse from the floor. Taking out a breath spray, she gave her mouth a couple of shots before dropping the spray back in her purse and balancing the purse on top of her boots. Then she spit on her fingers and twirled them around the tendrils of hair that had been allowed to hang artfully from her upswept do.

"Are you going to open the door anytime in the near future?"

The doorbell rang again. Eunice glanced over at Eve and smiled. "Is there lipstick on my teeth?" she asked without changing expression.

"Not that I can see." Eve's glasses were smudged from her frantic efforts to straighten up the place, but she didn't bother to tell Eunice. That would mean at least another minute delay while Eunice waited for her to clean the lenses.

"Does this smile show too much of my gums?" Eunice looked like a ventriloquist, talking like that without moving her lips.

"Eunice, open the damned door."

"Okay." Throwing back her shoulders, Eunice kept her smile in place as she opened the door. "Charlie! *Rick!* What a nice surprise!"

"Well, hel-*lo* there, Eunice." Rick's gaze took in the Niagara Falls plunge. "Talk about a nice surprise! I froze my ass riding over here with Charlie, but you make the sacrifice worthwhile."

"Eve invited me." Eunice twirled a loose strand of blond hair around her finger. "I brought wine."

"Excellent." Rick continued to block the door while he stared at her.

"I brought pizza." Charlie shouldered his way past his cousin and nudged the door closed with his knee. His dark-framed glasses fogged up immediately. "And it's hot, so we might want to—" He paused and squinted at Eve through the misty lenses. "Are you holding a whole bunch of clothes?"

She'd been so fascinated by the interaction between Rick and Eunice that she'd forgotten the bundle in her arms. "My dry cleaning."

"That's a boatload of dry cleaning."

She didn't think in Charlie's world that was a good thing. He didn't look like the kind of guy who liked high-maintenance women. "My washing machine's broken, so I've had to take stuff to Press 'n' Go." She found herself staring at his leather chaps and remembering how they'd framed his buns the first time they'd met. The chaps did a similar favor for his package.

"Your washing machine's broken?" Charlie shoved the pizza boxes against Rick's chest. "Here. Hold these."

Rick was so busy ogling Eunice that it took him a couple of seconds to respond and grab the boxes. "Uh, okay."

"I'm going to take a minute to look at Eve's washing machine." Charlie was out of his coat and boots and chaps in no time. Then he did a quick polish of his glasses before he padded over to Eve in his socks. "Where is it?"

"Really, that's okay." She was struck by how gallantly he'd leaped to her aid, and how seeing him in his socks made her wonder how he'd look with a few more items of clothing removed. "I wouldn't expect you to fix it. I'm sure it needs . . . something. I should have called a repair person, but I—"

"Ah, no reason to call somebody. I can fix it."

"He probably can," Rick said. "If it has moving parts, Charlie can fix it. He's pretty much the repair king."

"Then by all means, Eve, let the man do what he does best," Eunice said. "Rick and I can drink wine in the kitchen until you two come back."

Eve could see how this had played right into Eunice's hands. No telling what would happen in the kitchen if Eve and Charlie left Eunice alone with Rick and two bottles of wine. But one glance at Charlie's eager expression convinced Eve that she had to go along with the repair option. Rejecting Charlie's skills would be the same as rejecting him, and she wasn't about to do that.

"Okay, follow me," she said. "I'll drop these off in my bedroom on the way." She started down the hall.

"We'll be in the kitchen if you need us," Eunice called after her.

"Start on the pizza too if you want," Charlie said before following Eve. "This should be quick, but just in case it isn't, go ahead and eat."

"We might, at that, cuz," Rick said. "It smells great. I never could resist a piping hot pizza."

Eve wondered if he could resist a piping hot Eunice. If he couldn't, so much the better, because just like that, Eve had Charlie to herself. She hadn't expected it to be so easy. Who knew a broken washing machine could create a romantic opportunity?

"You won't have to hang around once I get into it," Charlie said. "You should grab some pizza before it gets cold."

Apparently he wasn't viewing this at all the way she was. She'd have to come up with a reason to stay. "Let me dump these clothes in my bedroom and then we'll see what the situation is. I'd like to watch and see how you do it." She stepped into her bedroom and laid the dry cleaning on the bed.

Then she turned to find Charlie standing in the doorway waiting for her. Charlie in the doorway of her bedroom was an unexpectedly arousing sight. Even without the benefit of a leather motorcycle jacket, his shoulders were satisfyingly broad. Add to that the appealing way his brown hair curled just a little, sending a softening wave down over his high, intelligent-looking forehead, and you had one hot-looking guy.

Ever since Monday afternoon, her hormonal reaction had been building in her system gradually, drop by drop. Now it had reached critical mass and she was helpless in the face of urges that shocked her.

She wanted him this very minute. If he walked into the room and threw her on the bed, they could do it on top of the dry cleaning as far as she was concerned. She probably wouldn't even notice unless a hanger poked her in the butt.

As she watched him standing in the doorway, her mouth began to water. Denise was so not getting her mitts on this guy. Eve wanted to strip off his flannel shirt and corduroy slacks to find out if indeed he wore tighty-whities as she suspected. Suddenly that seemed like the sexiest underwear in the world.

He, however, wanted to fix her washing machine. Somewhere between those two goals they might be able to find a meeting place.

"Mm." His murmur of approval caught her by surprise.

Was it possible that he'd read her mind? If she stayed right where she was, would he walk into the room and take her in his arms?

When he moved in her direction, her heartbeat changed dramatically. What a rush. She'd never been so in tune with someone that he acted out her internal impulses. Should she go to meet him, to let him know his instincts were right on target?

As she debated whether to hold out both arms in welcome, he cruised right past her and picked up the pamphlet on her bedside table.

"Properties of the Custom Rotary Engine." He flipped it open to the table of contents. "Now there's something I wish I'd had a chance to read before tonight. Can I borrow it?"

"Uh, sure." Damn, he'd been after her bedside reading material, not her. So much for being in tune. "It gives all the parameters. I skimmed it instead of doing an in-depth study of the specs. If I'd read it cover to cover, I might have avoided blowing up the first one."

"We're not going to blow up another one." Charlie started leafing through the pamphlet and nodding. "Yeah, this is great." Then he closed the pamphlet. "Now let's check out that washing machine."

"Okay." Getting Charlie to think about something human instead of mechanical might prove more of a challenge than she'd thought.

But right before he turned around to leave the room, he paused. "You have a round bed." He sounded surprised, as if he'd been so absorbed in the pamphlet that this was the first real look he'd taken.

Obviously the man wasn't plugged into the same sexual outlet that was powering her sex drive. "Yes." She'd had it so long that she'd forgotten it worked as a conversation piece. If the bed could jump-start a personal discussion, fine.

"Why round?"

If only she could tell him she'd bought it because it was supposed to promote great sex, but that would be intellectually dishonest and she'd never been capable of that. "I read somewhere that if you want to spark creative ideas, you have to shake up your brain, surprise it with the unexpected. So I ordered a round bed."

"Does it work?" He drew closer to the bed.

Want to test-drive it and see? But she knew the timing was wrong for a comment like that. "It did at first. I had some wild dreams and came up with the hovercraft concept."

"There's an endorsement."

"But I should probably change to something else."

"Trapezium?"

She laughed. "Wow. No two sides the same. That would shake things up."

"Just draw up some specs and I'll fool around with it."

Now there was a concept. Charlie making her a bed. That could lead to some interesting discussions. "Okay, I will."

"With this one, though, I would think you'd fall off." He glanced from Eve to the bed and back again.

She wondered if he might be picturing her in that bed. With luck he was also imagining a sexy negligee. The brightness of his eyes made that a definite possibility.

"The dimensions feel strange at first, but you get used to them," she said. "Then again, I don't move a lot in bed." *Except when I go there to do something besides sleep.*

He swallowed. "I, uh, do. I thrash around something terrible. Sometimes I wake up and I'm all tangled in the . . ." His voice trailed off as his glance met hers. "But I'm sure you don't want to hear that."

"I don't mind." She held his gaze, which was fun because she had to look up. When a girl stood five ten in her stocking feet, she didn't look up to a whole lot of guys. Charlie was at least six five.

And he had such great eyes to look up into, especially when the light didn't reflect off the lens of his glasses. Right now there was no reflection at all, and she could study those intelligent brown peepers for as long as she wanted. "There are lots of things we don't know about each other."

"Guess so," he said softly. His eyes got all warm and dreamy. He looked like a man thinking seriously about a kiss. Then he backed off and took a deep breath. "To tell the truth, I'm not very interesting."

Chapter Six

Whew. Charlie wasn't sure what had happened, but he'd been damned close to kissing Eve at least twice. It was that mouth of hers, those incredible lips that had helped make her famous.

Obviously he was as susceptible to that mouth as the rest of the world, especially when she used it to explain her theory about sleeping in round beds to shake up her brain and promote creativity. He'd also allowed himself to stand next to that round bed of hers for way too long.

Then he'd made the colossal mistake of offering to build her one in the shape of a trapezium. When was he planning to do that? He had places to go, jobs to interview for. He needed to forget about beds and sex and get his hands on something mechanical fast.

He tucked the pamphlet on rotary engines in his hip pocket. "So where's your washing machine?"

"Down this way. The washer and dryer are in a closet in the bathroom." She led the way down the hall.

The hardwood floors felt great under his socks. He was renting an apartment with the standard beige carpeting, and he'd never realized how much he hated it until now. He'd been renting for years, always telling himself that buying a house was the first step in admitting he'd never leave Middlesex.

But he liked the feel of Eve's house. Sure, the place was a little cluttered, but he'd decided that was Eve's style. Ordinarily clutter drove him nuts, but he was so impressed with Eve's thought processes that he forgave her the clutter. He suspected she had a much higher IQ than anybody guessed. Although he was pretty smart, she might be smarter, maybe even genius level.

She kept that brain hidden away, but the hovercraft was like a giant neon sign advertising her superior intelligence. He was drawn to that bright light like a moth. And he shouldn't be.

Eve's bathroom smelled of her perfume and shampoo, which sent Charlie's libido into operational mode once again. He pictured Hoover Dam and tried to block the incoming sensual messages.

"The washer's in here." Eve opened a pair of bifold doors.

The washer and dryer were piled with more clutter. In an attempt to forget that Eve was standing right behind him, so near he could hear her breathing, he started cataloging the stuff. He noted supplies for scrapbooking, several skeins of purple yarn, three empty flowerpots and a trowel—minus any dirt—a book on herbs, packets of seeds, a box of watercolors, a table easel, a book titled *How to Draw Nudes* . . . whoa. Maybe cataloging the clutter wouldn't work to take his mind off sex.

"I keep trying to have normal hobbies, but it never works out." She continued to stand very close.

"I never could get into the hobby thing, either." Being so near Eve felt like standing in a thermal belt. Ambient heat teased him, and he fought the impulse to turn and pull all that warmth right into his arms. Instead he picked up a stack of junk and started to put it on the floor so he could get to the washer.

"I'll take that," she said. "I really should get rid of some of this, because I never follow through. I just go back to working on that crazy hovercraft. If I didn't have all this stuff around, then I probably wouldn't have misplaced my hovercraft notes."

"You did?" This was how genius could flounder. No doubt the notes were brilliant, and they could be anywhere in this mess. What a crime. Maybe Eve needed someone around to help her organize, someone like him, only not him. Definitely not him.

"I'm sure I'll find them." She didn't look all that sure, though. "It's just that I lose other stuff, but I've never misplaced something from the hovercraft project. And I could swear I left the notes on the workbench, because that's where I keep them."

"But you had that explosion." He had an image of papers flying everywhere. Valuable papers.

"I know. Stuff can happen. That's why I keep the notes under my Darth Vader mask. It's cast in lead, and it's very heavy."

"Once we get this finished up and have some pizza, I'll help you look." He didn't like the idea of missing notes. Not at all.

"It's not like I have to have them. Most of it's in my head, anyway."

"Maybe you don't need them, but if you ever intend to market the hovercraft, you'll need all the notes you can put together, to convince the money people to invest in it."

She took a deep breath. "Right. We'll find them."

"Yeah, we will." He held up the pile of stuff in his hands. "Where do you want this?"

"I'll take it."

He handed her the pile, which involved some physical contact. Static electricity arced between them.

"Ouch!" She pulled back and almost dropped everything.

"Sorry." Instinctively he reached for her hand to steady her. No shock this time, just warm, soft skin. So soft. So very . . . He let go abruptly as he realized they were staring into each other's eyes again exactly as they had in the bedroom, when he'd come so close to kissing her.

"It's okay." She smiled at him.

No, it wasn't okay. It wasn't okay that he was wildly attracted to this woman who had bought a house in Middlesex and seemed to be putting down roots.

"You have a nice house," he said.

"Thank you."

"I guess you must like the area."

"I adore the area." Her expression softened. "When I was house-hunting there were sappy Halloween decorations everywhere. I could hardly wait for the cardboard turkeys at Thanksgiving and the plastic reindeer at Christmastime."

"You're serious."

"Absolutely. I *love* plastic reindeer. My parents wouldn't be caught dead with one, though. Middlesex is the hokey small town I used to dream of when I was growing up in Boston."

"Well . . . that's good, then." And they were miles apart. She was settling in and he could hardly wait to leave. Charlie turned back to the washing machine and lifted off the rest of her hobbies-gone-wrong material, which included the easel and her book on drawing nudes.

"I made the right choice, that's for sure, although I did expect to get into some of these hobbies now that I live in a small town. Hobbies and small towns seem to go together."

"I guess." He wished he could stop thinking of her drawing nudes. "Except I don't really have any."

"Isn't playing pool a hobby?"

"Absolutely not." He exerted some force to pop up the top on the washer. It didn't come easily, so he had to put more muscle into it. The effort felt good and helped get his mind off the image of Eve sketching a live model.

"It's not? Well, there goes my only shot at a normal hobby."

He gave a mighty heave and the top came up with a metallic bang. "Playing pool, if you do it right, is a science." He could never pose nude for someone. Rick had that kind of chutzpah, but he didn't.

"I suppose it is a science. That's probably why I like it."

"No doubt. You play like a pro." Sometimes Charlie wished he could be more uninhibited, like his cousin. Rick wouldn't worry about whether he was leaving town. He'd put the moves on a woman anyway.

"I do enjoy it."

For a moment Charlie lost track of whether they were talking about pool or sex. But his answer would apply to either one. "Me, too."

"That stick of yours is awesome."

"Thanks." Okay, it had been pool. He'd been thinking about sex while he talked about pool. But now he needed to stop all the talking and thinking and fix this machine.

He glanced down into the bowels of the washer and discovered that she was using the wash basket for storage, too. Right on top was a book called *Kill That Clutter!* That made him smile. He left the stuff where it was because it didn't interfere with the repair work.

"Now that I live three blocks from a place with a pool table, I should buy my own cue," Eve said. "That is, if you'll be willing to play with me."

He managed to turn a bark of laughter into a cough.

Then he cleared his throat. "Sure." This was the point where he should explain about his job change, but he couldn't bring himself to do that yet. She seemed so happy at the prospect of him hanging around for a friendly game of pool that he hated to tell her he hoped to be gone in less than a month.

Reaching down, he wiggled a couple of wires. One was definitely loose. And so were his thoughts. He fantasized about fixing the washer, turning it on, and propping Eve up against it to have sex. He'd heard that the vibrations of a washing machine could make a woman come in no time.

"I'm glad there's no hard feelings," she said.

"Not at all." Other parts of him were hard, but not his feelings.

"Some guys don't like it when a woman licks them."

He wished she'd chosen a different way to phrase it. "Doesn't bother me." He checked the hoses, and they seemed to be okay. This might be a really easy fix, once he had a screwdriver.

But once he had a screwdriver, they'd have to go back to the kitchen and join the party in progress. Although he was flirting with disaster by staying here with Eve, his ego loved the idea that she found him good company. He hated to give up that heady feeling.

"It's nice that we're well matched," she said.

He pretended to fiddle with the hoses. "Even if we weren't, that would be okay. It would be a learning experience for me." He studied the inside of the washer and pretended to be thinking very hard about the repair.

"Not many men are secure enough to learn something from a woman."

Charlie could think of no further excuses for staring into the innards of the washing machine, so he turned around. "Maybe not." He looked into her eyes and knew he'd be deliriously happy if she'd teach him anything at all. Underwater basket-weaving would be fine. The subject wouldn't matter—he'd be her willing pupil for the duration.

"That's something special about you, Charlie. You don't have those stupid macho hang-ups." She gazed at him, her eyes very blue behind the thin wire frames of her glasses.

"I like things to be straightforward." Like this, where they were both being totally honest with each other. He'd had no idea the chemistry would be this compelling or he would never have offered to fix her washer.

"Okay, so how's this for straightforward? Do you have a girlfriend?"

"I don't have a girlfriend."

"Oh." Chagrin flashed in her eyes. "Then you must not find me attractive, after all."

"Not true." He took her by the shoulders, more contact than he'd ever dared before. But he didn't want her thinking that she wasn't good enough. Never that. "I find you incredibly attractive, but why you would even care what I think is a mystery."

Her expression grew soft. "I like you, Charlie. I like you a lot."

"That's crazy." He had the sensation of sliding into a vast pit that would swallow him. Maybe he was never, ever leaving this town. She was the equivalent of a siren song, luring him to crash on the rocks of this Connecticut village and never make his journey out West. If he didn't believe his mother was a bastion of integrity, he'd think she'd bribed Eve to rope him and tie him securely to Middlesex.

"I don't know why you think it's so crazy," Eve said. "There's a lot to like about you."

He was aware she'd moved closer, dangerously closer.

Or maybe he was responsible for that. He might have been tugging her toward him. He did still have a grip on her shoulders. "I have to explain something, something very important."

"All right." She ran a tongue over her lips.

The urge to kiss her was so strong that he almost didn't get the sentence out, but he managed somehow. "It's all about Hoover Dam."

Of all the things Eve had expected to hear, Hoover Dam wasn't one of them. But Charlie was a complicated man, and she seemed to be stuck on him, so she might as well learn about this Hoover Dam thing. "Lay it on me."

"Do you have any idea how many kilowatt hours that dam produces per year, on average?"

"None whatsoever." Nothing was making sense so far, but Charlie was holding on to her, and that was such a marvelous sensation that she would listen to a lecture on the mating habits of tree frogs if only he'd keep his hands right there.

Or maybe not right there. Maybe other, more interesting places. But her shoulders were a start. A very good start.

"Four billion kilowatt hours per year." Charlie tightened his grip and his eyes sparkled. "Can you imagine that?"

"Amazing." She loved stats almost as much as she loved the enthusiastic way Charlie was squeezing her arms. "How many turbines?"

"Seventeen." He threw the number out with a proud flourish.

"Impressive! Output?"

"Brace yourself. Almost *three million horsepower.*"

"Wow! Now that's generating capacity!" She quivered. Charlie was generating a sizable amount of electricity, himself. And that electricity was pouring through her at the point of contact. She wouldn't mind having more points of contact.

"You're not kidding, Eve. It's an incredible facility. Absolutely incredible." His voice grew husky as he drew her closer.

She went willingly, drawn into his magnetic field.

"And I want to work there," he murmured.

"I don't blame you." Her heart beat furiously and she could barely breathe.

He took off his glasses and tucked them in his pocket. "I want to walk all ten acres of floor space knowing I'm part of an operation that huge."

"That would be wonderful." She pictured him striding along, glorying in the magnificence of the plant.

His voice vibrated with excitement as he gently pushed her glasses to the top of her head. "They uprated the plant in '93 and now they have all Francis-type vertical hydraulic turbines."

She moistened her lips. "I really love hydraulic power." Now that he'd pushed her glasses on top of her head, the only thing she could see clearly was his face, which was all she wanted to see, anyway. She was at a perfect angle to focus on his kissing equipment as she slipped her arms around his waist.

"I want to feel the power of those seventeen turbines spinning."

She sighed. *"Yes."* She'd always thought turbines were blatantly sexual with their shafts and rotors. There was even a small section at the very tip called an exciter. A part of her body was very much like that exciter, and currently it was yearning for some stimulation of the Charlie variety.

"Oh, Eve, you do understand." He leaned down, his mouth inches from hers. The closer he came, the better he looked—a nicely sculpted upper lip and a sensuously rounded lower lip made for the perfect combination. He cradled her head with one hand and urged her closer.

"I totally get it." She closed her eyes and lifted her chin, so he would have no trouble finding her in case his eyesight was worse than hers.

"I knew you would." And he kissed her, right on target.

On a scale of one to ten, the kiss rated a fifty. If she'd known Charlie could kiss like this, she would have asked him to fix her washer several months ago. She wondered how many women he'd practiced on to achieve this level of competence.

And then she decided not to think about that, because pure feeling was coming at her like the water pouring out of Hoover Dam. When Charlie wrapped her in his arms and the kiss went from American to French, the dam gave way. She moaned. Charlie moaned. Everything got hotter and wetter. This was turning into one big-ass kiss and she had the builders of Hoover Dam to thank for it.

The longer they kissed, the tighter Charlie held her, until there was no measurable space between them and no doubt that this kiss was generating all kinds of activity besides simple oral gratification. Eve's panties grew decidedly damp, and she figured the stretch factor of Charlie's tighty-whities was being thoroughly tested.

Quickly she figured her options. The bathroom door had a lock. The bathroom vanity had condoms. No worries on any front.

With a groan, Charlie lifted his talented mouth away from hers.

She had a good idea what he might want to say, so she answered the questions for him. "Lock on the door, condoms under the sink."

His breath was warm on her face as he struggled to take in air. "We can't."

"Sure we can." She tried to pull his head back down so they could go on kissing. Kissing would lead to good things. Talking wouldn't get them anywhere.

He resisted. "I can't have this and Hoover Dam both."

This sounded like something she'd have to deal with. She opened her eyes and gazed up at him. A flood of hormones interfered with her normal thought processes, but she managed to get a reasonable question out there. "Having sex with me now will mean you won't get the job at Hoover Dam?"

"It's a step in the wrong direction, that's for sure."

"Who do you think I am, a double agent for some international spy network?"

"Worse. You're crazy about Middlesex."

Chapter Seven

Charlie knew he couldn't have screwed this up any more if he'd tried. He'd meant to give Eve a simple explanation of his fascination with Hoover Dam and his lifelong dream to work there. Then he'd planned to tell her that because he was leaving and she so obviously loved it here, they had no future.

But he'd been guilty of premature kissing, which had led to a premature erection on his part and lots of enthusiastic body movements on hers, all before the full story was out. His excitement about the dam and his sexual attraction to her had brought them to this. Chaos.

She wiggled out of his arms. "So I'm crazy about Middlesex. So what?"

He fished his glasses out of his pocket and put them on, so he could assess her expression better. "What I mean is, you're a permanent resident." *And the most beautiful permanent resident I've ever seen.*

"My goodness. How *awful*. I should be ashamed of myself." She settled her glasses on the bridge of her nose and glared at him. "Allow me to point out the obvious. So are you, kilowatt boy."

"Not really. I'm renting, not buying. I'm temporary." He tried to ignore those full, moist lips. Tried and failed.

"Temporary? You've lived here all your life!"

"So far, that's true." He sighed and rubbed the back of his neck. "But I have other plans."

"Like Hoover Dam?"

"Exactly." He felt in tune with that dam right now. Lust was bottled up in him and the pressure continued to build.

She blew out a breath. "Look, I told you I understand about Hoover Dam, and I do. Working there sounds like your kind of fun. And pardon me if I'm getting into a sensitive area, but . . . why aren't you there yet?"

"Um, well, I had some dumb idea that I could institute some changes at the ML and P before I left town, sort of a good-bye gift. About the time I figured out that was hopeless, my dad's health got bad. Then after he died, my mom was depressed, naturally. But working with her sister in the bakery seems to be the answer there, so . . . I have an interview next week in Nevada."

"That's really sweet, that you've stuck around for such noble reasons." Her gaze softened and her voice grew gentle. "Charlie, I was ready to have sex with you. I wasn't planning to ask for your hand in marriage."

And that was the embarrassing part. He'd handled this whole incident wrong. "I'm sure that's true, but I still think I should have said something before we ever got to this point—"

" 'This point' being right before we're ready to rip each other's clothes off?"

"Pretty much." Heat shot through his veins as he imagined that scene. "Anyway, I should have found a way to explain my situation."

She crossed her arms over her chest. "So you think we shouldn't have sex because you're planning to leave town. Is that the gist of it?"

"When you put it that way, it sounds dumb." A really cool guy—a guy like Rick—would go for it. And even if the relationship turned out to be fantastic, Rick would leave the girl and take the job in Nevada. But Charlie knew himself. He could be talked into staying, and that would be bad.

"Not necessarily dumb. Noble, maybe. I'm thinking you have a noble streak a mile wide."

"I wouldn't say that." He wasn't being noble. More like cowardly, afraid he couldn't handle sex with Eve, afraid he'd trash his career plans so he could stay and have even more sex with Eve.

"I would." She uncrossed her arms. "And it's okay, Charlie."

He didn't know how to respond to that. It was an awkward moment, one Charlie didn't have all that much experience with. He'd never tried to discourage a woman from having sex with him. He must be out of his mind.

"Do you think you can fix the washer?" she asked.

"I'll need a screwdriver."

"They're out in the garage. I'll be right back."

After she left, he scrubbed both hands through his hair and massaged his scalp as he tried to think what to do next. He'd kissed her. He'd *kissed* her, for God's sake. And it had been one hell of a kiss, too. He deserved a medal for pulling away from that amazing liplock.

He also deserved a punch in the nose for getting into it in the first place. His instinct to fix anything mechanical in the vicinity had put him in the way of temptation, and he'd had so little resistance it was pathetic.

She kissed with a depth of soul that still lingered on his

mouth. Man, how it lingered. He couldn't allow another kiss to happen, and yet the craving gnawed at him. Good thing he didn't believe in love at first kiss, or he'd be in serious shit.

But that kiss didn't represent an instant love connection. No, it was undoubtedly the result of not having had sex for the past few months. He hadn't realized how sex-starved he was until he'd pulled Eve into his arms.

Her footsteps on the hardwood floor of the hallway announced her return. She came through the bathroom door and gave him a handful of screwdrivers of various sizes including several of the Phillips variety. "Rick and Eunice are gone."

He blinked. "What do you mean, *gone*?"

"As in, not in the kitchen. Your Harley's still parked in the driveway, though."

"It better be. I have the keys."

"Hmm." Eve paused. "They must have headed over to Eunice's house."

"Or they were both transported into a spaceship for sexual experimentation." He should have figured on this, knowing his cousin.

"I think they're at Eunice's house having sex," Eve said.

Probably. The concept made him uneasy, because Rick was doing what Charlie didn't have the guts to do. "That's not a given." He picked out a screwdriver and laid the rest on top of the dryer. Rick wasn't letting geography rule his sex life. Only Charlie, the uncool one, was doing that.

"I think it's a given. I—" She was interrupted by the sound of a phone ringing in the kitchen. "Excuse me a minute."

Charlie tightened a couple of loose wires while he debated whether he was being a complete idiot. What kind of guy turned down sex with someone who looked like Eve? A dope, that's who.

Disgusted with himself, he closed the top of the washer with a clang. Might as well turn the thing on and see if it worked. Twisting the knob into position for Permanent Press, he started the water. So far, so good.

He listened to the water pouring in and took some satisfaction from this tiny victory. He might not be man enough to take advantage of a ready-made sexual situation, but it looked as if he'd managed to fix the washer.

Fixing equipment had always been his deal. It had started because his dad, the most unhandy guy in the world, had insisted on trying to repair things, anyway. Charlie had decided at an early age that if he didn't learn something about electrical appliances, his dad might burn down the house. Then, to Charlie's surprise, he'd become fascinated by the subject of electricity.

Eve walked back into the bathroom, her cordless phone in her hand. She glanced at the washing machine. "Hey, it works!" Then her eyes widened. "Did you take out the—"

A loud thumping noise answered the question. They leaped for the knob at the same time and collided, which resulted in neither of them getting the washer turned off.

"I'll get it!" Eve pushed him aside and turned off the machine. Then she lifted the lid. "That's not pretty." She clanged the lid shut again.

"I'm sorry, Eve." Charlie's sense of victory evaporated. The one thing he'd accomplished had turned out to create more problems than it solved.

"It doesn't matter."

He sighed. "It does matter. I'd better take a look." Expecting something gross, he lifted the lid. Instead he became intrigued by what he found. "Hey, the candy's floating to the top. Did you know candy floats?"

"Nope. It wasn't floating when I looked." She braced her forearms on the top of the machine and leaned down to get a better view. "What do you know? I would think it's too dense to float."

"Yeah, me, too." The chocolate bobbed around in what looked like a pool of industrial waste. He rested his arms next to hers and hunkered down so their heads were at the same level.

Her shoulder touched his in a friendly way. "I didn't want any of that stuff in the first place, so it doesn't bother me if it's trashed."

When they stood side by side, their bodies touching at several points, Charlie couldn't bring himself to care, either. Every time she shifted her weight she created a soft friction that reminded him of how good she'd felt in his arms. Friendly was evolving into something much hotter.

"I'm not surprised that the subscription postcards from the magazines are floating, but I wouldn't have guessed the chocolate." He couldn't help himself. He deliberately moved, ever so slightly, so that his arm rubbed hers.

"Cheap chocolate."

"Ah." He noticed that her *Kill That Clutter!* book lay on its side looking extremely soggy. Too bad she was taking this disaster so well. He would have been more than willing to comfort her if she'd been inconsolable at the loss of this junk. He'd about decided that his former decision, whether noble, cowardly, or stupid, was a mistake.

Eve gazed into the washing machine. "I keep thinking of that scene out of *Titanic*."

"Yeah." Charlie nodded. "I hated that scene." Agreement caused his shoulder to bump hers. He longed to run his tongue down the curve of her neck and along the line of her shoulder. Then he'd nip her very gently before following the ridge of her collarbone back to the hollow of her throat.

"I hated that scene, too."

He thought it was a good sign that they agreed on which scene they hated. "But the scene in the car, where you see her hand against the steamed-up glass . . ."

"Very hot." She continued to stare down at the muck in the washing machine, but her breathing changed. "Have you ever been on a ship?"

"No."

"No matter where you are, you can still feel the vibration of the engines. I'll bet they felt it there, in the car, the whole time. Very erotic."

"Mm." Where was a cruise ship when a guy needed one?

"We should turn this machine back on and see what happens."

A working washing machine had been part of his earlier fantasy. He could back her up against it and they'd both feel that vibration running through them as they . . .

Oh, hell, what was he thinking? That was the kind of sexual experience that stayed with a guy forever. One up-against-the-washing-machine moment and he'd give up on Hoover Dam to stay in Middlesex for the rest of his life. Guaranteed. He wasn't Rick, so he'd be crazy to try and act like him.

"Let's do it." Eve reached for the knob.

"Wait." Charlie had to come up with a way to derail this impulse. Fortunately, he glimpsed something in the washer. Stuck between the pages of her clutter book was a type of metal fastener he'd been needing for a repair on his mother's garbage disposal and he hadn't gotten around to picking one up yet.

He plucked it out of the glop. "Did you get this for the hovercraft?"

She paused and looked at him for a full five seconds as the sexual heat building between them began to diffuse. "Uh, no. I thought I might need it under the dashboard, but I don't think it's quite right. I need the next size up, probably."

"Can I have it?"

"Be my guest. There's some other hardware stuff in there, too."

"Really?"

"Sure. I'm always collecting pieces of hardware."

He gazed at her in wonder. "Don't tell me you're one of those people who get their kicks strolling through a hardware store."

"Maybe." She smiled at him, but it was fondness rather than lust in her blue eyes. " 'Fraid so."

She really had the most amazing mouth, and he wouldn't have to move very much to reach it. Just one kiss. A kiss wasn't the same as washing machine sex. He could handle one little kiss. A haze descended over his brain as he leaned forward, focusing on that wide, welcoming mouth . . .

"Oh, Charlie." She sighed and reached up to cradle his head. The phone she was holding banged against his ear.

He reached for it. "Here, let me have that." He was thinking of dropping it into the washing machine, so it wouldn't ring any more and disturb them.

"Uh-oh!" She backed away from the machine, which meant backing away from him, too. "I almost forgot! I have to call Eunice and see if Rick's over there."

The haze began to clear from his brain. "Is someone looking for him?"

"Manny is. He said Rick wasn't answering his cell." Eve punched a number into the phone.

"Did you tell him that Rick might be over at Eunice's house?"

"No, because I didn't want Manny and Kyle running over there. Who knows what's going on?"

"Maybe nothing." Charlie couldn't convince himself of that.

"Maybe more than we care to know. Anyway, I said I'd check out what was happening with his cell. Manny and Kyle just got back from Hartford. Did you know they went to Hartford?"

"They ran an errand for the bakery." Charlie pushed the thought of the X-rated cookie cutter from his mind.

"Well, they're back."

"Did they change their minds about coming over to help with the hovercraft?" Charlie thought that might be good, to get more people into the project. Then he'd be less likely to end up alone with Eve, which was a responsibility he seemed unable to handle.

"I don't think they plan on helping. They said something about frosting cookies for Myrtle and Rose." Eve held the phone to her ear. Then she rolled her eyes. "Answering machine."

"Listen, maybe I should drain the water out while you're on the phone."

"Good idea." Eve turned back to the phone. "Eunice, if you're there, pick up. I need to talk to Rick." She tapped her foot on the bathroom tile as she waited.

Charlie listened to the water gurgle out of the washing machine. "I think they probably went to the movies."

Eve covered the mouthpiece. "You're delusional." Then she spoke into the phone. "Okay, I guess you're . . . unavailable. But Manny needs to talk to Rick, so call me back when you get this." She disconnected the phone. "Mark my words. They're doing it."

Charlie didn't want to think about it, because thinking about it only emphasized that Rick could enjoy sex for sex's sake and Charlie couldn't. He picked up the dripping clutter book. "If we take this stuff out I can run the machine through a complete cycle and make sure it's fixed. Do you have a big bucket?"

She blew out an impatient breath. "Let's forget about it."

"You can't exactly do that. It'll congeal." Leaving a mess wasn't Charlie's style, especially when he'd helped create it. "Then there's no telling if your machine will ever work right."

"I don't really ca—" She must have seen the look of dismay on his face. She paused and cleared her throat. "Charlie, it was wonderful of you to give this a shot, but I want you for the hovercraft, not my washing machine."

Hearing her say she wanted him, even if the rest of the sentence was about mechanical projects and not sex, drove out all thoughts of appliance disasters. Instead he found himself concentrating on her mouth and the memory of its moist, velvety interior.

Unless he got out of this cozy bathroom that had a lock on the door and condoms under the sink, he was liable to do something incredibly unwise. He closed the lid on the washer. "Let's go see about the hovercraft."

Chapter Eight

As they walked into the kitchen, Eve noticed the pizza boxes sitting on the table and remembered they hadn't eaten dinner. A hot number like Charlie could make a girl forget all about food, but now that he wasn't kissing her, she discovered she was hungry, after all. "Want to take some pizza and Cokes out to the garage so we can eat while we work?"

"Sure." Charlie walked over and lifted the lid on both boxes. "Looks like Eunice and Rick made off with the pepperoni and sausage. I hope it wasn't your favorite."

"Nope."

"What is?" He glanced over at her.

"Veggie, but I like other kinds, too."

He looked pleased with himself. "Then veggie it is. But it's not very warm."

"That's okay with me." She wouldn't expect it to be warm after all the time she and Charlie had spent in the bathroom fooling around with the washer and each other. "But I can nuke some for you, if you want."

"Nah. Cold is usually how I eat it, because I get involved in some project and forget until it's too late."

"Me, too. Besides, cold pizza isn't as messy, so you can work without getting food everywhere."

"Exactly."

They exchanged a smile of agreement, and that smile of his had way more impact now that she knew what a great kisser he was. It didn't matter, though. Charlie could hardly wait to leave Middlesex, while Eve had finally found a place she wanted to call home. As he'd pointed out, they were headed down different paths.

But they were in the same place right now, and she had to decide whether or not to ignore his noble reluctance and seduce him. A man who could kiss like Charlie might be able to perform other heterosexual tasks with the same level of expertise. After six months of abstinence, Eve found herself more than a little interested.

She grabbed a couple of Cokes out of the refrigerator. "Do you and Rick usually eat one pizza apiece?"

"No. Why?"

"I just wondered why you brought three. That's a lot of pizza, especially when you didn't know Eunice was coming over."

He started out toward the garage. "I wanted to make sure I had a kind you liked."

"That was thoughtful." And thought-provoking, too. He'd overbought on the pizza in order to increase his odds of hitting her preference. He was a guy who really wanted to please. She couldn't remember the last time she'd had a lover with that kind of mind-set. She wondered if he'd consider an affair if she promised not to keep him in Middlesex a minute longer than he wanted to stay.

"Charlie?"

"What?" He turned, the pizza box in his hand.

Want to have a no-strings affair with me? It was a showstopper of a line, but she couldn't deliver it. What if he said no? They'd never be able to work on the hovercraft together for the next few nights if that invitation and rejection hung in the air between them.

"I forgot napkins," she said. "Be right back."

Turning back to the kitchen, she took a deep breath. Might as well face the truth, the one that Charlie had already figured out. Neither of them were the type who had no-strings affairs. Therefore Charlie saw her as off-limits. She might as well be sitting inside a red circle with a slash across the middle.

Looking at the situation from her perspective, she was up against quite an obstacle—Hoover Dam, to be precise. Someone could even say she was in a pissing contest with that installation, and considering the volume of water churning through it, she wouldn't have much of a chance. Plus she didn't want to deliberately get in the way of Charlie's dream.

So although he was yummy, she would rein herself in and let any moves be his. If he kissed her, she'd kiss back. If he started undressing her, she'd start undressing him. If he inquired about the location of the condoms, she'd tell him exactly where to find them. He couldn't very well blame her for throwing a monkey wrench into his scheme if he'd been caught red-handed heaving the wrench himself.

With that settled, she headed back into the garage. She found Charlie studying something that looked like a page of her notes. "Did you find them?"

He glanced up. "Only this page. A corner of it was sticking out from under the hovercraft."

"That's weird." She put the Cokes on the workbench and got to her knees to look around the edge of the hovercraft.

"I did that already. I didn't find any other pages. You must have moved the notes and dropped this one in the process."

Still on her knees, she repositioned her glasses and gazed up at him. "I know my house is filled with clutter, but it's organized clutter. I know what's there. I wouldn't have picked up notes that were this important and dropped a page without realizing it. I just wouldn't."

"Then what do you think happened?"

"I don't know. I'm the only one who's been out here."

"Until Monday night."

She stared at him. "What are you saying?"

"I don't know." He shook his head. "Never mind. I shouldn't be casting suspicion on anyone."

"Did you see anybody go near the workbench Monday night?" Eve thought back over the discussion they'd had out there with Eunice, Rick, Manny, and Kyle. "Because I didn't."

"I don't think I did, either. But I was so engrossed in looking at the hovercraft that I can't be sure."

She got to her feet. "I would have noticed, and I don't think they did." Even when she'd been exchanging that meaningful glance with Charlie, she would have seen someone walk over and pick up her notes. Or at least she liked to think she would have. While trying to re-create the scene in her head, she walked over to the pizza box and took out a slice.

Charlie reached in while the box was open and took out a piece, too. "Anybody else have access to them since then?"

As she closed the lid on the pizza box, Eve thought of Eunice, the FedEx delivery, and the unlocked door. "Eunice has a key to the house. I gave it to her months ago so she could put any packages that are delivered to me inside the door. I get a lot of deliveries of parts, and I'm often out of town when they come."

"Would she come in and take the notes?"

"I can't imagine why. She's known about the hover-craft pretty much from the beginning. If she'd wanted to steal my notes, she could have done it long before now."

"Maybe she didn't think it was worth it before, but after Monday night, she realized the notes might be valuable."

Eve swallowed her bite of pizza. "That's just it—they're not of much value by themselves. You'd need more than that to market it. Plus the information about the fuel is wrong. I blew up an engine with what's in those notes. I don't know how anyone could make use of them."

"She might not know that."

"I'm sorry, but I can't believe Eunice would steal my notes hoping to make a profit." Even though Eunice liked designer shoes and handbags, she wouldn't stoop to theft. Would she?

When the doorbell rang, Eve jumped. Then she grinned self-consciously. "Guess I've managed to freak myself out."

"Maybe it's Eunice and Rick coming back."

"I doubt it." Returning her half-eaten piece of pizza to the box, Eve headed toward the kitchen. "They wouldn't be ringing the doorbell when they could just walk in."

"You mean because Eunice has a key?" Charlie followed her.

"She wouldn't need it. The door's unlocked."

"You don't automatically lock your doors?"

"Not usually when I'm here." She walked through the kitchen into the entryway as the doorbell rang again. "This is a small town. That's one of the reasons I wanted to live here as opposed to New York. I like not having to lock my door all the time." But she had to admit that finding her door unlocked when she'd come home tonight had been unsettling.

"I'm not sure that's a good idea, leaving your door open when you're here."

"Oh, come on." She didn't like this subject, didn't like feeling on edge about her personal safety. That was a New York issue, not a Middlesex issue. "Don't tell me you lock yourself in whenever you get home, because I won't believe you."

"No, but I'm a . . . an engineer."

She swung to face him. "You were going to say it's because you're a man, weren't you? Then you thought better of it at the last minute."

"Maybe." He had the decency to look uncomfortable. "Sorry about that."

"Damn straight. For all you know I'm a black belt who can take somebody out while you're still standing there figuring the odds."

"Are you a black belt?"

"No." She'd thought about taking self-defense classes when she'd lived in New York, but now it seemed unnecessary.

"Then I wish you'd lock your door."

"I refuse to live like an inner-city person when I'm not one anymore." But she turned around and checked the peephole before she opened the door. Some habits were hard to break.

"It's Manny and Kyle." She opened the door. "Hi, guys! I thought you were frosting cookies."

Manny stomped the snow from his shoes. "We were, but when we didn't hear back from Rick, we thought we'd come over and check to make sure everything's okay."

Eve glanced at Charlie, who gave a noncommittal shrug. No help there. "Rick and Eunice went over to her house for a little while," Eve said. "They'll probably be back any minute."

"Where does she live?" Manny asked.

"Right next door," Eve said. "They should be back any time. Would you like to come in and wait for them? We have extra pizza, and I might have a couple of beers in the refrigerator."

"No, thanks." Manny started to turn away. "We'll just go check on Rick."

"I'm sure that's not necessary," Charlie said.

"We think it is necessary," Kyle said. "We just heard from an important client of his. We're talking big money. Rick would definitely want to respond personally to this. He's given us strict instructions to let him know whenever this client calls."

"Then I'll go get him." Charlie reached for his boots and shoved his feet into them. "I wouldn't want him to lose a valuable client."

"I'll go, too." Eve started putting on her boots and coat. She had an urge to talk to Eunice, anyway. Maybe the subject of hovercraft notes could be broached, to see whether Eunice looked guilty. Eve couldn't believe that her neighbor had taken anything, but now that the thought had been planted, it had taken root.

"Then I guess we'll all go," Manny said.

Before they left, Charlie took Eve's keys from the metal key holder she had mounted by the front door. Silently he handed them to her.

"I was going to lock it, you know," she said, feeling a little belligerent.

"Glad to hear it."

She resisted the urge to stick her tongue out at him. Instead she opted for maturity as she stepped outside and locked the door behind her. Before all of this came up she might not have locked it, though. Running next door hadn't seemed like reason enough. She hated the idea that her concept of small-town living might be naïve.

On the way across the snowy yard, she leaned close to Charlie so Manny and Kyle wouldn't hear. "There aren't any lights on in the front of the house."

"I noticed." Charlie's boots crunched through the top layer of frozen snow.

"Do you really think he wants to be interrupted, no matter what?" Eve tried to match her stride to Charlie's but came up a little short. They'd never walked anywhere together before, and she hadn't realized what big steps he took.

"The Rick I used to know wouldn't want to be interrupted, but maybe success has changed his priorities. That's why I want to handle this instead of leaving it to those X-rated cookie frosters."

"X-rated? What do you mean by that?"

"Uh, nothing."

"Come on, Charlie. Don't make me ask Manny and Kyle."

"They're for a bachelorette party." Charlie sounded uncomfortable. "They're on the explicit side."

Eve lowered her voice. "Your mom and aunt are baking explicit cookies?"

"Yep."

"I guess I shouldn't laugh, but that's too funny."

"Yeah, it's hilarious."

Obviously Charlie didn't appreciate the humor in it. "Now I have to see one. I can't believe those two women convinced the guys to help frost. I love that."

"My mom and Aunt Myrtle could charm the birds from the trees. Listen, when we get there, you and I will block the doorway so that if Rick wants us all to go away, that's what we'll tell these overzealous assistants."

"I, um, would actually like to have a word with Eunice."

Charlie gave her a sharp glance. "So you don't think she's so innocent, after all?"

"I think she's innocent," Eve said quickly. "I just want to make sure."

"You'd better get that key."

"I suppose." She hated the idea of mistrusting anyone and couldn't imagine asking Eunice to return the key.

"Any other keys floating around?" Charlie's breath fogged the air.

"I sent one to my parents, and another one to my sister, Denise." Six months ago she'd been so proud of owning her own little house that she'd mailed the keys in a flourish of imagined hospitality. Her parents had not visited, which was probably just as well. Denise had been here once, right after she'd moved in, when she'd been able to blame the chaos on moving. Six months later she had nothing to blame but inertia.

"I guess we can eliminate them as suspects."

"Suspects?" She said it way too loud, loud enough for Manny and Kyle to hear. Instantly she lowered her voice again. "We don't have suspects. This isn't like a police investigation. The notes will turn up."

"I don't think so."

Eve didn't think so, either, but she didn't want to start accusing people. "If you're so intent on playing Joe Friday, you can grill my sister tomorrow night. I'll get out the rubber hoses and the spotlight."

"Your sister's coming to visit?"

"Yeah." Then Eve remembered Denise's reaction to the hovercraft. She'd told Eve to stop working on it immediately. Surely Denise wouldn't drive down here, use her key, and steal notes in a misguided attempt to save her baby sister from bodily harm. Surely not.

"Does she know about the hovercraft?"

"Uh-huh."

"What does she think?"

"Oh, she loves the idea." Eve wondered if her nose would grow. Charlie would find out soon enough what Denise thought of the project, but at the moment Eve didn't want to give him information that would land Denise squarely on his list of suspects.

As she climbed the steps to Eunice's snow-covered front porch, Eve wished Rick hadn't mentioned the hovercraft Monday night at the Rack and Balls. Everything had been running smoothly, with the slight exception of the explosion, until she'd unveiled her project. Now her notes had disappeared. No matter how much Eve wanted to believe otherwise, she didn't think that was an accident.

Charlie rang Eunice's doorbell and tried to concentrate on the matter at hand, but instead he kept thinking about those missing notes. He was convinced someone had swiped them. The project was a potential moneymaker that had no patent protection yet, and now several people knew about it. That put Eve and her invention in a vulnerable position.

Eunice came to the door wearing a pair of glow-in-the-dark antennae and not much else. Her black thong and tiny black bra might get her kicked out of a nudist colony, but she'd still be booked on charges of indecency if she stepped out of her house looking like that. The *X-Files* theme song floated from somewhere inside.

Eunice looked startled. "What is this, a posse?"

Although distracted by the bobbing antennae and the vast expanses of goose-bumpy bare skin, Charlie managed to stay on topic. "One of Rick's important clients wants to talk to him."

"And it took four of you to deliver that message? Oh, never mind. It's too cold to stand here and discuss this. Come on in." She stepped away from the door, shivering.

Charlie stomped the snow from his boots and took off his jacket as he walked into the dark living room. A shaft of bluish light from an open door down the hall indicated where the action was. No telling what kind of action involved green fluorescent antennae, though. The music came from that room, too. Charlie was afraid to speculate.

Once everyone had gathered in the cavelike atmosphere, Eunice closed the door, which shut out the light from the porch and made the room even darker. "Rick's tied up at the moment, so make yourselves comfortable while I go get him." She hurried down the hall and everything that could bounce, did bounce.

As they all stood around in the living room, the only sound besides the *X-Files* music was the rasp of zippers on everybody's coats. Charlie figured they all were busy processing the sight of Eunice in that getup. He started to take off his glasses to clean away the condensation and then stopped himself. Sometimes a little protective condensation was a good thing.

Finally Manny cleared his throat. "Seeing her reminds me of a *Star Trek* convention some woman dragged me to years ago."

"In that case, sign me up, Scotty," Kyle asked. " 'Cause I could go for some of that, especially after painting those cookies. They got me in the mood, you know?"

Manny snorted. "Give me a break. You are *always* in the mood."

Charlie edged closer to Eve. "Does she wear those antennae a lot?"

"I've never seen her in them. I'm guessing they're reserved for special occasions." Eve lowered her voice to a murmur. "Do you think Rick's tied up as in busy, or . . . ?"

"Could be both." His cousin had never been able to resist a wild woman, and Eunice definitely qualified.

Rick appeared more quickly than Charlie had expected.

Thank God he'd at least pulled on his slacks and wasn't wearing antennae or trailing any velvet ropes. Too bad he hadn't grabbed a shirt, though. A shirt would have spared Charlie a view of Rick's nipples adorned in concentric circles of fluorescent green paint. Charlie's glasses had chosen this moment to clear up.

A few steps behind him came Eunice tying the belt of her black silk bathrobe. She continued to wear the antennae. Charlie wondered if she'd skipped the bathrobe on her first trip out because the tie had been in use.

Rick barely glanced at Charlie and Eve. All his attention was focused on his assistants. "What's up?"

Manny's gaze, which had been directed at the fluorescent circles, moved slowly upward. "It's, uh, Peterson."

"Yeah, Peterson." Kyle continued to stare at Rick's chest. "I'm not so sure you should go painting things on yourself, Ricky. The skin absorbs whatever's in that paint, you know. Most paint is loaded with toxins. You could be poisoning yourself."

"Kyle, forget about the damned paint," Manny said. "Rick, Peterson wanted to make sure we were still on for that deal next week."

"Absolutely!" Rick stepped closer to his assistants. "You told him everything was in the works, right?"

"He wanted to hear it from you," Manny said, "but it seems you weren't answering your cell."

"Oh." Rick looked around, as if trying to locate his phone. "I might've accidentally turned it off. Want me to give him a call?"

"I think you'd better," Kyle said. "You know how he gets."

"I do know." Rick turned toward Charlie and Eve as if finally realizing they were in the room. "Temperamental client. It's important to keep guys like this happy, though."

"I guess so." Charlie found it difficult to think of Rick as a highly paid professional while he sported green rings around his nipples. But maybe green rings were all the rage back in L.A.

Charlie could only imagine the egos that Rick had to work with in the fashion world. He supposed they expected Rick to be available twenty-four/seven. But the Rick he used to know wouldn't have been so accommodating, especially if he happened to be in the middle of a hot episode.

People changed, though. Charlie had always thought of Rick as calling all his own shots, yet here he was coddling some prestigious client. Maybe Rick's success didn't equal freedom, after all.

"I'll get my cell." Rick headed back toward the blue-lit bedroom.

"Look under the electronic muscle stimulator," Eunice said.

Charlie's eyes widened. Maybe he was misinterpreting what he'd heard. He glanced at Eve to get her reaction.

She was staring at Eunice in alarm. "Uh, Eunice, I know Rick's a consenting adult and everything, but—"

"Don't worry," Eunice said. "It only administers a mild shock, the kind used for muscle therapy. Gonaug, that was my chief instructor from the planet Titillium, taught me that certain kinds of electrical stimulation used at the right moment can be *very* exciting."

Manny shifted his weight and looked uncomfortable, but Kyle listened in openmouthed wonder. "Yeah? You got abducted?"

Eunice smiled. "I did. It was wonderful."

"Damn." Kyle shook his head. "Why can't I ever have stuff like that happen to me?"

Rick walked through the shaft of blue light spilling out of the doorway as he returned to the living room and

Charlie shivered. This whole business was getting too weird.

"I called Peterson," Rick said. "Everything's cool."

"Good," Manny said. "Better keep that cell phone on."

"Will do. Thanks, guys."

Manny crooked a finger at Kyle. "Let's go. We promised to finish the cookies tonight."

"I know we did." Kyle glanced longingly at Eunice. "But threesomes can be nice. I could work the stimulator for a while."

"*Kyle.*" Manny's expression darkened. "We're leaving. *Now.*"

"Right." Watching Eunice over his shoulder, Kyle followed Manny to the door. He bumped into the jamb on his way out and stumbled out into the snowy night without closing the door. Manny had to come back and do it.

Charlie was ready to leave, too. Not only were the green circles freaking him out, the whole kinky-sex scene was giving him ideas he shouldn't be having, ideas about Eve spread-eagled on her round bed. Charlie wouldn't need anything electronic to turn that into a major experience. Seeing Eve naked on that bed would be plenty of stimulation.

A walk through the snowy yard should cool him down some. If not, he'd head straight for her garage and the hovercraft. Once he immersed himself in that, sex would take a backseat. At least he hoped to hell it would.

But Eve seemed in no hurry to leave. Instead she'd left her coat unzipped as she turned toward Eunice. "I had a few miscellaneous notes on my workbench and now I can't find them. You didn't happen to see them by any chance, did you?"

"Notes?" Eunice frowned. "Gee, I don't think so. Are they important?"

"Not especially. It's just frustrating that I can't find them."

"I'll bet. Do you think somebody took them when I accidentally left the door unlocked? I would feel terrible if I thought—"

"No, no, I'll bet they're around somewhere." Eve zipped her coat. "I thought I'd ask, but I'm sure they'll turn up. All set, Charlie?"

"Sure." He glanced at his war-painted cousin. "Are you going to need a ride home?"

Eunice linked her arm through Rick's as she gazed up at him. "No, he won't, will you, Earthman?"

Rick dropped into his John Wayne imitation. "Guess not, my little planetary pilgrim."

Charlie had to get out of there. If sex was catching, he was definitely coming down with one hell of a case.

Chapter Nine

Rick allowed Eunice to lead him back to the blue-lit bedroom. His cock was ready for the next alien adventure she'd promised, but his mind was still circling around the subject of those notes. He'd meant to find a way to put them back on the workbench without anybody seeing. But then Eunice had poured him a glass of wine and hovered over him, cleavage at the ready, and he'd lost track of his plan.

Amazing about that dress of hers, how a guy could just reach in and flip her tits right out into the fresh air. She'd promised to keep watch while he nipple-noshed in Eve's kitchen, but luckily nobody had interrupted the activities. He'd started feeling reckless after that and had let Eunice give him a blow job while he sat on one of Eve's kitchen chairs staring at the stainless steel fuel converter.

Needless to say, the notes had stayed folded and forgotten in the back pocket of his pants. At least Eve thought she'd misplaced them. Maybe he never had to put them back, which would make his life a hell of a lot easier.

But there was another thing he needed to find out. It

sounded like Eunice might have a key to Eve's house. If so, that was some news he could use. Peterson had graphically reminded him of what would happen if he didn't come up with the money by next week's deadline. Peterson's voice had been soft and gentle as he'd described the excruciating way Rick would die.

"Strip down for the next phase of Project Penis, Earthman." Eunice dropped her black silk robe in a puddle at her feet.

"You've got it, Space Girl." Rick was out of his pants faster than you could say galactic orgy. "By the way, what was that Eve was saying about notes?"

"I think I accidentally left her door open. Lie down on the rubber antigravity mat. I'm going to blindfold you."

His heart pounded with eagerness as he stretched out on the spongy surface. Sex like this could almost make him forget Peterson. "How would you leave her door open?"

"She gave me a key so I could take delivery of FedEx packages when she wasn't home." Eunice's generous tits bobbed above him. Then she laid a silk scarf across his eyes. "Lift your head."

He did, and she tightened the blindfold. Not being able to see made his heart race even faster. That, and knowing Eunice had a key he could quietly borrow. She'd dropped her keys in a bowl by the front door when they'd first come in the house. He'd bet Eve's key was in that bowl, too.

"And now, Earthman, it's space-slime time."

"Space slime?" It sounded gooey and wonderful, something to drive the thought of Peterson right out of his head.

"A special formula created by Gounag, himself." Somewhere in the darkness, a jar opened. "Gounag was well hung, much like yourself. He instructed me in the proper application of space slime."

Rick's breathing grew shallow. With Eunice, anything was possible. "Good," he said. "That's good."

"First, we must shave the testicles."

"What?" Rick started to sit up, but she pushed him back down.

"Quiet. Must I bind you again?"

He gasped for breath. "I don't think I go for the idea of a razor near my balls. I'll bet Gonaug didn't let anybody shave his boys, either."

"Of course he did." Her warm breath tickled his ear. Then she ran her tongue inside, a move that was guaranteed to drive him crazy. "Earthman," she murmured, "do you think I would ever damage something that can give me such incredible pleasure?"

"Oh." All the resistance went out of him. "Guess if it's good enough for Gonaug, it's good enough for me."

"Then lie very still."

That turned out to be extremely difficult. When the shaving cream hit, he yelped, and as she began stroking him with the razor, he groaned and resisted the urge to come. Coming could result in serious injury.

At last she was finished. "Now for the space slime. Enjoy."

"Ahhhh!" He trembled as she smeared the creamy, tingling stuff all over his balls. They tightened in response, and he fought back his climax, because he had a feeling she would . . . yes, she did. Up and down his rigid cock with the space slime. Mind-blowing. Incredible. His orgasm wouldn't be held back any longer.

But just before he came, he reminded himself not to forget . . . not to forget . . . what? Oh, yeah. The key.

On the way back to her house, Eve considered Eunice's reaction to her question about the notes. "I don't think Eunice took anything."

"Some people are really good liars," Charlie said.

"I know. I just don't believe Eunice is one of them."

"So you think she was abducted by Gounag from Titillium?"

"No." Eve glanced up and discovered the clouds had drifted away, leaving the sky brilliant with stars. She believed there were other life-forms out there, but she didn't think Eunice had met any.

"Aha!" Charlie sounded triumphant. "So if she'd lie about that—"

"But don't you see? She tells this outrageous story, but then she gives herself away with all the cheesy effects."

Charlie glanced at her. "So you're saying she might be a liar, but she's not very good at it?"

"That's my point."

"But what if that whole alien abduction thing is designed to disarm people so they won't take her seriously? What if she's deliberately outrageous to hide her crafty side?"

Eve laughed and shook her head. "Poor Eunice. She can't catch a break with you, can she?"

"She had motive and opportunity. She was the only one in the vicinity with a key. That's all I'm saying."

"If someone timed it right, they wouldn't have needed a key." Now that Eve was convinced Eunice hadn't stolen the notes, she had to accept that she'd misplaced them or that someone had taken advantage of Eunice's slipup. "When I got home tonight the door was unlocked. I think Eunice forgot to lock it after she let the FedEx man drop off the package."

Charlie groaned. "Great. How long do you think it stayed open?"

"Don't know. Could have been as much as twenty-four hours. We could check the FedEx slip or ask Eunice." Stepping up on her front porch, she fished her keys out of her pocket. She loved this porch, and come spring she intended to put wicker furniture out here. She'd never had her own porch.

"I guess it doesn't matter how long it was," Charlie said. "But that sure widens the list of suspects."

Eve unlocked her door. Maybe in the spring she'd paint the door and the shutters purple. "I wish you wouldn't keep using that word. It seems so—"

"Accurate?"

"Sleazy." She walked into her cozy little house.

Charlie followed her, closing the door and flipping the dead bolt. "You don't want to admit that Middlesex harbors any thieves, do you?"

"No, I don't." But she'd already lost interest in the discussion the minute she heard the dead bolt slip into place. Charlie had just locked them in. That meant Rick and Eunice couldn't come over unannounced. They probably wouldn't come over at all, but if they should for some reason, they'd have to ring the doorbell.

The click of the dead bolt signaled that she and Charlie were truly alone, with a locked door between them and the world. She wondered if he'd sensed the change in atmosphere, or if she was the only one on full alert. Her fogged glasses kept her from assessing his expression as she took off her coat and boots.

"We haven't made any progress on the hovercraft," Charlie said.

Did his voice sound a wee bit husky? Eve thought it might. "No, we haven't."

"We should at least get your new motor mounted on a stable part of the workbench."

That sounded incredibly sensual, somehow. "As a bare minimum. Before we quit for the night, that is." As her glasses cleared, she glanced over at him. He seemed to be breathing a little faster than their walk from Eunice's demanded. Beneath the green plaid of his shirt, his chest expanded as he drew in air. She remembered the softness of that flannel and the insistent pressure of his mouth. He'd tasted wonderful.

"You'd like to test another batch of fuel, wouldn't you?" His glance grew warmer by the second.

"That would be great." She noticed that Charlie smelled terrific, like a walk through the woods on a summer's day.

He cleared his throat. "I'd love to check out the undercarriage before we get into the fuel thing."

"Be my guest." His comment shouldn't have been suggestive, but Eve's personal undercarriage didn't seem to understand that. It was responding as if Charlie had begun an elaborate seduction routine.

"I'm fascinated by your use of magnets," he said. "And you know me. I'll have to look at every inch of your wiring."

"Of course." He could do whatever he wanted with her wiring. She had some hot spots that needed attention right away.

"If I'm going to help you, I need to be thoroughly acquainted with everything."

"Definitely." If a man could virtually undress a woman with his gaze, then Charlie was doing that now. She tingled under the assault of those penetrating brown eyes. "You're welcome to go over every tiny little part." Repeatedly. Until they were both wild with lust. "Ready to get started?"

He took a step in her direction. "I'm not going to kiss you again, Eve."

"I never said you were." Her chest tightened in anticipation.

"I'm here to work on the hovercraft." He moved closer.

"I understand that."

"But every time I think about you building that thing all by yourself . . ."

She gazed up into eyes that held the special kind of softness that made her toes curl. And here she'd been told the way to a man's heart was through his stomach. "I'm glad you like my invention."

His voice grew rough with emotion. "I'm crazy about your invention."

She wanted him so much she could hardly think, which explained her next idiotic statement. "Charlie, I wonder if we should consider one little sexual episode, just for the heck of it?" The minute she'd made the suggestion she wanted it back.

Left to his own devices, he might have kissed her again, and who knows how that might have turned out? But she'd had to push the issue, and now he was struggling to bring himself under control again.

Eventually he seemed to succeed. Backing up, he took a deep breath. "No sexual episodes."

"I didn't think so." She looked away. "I shouldn't have mentioned it. My bad."

"You were only mentioning what I was thinking."

She met his gaze. "That makes me feel better."

"I don't want you to be upset in the first place." He spread his arms and gazed up at the ceiling. "Why does this have to happen now?"

"What?"

"You!"

"What about me?"

"Okay, maybe I'm wrong in my conclusions. Say we got involved with each other. What would you be looking to get out of that?"

She answered as honestly as she could. "I'm still try-ing to figure it out, Charlie." Now that it seemed they wouldn't kiss, after all, she had a yearning to get to work to let off some steam. "Let's talk in the garage."

"Fair enough."

"We can mount the engine on the workbench, like you said." And that still sounded sexual, but she'd try to ignore her urges in that direction. Never let it be said that she'd forced herself on a guy.

Once they got out to the garage, Charlie helped Eve mount the engine on the workbench, all the while aware of her scent, her warm body moving around, her breathing, which seemed to become quicker whenever they accidentally touched. Somehow he managed to complete the job without grabbing her.

After that he made himself eat pizza and drink Coke because it gave him something to do with his mouth other than kissing Eve. She told him her theories for modifying her fuel, and he thought they sounded reasonable. At least the parts he managed to pay attention to sounded reasonable. Mostly he kept watching her mouth and fantasizing about kissing her.

A project like this should have the drawing power to keep his thoughts away from having sex with Eve. It didn't. He couldn't concentrate on the hovercraft without thinking about getting horizontal with its inventor.

"Do you want to put that additive in the fuel and give it a try?" he asked.

"Not yet. Why don't you check out whatever you want to on the hovercraft. You haven't had a chance to go over it thoroughly, the way I'm sure you want to."

He wondered if she had any idea what he wanted. Maybe. She kept giving him little glances, glances that sizzled wherever they landed and made him long to unfasten those overalls she was wearing.

But he'd inspect the hovercraft instead. Still holding his can of Coke, he got to his knees and peered under the belly of the craft. He found a movable flap that he hadn't noticed before. "Rudder?"

"Yep." She leaned against the workbench and munched on her pizza. "I've done some calculations on my computer, but I won't know for sure if it works until the first test flight."

"About that." He glanced up at her and fought the urge to pull her down next to him and kiss her until they were both breathless. "I'm going with you on that first flight."

She shook her head. "Nope. Can't risk it."

He wasn't about to accept that answer, but he decided to try logic before he resorted to coercion. "Do you have any experience with light aircraft?"

"You mean like a pilot's license?"

"Like a pilot's license." He took a swig of his Coke as he evaluated the shape of the rudder again. It should work, but this entire vehicle was experimental, so there were no guarantees.

"No pilot's license. And I don't know what you're getting at. A pilot's license wouldn't do me any good if I get picked up flying a hovercraft that's not legal in the first place."

"I'm talking about the flying experience, not the license itself. A person who's flown light aircraft would have a better feel for how to navigate in the hovercraft."

She frowned, looking uncertain for the first time. "You could be right. I hadn't considered that. Maybe I can get one of those software flight programs and brush up on it."

"There's nothing like actual hands-on experience." His groin tightened as he inevitably thought about another kind of hands-on experience that he longed to have.

"I don't have time to take actual lessons. Plus I doubt if winter is the best time to start."

"I have a license."

"You do?" She sounded completely astonished.

Although it was stupid, he let that irritate him. "I'm no Tom Cruise–type top gun, but I can fly a Cessna without crashing into things."

"Don't get defensive on me, Charlie. Most people can't fly a plane, so naturally I'm surprised to hear that you can. Lyle is the only other person I've known personally who has his license."

Lyle. Instinct told him this was an important name for him to know. He shouldn't care about guys in her past, but he couldn't help it. So although he was itching for information, he kept his tone casual. "Did you go up with him? Even that would be helpful."

She set her Coke can on the workbench and hunkered down next to the hovercraft. "No, but I've been in small planes before. I've had to take them plenty of times to photo shoots in out-of-the-way places. I usually sat in the back, but I paid attention." She beamed at him. "I'll bet I would know exactly what to do with the hovercraft, so no worries."

"You need me to go with you." He couldn't think how to get back to the subject of Lyle, so he let it drop for now.

"No." She met his gaze. "If something happened to you, I'd never forgive myself."

"If something happened to you because you went alone, I'd never forgive myself, either."

Determination firmed her jaw. "This isn't up for discussion. I appreciate any help you can give me in the garage, but nobody goes in this hovercraft the first time except me."

He'd never been so attracted to anyone in his life as he was to Eve as she crouched there in her overalls and bulky sweater, her glasses sliding down her nose and the gleam of purpose bright in her blue eyes. "We'll talk about it later," he said.

"No, let's talk about it now." She stood and started to pace. "Let me explain this so you'll understand."

He stood too and watched her walking the length of the garage. Strands of her lustrous brown hair were coming loose, and she tucked them behind her ears as she moved. She held herself with such grace, which made sense considering that she was a runway model. Here in this garage he tended to forget that.

"The thing is, I want to live in Middlesex forever, and I realize this . . ." She paused and gestured toward the hovercraft in a move worthy of Vanna White. "This is on the eccentric side."

"Not compared to alien abductions." He also thought of his mother's X-rated bakery items. Middlesex wasn't quite as boring as it used to be, not that he'd changed his mind about staying.

"I don't think the hovercraft itself will get me kicked out of town, but killing or maiming a favorite son would definitely make me a pariah."

"I don't know about that favorite son part." He loved watching her move. She made those baggy overalls look like high fashion.

"Oh, you're a favorite son, all right. Now I realize it was you that your mom talked about when I was buying cinnamon rolls at the bakery."

"Of course I'm her favorite son. I'm her only son."

"Another customer was in there, and she chimed right in about your valedictorian speech and your SAT scores. And there was the time you repaired the furnace in the gym. You are quite a legend at Middlesex High."

Charlie could feel a blush coming on. "That's embarrassing. I'll have to talk to my mom. I don't want her carrying on about stuff like that to anyone who walks in."

"Give her a break. She's a mom."

"She's making me sound like some kind of hero around here, and I'm definitely not that."

"Say what you will, but there's no doubt in my mind that if I let anything happen to you, I'd be run out of town. And I really like it here."

He blew out a breath. "That's something else I still don't get. I mean, plastic reindeer? What's that all about?"

"It's more than the plastic reindeer. You have Little League fields and a pumpkin patch in October. There's a parade every Fourth of July. I saw the pictures of last year's."

"New York has parades almost every day of the week!"

"Yes, but hardly any have little kids pulling wagons decorated with red, white, and blue crepe paper with their dog riding inside."

"Oh." Charlie had pulled a wagon exactly like that down Main Street when he was seven. His mother still had the wagon, but Charlie no longer had a dog. Owning a dog would have made moving more complicated. He'd lived his life in limbo for years.

"I want to be part of a community like this," Eve continued. "I know I'm not completely accepted yet, but I will be if I stay long enough. I'll blend in more and more, especially after my kids start going to Middlesex Elementary, and I become a Brownie leader or a den mother. I could coach soccer. I'm not too bad at soccer."

He listened in dazed wonder. "You're a highly successful model, and you want to be a *den mother*?" He didn't mention that she'd skipped over a critical step, finding a father for those potential children of hers.

"Yeah," she said softly. "Yeah, I do. I grew up on Beacon Hill in Boston in a world of nannies and boarding schools. My parents still live in the same elegant house, still worship affluence and prestige. They adored Lyle."

Charlie adjusted the fit of his glasses, as if that would help him absorb all the information she was throwing at him. This was the first time she'd mentioned wanting kids, and there was that name again, one that made him want to snort and paw the ground. "Does . . . Lyle figure into all this somehow?"

"See, that was the problem. Lyle's exactly like my father. He was very clear that he never wanted a lawn to mow or a basketball hoop to install over the garage. The thing he liked about boarding school was that he'd never have to attend a PTA meeting in the cafeteria and sit on those molded plastic chairs."

"Why is Lyle in the past tense?" Charlie knew he was still in trouble because Lyle in the past tense made him happy.

"Because the life he wanted gave me the heebie-jeebies."

"Heebie-jeebies are bad." And Lyle had given them to her. Charlie smiled.

"Heebie-jeebies make you break the lease on your New York apartment and go house-hunting in Connecticut. But my family had a fit. I'd rejected a proposal from a Wall Street phenom. Denise would have given her tenured position for him. But he wasn't what I wanted."

"I'm not, either." Charlie said it without thinking. "That sounded egotistical as hell. What I mean is—"

"I know what you mean. You're hoping I understand that you don't want the life I just described any more than I wanted Lyle's version."

Charlie didn't think her description sounded all that bad for some time in the far distant future. Very distant, both in time and miles from Middlesex. "It's just that I'm up to here with cardboard turkeys and pumpkin patches. I need a break from plastic reindeer."

She nodded. "And I'm up to here with taxicabs and skyscrapers. I lived the urban lifestyle because it was what I knew and it made sense for my modeling career. It didn't feel particularly good, but it did feel familiar."

"Exactly. That's exactly what I'm saying. Not good, but familiar." He gazed at her in complete understanding. Different needs, same sentiments. "So Lyle proposed and you ran away to Middlesex?"

"Pretty much. At first I thought maybe I was running from the idea of commitment, but that wasn't it." She paused again, her expression soft. "A little while ago you asked me what I'd expect to get out of a relationship with you. I know now."

He swallowed. "And what is that?"

"Much more than you're willing to give."

Chapter Ten

It broke Eve's heart to admit that Charlie was everything she wanted in a man, because he was out of reach and she didn't know if another guy would ever come along who was as perfect for her. Looking into his eyes, she could see the battle going on inside that superior brain. He obviously didn't like disappointing people.

Besides, he wouldn't mind scratching her itch. Kissing him had convinced her that they had chemistry going on. They could have a grand old time rolling across her round bed. She'd bet he was putting some thought into that option and wishing he didn't have to give it up for the cause.

"Poor Charlie." She walked over to the hovercraft. "I didn't mean to mess with your head."

His smile was self-mocking. "That's not the only part of me that you're messing with, but it's not your fault."

"Or yours. Would you rather not help me with the hovercraft?"

"No, I want to help you." He took a deep breath. "The timing sucks, doesn't it?"

"Uh-huh." And the longer he stood there looking hot

and gorgeous, the more she wanted him in her bed and in her life. Maybe she should make the decision to do without his help instead of leaving it up to him

"You probably think I should get over myself. I mean, what kind of fool would stand here looking at someone like you and rave on about his precious freedom?"

She shrugged, trying not to feel rejected. It wasn't her he was rejecting, just the concept of being tied down. Still, it stung.

"Eve." He started toward her.

She held up a hand to stop him. Then she shoved her hands in the back pockets of her overalls and faced him. "Look, I want you to help me with this project. You're the only person I know who I would trust to help me. We're both reasonable adults. We should be able to work on this hovercraft without grabbing each other's ass, don't you think?"

His surprised bark of laughter echoed against the walls of the garage. "I'll give it the old college try."

"I never went to college, so I'll have to give it the old boarding school try." She hesitated, debating whether to reveal her lack of scholarly training. Oh, what the hell? "I flunked out my junior year of high school. Just so you know."

"Lots of genius types didn't finish high school."

"Whoa! I am *not* a genius!" She backed up, both hands raised in protest. "Don't go pinning that label on me." The whole concept made her tummy churn.

"Ever been tested?"

"I don't know. Maybe. Nobody ever told me the results, and I sure didn't ask. I was lousy at school. If anybody in this garage is a genius, you are. Your mother thinks so."

"Like you said, she's a mom. I did well in school because I liked it and I'm . . . I guess I'm disciplined, although my behavior tonight doesn't show that."

"See?" She didn't want to think about his behavior tonight, because his most excellent kissing skills would get her into ass-grabbing territory. "You don't want to be a genius, either."

"It's not a question of whether I want to be or not. I'm not. End of story." His brown gaze softened. "You, on the other hand, are still a question mark."

She backed up a step. "I refuse to be a genius."

"You don't have any say in it."

"Sure I do. I reject the label."

"Then you might want to reconsider inventing purple hovercrafts, especially when you've had no engineering courses whatsoever. It would take a genius to—"

"I took some online courses. Spent lots of time on engineering message boards. I don't want you to get too impressed with my native abilities."

Charlie studied her for several long seconds. "What have you got against being a genius?"

"They're weird. In a town like Middlesex they could be looked at strangely. I can see it all now. 'I'm sorry, Mrs. Whosit, but you can't be a Brownie leader. We heard that you're a genius, and they can't be trusted with impressionable young minds.' "

Charlie rolled his eyes. "It's not like leprosy. It's a gift."

"Then you take it. I don't mind being known for regular smarts. In fact, I'd like that a lot, if nothing else to show old Denise that she's not the only one who—"

"Your sister, right?"

"Yes. My sister who is coming tomorrow . . ." Eve glanced at her watch and discovered that the time had really gotten away from her. She had a ton of cleaning to do before Denise showed up. "Let me ask you a question. I get that you're not interested in me."

"Wrong. I'm very interested in you. I'm fighting it."

"Okay, interested but fighting. Duly noted. Now let's say a brainiac showed up who taught economics at Yale. She's not into small towns at all, but she's convinced that there's no civilization worth mentioning outside of New England. Would she be a potential girlfriend or not?"

Laughter sparkled in his eyes. "Does she invent things?"

"Not that I know of. She's mostly all about the numbers, all about stock options, leveraged buyouts, boring stuff like that."

"Blah."

What a sweet word that was. *Blah*. The sweetest word she'd heard in a long time. Her mood improved exponentially. "I thought with your magna cum laude and everything, you might be interested."

Charlie groaned. "I suppose my mom told you about that, too."

"It was a slow day at the bakery. I was waiting for Myrtle to finish frosting my cinnamon roll. And you didn't answer my question."

"Eve, are you worried that I'll be attracted to your sister?"

"Maybe a little bit. After all, she is a college professor."

"Don't put me in the same category as Rick."

That confused her. "He has a thing for college professors?" Somehow Eve couldn't picture that.

"No, his general category is good-looking women, and as long as someone fits in that category, he'll dive right in. He doesn't care what else is going on with her, just so she's a babe. His girlfriends all fit the profile and are pretty much interchangeable."

"And your point is?"

"You implied that I'm the same way with female brainiacs. If they're smart, I'm going in, regardless of other factors. One's as good as another. But I don't happen to operate that way."

She was intrigued with this conversational thread. "Then how do you operate?"

"I'm a one-woman kind of guy."

The way he said that, looking straight at her, made squiggles of excitement dance in her tummy. "I see."

"Once I focus on someone, she's the only one I want."

She warmed herself in the heat of his gaze. "So once you're committed, someone could drop you into a room full of naked Mensa ladies and you wouldn't be tempted at all?"

"Nope. Not if I'm into someone else."

And he was into her. She had no doubt from the way he was looking at her. But he was fighting it. "Well, doesn't that suck the big one?" she blurted out before she could stop herself.

"What do you mean?"

"There you stand, the perfect boyfriend, and you've taken yourself off the market where I'm concerned! It's not fair." Her sudden burst of anger surprised her.

It seemed to surprise him, too. "Okay, look. I should go. You're right, it isn't fair." Then his glance strayed to the hovercraft. "Except, damn it, I really want to make sure you get this airborne without smashing yourself into tiny bits. And I'm worried that someone is trying to steal your concept."

She didn't want him hanging around because of some misplaced protective urge. If he was determined to fight his attraction to her, she would make it easier on him. "I won't smash myself into tiny bits, and there's no hard evidence somebody is trying to steal anything. I could still find those notes. Feel free to leave."

"But—"

"I mean it, Charlie! Your services are no longer needed around here." She was working up a good head of steam, now. Until he'd said that thing about being a one-woman guy, she'd been able to talk herself out of feeling gypped. But that was the last straw. She'd searched all her life for a man who could make that kind of deep commitment, and now that she'd found one, she couldn't have him.

He gazed at her, his expression troubled. "I really think that we should—"

The doorbell rang. She couldn't imagine who could be coming over at this time of night, but whoever it was might provide the perfect segue to get Charlie out of here. She hated the fact they were fighting and their friendship was in jeopardy, but she was probably foolish to try and hang on to that friendship when he'd be leaving Middlesex at the first opportunity.

"Let me see who that is." She started into the kitchen.

"Don't forget to check the peephole." Charlie followed her.

"I always check the peephole." She was feeling cross with him and frustrated by the situation. Why did he have to set his sights on Hoover Dam, anyway? What did Hoover Dam have that she didn't have? Oh, yeah. Big turbines. Men and their machines. Phooey.

When she looked through the peephole she saw Rick standing on her front porch blowing into his hands to keep them warm. She started to open the door and it wouldn't budge. Then she remembered that Charlie had locked it.

Charlie was unnecessarily freaking her out with all this door-locking and talk of people stealing things. She was in Middlesex, voted one of the ten safest towns of its size in the nation. The real estate agent had told her that early on. Eve hadn't thought the statistic had mattered all that much to her, but now she realized instinct had led her here, because she wanted to raise her kids in Middlesex.

Those potential kids would need a father, of course, and she'd been unconsciously searching for him, too. So what if Charlie looked like the perfect candidate for that, too? He didn't care to raise his kids in a place that ranked in the top ten safest towns for its size. Maybe he wasn't so damned smart, after all.

She unlocked the door and Rick came in looking as though he'd had one too many jolts from the muscle stimulator. His shirt was buttoned up wrong and apparently his coat zipper had jammed a third of the way up.

"Nanu, nanu," he said in a halfhearted imitation of Mork from Ork. "I needed a time-out. Hey, Charlie, how's it going?"

"Okay."

Eve told herself not to react to Charlie's soft tone, but her heart wrenched, anyway. Those two quiet syllables spoke volumes about his state of mind. He was upset. Well, so was she.

"I'd offer to help you guys." Rick tried to tame his hair, which was standing out in six different directions. "But I'm wiped. Maybe I could stretch out on Eve's couch un- -til Charlie's ready to go home."

Eve grabbed her opening. "Actually, Charlie's ready to—"

"I thought Eunice was planning to run you home," Charlie said.

"She was, but I couldn't talk her into quitting. She never seems to wear out." Rick looked dazed.

"Maybe you shouldn't have let her use that muscle stimulator," Eve said.

"Oh, that was cool. It was just the pace was brutal. I kept trying to convince her that we should take a break, but then she'd turn on the black light and start twirling her tassels or some such trick, and I'd be back at it."

Eve resisted the urge to glance over at Charlie, who was no doubt rolling his eyes at his cousin's lack of restraint.

"Finally I just grabbed my clothes and ran. Got dressed on her front porch. Then the local fuzz cruised by and I was afraid that paint job would glow in the dark, so I had to jump behind a snowy bush to finish the job."

"That explains the sprig of evergreen behind your ear," Charlie said.

"There is?" Rick reached back and pulled out a twig with a few pine needles attached. "After all that's happened, I didn't even feel that. I think the aliens gave her sexual superpowers, man. She's like some X-rated Energizer bunny."

"Rick," Charlie said. "There were no aliens. She made all that up."

"That's what you say!" Rick struggled with his jammed zipper. "You weren't there! I never knew there were so many ways to use a green glow stick. So, Eve, can I borrow your couch?"

Eve decided the evening had come to a fittingly weird ending. "Charlie, I think maybe you need to take your cousin home."

Charlie sighed. "Probably a good idea."

"I'd like that," Rick said. "But I can't seem to get this zipper unjammed."

"Let me see. I've dealt with a trillion cantankerous zippers in my life." She dropped to her knees in front of Rick and tackled the balky zipper.

"Thanks," Rick said. "Listen, Charlie, just to give you an idea of how much Eunice worked me over, I would normally look at a beautiful woman kneeling in front of me and start getting ideas."

"Well, don't." Charlie sounded irritated as he reached for his boots.

"Hey, no worries! Trust me, I'm not thinking of anything like that. It's like when someone offers you chocolate cake after you've eaten everything on the buffet table. You have nowhere to put it."

Eve glanced up at him. "I'm not offering you chocolate cake, Rick."

"Damn straight she's not," Charlie grumbled as he put on his coat.

"Oh, I know that! I'm just sayin'."

"Looks like the zipper on your lip isn't working any better than the one on your coat," Charlie said.

Eve wiggled the zipper and freed it up. "There." She zipped Rick's coat as she stood. The poor guy did look as if he'd ridden all the Coney Island rides ten times in a row. "Maybe you should stay away from Eunice," she said.

"Are you kidding? I just need to get my strength back. We're on again for tomorrow night, unless you really need me over here."

Eve wasn't sure what to say. "Well, I really—"

"I know," Rick said. "You really don't need me. I think Charlie invited me to be polite, and you went along for the same reason. Charlie's the guy you want, right?"

Right. "I'm not sure Charlie can make it tomorrow night," Eve said. "Don't you have a conflict, Charlie?" She glanced at him and wished she hadn't. He'd put on the chaps that showcased exactly what she could never have, damn it.

He gazed at her, cool as can be. "Not that I know of."

"Of course he doesn't have a conflict," Rick said. "You should have seen how excited he was about this project, all the research he did on biowhatzit. He wouldn't miss this for the world, would you, Charlie?"

"Sure wouldn't." Charlie continued to stare at Eve. "I figure tomorrow we can pool our resources on the fuel question. We didn't get to that tonight, but tomorrow we can get right into it."

"Great," Rick said. "So Charlie and I can ride over together. We can bring Chinese. Everybody likes Chinese."

Charlie lifted his eyebrows as he looked at Eve. "Do you?"

"Sure. Love it." She shouldn't let herself be roped into having Charlie come over for another night, but Denise would be here. Denise could chaperone.

And come to think of it, Eve wanted Denise to meet Charlie and figure out that her baby sister was capable of having a nerdy friend. In Denise's world, nerdy friends were a badge of honor. "My sister will be here, if you're deciding on portions."

"Oh, yeah?" Rick perked up. "Does she look like you?"

Eve barely kept from laughing. Rick was exactly as Charlie had described him. Even though Eunice had wrung him out tonight, he wasn't the least bit committed to her. If another woman came along who interested him even more, he'd jump ship in a heartbeat.

"She doesn't look much like me," Eve said. "She got the dark eyes and the dark hair from my father's side of the family. I take after my mother."

"Is she a model?" Rick didn't seem ready to let the topic drop.

"No, she's an economics professor."

"Oh." That seemed to dampen Rick's enthusiasm. "Any hobbies?"

"No." Eve realized that Denise was like her in that respect. Economics was her passion and the stock market was her hobby, but you couldn't really call it that because Denise took her investments as seriously as Eve took her inventions. In other words, neither of the Dupree girls liked wasting time on frivolous pursuits. Eve had never thought about that before.

"She doesn't sound like my type," Rick said.

"Maybe not." Eve wondered if a woman could ever feel secure with Rick. Apparently, he'd always be on the lookout for someone better than his current love interest. A girl could grab Rick and end up holding thin air, but if a girl ever got a good hold on Charlie, she'd have something. Unfortunately, Eve didn't think she had a hold on him at all.

"Then I guess we'll see you tomorrow," Charlie said. "Same time?"

"Okay." Eve tried to look on the bright side. Yes, she'd be tortured by being around a man who was exactly right for her and wasn't staying in town, but she'd also benefit from his research on biofuel. That was worth something.

Charlie started out the door and paused. "Listen, if you locate those notes, would you give me a call?"

He would have to mention those notes again, just when she'd convinced herself that the missing notes weren't anything to worry about. "I don't have your number."

"Let me give you my cell." He rattled off the number. "Want me to write it down?"

"No, I have it." She'd always been able to remember things like that. It certainly wasn't a sign of genius, though. She had no intention of letting someone slap that kind of label on her, least of all Charlie, who was doing his best to blow this taco stand called Middlesex.

"Then we'll see you tomorrow night," Charlie said as he went out the door. "Don't forget to lock up."

She didn't even answer that. No matter what he said, this was a safe town and she didn't have to worry about thieves. "See you later," she called after them. And who was he to lecture about personal safety when he was about to climb on a motorcycle and ride it through what had to be icy streets? "Drive carefully!" she added before they were out of earshot.

Then she closed the door. And locked it, but not because Charlie had told her to. She locked it because even in a town that was ranked among the top ten safest for its size, a locked door was a simple way to improve the odds. Nobody had said Middlesex was totally crime free.

After locking the door, she went in search of her notes. If she could find them, that would end this whole crazy paranoia that Charlie was promoting. They had to be here somewhere. Plus she still had a bunch of cleaning to do.

Charlie didn't usually have passengers on his motorcycle. Tonight he wished he didn't have this particular passenger. Rick leaned forward so that he could spend the ride relating more of what had happened over at Eunice's house. In Charlie's current frame of mind, that was too much information.

"She's beyond inventive, Charlie," Rick said. "I have to buy that alien story."

"No you don't!" Charlie had to shout over his shoulder to make himself heard, but shouting felt good. He was filled with nervous tension after the confrontation with Eve. Consequently, he drove the motorcycle fast, watching for icy patches on the road and swerving around them.

"Aliens, I'm telling you," Rick said. "Who but an alien would look at those rubber bands they put around bunches of broccoli and think cock ring?"

Charlie groaned. He didn't want to think about anything to do with sex. Tonight would be full of tossing and turning even without help from Rick's monologue.

"Then she puts these little suction cups all over you and tells you to imagine tentacles. Who would think of that except someone who'd had sex with a creature with tentacles? It drove me wild, thinking of her in bed with an alien octopus. I was constantly on the verge of coming, but then she'd put on the broccoli rubber band and I'd be good for a while longer."

Charlie stepped on the gas. The sooner he got Rick home, the better.

"Then there was the space slime. She said that came straight from Titillium."

"Never mind about the space slime!" Charlie had taken about all he could take.

"No, really! It was green and gooey, and she rubbed it all over my dick before I finally— Yikes, Charlie! Watch out!"

The bike went into a skid. Charlie corrected with his body weight and managed to come out of it. The skid scared him straight and he slowed down some. A wreck wasn't going to solve anything.

"Guess I'm distracting you, huh?" Rick sounded shaken. "Maybe I shouldn't be telling you about any of this while you're driving."

"Good guess!" Charlie concentrated on the pattern of ice and dry pavement, weaving his way back to his aunt's house.

Rick stayed silent the rest of the way home. "Want to come in for a beer?" he asked as Charlie screeched to a stop in the driveway. "I could fill you in on the stuff I didn't mention."

"That's okay."

"I'm telling you, that space slime had some ingredient that made it tingle, like menthol or something. She loved it when I put it on her. I put it on her nipples, of course, but she really went crazy when I put it on her clit. I rubbed it in really good, and she—"

Charlie revved the motor. "Sorry. Have to run. Work tomorrow."

"You don't know what you're missing." Rick fastened the spare helmet on the back of the bike. "I'm willing to share. It might give you some ideas."

"Appreciate the thought." Charlie took off before Rick could launch into any more vivid description.

He drove home at a more leisurely pace. Now that he'd ditched Rick, he was in no hurry to go back to his empty apartment. As he was cruising the dark streets of Middlesex, the cell phone clipped to his jeans pocket vibrated. He pulled over to the side of the road so he could answer it.

If Rick was calling him with more war stories, he wouldn't answer. But the number wasn't Rick's cell or his mother's land line. He answered the call.

"Charlie?" Eve sounded scared. Really scared.

"What is it?" Unconsciously he'd driven back in the direction of her house. He was less than two blocks away.

"My . . . my back door lock doesn't work."

"Why not?" He had a bad feeling about this.

"It looks like somebody broke it. On . . . on purpose."

Chapter Eleven

Charlie concentrated on every nuance of the road as he flew over the deserted streets dodging patches of ice. He stayed low and moved with the bike, aware of every slip of the tires that warned him of a slick spot. He was desperate to get to Eve's house, but he wouldn't be any help to her if the paramedics had to scrape him off the pavement.

The two blocks seemed like two miles, but finally he swerved into her driveway, parked the bike, and pulled off his helmet as he ran up to her front door. She must have been watching for him because she threw the door open before he could ring the bell.

"Oh, Charlie." Her face was pale as she drew him into the entryway. "It looks like they used a crowbar to get in. The door's all chewed up around the lock."

Charlie's chest was tight with the effort to breathe. He was so glad to see that she was okay. Theoretically the lock could have been jimmied anytime, but whoever had done it probably knew it was still broken. "I didn't think you had a back door other than the one that goes from the kitchen to the garage. Where is it?"

"At the end of the hall there's a little dogleg to the left. I forget about that door half the time, especially this time of year when I don't go out in the backyard. Come on, I'll show you."

Charlie glanced down at his boots. "I don't want to track—"

"Never mind that now." She started toward the hallway.

He glanced at the front door, and sure enough, the dead bolt wasn't thrown. "Eve, damn it, you haven't locked the front door. That needs to become second nature."

She turned back, startled. "Oh." With a sheepish expression, she walked back to the door and turned the lock. "I guess once you arrived I automatically started letting my guard down."

"That's dangerous thinking. I'm not some martial arts expert who can save you from anybody who comes along."

"I know." She gazed at him. "It isn't logical, but you have that effect on me, anyway. I feel completely safe around you."

"You shouldn't." And he wasn't only talking about personal safety. He wondered if she had any idea the kind of craving she inspired. Giving in to that craving could mean heartbreak for both of them, and his grip on those urges was tenuous at best.

"I'll work on that," she said. "In the meantime, I want you to take a look at the door and tell me what you think." She started back through the living room.

"I don't have to look to tell you what I think." He followed her down the hall. "You need to notify the police. I meant to say that when you called, but I was so rattled I forgot. I figured we'd do it once I got here."

"I don't want to notify the police, Charlie."

"Why the hell not? You had forcible entry. I'll bet whoever it was took your notes."

"I have a hard time believing the police will get excited about a missing set of notes. They'll probably advise me to fix my door and get an alarm system. End of story."

"At least there would be a report." Charlie had to agree with her, though. Those notes weren't something you could put a dollar value on, like a television or a sound system. He just wanted to find a way to get her more protection.

"Having a report is less important to me than taking a risk that they'd look at the hovercraft and want to know what kind of license I have for it."

Good point. Charlie was sure the moment she flew it she'd be in violation of some law. And he could only imagine what kind of red tape she'd encounter if she tried to get a permit. In doing that she'd only increase the number of people who knew about the hovercraft.

She turned the corner at the end of the hall, a corner he hadn't noticed before. Of course he'd been thinking about round beds and condoms in the bathroom during the time he'd spent in this part of the house.

"There it is."

At first glance in the dim light from the hall, the old wooden door seemed fine. He wasn't sure what he'd expected—maybe a hacked-out place where the lock should have been. Then Eve pulled on the knob and the door swung open, letting in a slice of cold air.

The other side had taken all the abuse. Claw marks indicated where someone had used a crowbar to pry open the door. Looking at it made the hairs on the back of his neck stand up.

"I guess we don't have to worry about how many keys you have floating around, do we?" he said.

"I figure they hacked their way in the back door and went out the front, leaving it unlocked. Maybe they even thought the unlocked front door would throw me off the track for a while, which it did. If you hadn't been so intent on having me lock everything up good and tight, I might not have checked this back door at all."

"Did you check for footprints?" He glanced out the door, but the snow looked trampled by many pairs of boots.

"I didn't think of that. When I first went out to see what had happened, I stomped around a lot because I was cold. I'm sure I messed up any prints that might have been there." She was shivering.

He didn't know if her trembling was from the chill or nerves, but for starters he closed the back door to eliminate the frigid draft. "For right now I'll nail some boards across here so no one will be able to get in. Tomorrow I'll get you a new door and a different lock." He unzipped his jacket in preparation for the work ahead. "An alarm system might be a good idea, too."

She made a face. "I hate those things. I never remember the code and I'm forever setting it off or forgetting to turn it on."

He had no trouble believing that. Alarms only worked for meticulous people. A scatterbrained genius like Eve would make a mess of an alarm system. "Then we'll come up with something else."

"Sleigh bells." The color was returning to her cheeks. "I'll hang sleigh bells on both doors so I'll hear anybody who comes in."

"When you're here. What about when you're not?" He figured the intruder had taken advantage of Eve being gone.

"I'll worry about that the next time I have to leave, which isn't until next week. I hope to have the hovercraft ready to test before then."

"We will have it ready." Charlie was busy rearranging his priorities. He had unused vacation days at work. Now seemed like the time to take them. "But the first order of business is boarding up this door"

She looked doubtful. "No boards."

"Come on. You must have boards somewhere Every homeowner has boards. My mother has a shed full of boards."

"Not me I like metal hardware and fiberglass and engine parts. I've never had the slightest urge to get into carpentry"

Charlie studied the door. "Then I'd better check out your hardware supply"

"Anything I have would be out on the workbench. Want me to take your jacket?"

"Thanks. And my chaps." He handed her his jacket and unbuckled the chaps. As he gave her those, he noticed the color was *really* back in her cheeks. Her eyes, magnified slightly by her glasses, seemed unusually bright, too

She fingered the chaps. "Soft leather."

"It needs to be flexible to give me plenty of mobility when I ride." And that was the God's truth, but it came out sounding vaguely suggestive. He could feel the sexual tension building. Apparently, it didn't take much to make that happen.

"I suppose so." She continued to finger the black leather

To sidetrack his instinctive urge to reach for her, he turned himself into the Answer Man. "People think cyclists wear leather for the looks, but it's the best protection you can have if you end up sliding across the pavement. It peels off in layers, which gives you a chance to literally save your skin."

She winced. "But you're careful, aren't you?"

He thought of the reckless way he'd been driving tonight while Rick had insisted on describing his sexual adventures with Eunice. "Most of the time."

"You should be careful *all* the time, Charlie. Think of how your mother would react if something happened to you. Moving out West is nothing compared to getting in an accident on your bike." A strong current of emotion made her tremble.

Charlie recognized that emotion. It was the same one he'd felt when he'd seen the busted door. It seemed that they'd started to care about each other, whether that was convenient or not. "You're right," he said. "I need to be careful all the time." He looked into her eyes. "And so do you. No more cavalier attitude about locks."

She nodded. "Don't worry. I'm convinced."

He took a deep breath. "Good. Okay, let's see what I can find on your workbench that could secure the door until tomorrow. Unless you've put them away already, I'll need the screwdrivers we left in your bathroom."

"I'll get them."

As Charlie walked back through the house he thought about his options after he secured the door. He didn't think he could just leave her and go home. Chances were the thief wouldn't show up while she was still there, and maybe the notes were the only thing the person was after, but still . . . Charlie wasn't wild about leaving her alone.

Staying would present its own kind of challenge, though. He was well aware of that. He could camp out on her couch, of course. There was always that option. Yeah, right. With the kind of sparks flying between them on a regular basis, opting for the couch would be a joke. She'd know it the minute the suggestion came out of his mouth. Sheesh, what a tricky situation.

Eve hung Charlie's jacket and chaps on the hooks by the front door. Every time she touched the chaps she got a sexual zing, and she was guilty of touching them a lot. The soft leather was sensuous all by itself, but when she thought about where that leather had been, she moaned with longing. She'd never thought of herself as a kinky person, but the image of Charlie wearing those chaps— and nothing else—was too potent to resist.

Maybe she'd been nudged in that direction by Rick's comments about his session with Eunice. Eve wondered if Eunice would divulge her side of the story. Apparently the poor woman had been so long without sex that she'd hated to let Rick leave.

Eve could relate. She had Charlie in residence and her hormones were telling her this was an opportunity not to be taken lightly. He might not be boyfriend material, but he had the right equipment to relieve the majority of her tension, with or without the added thrill of chaps.

Contemplating the wisdom of jumping his bones, knowing it was a temporary fix, she went back to the bathroom to get the screwdrivers lying on top of the dryer. Then she decided to peek inside the washer just for kicks. The gunk in the bottom of the basket was starting to smell funny, so she made a command decision and poured some liquid soap on top of everything. Aromatherapy.

Finally, as a last touch, she piled a few things on the lid to discourage Denise from going in there. Oh, God, Denise. Eve could picture her sister's face when she discovered the situation with the back door.

Denise would go into her bossy routine immediately and probably insist on one of those dopey alarms. Eve would have to remember that this was her house, not Denise's house, and resist the alarm campaign. Denise had one, and that was the main source of Eve's horror of them.

She'd made the mistake of staying a weekend with Denise a couple of years ago. During that one short weekend, Eve had managed to set off Denise's alarm a grand total of six times. The first few episodes had brought the

cops to the door, but eventually they'd figured out it was
Eve mishandling the system and had called before they
sent out a squad car. That had thrown Denise into a tizzy
because she was sure now the cops would ignore an actual
emergency.

Eve had felt rotten because it might be true—the little-
boy-who-cried-wolf syndrome. She'd tried really hard to
master the alarm sequence, but the pressure to get it right
in a certain amount of time had always been her weakness. Give her a relaxed atmosphere and she could perform most any task, but put her under time constraints
and she froze up. That was another reason to love pool. It
was a leisurely game.

After picking up the screwdrivers, Eve paused, listening for Charlie's footsteps. He must still be out in the
garage. She tried to picture what would happen after he'd
fixed the door and couldn't decide for sure what he'd do.
A guy like Charlie wouldn't feel right leaving her to face
the rest of the night by herself.

But they had issues. He might think sleeping on the
couch was the best alternative for dealing with those issues. Eve had other ideas. But if push came to shove, and
the birth control stayed inside the bathroom cupboard,
Charlie would probably be able to hang on to his virtue.

Setting the screwdrivers on the bathroom counter, Eve
opened the cabinet under the sink and took out the box
she'd put there. She'd moved the condoms from her New
York apartment along with all her other bathroom supplies. Although she'd had no immediate use for them
once Lyle was out of the picture, throwing them away had
seemed silly. They hadn't expired yet.

She hadn't thought of Lyle much until tonight when
she'd used his name in conversation without thinking. Or
maybe her subconscious had wanted Charlie to know that
Lyle had existed and why she'd turned him down. Despite

knowing she had no future with Charlie, she kept creating those tiny bonds, opportunities for Charlie to get to know her better. Maybe the effort was futile, but she couldn't seem to stop doing it.

Tucking a couple of condoms in the pocket of her overalls felt like clandestine behavior. But the more she thought about it, and she'd been thinking about it a lot recently, she wanted to have sex with Charlie. So what if it led to nothing? She'd had sex with Lyle, and that had led to nothing. But that had been her choice not Lyle's, and she realized the distinction.

She'd heard that Lyle hadn't taken their breakup very well. Some mutual friends had reported several nights of heavy drinking during parties he'd attended alone. But he was seeing someone now, and from all indications he was over her. Eve was happy for him. She had nothing against Lyle except the golden cage he'd wanted to put her in.

As for Charlie, she knew going in that he was planning to leave Middlesex. She wouldn't try to keep him here, either. Because she'd expect the relationship to be short-lived, she could prepare for that—assuming she could get Charlie to have sex with her in the first place.

"Hey, Eve!" Charlie called to her as he came down the hall. "Guess I won't need the screwdrivers, after all. I found your cordless . . ."

She spun around, putting her body between the door and the open box of condoms still sitting on the counter.

". . . drill." He paused in the doorway, a fistful of metal hinges in one hand and her cordless drill in the other. She didn't think he could see the condom box, but she probably looked both startled and guilty. She certainly felt startled and guilty.

She glanced at the cordless drill. "So you found the attachments? That's great!" Too hearty. She needed to tone it down.

"Yeah, I did." His gaze was difficult to interpret, but he was definitely cloaking his reaction.

She decided he'd either seen the box or he had a good idea what she'd been doing over there by the cabinet. But he was going to act as if he hadn't. It wasn't the sort of thing you could broach in casual conversation. *"I found your cordless drill! And I see you're getting out some condoms! Good to know!"*

Or maybe he was trying to think how to gracefully derail her obvious interest in having sex with him. Damn it, she'd wanted to be more subtle than this, but she'd blown it due to her tendency to get lost in her thoughts. Denise had tried to assign a bunch of alphabet letters to that tendency, but Eve hadn't paid any attention because it sounded too much like a stock market symbol. Denise loved to categorize things, but Eve didn't fit neatly into any category, which drove Denise crazy.

Nevertheless, Eve's meandering thought process had left her in the awkward position of being caught with her condom box open. She decided there was no getting around this embarrassing moment. Better to plow right through it.

"You're probably wondering what I'm up to," she said. "Standing here by the cabinet where the condoms live."

Charlie started to laugh. Pretty soon he had to lean against the doorframe because he was laughing so hard.

She couldn't help smiling herself, although she wasn't sure what the joke was. "What's so funny?"

"You." He gasped for breath. "Us. This whole ridiculous situation." He laid the hinges and drill on the bathroom counter, took off his glasses, and swiped his arm across his eyes. Then he put his glasses back on. "You really want to, don't you?"

"Don't you?"

"More than you can imagine." He cleared the laughter

from his throat. "But I don't see how it's a good idea, all things considered."

"We could pretend this is wartime."

"What?" Then his confusion faded and he started to grin. "Wait, I get it. I've just enlisted and am being shipped out any day. In the meantime, we're grabbing what happiness we can. Is that the routine?"

"It works in the movies."

That telltale warmth softened his gaze. "You are something else. I could gobble you up."

Her skin began to tingle. "I'd like that. I'd like that a lot."

"Me, too," he said gently. "But before we make any decisions, I have to fix your door." He picked up the hinges and the drill. "Let's go back there and get that done."

"Okay." She felt encouraged by his reaction so far.

"And bring your condoms."

Now she was *really* encouraged.

Chapter Twelve

Charlie was toast and he knew it. After all his inner debate about the ethics of going to bed with Eve, he'd walked down the hall and discovered her digging out the condoms. He didn't know how a guy was supposed to resist that kind of enthusiasm.

He could rationalize that she'd had a bad scare and he needed to stay and comfort her. Comfort could easily take the form of satisfying sex. On the surface that made perfect sense, but when faced with a hot woman supplied with condoms, all rationalization became unnecessary. He'd be a fool to reject what she was offering.

When he got to the damaged back door the wind had blown it partway open again. He closed it and laid the drill on the floor to hold it shut while he figured out exactly how he wanted to attach the hinges.

She walked into the small hallway. Even if he hadn't heard her footsteps on the hardwood floor, he would have known she was there because the temperature went up several degrees. Or so it seemed to him. He resisted the urge to open the door again to cool himself off. He needed to get this door secured before he let himself think about what the two of them might do with those condoms.

He picked up one of the hinges, placed it head high on the doorjamb, and used a small drill bit to scratch marks in the wood where the screws would go.

"The hinges are a good idea." There was a little quiver to her voice.

He was egotistical enough to think it might be because of him. And damned if that didn't feel wonderful, in spite of his misgivings about the direction they were headed. "They seemed like the best option."

There was a quiver in his voice, too. Well, what sort of man wouldn't have a quiver in his voice at the thought of having sex with Eve Dupree? "I was surprised to see them, though, if you're not interested in carpentry."

"If I tell you why I bought them, you'll probably laugh."

"Were they another impulse buy at Middlesex Hardware?" He glanced over his shoulder at her.

Whoops, he shouldn't take a chance on doing that. Looking at Eve when he knew she had condoms in her pocket was like his first glimpse of the erector set he'd gotten the Christmas he was nine. He hadn't been interested in anything else that day. His other presents, Christmas dinner, singing carols around the battered old piano—he'd been oblivious to all of it.

"Not that there's anything wrong with impulse hardware store buys." He forced himself to turn back to the job at hand. What had he been doing with this hinge? Oh, yeah. Holes had to be drilled. Screws had to be inserted. If they seemed like a metaphor for something else right now, he'd ignore the implications or risk doing this job while sporting a woody.

"There's a crawl space over the garage," she said. "A pretty big one, as a matter of fact."

"And you wanted to make a trapdoor." He chose a drill bit, positioned it in the jaws of the drill, and tightened it down.

"I did want to make a trapdoor." She sounded delighted. "How did you know that?"

"Lucky guess." He wasn't sure how he'd known. Maybe he was beginning to understand how that imaginative brain of hers worked, which was kind of cool. He turned on the drill and braced himself against the door as he pushed the whirling bit into the wood. "So what would you put up there?" Judging from the amount of stuff she had all over the house, she could fill a crawl space in ten seconds flat.

"The hovercraft."

He stopped drilling and glanced at her. "You're kidding. You'd need a forklift to get it up there."

"Or something similar." She looked smug. "I have some rough plans for a hydraulic system that would raise and lower it."

"Yeah?" God, she was sexy when she talked like that. "Hydraulics would definitely work. I could help you build it." She wouldn't be able to beat him off with a stick. He was all over that hydraulics idea.

Her smile dazzled him. "I thought you might like that part. I haven't worked out the kinks yet, but I think it's viable. Then it would be out of the way so I have the available space for whatever I wanted to invent next."

He nodded. "Nice." He wondered if any other man in the world would be turned on by this kind of discussion. He sure was. All he had to do was listen to her ideas for fascinating machinery and he was ready to go. She was the most exciting woman he'd ever met.

"It's a short-term solution, though. I can't store every invention in the crawl space."

"Do you already have an idea for your next invention?"

"Oh, yeah!" Her face glowed with excitement. "How about a personal rocket system that includes its own parachute? Forget about climbing ladders to fix that hole in the roof. Just shoot yourself up there and parachute back down!"

"That's great!" Charlie was sinking deeper with every minute. He wanted to be around for the next invention, and the one after that. He could be her guinea pig, her project consultant, her marketing adviser, her lover . . .

"Charlie."

"What?"

"You've stopped fixing the door."

"Oh!" Jumping to attention, he squeezed the trigger on the drill he was holding at crotch level and damn near ended his sex life. "Right."

Putting down the drill, he took screws out of his pocket so he could insert them partway into the holes he'd drilled. Once all the holes were made and the screws tucked inside, he'd take out the drill bit and use the screwdriver attachment to speed things up. With the potential of ending up in Eve's round bed, he didn't want to waste too much time on this job.

Thoughts of Eve's inventions mingled with images of Eve naked. His brain was on such overload that it was a wonder sparks weren't coming out of his ears. His hand-eye coordination was off and he had trouble getting the screws in the holes.

"About the personal rocket system."

"What about it?" He managed to insert the screws and start the next round of drilling.

"I'd appreciate it if you wouldn't mention that to my sister Denise."

"Eve, I wouldn't mention it to anyone." But he'd forgotten that Denise would be showing up tomorrow. Chaperone time. Tonight could be his one and only chance to be alone with Eve and her pocketful of condoms.

"I didn't think you would," she said. "You're the discreet type. In fact, I should have told you about the hovercraft immediately when we met for pool."

That still bothered him, that she'd told Rick years ago and then withheld the information from him, her knight in shining armor. "So why didn't you?"

She took a deep breath. "Once I heard your name, I figured out you had to be Rose Shepherd's son. I thought about your SATs and your magna cum laude and I was afraid to."

"Afraid to?" He abandoned the drilling and turned around. "That's the craziest thing I've ever heard. I may be a lot of things, but one thing I'm definitely not is scary."

"Oh, yes you are, Charlie Shepherd. You not only have an excellent brain, you know how to use it. You ace tests and you win academic honors and you march in graduation processions with special tassels hanging from your cap. I . . . can't seem to do any of that. I just fool around with inventions."

He stared at her in amazement. She was without a doubt miles ahead of him in brainpower, and yet she had no confidence in her mental abilities. Somebody, or several somebodies, had done a number on her. Her teachers might be partly to blame, but in Charlie's experience the buck stopped with the parents.

He hoped he was wrong. A genius born to unsupportive parents could live in agony. "I can't believe no one ever told you how smart you are."

"I had one science teacher who told my mom and dad that maybe I should go to a special school for gifted kids. My mom was willing to consider it, but my grades were horrible, and my dad said if they paid the money for anyone, the person who should go to a special school would be Denise, who was making straight As."

"And now she's an economics professor at Yale."

"Yep. She fulfilled her destiny. And so did I. When the science teacher, Mr. O'Hurley, suggested a special school for me, I was already doing commercials. My dad found me an agent who told my folks that I'd make a fortune in modeling. So I've fulfilled my destiny, too."

Charlie's jaw clenched. Her parents had been given an exotic flower with incredible potential, and instead of letting her grow in a fertile bed where she could send down roots and expand her abilities, they'd planted her in a pot that was way too small. Before he left this town he hoped to convince her that she was worth more than she'd ever dreamed.

He couldn't do that by holding himself aloof from her, either mentally or physically. He hated to think he might be the first guy who appreciated everything about her, but he could be.

"I think you might have some more destiny to fulfill," he said.

Her gaze held his. "You make me feel that way, Charlie. That's why I'm glad you offered to help. And I'm worried about the electrical system of the hovercraft. Structurally I think it's okay, but the electrical system may not be quite right."

"Don't worry. I'll check it all out." He blew out a breath. How he longed to take her in his arms and tell her how beautiful and smart she was. "I really need to finish this door."

"Go ahead. I didn't mean to distract you."

He smiled. "You would be a distraction just standing there."

"Want me to go in the other room?"

"No! I love knowing you're there." He picked up another hinge and positioned it halfway down the door.

"Why don't you tell me about Lyle?" He sensed her hesitation. "Never mind."

"No, I'd like to tell someone who would understand. God knows, my friends and family didn't. Which isn't completely their fault, because I'm not sure I completely understood it until just recently."

"What would Lyle have thought of you building a hovercraft?"

She laughed. "That's a funny thought, Lyle coming upon me building this hovercraft. He'd probably stroke out."

Just as Charlie had suspected, Lyle had been clueless about this side of his girlfriend.

"The fact is, I wouldn't have built a hovercraft if I'd stayed with Lyle," she said. "He would have expected me to become like my mother, a society matron who spends all her time with charity functions. I'm not knocking what my mother does. She helps plenty of people and she works damned hard at it. But if I had to live her life, I'd end up in a padded cell."

Charlie was in awe of what he was witnessing. By moving to Middlesex and starting to build her hovercraft, Eve had transplanted herself out of that confining pot she'd been placed in. He was lucky enough to be around when she was finally starting to grow.

He forced himself to work on the damned hinges. "So Lyle's proposal was what tipped you over the edge?"

"Absolutely. You know how you can be vaguely dissatisfied, but you don't let yourself face it because everyone tells you that your life is great? So you just convince yourself they're right."

"Believe me, I know." He dropped to his knees to drill the holes for the final hinge.

"I guess you would. Your Hoover Dam and my hovercraft have a lot in common. Anyway, Lyle had planned the quintessential proposal. He took me to dinner at Jean George's, and between the main course and dessert, he got down on one knee, popped open a ring box just like they do in diamond commercials, and asked me to be his wife. It was kind of embarrassing, to be honest. But Lyle likes the grand gesture."

"I take it Jean George's is fancy." Charlie drilled the holes with a vengeance. He didn't like this image of some slick Wall Street type proposing to Eve, but there was no point in pretending that he was worldly enough to know all about Jean George's.

"Oh, yeah, fancy. Lyle was in a suit. I was in a long, slinky dress, which I've since given to the Salvation Army. Did *not* want to wear that thing again."

"You might not have had a reason to, anyway. There's not much call for a long, slinky dress in Middlesex." All the screws were resting in their appointed holes, so he switched the drill bit for a screwdriver attachment.

"To be honest, that's one of the joys of living here, although I have a closet full of clothes I may never wear again." She paused. "But that gives me an idea. Would you like me to put one on?"

He glanced over his shoulder. "Now?"

"Why not?"

He looked down at his sawdust-covered flannel shirt and jeans. "Because I seem to have left my suit at home."

"That would make it more fun. Every time I've put on a sexy dress, I've either been on the runway, in front of a camera, or headed to some fancy party or elegant restaurant. I'd love to dress up for the benefit of one special person."

He gazed at her and couldn't imagine her looking more desirable. "You don't have to dress up to get my attention."

"That's what would be so great about it. You don't require me to do that, so it's a treat, a bonus . . ." She paused and uncertainty flickered in her eyes. "Unless you think I'm being vain? Trust me, looks aren't a big thing with me. I wouldn't want you to get the impression that I need the ego boost."

"I'm the one that would get the ego boost. I've never known a woman who would go to the trouble of dressing up when I'm the only person who will see her."

Her expression became luminous. "Then I'll do it. I'll be back in ten minutes. Let's synchronize our watches."

Instinctively, Charlie glanced at his digital watch, a marvel of craftsmanship calibrated to stay within a split second of Greenwich Mean Time. He'd bought it for himself a year ago.

Eve laughed softly. "I didn't mean that literally, but ten minutes should be about right. You should be finished by then." She started to turn away. Then she spun back to him and reached in the pocket of her overalls. "Here." She handed him three condoms. "What I have in mind doesn't have pockets." Then she hurried down the hall.

Charlie wondered if he could be dreaming this. In what reality did a gorgeous model hand him three condoms before going off to change into something long and slinky? In Eve's reality, apparently, and he was the lucky son of a bitch who'd stumbled into her world of hovercrafts and high fashion.

Some cool jazz drifted down the hall and snapped him out of the daze he'd fallen into the moment she'd placed the condoms in his hand. He checked his watch. He'd been standing there like a dork for a full minute. That left only nine minutes to finish up this job so he'd be ready for . . . whatever happened after Eve appeared in her slinky dress. He'd better start screwing.

Eve was beginning to believe that tonight would be her one and only chance to have a romantic interlude with

Charlie, and she might as well capitalize on it. Tomorrow Denise would arrive. If Eve could think of a way to keep her sister from showing up, she'd do it. But Denise was a force of nature. Once she was set in motion, nothing could stop her.

So Eve would have to make the most of what little time she had left with Charlie before Denise swept in and changed the dynamic completely. In her bedroom she flipped on her CD player and chose soft jazz to provide some atmosphere. Then she stripped down to her panties and started the transformation.

First came the makeup. Charlie deserved the complete package tonight. She grabbed the smudge-free stuff so he wouldn't get it all over him when they . . . whew. She'd almost jabbed herself in the eye with the mascara wand just thinking about what would happen between them tonight.

In less than five minutes she inspected the job in her magnifying mirror and was reasonably satisfied with the results. If they ever had a time trial for makeup application, she'd win hands down. Because she thought it was hideously boring she'd taught herself to do it at warp speed.

Next she had to rummage through the pile of clothes still in their dry-cleaning bags that covered her bed. Oh, wait. She didn't want a pile of clothes on her bed. With any luck, things were about to happen in that bed and she didn't intend to stage the event on a mound of dry cleaning, although Eunice would probably have found a way to make something kinky out of that.

She found the dress she wanted, tossed it on an overstuffed chair in the corner of the room, and gathered up the rest. Then she looked around for a place to put them. Theoretically they should fit in her closet, but in the absence of clothes being stored in there, other things had stacked up.

They were not going back in the guest room. Once Eve had moved a pile of something, she had a policy that it would not return to its original spot. She liked to keep her clutter in motion, like airplanes in the pattern over JFK.

They couldn't go on the floor, either. She and Charlie might trip on them during a critical moment. Pratfalls hardly ever added to someone's sexual experience. In desperation she finally hurried across the hall to the bathroom, pulled back her shower curtain and dropped the whole pile in the tub.

Something would have to be done about that when Denise came, but Eve decided to worry about it in the morning. She had a slinky dress to get into and a date to keep. On her way back to her bedroom she heard the rapid whirr of the drill spinning those screws into place. Charlie sounded like a man on a mission.

And she was a woman on a mission—a mission to make the next few hours unforgettable for both of them. She hoped while Charlie was striding around the facility of Hoover Dam he'd sometimes pause and think of her in this dress. The fabric was an iridescent dark purple that in certain kinds of light looked black. But even then, every time she moved the purple would flash.

One thin strap held the dress up on her left shoulder. From there the neckline swooped across and down, leaving her right shoulder bare. The material had just enough Lycra to mold itself to her breasts, waist, and hips. Eve had never worn a bra with it, and with a sense of daring she decided to forgo the panties, too.

Stripping them off, she stepped into the dress and wiggled herself into it. The slit up the side of the skirt allowed her ease of movement and gave anyone looking a view of her leg to mid-thigh. She'd always thought this approach was more effective than a miniskirt. Now you see it, now you don't.

With two minutes to go she'd zipped the dress and put on the deep purple five-inch sling-backs she'd bought to go with the dress. She didn't have time to do much with her hair, so she took it out of the pins and gave it several swipes with the hairbrush. Rhinestone chandelier earrings, a touch of perfume at her throat, and she was done.

No glasses, no contacts. She knew the way down the hall, and if everything was a little blurry, that would add to the gauzy, romantic effect. The soft jazz followed her out the door.

The cordless drill had gone quiet. Heart pounding, she started down the hall. Then she heard a slapping sound and realized he must be trying to get the sawdust off his clothes. Pausing, she waited for the sound to stop. It didn't. Instead the slapping was now punctuated with muttered curses.

Laughter bubbled in her throat. Poor Charlie. He had no idea that she found the matchup of a sawdust-covered guy and this elegant dress exciting. She wasn't worried about the dress. She was a favored customer at the Press 'n' Go, and they'd clean it beautifully.

She hoped that once Charlie caught sight of her he'd forget about the sawdust. Taking a deep breath, she started down the hall, heels clicking against the hardwood floor.

With that sound announcing her arrival, the slapping and muttered cursing sped up. Then she rounded the corner and he lifted his head. It took a second for the impatience to drain from his expression, and then . . . *there*. Even without her glasses there was no mistaking that look, a look she would tuck away in the deep recesses of her heart . . . forever.

Chapter Thirteen

Over the years Charlie had seen plenty of magazine spreads of models in fancy dresses. He thought he knew what to expect when Eve rounded that corner. *Not even close.*

. Now he understood that expression about taking your breath away. Looking at Eve, he felt as if somebody had rammed a basketball against his diaphragm. He struggled for air and tried to remember the mechanics of using his lungs. Air in, air out. Such a simple concept. So difficult to execute while this . . . *goddess* stood before him.

"I guess you like it," she said.

He nodded, incapable of speech. ·

She took a step closer, and the shiny earrings dangling almost to her shoulders swayed. .

He was semihypnotized watching the earrings move. But he still had some of his faculties. "Wait." His voice sounded as if he'd swallowed a handful of the sawdust he'd been futilely trying to get off his clothes. "I need . . ." He could think of only one thing that would make him worthy of being within ten feet of her in that dress. "A shower. I need a shower."

"Silly man." She kept coming, walking in time to that smoky jazz in the background.

"Seriously. I'm covered with sawdust, and you—well, you're covered in something dry-cleanable only. I'd lay money that won't go in the washing machine, not that your washer is in any shape to clean anything after the job we did on it with candy, and magazines, and your decluttering book, so I—"

"I love contrasts." She moved in and reached for the cell phone he had clipped to his jeans pocket. "You won't be needing this." Leaning down, she laid it on the floor, giving him a glimpse of mouthwatering cleavage.

Then she wound one arm around his neck. The contact sizzled, and he knew that if she persisted, he'd cave, sawdust or no sawdust. The wail of a saxophone urged him to give in, give in, give in. He was a sucker for saxophones.

With her free hand Eve took off his glasses and tucked them in his shirt pocket. "Thank you for fixing my door."

He held his arms out, scarecrow fashion, so he wouldn't make the mistake of touching her with sleeves that had picked up sawdust like Velcro. Then he made one last stab at reasonable behavior. "Eve, you're going to get all messed up."

"Mess me up, Charlie." She cradled the back of his head and massaged his scalp lightly with her fingertips. "Mess me up real good."

He moaned softly. "You should let me get cleaned up first."

"And take all the fun out of it? Not likely." Her heels gave her enough height to bring her mouth exactly even with his. "Let's kiss."

"But you have on all that lipstick and stuff." He found

it incredibly sexy to look at that red, red mouth that glistened and tempted him to dive in. Even a guy not wearing his glasses could find a target like that.

"Afraid to get it on you?"

"No." He wanted it on him. He wanted to drown in her, but she looked so perfect, and if he gave in to his needs, she would become smeared beyond belief. He couldn't imagine that she really meant what she said about getting messed up. Women didn't like that, at least not the women he knew.

"This is professional-grade makeup. You could kiss me all night and it will stay put. If you don't believe me, feel free to test it out."

He held on for another couple of seconds. Then she ran her tongue slowly over her mouth, which only made it wetter looking.

"Oh, what the hell." A guy could be expected to put up only so much of a protest. Charlie wrapped both arms around her, sawdust and all. "Let the kissing start."

"Hallelujah."

She tasted like raspberries. Whatever this professional-grade stuff was, they'd flavored it with fruit, and raspberries were fast becoming his favorite taste thrill. The delivery system was outstanding. Eve had a way of kissing that made him forget everything but the feel of her mouth on his—moist, supple, open . . . oh, yes, very open. Exceedingly open to exploration, and he would do that. He most certainly would do that. Mm, sweet. Wet. Good.

He would have sworn that he was only aware of her mouth, but that must not have been entirely true, because before he realized it he'd backed her up against the wall, and his awareness had extended slightly lower. One moment he was totally involved in mouth-to-mouth action, and the next he was incorporating other areas—her chin, her throat, her collarbone, her shoulder.

His breathing shut out all but the deep bass coming down the hall. But deep bass fit the rhythm of his thoughts—his heated, incredibly focused thoughts. He wanted . . . everything.

This dress. Oh, God, this dress. The material was stretchy. He loved that about clothing. The thin strap over her left shoulder went down without a fight, not even threatening to tear. He could live with getting sawdust all over, especially now that she'd said how much she loved contrasts, but ripping was not acceptable.

She must have been helping him out in some subtle way, because he wasn't sure he could have found the zipper by himself. It was sort of hidden in the back, and she had to arch away from the wall to let him find it. While she was arching, she thrust her breasts forward, and that kept him occupied for a while so he delayed on the zipper situation.

The thing was, she didn't have on a bra, so her nipples poked against the shimmery material and he couldn't resist that. He had to play with those nipples until she made little whimpering sounds in the back of her throat. Touching her through the material worked him up so much that finally he had to make use of that zipper in the back so he could get rid of the top part of the dress.

By the time he got the dress pulled down to her waist, damned if she didn't have some sawdust sprinkled on the prettiest 36B breasts he'd ever seen. It was his duty to brush off that sawdust. Some of it wouldn't budge, so he had to resort to licking it off. He'd never eaten sawdust before, but under these conditions he didn't find it objectionable at all.

Inspecting his work, he decided that her nipples looked their absolute best when wet and quivering, so he endeavored to keep them in that condition. From the way Eve was quaking and moaning in his arms, he thought she might be happy with his efforts.

He was beyond happy. Her breasts fit perfectly in his cupped hands with exactly enough gentle weight to be supported nicely against his palms. He imagined himself as a human underwire. And as much as he loved the sensation of rolling her nipple against the roof of his mouth, she seemed to love it even more. And when he tugged softly with his teeth, she shivered.

Her shiver made the dress rustle against the denim of his jeans, denim that was under a strain at the moment. The situation below his waistband was fast becoming critical. A man with more finesse, the kind of man who dressed in suits and dined at Jean George's, would suggest moving to the bedroom.

But Eve hadn't liked a man with that approach. Maybe she was the kind of girl who liked it in a dim hallway up against the wall. Charlie hoped so, because he suspected that was how she was going to get it.

Vaguely he remembered there was something special about this dress besides the shimmery, stretchy fabric. Then the special part flashed across his brain like a streaking comet. As she'd walked toward him, each step had given him a breathtaking view of one long leg. The dress had a slit up the side, a deliciously long slit, long enough to send his imagination into very erotic territory.

Kissing his way back to her mouth, he slid one hand down her hip.

She put an inch between her lips and his. "Looking for something?" she murmured.

"A way in." He barely recognized his own voice. The rough urgency was unfamiliar, but so was this desperation. He'd never known such driving sexual hunger.

Her quick, shallow breaths tickled his mouth. "Keep going."

At mid-thigh the material gave way and he slid his hand through the opening to touch her warm skin. The tactile pleasure of that brought a growl of delight from his throat. He pushed on, expecting to find the kind of silk and lace he'd seen draped over her kitchen chairs Monday night.

Instead he discovered nothing but . . . Eve. He drew in a sharp breath.

"Surprised?"

He gulped. "Grateful." Smoothing his hand over her taut bottom, the blood pounding in his ears, he slipped his fingers between her thighs. There he found the wet welcome guaranteed to drive a man around the bend. His brain short-circuited and he was left with nothing but raw need.

He lost track of the sequence of events after that. He remembered kissing her hard and using his tongue to let her know what was ahead. She must have unzipped his jeans and shoved down his briefs, because he didn't think he'd done any of that. Somehow he located the condom packet, ripped it open and rolled the latex over his quivering penis.

When he picked her up, her skirt magically drifted to one side, or maybe she pulled it over to give him access. The details blurred, except for that defining moment when she held on to his shoulders and wrapped her feet around her hips and he pushed deep inside her. That sensation burst upon him with such clarity that he expected to remember it when he was a hundred and two.

One of her stiletto heels poked him in the small of the back, but he didn't care. Nothing mattered but the rhythm of his thrusting and the glow in her eyes. Her lips parted as she gasped for breath and her delicate nostrils flared.

Every time he pumped, her dress rustled and her long earrings swung, brushing her shoulders. Although he shouldn't know anything about her responses, had never mapped the quickest route to her pleasure, magically he seemed to know everything. He played to the excitement building in her eyes, gauged the pattern of her breathing and moved in tune with her.

Maybe this was how making love was supposed to be. Instinctive. Easy. Filled with wonder. And so good. So very, very good. He felt her tighten around him and joy surged in his heart that he would be able to give her this.

She said his name once, the two syllables trembling and vivid with emotion. And then she came, her back arching, her shoulders pressed against the wall, her thighs quaking as the spasms massaged his penis. He managed a few precious seconds more, giving her a chance to revel in the sensation.

Then he couldn't hold back anymore. With a groan of release he locked his hips against hers, closed his eyes and abandoned himself to the most powerful climax of his life. The force of it left him barely able to stand.

Afraid he might collapse and damage all sorts of valuable parts, both his and hers, he leaned his head against her shoulder and fought to stay upright. He'd give this position a ten for sexual excitement, but a one for ease of recovery. He was the structural support for this operation, and the structure was definitely compromised by the orgasm of a lifetime.

Then there was the problem of his jeans. Sometime during the action they'd fallen with a clank of the belt buckle down around his ankles. His briefs hung by the elastic around his knees. And he was still wearing a condom.

Maybe this was why he'd never done it up against the wall before. The after-party could turn awkward. Nobody ever showed that part in the movies. He could use a good fade-out right now.

She stroked her fingers through his hair as her breathing slowed. "Incredible."

"Mm. Amazing." He hoped he wouldn't ruin the

moment by falling down and getting hopelessly tangled in his clothes.

She moved her lips close to his ear. "You can let me go, now."

Gradually he became aware that he was gripping her bottom as if she were the handlebars of his Harley. Instantly he relaxed his fingers and hoped to God he hadn't bruised her.

Still feeling pretty damned vulnerable and shaky, he found the strength to lift his head and look into her eyes. "If I left marks, I'll never forgive myself."

She smiled at him, and her expression was all warm and misty. "If you left marks, I'll cherish each and every one. But now we have to figure out how to untangle ourselves, don't we?"

We. She was willing to take equal responsibility for making this turn out okay. He didn't get that a lot. As an only child, the smartest person in his graduating class, and the go-to guy at the power company, he felt mostly like the Lone Ranger. Everyone usually looked to him for the answers.

"Got any ideas?" he asked, thoroughly enjoying the idea of handing the problem to her to solve.

She gazed at him, and the corners of her mouth twitched as if she wanted to keep from laughing. "First we have to gracefully do the disconnect thing."

He could see how laughing might be a problem at a time like this. "I don't think there's a really graceful way to do that. I mean, sex is fantastic while you're doing it, but afterward, especially when you're vertical, there are . . . issues."

"That's why we'll both keep gazing fixedly into each other's eyes. Whatever you do, don't look down."

"You mean like those Olympic figure skating pairs, who do all sorts of complicated things with their lower body while staring straight at their partner's face?"

"Exactly." Her eyes sparkled and she caught her lower lip between her teeth. Then she cleared her throat. "We'll be just like those skaters."

"Are you going to talk us through it?"

"Sure. Just don't make me laugh."

"I should warn you. I'm one of those people who can be funny without meaning to."

Her expression softened. "I know. I like that about you."

"You like that I'm clueless?"

"Whoops, now you're making me laugh." Her body quivered against his.

"See what I mean? I don't even have to try." Despite the jeopardy that put them in, he enjoyed the sensation of being tucked inside her while she laughed.

"All right." She swallowed a giggle. "I'm calm again. Just look into my eyes. I'm going to loosen my hold on your hips. When I do that, you should ease back a little."

"So we'll make this a gradual unhitching."

"Unhitching." She grinned. "You do have a way with words. Now, here we go. I'm loosening."

"And I'm easing."

"Loosening."

"Easing." He felt her balance shift and started to lower his head to check out the situation.

"Don't look down, don't look down! I'm maintaining just fine."

"Okay." He locked in on her gaze again.

"One foot on the floor."

The moment came when he lost that magic connection, and he moaned softly.

She paused in midmotion. "Problems?"

"No." With his gaze fastened on hers, he couldn't hide his emotions. "It's just that I miss you already."

Her eyes shone. "I miss you, too. But the night's not over, Charlie."

"You're right." Yet he wasn't thinking about tonight. He knew she'd want him to stay until morning. He was thinking about the day he'd take the road out of Middlesex. He had to go. If he didn't, he'd always wonder how it would have been. But she'd just made leaving ten times tougher.

"Two feet on the floor. You can move your hands, now."

He didn't want to, but they couldn't complete the maneuver unless he let go of her silky derriere. Reluctantly he pulled both hands from underneath her skirt. "Now what?"

"Give me a minute. Keep looking into my eyes."

He did, but he could tell from the rustling around that she'd pulled her dress up. Then a zipper rasped.

"Now I'll turn and walk down to my bedroom," she said. "You can follow when you're ready."

"I'm impressed." Then he had an unwelcome thought. "You've done this before."

"No, never."

"But you choreographed it so perfectly."

She smiled. "It's like building a hovercraft. You might not know what you're doing in the beginning, but if you take it one step at a time, you'll get where you want to go."

"Guess so." For a guy who had always relied on directions and diagrams, it was a stunning concept. "Listen, do you want me to give you a certain number of minutes to yourself?"

"Not necessary. All I need to do is take off this dress and climb into bed."

Whoa. His blood heated at the implied promise, that he was welcome to climb in there with her. "Okay." The casual response had nothing to do with the fire racing straight to his groin.

"See you soon." Turning, she used her runway walk as she moved toward the end of the short hallway.

He, of course, stood watching her go because he was mesmerized by the sway of her hips, those same hips that had recently cradled him so beautifully. It wasn't until she was about to turn that he realized she could easily glance back and take in exactly the ungainly sight he'd been hoping to avoid having her see.

He couldn't move fast enough to prevent it. "No looking!" he said.

"I won't." She kept her head turned away from him. "I'll always play fair with you, Charlie." And she rounded the corner, her heels clicking on the hardwood floor.

Once she was gone, Charlie wasted no time getting himself together. He planned to duck into her bathroom for a quick cleanup, and then he'd be bedroom bound. He'd loved the slinky-dress routine, but he was looking forward to a completely naked experience. Looking forward? Hell, he was like a power surge waiting to happen.

As he gave the door one last check to make sure the hinges would hold, his cell phone rang. His mother's ring. Damn it. She was calling from the bakery. That wasn't unusual. Many times the two women were down there late at night baking and ran into a problem with one of the ovens or the large dough mixers.

Charlie tended to stay up late, so they thought nothing of calling him in to handle the electrical emergency. But he didn't want to go now. Not tonight, a night that might never be repeated.

Flipping the phone open, he answered the call. "Hi, Mom."

"I hope I didn't wake you." His mother always said that. She didn't want to be a problem to him, but sometimes she couldn't help it.

He needed to find her a good electrician before he left

town. "I'm awake," he said. "What's up?" Then he swallowed the laughter that almost gave him away.

"The mixer quit. I hate to bother you, but if we don't get it going, we won't have a good supply of booby buns. And they've been selling really well recently."

So the booby bun craze hadn't died. If he didn't go down there and repair the mixer, he'd feel responsible if sales were slow at the bakery tomorrow. But if he did repair the mixer, he might regret missing the opportunity with Eve for the rest of his life.

As he stood there trying to come up with a solution, his mother spoke again. "Charlie, it's okay. I shouldn't call you all the time. Myrtle and I can probably figure out how to fix it."

He had grisly images of the two widows electrocuting themselves while they labored over a machine he could repair in ten minutes. "No, don't do that." He thought of the guys he worked with and wondered if he could call in a favor.

It was after midnight. That was some favor, to ask somebody to leave a cozy home in the middle of winter so that the citizens of Middlesex could have their booby buns. Besides, Charlie wasn't crazy about the guys at work discovering firsthand the new direction the bakery was taking.

Eve appeared in the hallway wearing a white silk robe. "What is it?" she asked softly.

The robe clung to her in all the right places, as if to advertise what he would miss if he went down to the bakery. Besides, Eve had been through a shock. The door would probably hold, but he didn't want to leave her alone with her imagination right now. She had one powerful imagination, and she wouldn't sleep a wink as she tried to figure out who had pried open her door and stolen her notes.

"Mom, can you give me a second?" Putting his thumb

over the mouthpiece, he glanced at Eve. "There's an electrical emergency at the bakery, but I'm not going."

She looked upset. "I hope that's not on my account. We can . . . take a rain check."

He wasn't so sure about that. Once the spell was broken, they might never recapture what they had tonight. But that wasn't the only issue. "I don't want to leave you alone." He tipped his head toward the back door. "All things considered."

"Then don't. I'm not crazy about being by myself tonight, either. Let me get dressed and I'll come with you."

"You have no clue what the repercussions of that would be. My mother would book the church."

Eve shook her head. "Doesn't matter. You and I know that's not going to be the outcome, and I can make sure she knows that."

"Good luck."

"It'll be fine, Charlie. And after you've fixed whatever needs to be fixed, we can come back here."

He could see that he wouldn't get away with refusing his mother's request, not while Eve had anything to say about it. And he had the prospect of continuing where they'd left off once his duties were completed. "All right," he said. "Want to take the motorcycle?"

"Charlie, I would love to ride on your motorcycle."

"You would?" That pleased him.

"I would. Tell your mom we'll be there in fifteen minutes." She hurried back down the hall.

Charlie put the phone to his ear. "Hey, Mom? I'll be there in fifteen minutes. And I'm . . . bringing Eve." His announcement was greeted by silence. "Mom? Are you there? Did you hear what I said?"

"I most certainly did, Charlie. I was just taking a minute to thank God for my blessings."

Chapter Fourteen

Eve was determined not to stand between Charlie and anything—not his dream of Hoover Dam or his obligations to his mother. He'd had enough obstructions in his life and she wasn't about to become another one. Once she saw the conflict in his expression she knew they'd be making a trip together down to the bakery.

Throwing on jeans, a sweater, boots, and her quilted nylon jacket, she was good to go. Charlie had insisted she wear a helmet, so she'd put it on to please him, but she would have liked speeding down the dark streets with her hair flying out behind her. She would have liked to nestle her cheek against Charlie's broad back, but the helmet had a face guard that got in the way of doing that.

Still, she got to wrap her arms around his waist and hang on. She would have loved the sensation of riding with Charlie even before they'd had sex, but after they'd had sex . . . oh, baby. The crisp air laced with the scent of leather and fine machinery was an aphrodisiac.

Instead of resting her cheek on the back of his leather

jacket, she leaned forward to murmur in his ear. "Want to know one of my fantasies?"

He had to yell his response. "What's that?"

"I'm naked, and you're wearing nothing but these chaps." She stroked his leather-covered thigh.

Charlie swerved abruptly to the side of the road and squeaked the tires as he stopped and put both booted feet on the pavement. Then he sucked in air. "God, I almost wrecked."

"Whoops. Sorry."

He glanced over his shoulder. "And here I was thinking you were the girl-next-door type."

"I am the girl-next-door type . . . with ideas."

"No kidding." He blew out a breath. "Sex in leather chaps. I honestly believe you'd like that."

"I honestly believe I would, too. Am I shocking you?"

He made a sound low in his throat. "No, but you bring up a good point. You're way too wild to hang out at my mother's bakery."

"Oh, for heaven's sake. I would never embarrass you in front of—"

"I'm going to call and tell her I can't make it, that something has *come up* and I have to take you home ASAP." He unclipped his cell phone from the pocket of his jeans and started to take off his helmet.

"Wait." Laughing, she caught his hand before he could punch any cell phone buttons. "I can't have that on my conscience."

He brought her hand up to his mouth, took off her glove, and started nibbling on her fingers. "I don't know how you expect me to repair my mother's bakery equipment when I'm thinking about sex and leather."

"Then think about something else, because this repair needs to take place. What would take your mind off sex?"

"With you and your ideas hanging around? Absolutely nothing. Ever since I walked into your kitchen Monday night and saw that purple underwear, I've been thinking of nothing but sex. With you."

"You have?" She shivered as he sucked on her index finger. "I thought you were all engrossed in my stainless steel converter."

"With your purple bra dangling five inches from my nose? Not likely." He licked the space between her index finger and ring finger. "Don't get me wrong. The converter's a masterpiece of engineering. But so's the purple bra, and I'm just a guy, after all."

His tongue felt so warm compared to the cold night air—another contrast to fall in love with. But she'd have to be careful not to fall in love with the guy himself, because he wouldn't be around long. "Charlie, we need to get going. Your mother is waiting."

"I don't have a plan yet for behaving myself while I'm there."

"My fault. But there must be *some* mental trick to keep yourself from getting an erection in your mother's bakery. Think hard, Charlie."

"Thinking soft would make more sense."

"Ha, ha. Come on. This is serious. How about the multiplication tables?"

"Too easy. I could have an entire round of sex while mentally reciting the multiplication tables. But you're on the right track. I'd forgotten that trick. When I was younger and didn't have great staying power during sex, I'd take a number, any number, and figure it to the twelfth power so I wouldn't come too quick."

As heat surged through her, she moaned and hugged him tight. "Thanks. Thanks a whole hell of a lot. Now all I'll be able to think of is you and your well-developed staying power."

His voice grew husky. "I didn't demonstrate that so well tonight, did I?"

"Wasn't needed. Ever since Monday night, I've been thinking about sex. With you."

"Want me to call my mom and cancel?" he asked softly.

"No. I would feel incredibly guilty."

"I'll bet you'd feel just plain incredible. At least I thought so the whole time I was—"

"Stop it, Charlie. Point this hog of yours toward the bakery, okay?"

"Okay." With one last brush of his lips over her fingertips, he released her hand. "And don't touch the chaps."

"Because you're a hunk of burning love ready to go up in flames?"

"You've got it." Charlie revved the motor and took off down the deserted street.

As Charlie drew close to the bakery, he tried to get his head on straight. He knew Eve had been kidding when she'd thrown out the "hunk of burning love" comment, but she didn't know how close she'd come to the truth. He'd been in love a couple of times in his life. It hadn't worked out either time. Cindi had been way too young, and Mariah had hated his plan to move to Nevada.

After Mariah, he'd told himself to be careful about this love business. But along came Eve. Maybe because of her appealing nerdiness and her most excellent brain, he hadn't remembered to be careful. And sure enough, judging from the signs, he was coming down with the beginning stages of lovesickness.

The evidence was all there. To begin with, he'd volunteered to work on the hovercraft, but he'd spent more time learning about her than her invention. Totally uncharacteristic. Then he'd allowed his sexual frustration to turn him into a reckless driver tonight. Also unlike him.

Those were the big things, but there were a million little things. He'd noticed just now that she didn't wear rings of any kind, and he'd started wondering what kind of wedding band she'd want. He got a real charge out of every time he made her smile, and when she laughed, especially if he'd had something to do with that reaction, he felt warm all over. Yes, the sex was amazing, but he also remembered how cute she'd looked trying to hide the fact she'd been gathering up condoms, just in case.

He'd begun to catalog the small things—the graceful gestures she made as a result of runway training, the soft wisps of hair that grew at the nape of her neck, and the little indentation her glasses made on the bridge of her nose. She was working her way into his heart, and he didn't know what to do to stop that from happening.

Abandoning the relationship wouldn't work, not when she needed him to help her with her invention and potentially keep away whoever was trying to horn in on it. That crowbar job on the door looked more like a man's work than a woman's, but a woman who kept in shape might be able to accomplish it. One thing was fairly sure—it hadn't been a professional thief. A professional would have picked the lock.

Or maybe it was a professional and they'd used the crowbar to make it look amateurish. When Charlie considered that, he realized that he didn't know much of anything about who had broken into Eve's house. The missing notes, if in fact they were missing, were the only thing connecting the break-in to the hovercraft. Someone even might have broken in by mistake, figured out they didn't have the right house, and left.

All Charlie could do was stay close and try to keep it from happening again. That meant that he was leaving himself wide open to the onset of lovesickness. He thought of it as a disease, one he didn't want to catch right now. But it didn't seem as if he had much choice.

Guiding his bike down an alley and steering around the shoveled mounds of slushy snow, he parked in his usual spot behind the bakery, right next to his mother's Volvo. His mother and Aunt Myrtle would have left the back door open. They weren't much better about locks than Eve.

Eve climbed off the bike and immediately Charlie missed the contact of her thighs and breasts. Why did this bakery gizmo have to malfunction tonight? No matter how quickly he fixed it, and he planned to do it at warp speed, he'd still lose a good hour with Eve. And it would have been a good hour, too.

"What should I do with the helmet?" She took it off and tossed her head so that her hair fell loose around her shoulders. The back door light reflected off her tumbling hair so that sections of it turned the color of burnished copper.

Charlie sat on his bike and took in the show, unable to stop staring. He ached to bury his fingers in all that glorious hair, to have it rain down around his face as she leaned over him, to watch it bounce and wiggle as they writhed on her round bed.

"Charlie?" She held out the helmet.

"I love your hair."

She looked startled. Then she adjusted the fit of her glasses. "Thank you. It's just hair."

"That's like saying Hoover is just a dam. Your hair is amazing."

"I never thought so. I always wanted to be a blonde."

"Then why aren't you?" He'd dated several blondes in his life. Three he knew for a fact weren't natural blondes. The others were an unknown—the relationship hadn't progressed to the bedroom stage where he'd inevitably find out. But all the women he knew, including his mother and his aunt, had whatever color they wanted.

"Models aren't supposed to color their hair."

"I didn't know that. But I'm glad you don't. It looks perfect the way it is."

She picked up a strand and studied it. "It's okay, I guess. At least the ends look better now that the frizzed part from the explosion is gone."

"You singed your *hair*?"

"Just a little."

"You could have been killed." That settled it. He wasn't letting her do any more testing without him around. Accidents could so easily happen, but if he double-checked all her work, then . . . his mind stalled as a horrible thought came to him. What if the explosion hadn't been an accident? What if someone had wanted to stall the development of the hovercraft until they could steal her notes?

"I have fast reflexes," she said.

"Thank God." But the more he thought about this, the more worried he became. The explosion had delayed Eve's progress, and someone might have wanted that. "Listen, was Eunice the only person who knew about the hovercraft before we all came over on Monday night?"

"I think so. Unless somebody caught a glimpse of it when I opened my garage door, which I didn't do very often. A couple of weeks ago I accidentally hit the button and it opened, but the only person outside was Eunice, who was shoveling her driveway."

"Does she usually shovel her own driveway?"

"Usually. She thinks it builds up her boobs. Why?"

"Just thinking." A woman who shoveled her own driveway on a regular basis would have the necessary muscles to use a crowbar on Eve's back door. But Charlie wasn't ready to point the finger yet. He needed to find out more about Eunice before he started making accusations.

"Look, Eunice isn't behind any of this. I knew that the minute I saw somebody had gone after my door with a crowbar."

"If you think that lets her out because she has a key, think again. She could have used the crowbar on purpose, to cast off any suspicion."

"She didn't use a crowbar on my back door, Charlie."

"How can you be so sure? If she shovels her own walk, she'd be strong enough."

"Strength isn't the issue here. It's nails."

"Nails? There weren't any nails in that door. Just the lock."

"Fingernails." Eve waved her fingers at him. "Shoveling snow is one thing. You can wear gloves and be careful. But using a crowbar on a door is a whole different ball of wax. You can't predict exactly how it will go and when something will give way, so you stand an excellent chance of breaking a nail on a project like that. Eunice wouldn't risk it."

As Charlie studied her, he tried to decide if her theory made sense. She certainly knew more about women's manicures than he did. "Obviously you have been thinking about who did this."

"Of course I have." She smiled. "In between thinking about having sex with you, that is."

He pushed away his immediate response, which was to grab her and carry her away into the night so they could get naked. "And do you have any idea who it might be?"

"I hate to throw out accusations."

"I know. Me, too. But somebody broke into your house while you were gone, and until you find those notes, we have to assume that was the reason. I'm not ruling the explosion an accident yet, either."

She waved a hand, dismissing that part of his statement. "It was an accident. The vandalized door was not. The only people I can think who might have done it are . . . and I hate to say this . . . Manny and Kyle."

Charlie had thought of them, too. "Motive?"

"They're lowly assistants, working for a high-powered, successful photographer. Maybe they're sick of being errand boys who are helping to build another guy's career, and they want to make a chunk of money so they can go off on their own. You and Rick let them know the hovercraft could be worth money, so they might be trying to peddle the concept."

"I guess it's possible." Charlie let the idea simmer a moment. Yeah, it was definitely possible. "Too bad they ended up getting in on the discussion Monday night and had to be invited over. But there wasn't much else we could do."

"And I could be wrong about them. That would be horrible, to accuse two innocent guys when it's really someone else."

He had a feeling that she had another person in mind who might be responsible, and she wasn't saying. "So those are the two you came up with, Manny and Kyle?"

"I don't know who else it could be."

Charlie thought he had to say it, to be fair. Maybe then she'd come out with her other name. After all, she had told her sister, who didn't live all that far away. And her sister could be insane with jealousy. Family dynamics could get very weird.

"We can't forget my cousin," he said. "He was there Monday night, too. He believes the hovercraft's a moneymaker."

"Rick? Why would he jeopardize a great career, one that's pulling in insane amounts of money, by the way. Do you have any idea how much top photographers get these days?"

Charlie didn't. "Are you telling me that maybe his Rolex isn't from China?"

"Not from China. Why do you think Eunice is putting on her alien sexual show with all the fanfare and props? Sure, she thinks he's cute, but she also knows he's loaded." She gazed at him. "Look, I have to ask, and then we can drop the subject. Did you offer up your cousin to see if I'd offer up my sister?"

She looked so vulnerable that he could only come up with one answer. It might be a white lie, but he'd take the consequences of telling one this time. "I'm sure it's not your sister."

"Yeah, me, too. I'm glad we agree on that."

From the soft way she said it, he didn't think she was at all convinced. But he wasn't about to press on that sore spot, and she'd desperately needed to hear that he didn't list Denise as a suspect. "We're not going to solve it now, anyway."

"No, we're not. Come on, Charlie, let's go in. I want to get a look at those cookies."

"Yeah, because it's not your mother making them." But Charlie was feeling better about braving the X-rated pastries with Eve by his side. Eve helped him maintain his sense of humor about such things.

"Speaking of cookies, how could two guys who got talked into frosting those cookies take a crowbar to my back door? It doesn't make sense that they're the ones, when I think about how your mom and aunt are wrapping them around their little fingers."

"Right now, only one thing makes sense."

"What's that?"

He put an arm around her waist as they walked toward the back door of the bakery. "First of all, repairing the damned mixer."

"And then?"

"Going straight to bed."

She laughed, and he felt that suspicious warmth invading his heart. No doubt about it. He was coming down with a bad case.

Chapter Fifteen

Eve hoped either Manny, Kyle, or both of them together had done that number on her door. If they hadn't, then Denise was next in the lineup. Denise worked out every day. No flabby muscles would dare cling to her athletic frame. And she might be determined to protect her baby sister from doing something dangerous.

Denise would be smart enough to break down the back door to make it look as if the culprit didn't have a key. And Denise would rationalize it as all for Eve's own good. Eve didn't think Denise would be the least bit conscience-stricken if she thought her actions would save her little sister from her own stupidity.

But Eve wasn't about to help focus the laser beam of Charlie's intellect on Denise. She appreciated his protective tendencies, but a false accusation would rip apart a sisterly bond that was already worn in several places. Eve could kick herself for giving in to the urge to tell Denise about the hovercraft.

Charlie opened the back door of the bakery without knocking and they stepped into a world that smelled of family, Christmas, and lazy Sunday mornings. Or at least that's what Eve imagined the warmth and soothing aromas could mean in the right hands.

There hadn't been any baking going on in her parents' house, not with all the charity work her mother had to do. Christmas had been efficiently dispensed with because the holidays were high season if you were running charity balls and teas. Lazy Sunday mornings hadn't existed, either. Church early in the morning and a big brunch at the country club had taken up the biggest part of the day.

Eve's reverie ended abruptly as she realized Charlie had opened the back door of the bakery without a key. "The door wasn't locked?" She'd become fixated on the subject of locks recently.

"It's a problem with several people in my life these days," Charlie said as they stepped inside. "They say locking the door causes too many problems, like when Aunt Myrtle comes into the alley for a breath of fresh air and locks herself out."

"She goes outside in this weather?" Eve found herself in a little curtained alcove. A small bathroom was off to the right, and a large fuse box was mounted on the wall right next to the door.

"It's a habit left over from her smoking days."

"BS. She's sneaking a cigarette." Eve had been around too many people who had supposedly quit to believe that Aunt Myrtle went to the back alley to suck up plain old air. She was after nicotine.

"Charlie?" Rose Shepherd, a voluminous apron covering her pale green pantsuit, pushed back the curtain. "I thought I heard people talking back here. Hello, Eve!"

"Hello, Mrs. Shepherd." Eve winced at the heartiness of the greeting. No doubt about it, Rose was salivating for a daughter-in-law prospect, and by showing up tonight at this hour, Eve was implying a connection with Charlie that could lead to Something Big. Too bad for Rose.

"You should call me Rose," she said. "After all, you and Charlie are friends, so it seems silly to stand on formality."

"Thank you. I'll do that, then." Eve avoided looking at Charlie. He'd warned her this would be the result of her tagging along, but she hadn't been able to figure out an alternative. "Listen, as long as I'm here, what can I do to help while Charlie's repairing your mixer?"

"She can frost!" The raspy voice could only belong to Myrtle, the pseudo ex-smoker. "Manny's doing fine, but Kyle's flagging. We could use reinforcements."

Eve's stomach lurched. She glanced at Charlie for moral support. He winked, which helped relieve her jitters, but it still felt weird to be diving into a communal project with the very men she and Charlie had discussed as prime suspects in the break-in. It looked as if she'd end up frosting X-rated cookies with them.

"It'll be fine," Charlie murmured as he held the curtain aside.

Of course it would, she told herself. After all, Charlie was here. Comforted by that thought, she stepped into the warm and fragrant back room. Gleaming stainless steel appliances lined the walls, giving it a high-tech feel. A seriously insulated door on one wall obviously led to a walk-in refrigerator.

A butcher-block island took up space in the center of the room, and there Manny and Kyle perched on stools, each man wearing clear plastic gloves. They didn't look much like criminals while surrounded by an array of cake-decorating tools. Eve wasn't close enough to inspect the shape of the cookies they were working on, but she had a pretty good grasp of the concept already.

Kyle glanced up eagerly. "Are you here to help? I mean, this used to be fun and all, but after you've decorated fifty couples doing it, the thrill is gone. I never thought the day would come that I didn't care about sex, but after fifty cookies, a guy gets jaded."

"Kyle." Manny placed his cookie to one side and picked up another one. "You haven't done fifty. You've only done twenty."

"Really? It seems like more."

"Actually, it's less," Myrtle said from her station over by one of the large ovens. "You ate one. So your count is only nineteen to Manny's thirty."

"Manny's done thirty? No way."

"Thirty." Manny's hands looked huge wielding the parchment cone filled with frosting, but despite that he delicately squirted two dabs of red frosting on his cookie. "This will be thirty-one. You, on the other hand, are not currently frosting diddly-squat, are you?"

"I'm resting my fingers," Kyle said. "All that squeezing was giving me finger cramps. I might get carpel tunnel of the pinky doing this."

Manny snorted and picked up a cone filled with yellow frosting.

Eve had a tough time imagining two guys who were squabbling over how many cookies they'd each frosted taking a crowbar to her back door. But maybe that was the idea. The cookie-frosting caper was protective coloring. And she'd much rather think they did it than her sister.

As she stepped closer to the island she saw the purpose of the two dabs of red on Manny's cookie. Nipples. The cookie portrayed the woman on her back and the man in a sideways scissors position, so you got him in profile, but she was sporting full frontal nudity.

Eve felt warm breath on the back of her neck and glanced over her shoulder to find Charlie standing there, hands on hips, his gaze intent on the cookie Manny was decorating. Both couples were being given blond hair . . .

everywhere that hair was appropriate. Charlie seemed to be fascinated by Manny's technique.

"So what do you think?" she asked, just to get a reaction out of him.

Charlie's color was high as he met her gaze. "Looks complicated. But doable."

She was a bad girl to tease him, but she couldn't resist. "The decorating or the position?"

He swallowed. "Uh . . . both, I guess." Then he stepped back and turned toward his mother. "All righty, then! Let's see about that mixer."

"I don't know how it happened." Rose led him away toward a far corner of the room. "One minute it was kneading the dough great, and the next it gave a groan of protest and quit working entirely."

"Sort of like Kyle, over there," Manny said.

"Boys, boys," Myrtle said. "Don't fight." Opening the oven door, she took out a giant tray and smacked it down so hard on the butcher-block island that the cookies jumped. "Here's another twenty-five, kiddos. Let 'em cool off a little before you start. Eve, you'll have to tie back your hair if you're going to help. Health department regulations."

"Oh. Right." Eve didn't know much about the food business, but she'd noticed that employees didn't have loose hair flying around. "I didn't bring anything."

"Here." Manny took off one glove, reached in his pocket and pulled out a red bandanna. "It's clean."

"Thanks." She couldn't imagine that a guy who would break down her door would turn around and offer her a bandanna for her hair, but who knew how criminals thought? She tied her hair back with Manny's bandanna.

"If you're all set in here," Myrtle said, "I'm going out for a breath of fresh air." Pulling off her oven mitts, she headed out through the curtained doorway.

"She's going for a smoke," Kyle muttered.

"Which she can have if she wants," Manny said in a low voice. He pursed his lips as he finished up his cookie. Then he drew back and admired it. "Not bad. Not bad at all."

"Smoking is bad for her," Kyle said.

Manny took another cookie. "You aren't some judge and jury, you know. The poor lady's had a hard life, losing her husband early. I think she showed pluck, starting up this bakery. She can have the occasional cigarette without going to hell."

"It's not hell I'm thinking of," Kyle said. "It's the hospital, which is worse. Cigarettes will land you in the hospital sooner or later. Everybody knows that." Then he looked at Eve. "Am I right?"

"Probably, although some people get away with it." Eve glanced over to where Rose and Charlie were engrossed in the mixer repair. Charlie was making enough noise taking it apart that she doubted either he or his mother could hear this discussion.

"I say Myrtle shouldn't take those odds." Kyle looked worried. "I tried talking to her about it, real quiet so Rose wouldn't hear, because Rose acts like she doesn't know. But Myrtle's in total denial about the risks."

"Kyle, you can't make her give up smoking if she doesn't want to," Manny said. "But you could help her by frosting a few more cookies."

"Okay." Kyle sighed. Then he glanced hopefully at Eve. "Ready to glove up and take a turn? This would be easier without the gloves, but we're not allowed on account of the sanitary issues. If you're not used to working with gloves, I can show you a few tricks."

"I'd appreciate that." Eve reached for the box of plastic gloves and pulled out a pair. As she put them on she wondered if Kyle had handed her a clue. Anybody who knew his way around plastic gloves might be used to them because he always made sure not to leave fingerprints whenever he took a crowbar to somebody's back door.

But as Kyle demonstrated how to manipulate the parchment cones filled with frosting and the various attachments, Eve felt less and less inclined to think of him as a crook. Crooks could be charming, she reminded herself. *Dirty Rotten Scoundrels* had become a Broadway hit based on that very premise. She shouldn't eliminate Manny and Kyle because they seemed like decent guys.

As a cookie froster, Eve turned out to be passable, better than Kyle but not nearly as accomplished as Manny. She did discover that staring at the sex act while squeezing frosting from a parchment cone made her think about getting back to her house ASAP. She didn't mind helping the cause, but she hoped Charlie would finish the repair in the next hour or so.

Logically she should be exhausted. It was nearly one in the morning, after a long day and an eventful night. But she was keyed up and eager to finish out the hours of darkness with a guy who did nice things for a pair of black leather chaps. Instead she was dabbing nipples on a sugar cookie while Charlie had his head buried in a dough mixer.

"You're doing a great job," Rose said as she walked past carrying a large bag of raisins.

"Thanks," Eve said. "Manny's the cookie maestro, though. He's finished another five while I'm still on my second one."

"Every little bit helps." Rose paused and switched the bag of raisins to her hip, as if she were carrying a toddler. "We promised two hundred cookies for that bachelorette party Friday night."

"Two hundred?" Eve stopped working and glanced up. Her next order of business was squeezing pubic hair onto her cookie lady, and she couldn't do a good job and talk at the same time. "How many people will be at this party?"

"Most of the women in town, including me and Myrtle." Rose looked wistful. "In Middlesex the whole community gets behind a wedding." Then she brightened. "You could come to the bachelorette party, too!"

"Oh, I don't think so." Eve wanted to save her evenings for the hovercraft. "I'd feel funny going without an invitation."

"I could get you an invitation. I'll bet Jill didn't think you'd be interested, considering you're so busy with modeling and all. But you might as well go. Charlie will be at the bachelor party for her fiancé David. They're holding it at the Rack and Balls."

Eve was sure Charlie had spaced that particular social obligation. And Rose's invitation had put her smack-dab in the middle of a dilemma. She didn't want to be thought of as stuck-up. The whole point in moving to this small town was to be part of the life here and lose that big-city glamour role. "My sister's coming to visit tomorrow," she said. "I couldn't very well abandon her."

"Bring her!" Rose beamed at Eve. "The more the merrier. Is she a model, too?"

"She's an economics professor," Eve said. "She knows everything about Wall Street."

"Oh, yeah?" Manny stopped decorating and looked up. "I dabble in stocks, myself. Think she'd give me some tips?"

Eve thought about what could happen if someone turned Denise on to her favorite subject. "You have to know how to frame your questions. If you're not careful, she'll give you a complete analysis of the New York Stock Exchange and throw in an evaluation of Nasdaq for free."

"I wouldn't mind. When's she coming to town?"

Eve glanced at her watch. "In approximately nine hours." When she considered how little housecleaning she would get done between now and then, her tummy fluttered with anxiety. But if it came down to cleaning house or spending time in bed with Charlie and his chaps, she had no trouble making the decision.

Manny grimaced. "With luck we'll be finished with these cookies by then."

"Oh, goodness." Rose patted him on the shoulder. "You can stop now. You can all stop now. I'm feeling guilty. Myrtle and I shouldn't be keeping you young people from your fun and games."

Eve felt the heat climbing up her neck. Rose hadn't looked directly at her when she'd made that comment, but she knew what Rose must be thinking. It was true, except there would be no happily-ever-after part, and that was the part that Rose was probably counting on.

Eve decided to set the record straight and give the printable reason why Charlie was spending time with her. Charlie's mother wasn't likely to cause her problems if she knew about the hovercraft. "Charlie and I are collaborating on a project of mine," she said. "We're trying to keep it under wraps until I can test it. After that we'll try to market it, but for now, it's in the experimental stage, so we only tell the people we can trust."

"You can certainly trust me," Rose said.

"Me, too." Myrtle came in through the back curtain. "I have no idea what you're talking about, but I'm great at keeping secrets. Isn't that right, Rose?"

"You're pretty good at it, Myrtle."

"I'm more than pretty good. I never told a single person that you had that tummy tuck, now did I?"

"You just did!" Rose blushed as she glanced around the room. "I assure you it was minor. Extremely minor."

"It wasn't, but that's neither here nor there," Myrtle

said. "We're talking about Eve's secret." She glanced over at Manny and Kyle. "What about these two boys? Can they hear about this?"

"They already know," Eve said.

"And did they swear on a Bible that they wouldn't tell?" Myrtle gave both men the evil eye.

"I don't expect anyone to swear on anything." Although now that Myrtle had brought it up, some kind of agreement might have been a good idea. It wouldn't mean much if Manny and Kyle were the crowbar crew, though.

"I think we should all swear an oath of silence," Myrtle said. "That's how it is with secrets. You're supposed to take them seriously and swear not to tell, but the problem is, we don't have a Bible. All we have is . . . wait, I've got it! We'll say that the sack of raisins is really a Bible and swear on that."

Rose groaned. "Myrtle, for pity's sake. If I didn't know better, I'd think you were mixing up old-fashioneds in the bathroom. We are not swearing on a sack of raisins. That's silly and it might even be sacrilegious."

"Is not." Myrtle stuck her chin in the air. "I'm a very devout person. Mostly. Don't think of it as a sack of raisins. Think of each raisin as a nugget of wisdom from the Scriptures. Don't look at me like that, Rose Alice. It's a perfectly good idea."

"It's not, either, Myrtle Marie! We can't just say presto-chango, this bag of raisins is a Bible."

"Why not?" Myrtle put her hands on her skinny hips. "Jesus turned water into wine. Lots of things represent other things in the Bible. It's called being allegorical. So plop that bag of raisins up here and we'll all put our hands on it and swear."

Rose sighed and sent a glance of apology around to the group. "I can see you're determined on this point, Myrtle. So we might as well, because you won't rest until we do."

"We're doing what with raisins?" Charlie walked over to the island, a wrench in one hand. "I'm finished, by the way. The mixer works."

"Thank you, Charlie." Rose smiled at him. "And the raisins are your aunt Myrtle's brainstorm. She thinks we should all swear not to reveal the secret of Eve's project."

"On a bag of raisins?" Charlie looked confused. "What am I missing?"

"You're not missing anything," his mother said. "It's your aunt Myrtle who's missing a few slices from her loaf."

"Hey!" Myrtle swatted at her sister. "I'm trying to make sure Eve's secret doesn't get spread all around town. Do you have something against that?"

"Not a thing." Rose positioned the sack of raisins on the butcher block and placed her hand on it. "I solemnly swear not to reveal Eve's secret to anyone outside this room."

"Mom." Charlie sounded concerned. "You're swearing on a sack of raisins."

"Just go with it," Rose said. "Myrtle wants us to think it's a Bible, and once she gets like this, it's pointless to argue with her."

"This is a very good idea," Myrtle said. "You'll see. It's the symbolic nature of this that is important." She started to put her hand on the bag and then she snatched it back. "Hold it. Is anybody else in on it? What about Rick?"

"He knows," Eve said. "And so does my next-door neighbor, Eunice Piven."

"The alien abduction lady," Myrtle said. "She's a good Pastry Parlor customer, so I'm willing to trust her. And Rick's not a blabbermouth. I didn't raise him to be a gossip."

"I just thought of two other people who might have

heard something." Charlie glanced at Eve. "When we were talking about this at the Rack and Balls Monday night, do you remember the guys who came in?"

"Yes. I didn't know who they were, though."

"Darrell and Ed," Charlie said. "They own the Christmas tree farm outside of town."

"And they're both fruits," Myrtle said.

"Myrtle!" Rose glared at her sister. "I've told you a million times not to say it like that. The word is *gay*."

Eve met Charlie's gaze and could guess he was picturing her damaged back door, a door that could easily have been pried open by two guys who worked outdoors all day at their Christmas tree farm. "They might have heard something about the project, but it's hard to believe that they would—"

"I don't know," he said quietly. "Anything's possible."

"Darrell and Ed stay mostly to themselves," Myrtle said. "I don't think they would talk. Still, it's too bad we don't have everyone here to swear an oath of silence."

"You'd need a bigger bag of raisins, Aunt Myrtle," Charlie said solemnly. Then he winked at Eve.

Myrtle glared at him. "Are you making fun of my raisins, Charles Edward Shepherd?"

"Nope." Charlie laid his hand on the bag. "I solemnly swear not to reveal Eve's secret to anyone outside this room."

Eve melted. She was a sucker for a guy who went along with whatever craziness his relatives foisted on him. "Should I swear, too?"

"Why not?" Myrtle said. "We don't want you going around blabbing about this."

"I won't, except that I just thought of the other person who knows. My sister Denise."

"The economics professor," Manny said.

"Right. But she's not a problem." Eve hoped that was

true. She would have a much better idea after Denise arrived. Picking a spot right next to Charlie's hand, she laid her hand on the bag of raisins. Her pinkie touched his thumb. "I solemnly swear that I won't reveal my secret to anyone who doesn't already know about it."

"See, that's a better thing to swear," Myrtle said. "Maybe we should start over."

"No!" said Manny and Kyle together, slapping their hands on the bag. They each recited the pledge in turn.

"Then I'm the last." Myrtle laid her hand on top of everyone else's. "I solemnly swear, on this bag of common raisins, which has been transformed through the miracle of human inspiration into the embodiment of the Holy Word of God, that I will never reveal, on pain of death, or whatever punishment is deemed most fitting for the—"

"Myrtle!" Rose bumped her hip against Myrtle's. "Cut the dramatic monologue and take the pledge."

"I swear I won't tell." Myrtle lifted her hand. "There. It's done. Okay, Eve. Spill your guts."

While Eve described her hovercraft to Rose and Myrtle, she tried to gauge Manny and Kyle's reaction to see if talking about the hovercraft made either of them squirm or fidget. Guilty people tended to do that.

Manny and Kyle sat quietly, giving nothing away. Either they weren't guilty of breaking and entering, or they were experts at hiding their guilt. Their expressions were impossible to read one way or the other.

Too bad. She'd still like to pin the theft of her notes on them. They were strangers in town, so if they were the culprits, her idealized picture of Middlesex wouldn't be smashed to smithereens.

In any case, she was getting a kick out of talking about her project. She tried to keep her explanation as free of technical jargon as possible, and references to Michael J. Fox and the hover boards in *Back to the Future Part II* seemed to help Rose grasp the concept. Myrtle, however, never looked the least bewildered.

When Eve finished, Myrtle bounced with excitement. "I've read up on this! Biofuel is the wave of the future!"

"I hope it is," Eve said. "Maybe my hovercraft will help pioneer that. It will be a toy at first, but once people see that they can power a vehicle with something other than fossil fuel, they might want to expand the concept."

"What about powering it with used cooking oil?" Myrtle said.

Eve was startled. She hadn't met too many people who were versed in this subject. "It would work, too. I haven't considered that for my project because I don't cook with oil, myself, and I . . ." Then it dawned on her that she was standing in a bakery. Used cooking oil would flow from this place like water. She looked at Charlie.

"I thought of it," he said. "But I wasn't sure if you wanted to get other people involved."

"Other people?" His mother sounded insulted. "We're not 'other people.' Didn't we just take an oath of silence on a bag of raisins?"

"Sorry." Charlie looked sheepish. "I figured Eve had already thought of that angle and discarded it."

"I didn't think of it," Eve said. "Sometimes you miss the most obvious things." Maybe she didn't use cooking oil, but other people did. She should have considered it, but she'd allowed her single-track mind to take over on this one.

"We would be happy to give you our used cooking oil," Rose said. "If you want it, that is."

"I definitely do. I have to admit I've been struggling with my veggie fuel. I still want to make it work, but used cooking oil might speed up the development phase, which might mean I could test the hovercraft that much sooner."

"Then let us send you home with a supply," Myrtle said. "And you should both take off right now, so you can get to work."

Rose glanced at her. "Myrtle, it's almost two in the morning. You can't expect them to work at this late hour."

"Ah." Myrtle waved a dismissive hand. "At their age, they can stay up all night."

Eve bit her lip to keep from laughing. She hoped, at least in Charlie's case, that was true.

Chapter Sixteen

Rick's cell phone woke him from a dream about purple spaceships and little green men. Sitting up in the bedroom he'd had as a kid, he turned on the Power Rangers lamp on the nightstand and grabbed his phone. It wasn't a programmed ring, so it could be anybody, even Eunice trying to coax him back for another round.

Then he checked the number and immediately answered. God, when did the man sleep?

"I've done some checking," Peterson said in his soft, smooth voice. "My sources tell me that Myrtle Bannister could hock everything she owns and it wouldn't raise enough to pay your debt to me."

Rick's vocal cords tightened. "I know." His voice was too high, too clearly telegraphing fear. He cleared his throat. "I could see that immediately. That's why I have a different plan."

"Oh, really? Then maybe you'd better tell me about it."

He didn't want to be specific. A man like Peterson couldn't be trusted with the names of innocent people like Eve Dupree. So he described the plan in general terms.

"You're making this up, aren't you?" Peterson said.

"No, I swear I'm not!" Rick began to sweat. When he rubbed his hand over his chest, green paint came off.

"Then give me a name. Who's building this crazy thing?"

Reluctantly, Rick told him.

"Sounds very unlikely, Mr. Bannister. Very unlikely. Can you prove any of this to me?"

"I'll get pictures," Rick said. He'd need to do that anyway. He just hadn't wanted to carry his camera along the first time, when he'd had to break down the back door. But now he had a key.

"Perhaps I'll go with you while you do that."

"Go with me?" Rick struggled to breathe. "But you're in California!"

"Coincidentally, I had some business in New York. Look out the window, Mr. Bannister."

Rick stumbled to the window of his second-floor bedroom. In the street below idled a black Lincoln Towncar. Rick felt as if he might pass out.

"Ready to take a little ride to Ms. Dupree's house?" Peterson said, his voice gentle.

"You don't need to go," Rick said as spots danced before his eyes. "Really. I'm sure you could use some rest. I'll take care of it."

"I'm not so sure you will. I'm losing my faith in you, Mr. Bannister. And as you know, that can have serious consequences." Then Peterson laughed softly. "I'd advise you to be down here in five minutes." Then he hung up.

Charlie drove with exquisite care on the way back to Eve's house. Eve held on to him with one arm while she used the other to balance a small covered trash can full of cooking oil on her knee. It was a precarious arrangement, and for the first time since owning the bike Charlie questioned whether a car might not be a smarter option.

For all these years the bike had served as a reminder of the freedom he would have someday. He'd ridden in every kind of weather and never minded a bit. But it wasn't the safest mode of transportation for Eve, especially when she was trying to hold on to a couple of gallons of cooking oil.

He'd had no choice tonight, though. He couldn't very well switch vehicles and ask his mother and Aunt Myrtle to take his bike. Besides, Manny and Kyle needed a ride back to his aunt's house.

Charlie wondered if the cooking oil had changed any of Eve's plans for the rest of the night. She'd been handed a new option to fool with, and she might want to begin experimenting right away. Someone with a genius mentality like Eve's could very well get locked onto an idea and not allow herself to be distracted by something like, say, sex.

He was eager to find out how the cooking oil worked, too. But not so eager that he'd sacrifice the original plan, the leather chaps plan. He was no genius, but for the moment he seemed to have a one-track mind, too. With luck he and Eve weren't chugging along on entirely different tracks.

Once they got to her place and unloaded the cooking oil, he'd tell her that he was going to take a couple of vacation days from work. Maybe if she knew that she'd have him around to help the rest of this week, she wouldn't feel so desperate to begin working on the new fuel option right this minute. He hoped she'd look at it that way, because in his current condition he didn't know how well he'd be able to concentrate on the hovercraft.

Slowing the bike at her driveway, he made a gentle arc as he glided in and parked beside her Civic Hybrid. After turning off the engine, he held the bike steady while Eve climbed off and set the can of cooking oil on the icy driveway.

She reached in her pocket, pulled out her keys, and beeped open the passenger door of her car. "Let's put your bike in the garage." She leaned in and activated the garage door opener clipped to the sun visor.

"Uh . . . okay." He watched the door rumble upward and estimated the available room in the garage. "But won't my bike be in the way?"

She turned back to him, looking extremely cute in his spare helmet with the clear face guard flipped up. "In the way of what?"

"Well, we'll need the space when we work on the . . ." His heart began to pound. "We're not going to work on the hovercraft, are we?"

She took off the helmet and then untied the red bandanna she'd been wearing at the bakery. She tucked the bandanna in her coat pocket. "That depends. What would you rather do?"

Obviously she had no clue as to the degree of lust that permeated his entire body. "I—"

"I mean, you can leave your bike out here if you want." She stood there looking uncertain. "I just thought, considering that some people in this neighborhood get up early, that you should—"

"You bet." Charlie started up the bike and drove into the garage so fast he almost knocked over the can of cooking oil on his way by. As he dismounted, the garage door thumped down behind him. Anal retentive geek that he was, he wasted a couple of seconds wondering if she'd remembered to lock her car and bring the cooking oil inside.

But then he turned around and there she was, walking toward him with that runway stride, unzipping her coat on the way. So the cooking oil would freeze and the car would be stolen. Who the hell cared? Laying his helmet on the seat of his bike, he reached for her. "Let me help with that."

With a lazy smile, she moved sideways, out of reach. "You handle yours and I'll handle mine." She opened the kitchen door and walked inside. "I'll meet you in the bedroom. Oh, and bring your chaps."

Charlie gulped. When he'd fantasized this scene, he hadn't imagined how he'd get from point A, him fully dressed, to point B, walking into her bedroom wearing only his chaps and an erection. He couldn't do that any more than he could pose nude for an art class.

But he wanted to get to the part where he had sex with Eve while wearing his chaps. She'd fired up his imagination with the idea, and he wasn't about to wimp out when the opportunity was presented. He just had to work out how he'd accomplish this maneuver with some class.

By now she had time to walk all the way through her house, possibly stripping as she went. The thought of that sent a jolt of electricity through him, propelling him through the kitchen doorway. He locked the door behind him.

Once he was inside he could hear the music she'd chosen for round two. No smoky jazz this time. Instead she'd decided on something a little faster, with a syncopated beat.

Charlie reacted to that beat by getting hard. Well, now, maybe he could sashay into her bedroom wearing the chaps, after all. Then again, maybe not. Every time he pictured doing it he started to sweat. Besides, she'd asked him to *bring* his chaps. She hadn't said he should *wear* his chaps.

In that case, how should he arrive? She was the expert at making an entrance. It might not have occurred to her that everyone wasn't used to parading around in a costume.

Most people put on clothes and took off clothes as a practical consideration. It wasn't considered performance art.

Oy. Maybe he should begin by taking things off and finding out when he'd hit his comfort level. He could certainly ditch the leather jacket. He hung it over the back of a kitchen chair.

Logically he'd have to take the chaps off in order to put them on again. Unbuckling them, he laid them over another kitchen chair. The boots could go, too. He sat in the chair, moving gingerly because his jeans were getting tighter the longer he listened to that rhythmic beat.

After pulling off his boots, he set them side by side on the floor. The socks also could be eliminated. For sure he wasn't going in there wearing socks. He tucked a sock in each boot.

Then he looked at the scene he'd created—his jacket hanging neatly on one chair, his chaps on the other, his boots lined up on the floor and a sock carefully tucked inside. Unfortunately, none of this indicated a man who made love with his chaps on. This indicated a man who'd been president of his high school chapter of the National Honor Society.

But this time he'd overcome his natural inclinations, damn it! Standing, he wrenched his shirt from the waistband of his jeans, unbuttoned it and took it off. Instead of draping it neatly over another chair, he balled it up and threw it in the corner. It landed on top of the converter and he resisted the urge to move it.

He would be wild and crazy, by God! His T-shirt sailed into the other corner and landed on the floor. Now he was getting into the swing of things. With a flourish he unclipped his cell phone from his jeans pocket and lobbed it into one of his boots. Two points.

Then he reached for the metal button at the waistband

of his jeans. As he was undoing it, he remembered two things. Once the jeans were gone he was down to his briefs. Walking into Eve's bedroom wearing only his briefs and a hard-on was only marginally better than making his entrance in the chaps.

The second thing he remembered were the two condoms still in the pocket of his jeans. He'd carried them all the way to the bakery and back. And he'd be needing at least one of them shortly.

So it was decided. He'd go in there wearing his jeans and his briefs. He'd carry the chaps. Somehow, in the course of events, he'd get rid of the jeans and briefs and put on the chaps. Or maybe she'd help. There was an encouraging thought.

Taking a deep breath, he picked up his chaps and started toward her bedroom. He hoped he hadn't taken so long to get down there that she'd given up on him and fallen asleep.

Eve had made a bet with herself as to whether Charlie would follow through with the chaps. She'd kept to her part of the bargain. She was lying naked in her round bed under her custom-made, fluffy round comforter.

Before coming in here she'd darted into the bathroom and snagged a couple more condoms, in case Charlie had left his jeans in the kitchen. She didn't think he'd forget that item, but it didn't hurt to have backup. Then she'd stripped down and crawled under her comforter.

And waited. Talk about torture. Now that she knew how expertly Charlie used his equipment, she wanted more of that, the sooner the better. Maybe she shouldn't have mentioned the chaps fantasy. Charlie might be struggling with that part of the plan.

Well, of course he was. In order for him to walk in here wearing only his chaps, he'd need a personality transplant.

She should know. The only way she managed that long walk down the runway during fashion shows was to leave her glasses behind. The audience became an indistinct backdrop that she could ignore.

Once Charlie got into this, he wouldn't be wearing his glasses. That might help. What she had in mind was mostly about sensation, anyway. Mostly. She had her glasses on, in case he really did walk in dressed in only the black leather chaps. A girl couldn't be expected to let that pass in a blur of nearsightedness.

She watched the doorway with such intensity that she must have fallen into a semitrance. When Charlie actually appeared, she blinked to make sure she hadn't imagined him there. But no, he was standing in her bedroom doorway, naked from the waist up and the ankles down.

He wasn't wearing the chaps, but he was holding them in one hand. Seeing them made her shiver in anticipation. She was also gratified to discover that Charlie had nice pecs, for an engineer. Correction. He had nice pecs, period.

And after spending most of her adult life looking at men who shaved their chests for the camera, she enjoyed seeing a growth of healthy hair. It added interest to the scenery, plus there was that fascinating line of hair that blazed a trail down under the waistband of his jeans. The top button was undone, and she wondered what that was all about. Maybe that was where he'd lost his nerve.

All in all, he'd done well, though. He was gazing at her with obvious hunger, and a telltale bulge behind his fly told her he was interested in what lay under the fluffy quilt. But he looked nervous, too.

"I'm glad to see you," she said. Her voice quivered a little. That's when she acknowledged that she was nervous, too. Their first encounter had been spectacular. What if that had been a fluke? She might not have Charlie for very long, but she wanted the short time they would share to be memorable.

"Eve, I don't . . ." He looked at the chaps in his hand. "I don't know what to do next. I'm good at fixing things, but I'm not good at . . . sexy stuff."

She thought he could be very good, sinfully good, if she could loosen him up a little. But he couldn't do much of anything while he was clutching those chaps like a lifeline. "You could put those on my dressing table."

He glanced doubtfully at the table that held her makeup supplies, a hairbrush, styling gel, and a blow dryer.

"It's fine. Right on top of that stuff."

He laid them carefully on the table, creating one of those contrasts she liked so much—girly paraphernalia and black leather motorcycle chaps. Contrasts turned her on. She didn't need the added stimulation with Charlie in the building, but she wasn't objecting to a few extra thrills.

And now she was going to lower his anxiety level. She knew from experience how this could take the edge off. "You can leave your glasses on the table too if you want. So you can find them later."

He nodded, took off his glasses, and put them on the corner of the table.

"So, Charlie . . ." She moistened her dry lips. "How about taking off the rest of your clothes?" She hadn't gotten a good view of his package earlier tonight. She'd only felt the glory of what it could do.

He reached for the zipper on his jeans. "You know that book you had on drawing nudes?"

"Yes." She was impressed that he'd remembered that, with all the clutter he'd found on top of her washing machine. But he probably remembered everything.

"Did you ever have a live model?" he asked.

"No." She couldn't believe Charlie was offering to do that, but stranger things had happened. "I didn't take a class. I just bought the book. Why? Do you want to pose for me?"

"God, no!" He stepped out of his jeans. "I'd rather rewire the Eiffel Tower!"

And speaking of phallic symbols . . . her breath caught at the sizable tent and flagpole effect he had going on. The rest of him was damned good to look at, too. She supposed he didn't think much about his body because he lived in his mind, but he'd been gifted with a statue-worthy build. A different kind of man would have capitalized on that gift and spent hours in a gym to enhance that physique.

But Charlie wasn't that kind of man. Eve guessed that he took his body for granted and if he thought about it at all, he was simply grateful that all systems worked okay. As an engineer, he might admire the delicate wiring and connectors, but she couldn't imagine him standing in front of a mirror for any length of time.

As for her, she could look at him forever. The briefs were the only thing standing between her and an excellent view. If she ever wanted to draw a nude male, she couldn't do any better than Charlie.

"One last thing," she murmured.

He took off the briefs.

Oh, yes. He was proudly, classically erect. Sights like this were what guaranteed the continuation of the species. Eve was ready to propagate, be fruitful and multiply, celebrate the glorious difference in the genders.

For a little while she allowed herself to hate the builders of Hoover Dam. Mentally Charlie was perfect for her, and now she'd discovered that he was sexual eye candy, besides. What a joke on her. She'd found exactly what she'd been looking for, and he could hardly wait to move on to those giant turbines.

But he wouldn't be leaving tonight. And he'd brought his chaps. She had a feeling that she'd have to coax him into those, but she accepted the challenge. Victory would be well worth it.

She eased back the comforter. "Would you . . . bring the chaps over here, please?"

He squinted slightly, obviously eager to see her better. "You're even gorgeous out of focus." He turned back to the dressing table. "Maybe I should get my glasses."

"You'll have more fun without them."

He paused. "What do you mean?"

"Well, for one thing, they'll get in the way during . . . certain things." She was thinking specifically of oral sex. She hoped he was thinking of it, too. But first she really wanted her chaps experience.

"Um, you're—" He coughed. "You're right."

She would bet he'd gotten her message. "Here. I'll take mine off, too. Now, all that's left is for you to bring over the chaps." She was sure, once she eased him over the embarrassment hurdle, he'd get into it.

He started to pick them up. Then he stopped and turned to her. "It feels kind of silly, Eve. I've never had them on when I wasn't wearing anything, and definitely not when I'm . . ."

"Aroused?"

"Yeah."

She tried to put herself in his place. She'd been desensitized to the limelight fairly early, but her shyness had never gone away totally. Taking off her glasses before a fashion show helped, but even then she got butterflies. That was when she'd start estimating the wattage of the footlights and calculating the square footage of the runway.

"Arousal is so amazing," she said. "Your brain sends a signal, and blood flow increases to the exact area needed for participation. The increased blood flow creates a solid rod, which allows for maximum penetration of the intended sleeve. Don't you find that fascinating?"

"Mm." His breathing grew ragged.

"It's an engineering marvel, Charlie. Take my system, for example. Think of all those neurons firing, which prompts the release of lubrication and readies the sleeve to accept the insertion of the rod."

He made a sound low in his throat.

"You're programmed to initiate a pistonlike action, which increases lubrication in the complementary components. That, in turn, allows for faster motion and greater friction."

With a soft groan, he started toward the bed.

"Bring the chaps," she murmured.

He snatched them from the dressing table, sending lipstick tubes flying. While he buckled on the chaps, she ripped open a condom packet. But before she handed him the condom, she took one good look at Charlie naked except for his chaps. She almost came right then.

He wasted no time putting on the condom and climbing between her open thighs.

Up close she could see the fire burning in his gaze. When he thrust deep, bringing the soft leather in contact with her inner thighs, she arched upward as the first spasm gripped her. Oh, this was going to be good.

"I love it when you talk like that." He pulled back and shoved home again.

Once again the leather caressed her skin and the cool buckle pressed against her tummy. The subtle kinkiness was all it took to kick-start her climax. As it roared to life, Charlie began pumping fast, rocketing her down the pleasure highway while that wonderful leather slapped against her thighs. She'd never yelled so loud in her life.

Charlie laughed, one of those exultant sounds that only comes with triumph. Then his laughter turned to a wild groan of release. Eve held him tight as he trembled in her arms. Slowly she began to smile. Victory.

As she basked in the glow of satisfaction, both sexual and mental, she thought she heard a noise coming from another part of the house. It sounded like a soft click, as if a door had been closed. But then again, Charlie was still breathing pretty hard. It could have been one of those little clicks a person's throat makes when the epiglottis quickly snaps shut. Yeah, that was probably it.

Chapter Seventeen

The last thing Charlie wanted to hear right now was a suspicious sound. But damn it, he heard one anyway. Lying there in the kind of euphoric state he'd thought could only be achieved through heavy drugs, not that he knew from personal experience, he didn't want to move for a long, long time, maybe not ever. Round beds were awesome.

He tried to talk himself out of going to investigate. Maybe the sound hadn't been of a door closing. Maybe it had been the oil heater turning on. Or shutting off. Except there hadn't been the sound of a fan either before the sound or after the sound.

Charlie was pretty good with sounds. Changes in sound were the best way to troubleshoot any machine, if you had the ear for it. That soft click hadn't been some automatic relay, which left him with the conclusion that it had been a door closing. If he had to guess, and he was lying there doing exactly that, he'd say it had been the front door.

Finally he couldn't put off the moment. God, how he hated to move. He turned his head so his mouth was close to her ear. "Eve."

She stroked his butt and snuggled against him. "You were incredible, Charlie." She sighed happily. "And the chaps were incredible. Thank you."

"I think I heard something." Plastered against her the way he was, he could feel her lazy contentment disappear, to be replaced by the tight muscles of anxiety. Damn it to hell. "I could be wrong, though."

"I heard something, too."

That pretty much clinched it. One person could have imagined the noise. Two people—not so likely. "Was it like the front door closing?"

"Yes. Very quietly."

"Did you hear it open?" He hadn't, but maybe he'd missed that sound.

"No. I only heard it close. Maybe I was wrong, though. Maybe it was only the house settling."

"Maybe." But he didn't think so. And as the implication dawned on him, every individual hair on his body stood upright. If they'd interpreted the sound correctly, then whoever had been in the house was no longer there. But chances were they had been there, probably listening, maybe even watching, while he and Eve had been having sex.

"Charlie, what if they were here the whole time we were—"

"Let's hope not." He disentangled himself from her warmth. "I'll go investigate."

"I'll go with you."

"No. Stay here." Standing with his back to her, he reached for the tissue box on her nightstand and dispensed with the condom.

"I don't want to stay here." The sheets rustled as if she might be getting out of bed.

"No, seriously," he said over his shoulder as he unbuckled his chaps. "Lock the bedroom door after I go out, just in case. That's what the cops say to do. Lock whatever door you can and call 911." He climbed out of his chaps, all the while watching the door and wishing he had better vision. He didn't want to face an intruder, but he especially didn't want to face one while he was naked and couldn't see worth a damn.

"I'm not calling the police until we know whether we actually heard something or just imagined it. We both might be spooked by the earlier break-in. And for the record, you have a great butt."

"Thanks." Grabbing his briefs off the floor, he turned to find her getting dressed on the far side of the bed. Even though she was blurry, he could tell she'd already put on her glasses.

"I'm not just saying that to take my mind off this potential home invasion."

"You're not?" He quickly put on his briefs and grabbed his jeans as he went over to her dressing table to retrieve his glasses. Once he could see clearly again, he shoved his legs into his jeans.

"Well, maybe partly. But that doesn't mean it's not true." She came around the bed wearing her sweater and jeans. "You have excellent buns, and I'd much rather think about them than some jerk who might have been standing in the bedroom doorway while we played mattress bingo."

"I understand completely." He buttoned and zipped his jeans. At that point, he'd put on all the clothes available to him. The rest were in the kitchen. "And for the record, you have outstanding tits, and I'm not just saying that, either."

"Thanks."

"You're welcome." He'd much rather think about her tits than the other subject crowding into his mind. Whenever he allowed himself to consider the possibility of someone hiding in the house while he'd gone through his undressing routine in the kitchen and Eve had waited alone and naked in the bedroom, he got the shakes.

He was reasonably sure that had been the scenario. He didn't really think someone was still in the house. They'd left five minutes ago through the front door.

What if his repair on the back door hadn't held up? If he'd had any sense whatsoever, he would have checked that door the minute he and Eve had come home from the bakery. Had he done that? No, he hadn't. He'd been too busy thinking about getting naked with Eve.

He glanced at her. "At least let me go first."

"Okay." She looked scared.

"If someone was out there, I don't think they're around anymore."

"Right." She nodded and tried to muster a smile, but it looked fake and her pupils were still dilated.

He couldn't blame her. It wasn't only the thought that someone had been in the house. It was also the thought that they'd stayed for the show in the bedroom.

That was the only explanation for the timing of the exit. They would have had a better chance of leaving undetected if they'd taken off right in the middle of the activities. Instead they'd left after the main event was over. Creepy.

He peered out the doorway, looking right and left. "Where's the switch for the hall light?" At this point he was ready to turn on every damned light in the house. He wanted no shadowy corners anywhere.

"At the far end, right before you go into the living room, and another one by the back door."

Then neither one would help light his way in advance. "Then maybe you'd better stay here. I want to take a look at the back door."

"Are you kidding? Wherever you wander, there I'll be, cowboy."

He glanced down at her. "I suppose that's better than splitting up, now that you mention it."

"You think?" Her eyes rounded in mock amazement. "I can tell you haven't seen enough scary movies or you'd never suggest splitting up. That's the kiss of death. When somebody says 'you stay here, while I go look around,' then you know one of them is going to get whacked."

"Neither one of us is going to get whacked." He started slowly down the hall. "If they'd had that idea, they could have done away with both of us very easily."

"Don't remind me." She followed close behind, her hand on his bare back. "I'm feeling extremely traumatized. I'm worried that I'll never want to have sex again."

Finally his sense of humor reasserted itself. "It's just like falling off a horse. You have to get right back on."

"Is that right?" She slid her hand down his back and squeezed his butt. "Are you offering to be my riding instructor, smarty-pants?"

"Why not? Are we going to let some voyeuristic intruder ruin our evening?" He was secretly afraid that he was as traumatized as Eve.

But he also was attracted to the cure he'd tossed out originally as a joke. He was especially attracted to it after she'd squeezed his butt. That brought back the warm sensation of lying between her thighs, his extremely happy dick buried deep inside her as she'd stroked his naked backside.

So yeah, once they were satisfied that the house was secure again, they should probably get it on and wipe out all the scary associations. He didn't know if he'd ever have sex with her again after tonight, and he didn't want the lingering memory to be the icky feeling of being spied on.

In the meantime, they had to go over every inch of this house while they tried to figure out what the hell was going on. He turned the corner expecting to find that the back door had been pried open once again. But no, his hinges were still screwed firmly in place.

Eve stood beside him. "Maybe we really did imagine the whole thing. Wouldn't that be great?"

"Yeah, it sure would." Charlie flipped on the light to make sure he wasn't missing anything, but the door looked exactly as he'd left it. No one had come through this way. "Guess we go to the front door next." He started back down the hallway.

Eve hurried after him. "I just had a horrible thought."

"More horrible than some creepizoid getting his jollies by watching us in bed?"

"I'm not sure I locked my car. The garage door remote is inside the car."

"Then we'd better start with the garage." At the end of the hallway, Charlie veered right toward the kitchen. But the minute he got there, he remembered that he'd locked the kitchen door. "Nope. Even if somebody got into the garage, they wouldn't have made it through this door without jimmying something." He pulled at the door and it didn't budge.

When he turned around, Eve was smiling at him. "What?"

"Your clothes." She used her Vanna White gesture to indicate his stuff scattered around. "It tells a whole story. Jacket neatly hung on the chair. Boots lined up and socks inside. Then, judging from the shirts tossed in each corner, something must have snapped."

"In case you hadn't noticed, wild and crazy doesn't come naturally to me."

"Not yet." She stepped forward and slid both hands up his bare chest. "But you're making progress." Leaning forward, she kissed him.

He'd known the kiss was coming and he'd told himself

not to get too involved. They hadn't finished casing the house for clues. But her wide, generous mouth was magic. Before he could stop himself, he'd pulled her close, and in no time, tongues were involved.

Kissing Eve was a stress-buster to end all stress-busters. As he combed his fingers through her silky hair and cupped the back of her head to deepen the kiss, he managed to convince himself that no one had been in the house, after all. The click had been a branch rubbing against the eaves, a piece of ice falling off the roof, an owl dropping a pebble into the chimney. The longer Eve kissed him, the more creative he became in explaining away the noise.

She was the first to pull away. "Oh, Charlie, I just thought of something else."

"Me, too." He slipped his hand under her sweater, gratified that she hadn't put on a bra. "A couple of things, actually."

"No, about the intruder."

He cupped her breast and rubbed his thumb over her nipple. "I think we overreacted. I'll bet it was something else, and we leaped to conclusions."

She moaned and closed her eyes. "I hope you're right, but . . . oh, that feels so good."

"It's supposed to." He had a fantasy of doing it in the kitchen, with Eve braced up on the counter. First he'd get on his knees for a little oral sex, and then, once he stood, he'd be at the perfect height for the next stage.

He still had his two condoms, because she'd come up with one while they were in the bedroom. She must have snagged it from the bathroom, but that left him with—

"They could have . . ." She took a shaky breath. "They could have relocked the door."

"What door?" Somehow he'd lost track of the conversation, probably because he was hard as a rock, which meant his blood had drained south, exactly as she'd described back in the bedroom. That had been some monologue. He hadn't realized you could be nerdy about sex. And boy, did it work for him.

"The kitchen door. It's one of those old-fashioned locks you can open with a credit card. They could have done that and then relocked it."

His hands, which had been so busy under her sweater, stilled. *Shit*. Sex was making him stupid. How could he have looked at that locked door and made the assumption that no one had gone that way? She was right about the ease of opening a lock like that. Any marginally intelligent person would have come into the garage, used a credit card on the kitchen door, and locked it behind them.

With a bitter sigh of regret he withdrew his hands from under her sweater. "You're right. Obviously I don't have a brain cell working."

There wasn't a smidgen of blame in her blue eyes. "It's been a long night."

"We might as well check the front door and then we'll go outside and find out if you left your car open." He walked over to the converter and snagged his flannel shirt. "And this time I promise to concentrate." He buttoned the shirt as he walked back toward her.

"You've been concentrating." She stood on tiptoe and gave him a quick kiss. "Just on other things."

"I don't have that luxury right now." Cupping her cheek, he gazed into those incredible eyes. "I haven't told you, but I'm taking the next two days off work."

"For me?"

"Yep. You and your invention."

"That is so sweet!"

He could live on that sparkle in her eyes. "And necessary. You and I need to get this hovercraft operational so you can take the design to New York. I think someone's trying to steal your concept, but if we start negotiations with a viable company, we'll make the thief irrelevant."

"Sounds like a plan." She hesitated. "Um, does that cut out your 'getting back on the horse' idea?"

If he hadn't been falling in love with her before, that question tipped him right over the edge. He wanted her so much at that moment that he couldn't speak. Finally he cleared his throat and managed an answer. "I don't think it has to."

"Oh, good."

Yeah, he was done for. How he'd ever reconcile that with his future plans was anybody's guess. He might have to clone himself.

If she had to be in this situation, Eve was glad she was in it with Charlie. Granted, she hadn't been in this situation until she'd revealed her hovercraft concept to Charlie, his cousin, and his cousin's two assistants. Until that night at the Rack and Balls, she'd muddled along on her own, with only a minor explosion.

But as she walked with him to the front door, she wondered if the explosion had been her fault, after all. She didn't want to suspect Eunice, but it would be just like Eunice to enter the house for her own purposes and then decide to stay and watch the sexual show in the bedroom.

When it came to that, Eunice was the only person Eve could picture doing something like that. And the woman was frustrated by her inability to buy the finer things of life. Yet that didn't explain why she'd sabotage a project that she wanted to steal.

And there was the broken back door. If Eunice could get in with a key, would she break down the door to confuse the issue? That seemed like a lot of extra work when she could slip in and out undetected.

Charlie walked into the entryway and stopped. "Damn it. The door's unlocked."

Eve stared at the position of the dead-bolt lever and shivered. It was open.

"You didn't leave it that way by accident when we left, did you?" Charlie asked.

A headache was coming on. Eve put her fingers to her temples and began a slow rotation. She pictured leaving the house on the way to the bakery. She'd been aware of Charlie watching her to make sure she'd locked the door. And she had locked it.

"I wish I could say I wasn't sure." She looked at him. "But I am sure. I remember thinking that you'd give me a lecture if I didn't lock the dead bolt. But I would have locked it, anyway. I'm not casual about that anymore."

They both looked at the door in silence for several seconds.

"Maybe it has fingerprints on it," Eve said at last.

"I doubt it." Charlie sighed. "Whoever is doing this is trying to confuse the hell out of us so we won't guess. I'm going to bet they're at least smart enough to wear gloves."

"They were here when we had sex, weren't they?" Eve looked at Charlie in growing horror. When it had been only a possibility, she'd been able to keep the creepy crawlies at bay, but now, facing the unlocked door, she couldn't deny the obvious.

"That doesn't mean they watched."

"Yes it does!" Eve began to shake. "Otherwise, why did they wait until it was over before they left?"

"Could have been coincidence." He gathered her into his arms and nestled her head against his chest.

She rubbed her cheek against the soft flannel and wound her arms around the solid comfort of his body. "Some coincidence."

"No, really. They could have been rummaging around getting whatever they were after and they happened to be ready to leave right then."

"You're just trying to make me feel better."

"I'm trying to make us both feel better." He nestled his cheek against her hair. "That's a yucky thought, that someone could have been . . . standing in the doorway while we—"

"Don't say it. Let's decide it was a coincidence." In her gut, Eve didn't believe the coincidence theory, but she'd work on convincing herself.

"Fine with me. It was a coincidence."

Eve thought she'd have an easier time with the coincidence theory the longer she stayed tucked in Charlie's arms listening to the steady beat of his heart. "Can we assume they have a key?"

"Not until we go outside and check your car. If you left it unlocked, then they could have come through the garage, like you said. Then, just to drive us crazy, they could have locked the kitchen door after them, but not this one."

"I would have recognized the sound of the dead bolt being locked," Eve said. "I wasn't sure about the door closing, because it was only a soft click, but that dead bolt going in is a much louder noise."

"And that could be why they didn't lock it. Both of us would have been out of bed like a shot."

Eve remembered the sated, lazy feeling of lying in bed with Charlie. "Maybe not quite that fast."

"As fast as humanly possible, then. It was only that I wasn't sure of what I'd heard, and I wanted it to be something else."

"Me, too." She'd felt so warm and cozy with Charlie's body tucked in around hers. "You have a nice way of not crushing a girl afterward."

"Weight distribution. My forearms and my knees can keep approximately half the weight elevated."

Eve did her best not to laugh, but she had to swallow hard. Between the scary parts of tonight and the lusty parts, all her emotions were turned up to full volume.

"And since the other half is evenly distributed," Charlie continued, "it puts minimal stress on—"

A snort escaped, despite her best efforts.

Charlie sounded offended. "What's so funny?"

"You." She lifted her head to gaze into his wonderful, intelligent face. "You are such a nerd. And I love that about you." The words were no sooner out of her mouth than she wanted them back. The nerd part was fine, but she could have gone all night without making a comment that included the l-word.

His expression registered the impact of that word, too. She could tell he was trying to think of a response that wouldn't embarrass them both.

"I didn't mean that the way it sounded," she said. "It's just one of those expressions everybody uses."

His gaze told her that he didn't buy it. But he smiled like the nice guy he was. "Yeah," he said softly. "I knew that."

Chapter Eighteen

Close call, Charlie thought as he released Eve and went back to the kitchen to get his jacket and put on his boots. Good thing they had something to do right now, or no telling what kind of confessions they'd both make. Instead, they could concentrate on this breaking-and-entering situation.

By the time he came back to the entryway, Eve had on her jacket and boots and was smiling brightly. She was smiling a little too brightly, as if mentioning the word *love* in connection with him had all been a silly misunderstanding and she was moving past that moment as fast as possible.

"After we check the car, we need to see if anything's been disturbed in the garage," she said.

"Yep." He pretended to be all business, when all he could hear ringing in his ears was *"And I love that about you."*

If she only knew how close he'd come to blurting out his feelings for her, too. That wouldn't do either one of them any favors. He tried not to think about the fact that she might be falling for him just as he was falling for her.

But he thought about it anyway as they walked out the door. She took her keys and made a production of locking up once they were outside on the porch. He was glad to see she was being extra cautious. He didn't want to contemplate what he'd do if anything happened to her. She was fast becoming the most important person in his life.

Hell, what a mess. She was everything he'd ever wanted—brainy, fun to be with, creative, sexy. He was also aware of her beauty, but that wasn't the tipping point for him.

He was falling for her because she got him. And he liked to think that he got her, too. They might be—what was that corny term? *Soul mates.* He'd never believed in the concept before, but then he'd never seriously considered Eve as a life partner. And he still couldn't do that.

Because of the way he felt about her, he could never ask her to give up her dream of living in what she considered the ideal little town. He'd researched the area around Hoover Dam. There were no quaint little villages there.

Vegas itself was big, modern, and busy. He found the concept exciting, but she wasn't into exciting cities at the moment. Sure, the neighboring towns of Henderson and Boulder were smaller, but they weren't anything like Middlesex. New England generated its own brand of cozy little community, and Middlesex was a perfect example. If she loved this, he couldn't imagine her loving Nevada.

He could change his plans and stay here, of course. That option had crossed his mind more than once, and he'd ended up rejecting it every time. The thought of staying in Middlesex forever caused something vital in him to start withering. He'd end up resenting the sacrifice, one Eve probably wouldn't let him make, anyway.

"I don't know which to wish for," she said as they crossed the yard.

He was startled. Had she been reading his mind? "What do you mean?"

"If the car's locked, then we know the person has a key, so that narrows it down to Eunice."

And your sister, he thought. He didn't say it, though. She was probably thinking the same thing. "At least then you could confront Eunice and get to the bottom of it."

"I don't want it to be Eunice. I don't want to think that I bought a house right next door to someone like that. This town is supposed to be my safe haven. So if the car's unlocked, we still have no idea who's doing this. It could still be Manny or Kyle, for that matter."

"They'd have had to make a speedy trip. When we left they were still frosting cookies." He considered how long he'd diddled around in the kitchen while he'd tried to decide how to manage the chaps. "And I hate to admit this, because I like to think of myself as having more staying power, but it wasn't as if we spent a lot of time on the main event."

"We spent exactly the right amount of time."

"I'm glad you think so, but it still wouldn't have given Manny and Kyle much opportunity to do anything."

"But we have no idea what they intended to do," Eve said with perfect logic. "It could have been a short-term thing."

"Yeah, but if someone had access to the garage and they were after whatever was in there, why wouldn't they just leave the door open and go back out that way? Why bother to close the garage door and go out the front?"

They reached the driveway, where the Civic sat there looking the same as it had when they'd arrived earlier. The footprints in the thin layer of snow beside the car could have been anybody's. Charlie supposed a crackerjack crime team might be able to take some impressions, but a crackerjack crime team wouldn't be bothering with this trivial stuff. The cooking oil was undisturbed.

"They closed the garage door and went out the front because of what you said a while ago," Eve said. "They want to confuse us so we don't know who it is." Grabbing the passenger door handle, she pulled it open.

Charlie took a deep breath. He'd been hoping the car would be locked. That way they could narrow it down to Eunice or Eve's sister Denise. Because he didn't really think her sister was the culprit, then Eunice could be nabbed and the threat would be gone.

Now they were back to square one. "Is your opener still in there?" If someone had swiped it, they had another problem.

"It's still here." She pressed it and the garage door opened.

They stood together watching it go up as if waiting for a play to begin.

"Everything looks the same," Eve said.

"We have to check it out, though. Something could be missing."

"That's true." She started forward.

"Wait. Lock your car."

"Whoops." She aimed her automatic key at the car and the parking lights flashed as the doors locked. "Now, see? I almost forgot that, again." She paused and looked at him. "If only I could believe I forgot to lock the front door and that we imagined the click of the door closing, we'd have no evidence of any wrongdoing."

"Except for the fact that someone took a crowbar to your back door. That falls in the category of blatant wrongdoing, if you ask me."

"Well, yeah. There's that. I keep conveniently forgetting about the back door, maybe because I don't want to remember." Her breath hissed out between her teeth and formed a little cloud in the air. "I really hate this."

"I know. Me, too." He let his glance rove the interior of the garage, hoping something—anything—would look obviously out of place. Instead it all looked normal, or as normal as any garage that contained a purple hovercraft.

"Well, it's getting cold out here," Eve said, picking up the cooking oil. "I vote we go in and put down the door so we can thoroughly check out my work area. Maybe we'll find some sort of clue as to what happened."

"Wouldn't that be nice?" Charlie would love to have at least one of these problems solved. If he couldn't figure out what to do about his relationship with Eve, at least he'd like to solve the mystery of the break-in.

Twenty minutes later the garage was warm and cozy thanks to the space heater. They'd both taken off their coats and laid them over his bike, and they'd scoured every inch of the garage for clues.

Eve gazed at him, her expression bewildered. "I don't see anything different from the way we left it," she said.

"Maybe we came home before they could do whatever it was they'd planned."

"That would eliminate Manny and Kyle," she said. "No way did they beat us here." She made a face. "Shoot. I don't want to eliminate Manny and Kyle."

"I know." He leaned against the workbench. "I'm only trying out theories. But say someone was here ahead of us."

"Which means whoever it was didn't use the garage door opener. They had a key." She started pacing again. Apparently she liked to move while she thought things through.

"Yeah, they had a key." Eunice was still his prime suspect, and he would stick with that until proven wrong. "So if they were here and about to do something, and we came home, they'd have to run into the house and hide somewhere until it was safe to leave."

"Hold on." She stopped in mid-pace and swung to face him. "If what you say is true, then they would have had to open the dead bolt to get out. I didn't think of that before, but the dead bolt makes just as much noise being opened as being locked."

Charlie had an answer for that one, too. "They opened the dead bolt earlier, in case they got caught and had to make a run for it. They might have thought they could get all the way out the door, but decided at the last minute it was too risky."

"But where in the world would they hide? My closets are stuffed to the gills. Even the bathtub has all my dry cleaning piled in it."

If the situation hadn't been so dire, Charlie would have laughed. One advantage of so much clutter might be that intruders had precious few hiding places. But there was still one. "She could have ducked into that little alcove where the back door is."

Eve's gaze sharpened. "You just said *she*."

"That's because I think I know who it might be."

She began nervously drumming her fingers against her thigh. "But we have no proof."

"No." He realized he was treading on thin ice. "Except that we only know of two people who have a key. And I'll bet you'd rather pin this on Eunice."

"I don't want to pin it on either of them." She resumed her pacing. Charlie could almost hear her thinking, trying to come up with a way that wouldn't implicate either her neighbor or her sister.

Finally she turned back to him, her eyes alight with a new idea. "What if it's someone who knows how to pick a lock? I mean, what do we really know about Manny and Kyle? They could have those skills. They could have criminal records, even! Rick might have no idea what kind of men he's dealing with."

Charlie blew out a breath. "I understand that you want it to be Manny or Kyle, or both of them working together. But everything points to Eunice. She can't be making a lot of money working at the insurance office."

"No."

"So she has motive." Charlie held up a finger. "And if money wasn't enough motive, she also envies you."

"I guess." Eve didn't look happy about admitting that.

Charlie held up a second finger. "She has opportunity. She lives right next door and she has access with the key you gave her."

"I just don't see her as the kind of person to take what isn't hers. I know she envies me, but she's fairly open about it, and she's already supplementing her income with the—" Eve stopped abruptly and looked away. "Anyway, I can't believe she'd try to steal the concept for the hovercraft. It doesn't fit."

"How's she supplementing her income?"

She sent him a pleading glance. "I've promised not to say."

"You don't have to say if you don't want to. But it seems like we need all the info we can get if we're ever going to solve this." Hearing that Eunice had a secret source of income only increased his suspicion.

"This has to stay between us."

He was insulted that she'd even feel the need to say so, but maybe she was used to another kind of guy. "We already have several things that have to stay between us. Me naked except for a pair of chaps would be one of them."

"Good point." Her eyes sparkled.

He hoped that expression meant she was remembering those moments with lust and not hilarity. The experience had been intense, but looked at from a certain perspective, it could be funny, too. Maybe someday he'd be able to laugh at what he'd done, but right now it was too sensitive a subject for that.

"Eunice takes 900 calls," Eve said.

"After the paint and the muscle stimulator, I'm not surprised." He wondered if Rick had gotten wind of the 900 calling thing. Rick was intrigued as it was, without adding another element to rope him in. Oh, well. Rick's life. If Eunice turned out to be the person who'd been breaking into Eve's house, Charlie didn't have to worry. Eunice would end up in jail.

In the meantime, though, Charlie thought he should warn Rick that he might be getting mixed up with the wrong woman. "Look, I won't tell Rick about the 900 calls." And it might be just as well if he never found out. "But I think he should know about our suspicions."

"I really hate to accuse her, Charlie. I mean, what if she's innocent and she and Rick have a future together?"

"What if she's guilty and somehow manages to swindle my cousin out of a bunch of money? You throw sex into the mix and his judgment isn't all that clear."

"How would she get money out of him?"

"I don't know." But he had a potential suspect and he wanted to be right. "Maybe blackmail. She could have taken pictures of him while they were doing weird things with green paint."

Eve started to laugh.

"It's a decent theory."

"No it's not." She grinned at him. "You obviously don't know much about the L.A. lifestyle."

No, he didn't. And his lack of big-city experience was a sensitive topic. "I'm not particularly worldly, if that's what you mean."

Her smile disappeared. "I'm sorry. I didn't mean to

poke fun. It's just that a bachelor like Rick couldn't be blackmailed with pictures of him involved in kinky sex. Heck, he might want to show them around."

"Then maybe she'd get him to buy her expensive presents."

"Maybe." Her expression softened, as if she didn't want to be confrontational. "But there's nothing criminal about that, Charlie. Lots of men buy women presents."

"I suppose." He wouldn't mind shopping for Eve, now that he thought about it. He could find a bunch of cool stuff she'd like at the hardware store. For the first time in his life he'd have fun picking out a gift for a woman.

"I have to go with my gut on this one," she said. "I don't think it's Eunice."

"And I don't think we're going to solve it tonight."

She gave him a long look. "So . . . wanna work on the hovercraft?"

Just like that, he lost all interest in the mystery *and* her invention, two things that ordinarily would have kept him occupied for hours. He couldn't believe how quickly his libido short-circuited his brain and turned him into a heat-seeking missile with one goal in mind.

Her smile returned, but this time there was a seductive tilt to her mouth. "Your breathing just changed."

"If you think that's something, you should see what's happening to the rest of me."

She lifted her eyebrows. "I take it that's a *no* on the hovercraft project?"

"Let's say I'd like a rain check." He stepped toward her.

She backed toward the kitchen door. "Can I interest you in an alternative, then?"

"You already have." The remembered taste of her was still on his tongue, and he hadn't been given a real chance to explore. He wanted that chance, now.

"Just one thing." She turned and unlocked the kitchen door. "I don't relish having someone observing us again."

"Neither do I." Although he had very little blood going to his brain, he was able to focus what little intelligence he had left on the problem and come up with a solution. "Pots and pans."

She paused. "Excuse me?"

"Do you have any?"

"A few. Are we going to use them as weapons?"

"Nope. Early warning system."

Moments later, Eve had arranged several pans in front of the kitchen door, so that anyone opening it would trip over them and make noise. But that exhausted her supply, which left them with nothing to arrange across the front door. Charlie was aching to get into that bedroom, but he forced himself to think of a solution for the other door. They wouldn't have much fun in her round bed if they were both worried about somebody sneaking in the front door.

"Maybe we should pile all your discarded hobby supplies across the front door," he said as they stood in front of it.

"That's mostly soft stuff. I don't know if it'll make enough noise."

Charlie dredged up some memories from his college days. "What we really need is marbles."

"Marbles?"

"If you scatter marbles over the floor, then if someone walks in they step on them, lose their footing, and fall down. At least that's the way it's supposed to work. I've never actually tried that one."

Eve snapped her fingers. "I have beads! Be right back."

While she was going after the beads, Charlie stood with his hands on his hips, gazing at that front door. It had to be Eunice. Nothing else made sense. But Eve wasn't buying it, so he'd have to hope more proof came along, and soon.

He wanted Eve to ask for the key back, but he didn't think she'd agree to do that. She was still holding on to the hope that her view of Middlesex wouldn't have to change. Besides, it might not matter whether she retrieved the key or not. Eve had had plenty of time to get a second one made.

Eve came back holding a plastic bag with beads in every color of the rainbow. "Will that work?"

"Absolutely." He took the beads and opened the package. "We'll just sprinkle them all along here by the threshold." He crouched down and started pouring the beads out. They clattered and bounced on the hardwood floor like the Mexican jumping beans Rick had brought him once from Tijuana.

"I'm glad something I bought is turning out to be useful."

"We just have to remember they're here." He stood and surveyed the bead-strewn floor. "We don't want to be the ones crashing to the floor."

She glanced at him. "For someone from a small town with a low crime rate, you know a lot about booby-trapping a house."

"College stuff. My buddies and I didn't have much money for fancy alarms, and we had a ton of electronic equipment in our apartment, so we were always brainstorming ways to keep from being robbed. And it also worked for those times you had a girl in your room and didn't want anyone barging in."

"Well, guess what?" She caught his hand and began tugging him through the living room to the hall. "You're about to have a girl in your room."

Chapter Nineteen

Eve wasn't in the mood for games this time around. They'd had a long night, and now it was time to get down to basics. Two naked people making use of both the diameter and the circumference of her round bed—that was as complicated as she wanted things to get.

Fortunately Charlie seemed of the same mind. They stripped down to nothing, ditched their glasses, and tumbled onto the bed. Charlie, not being used to the shape, almost tumbled off again.

Eve grabbed one nicely muscled arm and hauled him back. "Easy does it there, big fella."

He rolled on top of her, his erect penis brushing her thigh. "I'd better keep close track of you. You know this territory better than I do."

She gazed up at him, his hair tousled and falling down over his forehead, his deep brown eyes gazing straight into hers. She could feel him trembling, feel the rapid beat of his heart against her breast. How sweet to be wanted this much.

She cupped his face in both hands. "Can you see me okay?"

"Up close I do great."

"Me, too. Come closer."

Smiling, he leaned down. "You have such big poufy lips."

"The better to kiss you with, kilowatt man."

"You can say that again."

"The better to kiss you with, kil—"

"Smart aleck. Don't talk. Just let me get at that gorgeous mouth."

She lifted her chin to put herself in better position. From the eager way he swooped down, she expected the kiss to be deep and wet, with lots of tongue. He surprised her.

His trembling increased, which showed how much he was restraining himself. His mouth barely touched hers. "I want you so much. I'm a fuse about to blow," he whispered.

Her pulse raced as she thought of all that power ready to be unleashed on little old her. She could hardly wait. "Or like Hoover Dam about to crack," she murmured.

"I am cracking." His breath was warm on her face as he brushed his lips over hers. "I had everything figured out, and now . . ."

"Now you'll still go." She kissed him back with the same light pressure.

"How can I?"

"How can you not?"

"Eve." Her name was a groan of surrender as he gave her the kiss she'd been expecting, the one that erased the boundaries between them, the one that made her forget everything but the taste and feel of his mouth.

She was so involved in the power of that kiss that she didn't realize he'd reached between her thighs until his fingers slipped without resistance into her moist heat. She moaned in pleasure.

He lifted his head, his mouth hovering over hers as he stroked her gently. "There's that lubrication you were telling me about." His words were thick and heavy with lust. "Ready to make those neurons fire?" He increased the pressure.

She gasped. "All . . . systems are up . . . and running."

"Let's switch to alternate current."

She didn't understand what he meant at first. Then he slid down between her thighs and she knew exactly what he meant. Here was a guy who generated enough electrical impulses to power the town of Middlesex, if someone could figure out how to harness that energy. She was sure that the friction of his tongue alone could make her glow in the dark.

The fireworks began slowly, little showers of stars raining down on her quivering body. Then the explosions grew in size, coming faster, and faster yet, until her world filled with a regular Fourth of July display. She greeted the grand finale with enthusiastic cries of appreciation.

As the sparkling stars gradually faded, Charlie eased back up, kissing her belly, her breasts, and her throat on his way to her mouth. She had never felt so thoroughly loved in her life. That Charlie put on quite a spectacular show.

She tried to find the words to tell him, but before she could he was kissing her again in that deep, soul-satisfying way of his. All she had to do was hang on and enjoy. She realized that he was completely in charge, and with moves like that, he was welcome to the job.

Finally he lifted his mouth from hers once again. He was breathing hard as he leaned his damp forehead against hers. "I never want to stop kissing you."

She gulped for air. "I never want you to."

"But if I don't stop kissing you, I'm going to come. It's high school all over again."

She responded to the desperation in his voice. "Condoms. Nightstand drawer."

"Thank God." He dragged in a breath. "I was afraid I had to go get my jeans." Lifting himself away from her with a groan, he pulled open the drawer and riffled around inside it. "Got one. Magnificent invention."

She opened her eyes. He was holding the condom packet as if he'd managed to get his hands on the Hope Diamond. "You actually *like* condoms?"

"I actually hate condoms." He sat back on his haunches and ripped open the packet. "The day I don't have to use them will be a great day." He rolled it expertly down over his penis. "But tonight . . . they make everything possible."

Not everything, she thought with a stab of longing. Everything would be a future with this man who was the essence of all she was looking for. Everything would be planning for the day when they could throw away the condoms and make babies together. Everything would be barbecues in the backyard and Little League games in the summer, snowball fights and cocoa by the fire in the winter.

But then Charlie moved over her, and with one sure thrust made that intimate connection she craved. It wasn't everything, but for tonight, it was enough.

A screech and a loud thud brought Charlie awake. Startled, he sat up too fast and fell on the floor. Where was he? And who was out there swearing so loud at this time of the morning?

"Oh, God." Eve leaped out of bed and grabbed Charlie's flannel shirt. "Denise! Stay where you are! You might have broken something!"

Charlie sat in a daze as Eve hopped over him and ran out of the room, buttoning the shirt she'd swiped as she went. *Denise? The sister? What the hell?* And then it came back to him. The bead booby trap.

Scrambling to his feet, he grabbed his jeans and put them on without bothering with underwear. He'd never met Denise. Assuming she'd taken a header on the beads he'd scattered in front of the door, he didn't suppose the meeting would be auspicious. He'd rather not go into it naked.

As he carefully zipped his jeans, he listened to Eve trying to calm her sister, who sounded furious. Charlie started to feel guilty about giving Denise a tumble, but then he began to wonder if the beads had worked, after all. Had they caught their suspect sneaking into the house?

He located his glasses and his watch and put them both on. Two minutes after ten. Denise had arrived right on time. A person couldn't really sneak into a house when they were expected, but she'd obviously used her key. Charlie supposed that was logical enough. No reason to stand there ringing the doorbell if you could just let yourself in.

He felt at a definite disadvantage wearing only his jeans and needing both a razor and a toothbrush before he'd feel ready to meet someone as pivotal as Eve's only sister. But he couldn't very well hide in the bedroom until she left. Eve had said she'd be staying a few days.

In fact, Denise's impending arrival had been the justification for having all that sex last night. As of now, he and Eve had a chaperone. Might as well suck it up and go out to meet her.

Walking down the hall, he listened to the conversation between the two sisters. Eve was still trying to make amends, but Denise didn't seem to be buying it.

"You knew I was coming," Denise said. "You could have called my cell and warned me to ring the doorbell." Her voice was a lot like Eve's, only with an edge to it that Eve's didn't have.

"I should have remembered to do that," Eve said. "I'm so glad you're not seriously hurt."

"I'll probably have a bruise on my butt. Fortunately, I'm not dating anyone right now, so I'm the only one who will see it. These slacks are a mess, though. Somebody must have been tracking dirt in here, and now it's all over the back of my pants."

Charlie came to the end of the hall where he had a view of Denise, who was facing away from him. She was shorter than Eve by a good four inches, and her dark hair was cut in a no-nonsense style not unlike Charlie's. She held a red leather jacket folded precisely over her arm like a maître d's towel.

Under the jacket she'd worn a navy suit, and sure enough, the slacks had dirt smears all over the seat. He was probably responsible for that, too, because he'd been the one who'd left his boots on when he'd come to see about Eve's back door.

Denise brushed at the dirt. "At least they're washable. I can change into something else and toss the whole suit in your washing machine."

Eve glanced toward the hallway where Charlie was standing. "The washing machine's out of commission, right now. But I can run it down to the Press 'n' Go. They can have it back in—"

"That's silly," Denise said. "That's why I buy washable clothes, so I won't have to spend the money on dry cleaning. What do you mean, your machine's out of commission? Don't they have repair people in this town?"

"I'm sure they do." Eve sent Charlie a look of apology.

"Well, here's Charlie! Charlie Shepherd, I'd like you to meet my sister, Denise."

Denise spun around. "A man? You didn't say there was . . ." Denise took in Charlie's bare chest and bare feet. Then she glanced back at her sister, who wore what was obviously a man's flannel shirt. "Eve, you could have warned me."

"She didn't have time," Charlie said, coming forward. "This was completely unexpected." He extended his hand to Denise because she looked like the kind of woman who liked to shake hands. Although she was attractive, her features were a little too sharp for anyone to describe her as pretty. But intelligence shone from her blue eyes. Charlie could believe that she'd cut a wide swath on Wall Street.

Denise had a firm handshake. And some of her prickly behavior seemed to disappear as she continued to gaze at Charlie. "Eve said something about a break-in. I guess it's a good thing you stayed with her, then."

He was slightly encouraged by that show of sisterly caring. "I'm also the one who suggested the beads," he said. No reason for Eve to take all the heat on that score.

"But I was the one who knew Denise was coming at ten," Eve said. "I should have set my alarm."

"I have one on both my watch and my cell, for what good that did." Charlie tried to imagine either of them thinking of setting an alarm in the state they'd been in. First had come the unbridled lust, and then the sleepy collapse into each other's arms. He'd never slept so deeply in his life.

Denise glanced around at the beads scattered all over the hall. "So you think someone is trying to steal the design for your . . . what did you call it, again?"

"Hovercraft," Eve said. "And we don't have any proof that's what they're after. But someone broke through the back door while I was in New York this week and last night someone . . ." She paused to take a shaky breath.

"Someone was in the house when we came home from my mother's bakery," Charlie said.

Denise's eyes widened. "How do you know that?"

"We heard them leave." Charlie decided there was no reason to give Denise the lurid details.

"What do you mean?"

"There was a click, like the front door closing," Eve said. "We both heard it."

Denise shuddered. "That's creepy. Are you sure you didn't imagine it?"

"We thought so at first," Charlie said. "But when we checked the front door, it was unlocked. Eve's sure she locked it when we left for the bakery."

"Well, you can't trust that information, Charlie." Denise glanced at her sister with a patronizing smile. "This one would forget her head if it weren't attached. She's the original scatterbrain."

Charlie's jaw tensed. "Oh, I wouldn't say that. She's managed to put together one hell of a hovercraft, not to mention the fuel converter she designed herself. I don't know too many engineers who could have done as well, and I know a *lot* of engineers."

"Thanks, Charlie." Eve smiled at him.

God, she was something. He'd been too engrossed in the awkwardness of the situation to register how cute she looked standing there in his plaid flannel shirt. The sleeves covered all but the tips of her fingers and the bottom hem reached to the middle of her thighs. And those were damned sexy thighs, too. Her hair fanned out in luxurious waves around her shoulders and her cheeks were pink from sleep and good sex.

Charlie wasn't up on sibling rivalry. He'd never had a sibling, so he wasn't sure how the whole dynamic worked. But watching the way Denise looked at Eve, he was getting a pretty good education on the subject.

"I drove here today exactly because of that hovercraft," Denise said. "Eve doesn't have an engineering degree, and she tends to go off half-cocked. If you had a few hours I could tell you stories of what she did when we were kids."

"I learned a lot from those experiments," Eve said.

Charlie was glad to see her standing up for herself. "I'd like to hear about them one of these days. Sounds like fun."

"The point is," Denise continued, "Eve has no business constructing something that will fly through the air. Someone is liable to get hurt."

Charlie had some of those same concerns, but that didn't diminish his admiration for what Eve had accomplished. "There's an element of danger in every experiment," he said.

"That's the key." Denise faced him, her chin jutting with determination. "An *element* of danger is one thing. When I take risks in the stock market there's always an *element* of danger that it won't work out. But those risks are carefully calculated. I'll guarantee that Eve's project has at least a ninety percent chance of failing spectacularly."

"I don't agree with those odds," Charlie said quietly. "The concept is brilliant and the execution is close to flawless."

"And you know this because?"

"I'm an electrical engineer with some background in mechanical engineering. And I'm putting my knowledge at Eve's disposal, although she's already done most of the heavy lifting. I'll only be helping her fine-tune things."

Denise looked him up and down, as if taking his measure. "Are you currently unemployed, then?"

"He has a great job!" Eve said. "He's an electrical engineer for the Middlesex Light and Power Company. And one day soon he's going to be taking a position of great authority at Hoover Dam. Right, Charlie?"

Charlie met the challenge in Denise's gaze. "I think your sister is wondering why a man with a normal job is standing barefoot in your entryway at ten o'clock on a Thursday morning."

"That has crossed my mind," Denise said. She all but tapped her foot as she waited for an answer.

"The fact is, I should be at work right now. I probably have a call on my cell wondering where I am. No doubt I've caused several people some concern, because I'm never late for work. As I mentioned, this was an unexpected development."

Eve gasped. "I hadn't thought of that. You'd better call in right away. I'm sure people are wondering what happened to you. They might think you've been in an accident or something."

"I'll call in a minute." Charlie felt as if he and Denise were having a high-noon sort of encounter. And he wasn't going to blink. "Maybe it's good for them to realize I'm not perfect."

"I feel the need to point out that this is what can happen," Denise said. "Schedules thrown off today, dangerous accidents tomorrow. I should know. I lived with her for almost fourteen years. No telling what she got away with after I went off to college and wasn't there to keep an eye on her."

"That's not fair, Denise." Eve combed her hair back from her face. "I'm not a kid anymore. You can't judge what I'm doing now based on twenty-year-old memories."

"Yeah, you're older, and your projects have just become bigger and more dangerous!"

"I'm taking precautions."

"And I'm helping her do that," Charlie said.

"I'm sure you are, which is admirable. But look what's already happened. You're missing work."

"The world won't come to an end." But Charlie felt guilty about it. He should have at least left a message on the company voice mail sometime during the night.

"I'm sure it won't come to an end. But you seem like a nice, steady guy. Don't let yourself get sucked into this. Instead of aiding and abetting, you should be helping me convince her to stop this nonsense. Then we'd all sleep better at night."

"Thanks for the advice." Charlie looked at Eve, who seemed to be trying hard to maintain a brave front in the face of her big sister's assault. "And for the record, I slept great last night. Now, if you'll excuse me, I'll go locate my cell phone and call the office."

As he walked back to Eve's bedroom, he tried to sort through the waves of concern and envy that poured from Denise in equal amounts. After meeting Denise, who had a key to the house and was a very smart woman, Charlie was no longer sure that Eunice was the prime suspect.

Chapter Twenty

"He's cute." Denise gazed after Charlie as he ducked into Eve's bedroom.

"He's temporary," Eve said.

Denise glanced sharply at Eve. "What do you mean by that? Isn't he good enough for you?"

Eve sighed. She didn't know why she and Denise couldn't have conversations like normal sisters, the loving sisters that inspired all those gooey e-mails that circulated on the Internet. "He's perfect for me," she said. "But he's not staying in Middlesex. And I am."

"Which is something I'll never understand, you in this backward little town."

Eve decided not to respond to that. Denise had put her finger precisely on the problem. She would never understand Eve. Eve was beginning to wonder if Denise had ever tried. "Listen, do you want some coffee? I could go for some." She started toward the kitchen, stepping around beads to make sure she didn't end up on her fanny like Denise.

At first she'd been horrified, but Denise was in one

piece, so now Eve could see the funny side of it. She would love a video of Denise barreling through the door ready to organize the troops and falling flat on her ass.

"Don't you think we should pick these beads up before we think about coffee?" Denise asked.

"You know, I think we should have coffee first." Eve continued on into the kitchen. For one thing, she wasn't wearing anything under this shirt of Charlie's, and bending down to pick up beads would have interesting consequences.

"Then I'll do it."

Eve paused in her retreat. With her back toward Denise, she was free to mouth a pithy swear word. "Just leave them, okay?" she said brightly. "You're a guest. I'll do it later."

"It'll only take a minute. Someone could come along and trip on them like I did. You could get sued. I'll bet you don't have an umbrella policy in force, either. Accidents like that can wipe you out if you're not careful."

Eve closed her eyes and bit back her response, mostly because she *didn't* have an umbrella policy. She didn't think it would cover accidents connected to the hovercraft, anyway. Much as she hated to admit it, the hovercraft did have the potential to be dangerous. That was part of the excitement. Besides, she was the only one who would climb into the cockpit until the hovercraft had been thoroughly tested.

"I'll bet you bought these because you thought you'd get into the beading craze, didn't you?" Denise didn't wait for an answer. "They're pretty, though. I'm sure you'll want to save them. Somebody might be able to use them someday. Do you have something to put them in?"

"Denise." Eve turned back, ready to take a stand on the stupid beads, which could stay on the floor until hell froze over, as far as she was concerned. This was her house, and if she wanted beads on the floor—or trained monkeys swinging from the light fixtures, for that matter—she had that right.

"What?" Crouched on the floor, Denise looked up. She'd laid her leather jacket neatly over the handle of her rolling suitcase and she'd already picked up a handful of beads. "Anything will work. A bowl or a pan. Anything. Look, I've already picked up about thirty percent of them. I can get the rest in no time."

The fight went out of Eve. What was the point? Denise was never going to change, and the sooner Eve stopped letting it get to her, the better. Knowing Charlie believed in her and her project helped. It helped a whole hell of a lot. No matter what happened between them in the future, she would always be grateful that he'd given her that confidence.

"I know exactly where to find a pan," she said. "Be right back." She walked into the kitchen and grabbed one of the pans from the floor where she and Charlie had arranged them before going into her room to have great sex. And it had been great—providing the kind of full-scale orgasms that a girl could become dependent on.

He knew his way around the oral sex routine, too. Maybe it wasn't fair to judge a guy on whether he was good at that, but she did, anyway. Lyle had never been very enthusiastic about such activities. Until this moment she hadn't admitted to herself that had been another reason she'd run screaming from a commitment to him.

But Charlie . . . now there was a man who had all the moves she could ever want, even when he was a little disoriented by the round bed. Thinking about those slow, deliberate thrusts he'd used in their last encounter got her very hot and bothered. She wondered how Charlie felt about morning lovemaking. Morning had never been a prime time for her, but that was before Charlie. She could easily imagine—

"Eve, I thought you said you were getting a pan?" Denise called from the entryway.

Eve blinked and stared at the pan she'd been holding for at least a full minute. "Coming!" she called out. Then she had a fit of giggles, because the potent memory of Charlie between her thighs had nearly made her do exactly that. She pinched herself to make herself stop laughing, but she was still grinning as she walked out of the kitchen, pan at the ready.

And there was Charlie, on his hands and knees next to Denise, helping her pick up beads. As he moved, his hair fell down over his forehead and his glasses slipped down his nose, which made him look boyish. But the rest of him was all man.

Crawling around on the floor made his biceps stand out and the muscles in his back flex. Then there was that sexy little gap in the waistband of his jeans where the small of his back curved in and the denim didn't. A wave of heat hit her. If Denise hadn't been there, Eve would have dragged him off to the bedroom to have her way with him.

He glanced up. She decided that she liked the rakish look of a beard starting to grow. He was the kind of guy who would wear a beard well, and it might make for a fun tickle factor on her face and . . . elsewhere. Maybe she'd suggest that he not shave it off.

As he pushed his glasses back into place and met her gaze, he seemed amused. Maybe he was beginning to appreciate the humor of the situation. But the lust Eve was feeling must have shown on her face, because his expression gradually changed. If eyes could actually smolder the way romance novels claimed, then that was what Charlie's were doing. They were producing enough heat to start a charcoal grill, no problem.

Although Eve was loving this scorching exchange, she didn't want Denise to catch them at it. She looked away and cleared her throat. "Here's a pan for the beads."

"Oh, thanks." Denise glanced up. "I finally figured out I could put them in my pockets."

"You know, you're welcome to these beads if you can make use of them." Keeping her distance from Denise, Eve walked right up to Charlie and held out the pan. If he could see up her shirt while she was doing it, so much the better.

Denise resumed her bead gathering. "Oh, I don't have time for anything like beading, unfortunately. I've agreed to chair a task force that's looking into making some major changes in the university's investment portfolio. I don't have to tell you how critical that is."

"Nope, sure don't." Eve smiled down at Charlie.

"Thanks for the pan." Charlie's voice bordered on husky as he sat back on his heels and reached for it. He looked as if he'd like to reach for something else.

"Did you contact your office?" She had the urge to put her bare foot on his shoulder and give him a real show, but of course she wouldn't dare. In fact, she'd better get out of there before Denise picked up on the sexual vibes swirling through the air.

Charlie swallowed. "Yeah. I said something had come up."

She pressed her lips together hard to keep the laughter inside. Did he realize what he'd said? She couldn't be sure. "Any problems?" The question came out kind of strangled.

"Nothing major." As he gazed up at Eve, he seemed to have completely forgotten the pot he held in one hand and the beads he clutched in the other. "I'll go over there this morning, but once everything's under control, I'll take off the rest of today and tomorrow. I think we need to get busy on the hovercraft."

"Great." Maybe Denise was a blessing, after all. Without Denise around Eve and Charlie would get busy, all right, but it wouldn't have anything to do with the hovercraft. "I guess you need your shirt." To tease him, she started on the top button.

"Um . . ." He stared at her as if he couldn't believe she'd do it but was halfway hoping she would.

She wouldn't do it, but the impulse was there, not only to taunt Charlie but to shock Denise. Fifteen minutes into Denise's visit and Eve was already reverting to the little sister who was always doing crazy things and getting into trouble. She was trying to outgrow that image, but having Denise around wasn't helping.

"That's the last bead," Denise announced, standing and brushing dust from her knees. "Now it's safe to go in and out your front door." She took the pot Charlie still held and emptied her pockets into it with a clatter of beads.

"Thanks, Denise," Eve said.

"No problem." Denise held the pot out to Charlie, who snapped to attention and dumped his handful of beads into it. "I couldn't just leave those beads all over the place."

"So I noticed," Eve said.

"And now I'll go make some coffee. Is your phone book in the kitchen? I can call somebody to repair your washing machine."

"Fine," Eve said. "Phone book's in the drawer closest to the back door." She was definitely reverting to her ten-year-old self. As a kid, she would have made that mess in the washer on purpose to get Denise in a tizzy. This time the mess was premade, and all she had to do was wait to enjoy Denise's reaction.

Charlie looked alarmed as he got to his feet. "Eve, don't let her call anyone. I'll take care of it. After all, I'm the one who—"

"Let Denise handle it," Eve said. "I don't want to waste your talents on a silly old washing machine."

"Yeah, but there's all that—"

"Stuff to do," Eve finished for him. "On the hovercraft. I know. Denise can supervise the repair person while we work. How about that for a plan?"

He frowned and glanced toward the kitchen where Denise was clattering around making coffee. "Look, I won't pretend that I understand the dynamic here, but I have a feeling if I get in the middle of it, I'll end up roadkill."

"Eve," Denise called from the kitchen. "Is this pre-ground the only coffee you have?"

"Yep," Eve called back. "Which is fortunate, because I don't have a coffee grinder."

"I knew I should have brought my own. Oh, well, I'll make do."

"Thanks, Denise!" Eve motioned Charlie into the living room and lowered her voice. "I think this is the best way to deal with her. As you can see, she has to march in and organize everything. I don't want her interfering with the hovercraft project, so if she has something else to straighten out in my life, maybe she'll leave that part alone."

"Don't count on it," he said quietly. "She's riddled with jealousy. I think she's concerned about you, but that jealousy is powerful. I'm wondering how far she'd go to keep that hovercraft from ever getting off the ground."

Eve's tummy started to hurt, because she'd been wondering the same thing. In spite of that, she shook her head. "She wouldn't break down my back door, not even to throw us off the track of suspecting someone who had a key. She's too neat to do anything so crass as pry open a door with a crowbar. That's not her style."

"Unless she's desperate to keep you from succeeding."

Eve couldn't bear the thought. "I know we're not as close as sisters could be, but I refuse to believe she'd sabotage me."

"Are you kidding? I'll bet she's been mentally sabotaging you all your life. Why not add some physical intimidation?"

"Because she's my sister, that's why."

"Right, and in addition to the sibling rivalry, she's genuinely afraid you'll hurt yourself, so she could convince herself that her actions are necessary to protect you."

Eve looked into his eyes. "We think so much alike it's scary."

"So you agree it could be her?"

"It could, but I can't let myself believe it is."

Charlie held her gaze for a long time. "Okay," he said gently. "But just in case, I've got your back."

Almost immediately, the weepies threatened to swamp her. She blinked, determined not to turn into some out-of-control water faucet because of such a simple statement. But the thing was, nobody had ever had her back. Mostly she'd felt all alone in the world, unsupported and misunderstood.

She swallowed the lump in her throat. "Thanks. You're . . . a good guy."

"No, I'm not. I'm just—"

"You are too, so don't argue. Now, if you'll excuse me, I'll go change into something less comfortable."

He nodded.

"Want to come and help?"

"You know I do. I think I'll stay right here."

She took a long, shaky breath. "I appreciate that you're taking time off from work to help me. We really are going to get that hovercraft working."

"You'd better believe we are."

"And nobody is going to stop us."

He held her gaze. "Not if I have anything to say about it."

She smiled at him. "Then it's as good as done." Turning quickly, she headed down the hall toward her bedroom. She didn't want him to pick up on the sudden grief that had come over her as she thought about the hovercraft project.

He would make sure he helped her finish it. That much she knew for sure. After that, he'd be on his way out of town. As his friend, the person who owed him the best she could give, it would be her duty to help him leave.

Charlie wasn't wild about abandoning Eve while Denise was there, but he couldn't see any way around it. He needed a shower and a change of clothes, plus he needed to pick up his prescription safety goggles so he could help Eve with the hovercraft. In his initial excitement the night before, he'd forgotten them.

Then he had to stop by the power plant and tidy things up in preparation for leaving for a couple of days. Last of all he wanted to find Rick and tell him what was going on. Eunice was still very much on Charlie's list of suspects, and Rick needed to know that before night fell and Eunice drew him back into her alien web.

So once Charlie had his shirt back, he declined Eve's offer of coffee, put on his chaps and leather jacket and hopped on his motorcycle. As he buckled on the chaps he avoided looking at Eve. He wondered if he'd ever wear them again without thinking of her. Probably not.

Minutes later he was back in his apartment. Before

hitting the shower he decided to call his cousin. Fortunately Rick answered his cell phone right away, and Charlie quickly arranged to meet him at the Rack and Balls for lunch, adding that he'd like Rick to come alone. Then he finally headed for the shower.

As he started to throw his flannel shirt into the hamper, he paused and held it to his nose. His shirt smelled like Eve. The scent made his groin stir, but the reaction went deeper than that. Memories of loving her went beyond sex, beyond the incredible time they'd had in bed. He heard her laughter, saw the sparkle in her eyes, felt her vulnerability when she'd told him she'd flunked out of high school.

She was fast becoming an essential part of his life, and he didn't know how to stop that process. He didn't even know if he wanted to stop it. That kind of human connection didn't come along very often, and he was smart enough to realize that. He knew they also had a problem with no solutions. It wasn't enough to keep him away from her.

He tossed the shirt in the hamper. Keeping it unwashed for sentimental reasons was goofy, even for him. He'd wash the shirt and wear it again, just as he'd keep wearing his chaps whenever he rode his bike. They'd remind him of her, but so what? He wasn't ever going to forget her, anyway.

An hour and a half later he'd squared away everything at the power plant. Good thing he'd asked Rick to meet him for lunch because he was starving. A few pieces of cold pizza were all he'd had since lunch the day before, and he'd burned a lot of energy recently. Good energy, though. Despite the lack of sleep he felt great. Fantastic sex could do that for a guy.

The Rack and Balls was deserted this time of day, which was exactly the way Charlie wanted it. Archie used the daylight hours to do routine maintenance around the place. Today he was on a stepladder dusting the large set of elk antlers that hung above the bar.

Charlie walked over to the bar. "Hey, Archie, how're they hanging?"

"Nice and loose, Charlie. And yours?" Archie's grin peeked out from his bushy gray beard.

"Couldn't be better." Charlie had never meant that more than today. Funny how a woman like Eve could put a spring in your step.

"Hey, that's good to hear." Archie climbed down from the ladder and stuck the feather duster into his back pocket. "Anybody I know?"

Charlie laughed. "Nice try."

"That's okay. You don't have to tell me. I admire a man who can keep his mouth shut." Archie washed his hands at the bar sink. "What'll you have?"

"Coffee." Charlie felt terrific, but sitting on a stool in the dim bar, relaxing for the first time in many hours, he could feel his energy level dipping.

"I just put on a new pot. It'll be done in a few minutes." Archie leaned his forearms on the bar. "I never see you here during the day. What's up?"

"I'm meeting my cousin Rick. We have a few things to discuss. You got anything cooking back there?"

"I got some homemade beans and Polish sausage."

"That'll work." Charlie's mouth began to water. He wondered if Eve had anything at home to eat besides leftover pizza. She'd been out of town for two days. He should have asked if . . . oh, hell, she was a big girl. He couldn't start worrying about whether she had food in the refrigerator. Next he'd be wondering whether she'd had her car's oil changed recently.

He could imagine her forgetting stuff like that. She needed someone around who could help her with those little details. He was outstanding at those kinds of details. But he wouldn't be around. How many times would he have to remind himself of that so that he would quit daydreaming about a life he never intended to lead?

"Here's your coffee." Archie put a steaming mug in front of him. "And excuse my saying so, but you look a little spacey today."

"I have a lot on my mind." Charlie took a reviving sip of the coffee. "Ah, that's better. Say, Archie, just between us, do you think Ed and Darrell are in financial trouble with that Christmas tree farm?"

"Yeah, I think they're sinking deeper into debt every year. So many people are using fake trees these days, and neither of them are all that cagey when it comes to the business, either. I'm amazed they're still afloat, to be honest. Why? You want to buy that property?"

"No, God, no."

"It would be a great place to raise a family."

"That's a long way off for me, Archie." Charlie couldn't help thinking how Eve would love the idea of living in the middle of a Christmas tree farm. But if Ed and Darrell really were struggling that bad, he also had to wonder if they would think stealing a hovercraft concept was the way to bail themselves out. Damn it—there were way too many people with a good reason to break into Eve's house.

Chapter Twenty-one

Eve had thrown on a bathrobe so that she could return Charlie's shirt to him. Although she'd hated to see him leave after that, she didn't have anything to offer him for breakfast except cold pizza, so maybe it was just as well that he'd left so he could get some decent food.

The reject of the three pizzas, the plain cheese, still sat on the kitchen table. Denise opened the lid and made a face. "Gross. This could attract all kinds of pests. And didn't you say something about mice?"

"Um, yeah, but—"

Denise reached for the phone book and started flipping through it. "Exterminators. Here we go." She grabbed the cordless phone from the kitchen counter.

"The thing is, I don't really have—"

Denise was already talking to someone. "Mice. Yes, that's right. No, I have a washing machine repairman coming then. Three? That should work." She hung up and gave Eve a smug smile. "Handled."

"I don't really have mice." Eve had decided the relationship with her sister was shot, anyway. She had nothing to lose by being honest.

"That you *know of*. But with food sitting around, I'll bet you do. It won't hurt to get the place checked out. I'll bet you haven't done that."

"No," Eve said. "If I saw any, I'd buy one of those little cage traps."

"Then what?"

"I'm not sure. Turn them loose . . . somewhere."

Denise rolled her eyes. "I'm sure your neighbors would love that." She clapped her hands together. "So! Where's this hovercraft? The washing machine repairman will be here in an hour, and I should probably do some grocery shopping before then."

"I thought we could go to the Pastry Parlor and get something." Eve didn't usually treat herself, but having Denise around made a girl deserve a cinnamon roll. She was curious about whether they were all made with one raisin in the middle, now.

Denise shuddered. "The Pastry Parlor? Sounds like a hangout for carb addicts."

"Pretty much." Eve couldn't help herself. Denise really begged to be taunted. "But not completely. There's some fruit involved. The Booby Buns have a raisin on top."

"The *what*?"

"Or maybe you'd rather try the Bawdy Breadsticks. They're the size of your average penis." Charlie's, she was proud to report, was above average.

Denise's jaw dropped. "You have an X-rated bakery in this town?"

"I'm not sure you could go that far, but the bakery has recently started offering a few interesting items. Charlie's mother and his aunt Myrtle own it, and they discovered that a touch of sex sells baked goods. Last night I went over there and helped frost some cookies for a bachelorette party. The pose reminded me of something out of the *Kama Sutra*. The guy was coming at her sort of sideways."

"I can't believe this."

"Oh, I'm sure the pose is possible." Eve had meant to ask Charlie if he wanted to test it, but they'd been too hungry for each other to get involved in unusual positions. Maybe another time. She hoped there would be another time.

"I meant the bakery, not the pose. This is a small town. Small towns are supposed to be conservative. They're not supposed to have—"

"Frosting the cookies was fun." Eve decided to keep it up. She seemed to have thrown Denise off balance, and this time she hadn't even had to use beads. "The tricky part was getting the red frosting dots of her nipples exactly right. A couple of times I had them way too close to her neck."

"Incredible."

"So, are you up for a trip to the Pastry Parlor? You can't very well leave town without at least taking a peek, right?"

"I . . . we'll see. First I want to inspect this thing you've built. Where is it?"

Eve considered telling her sister that the hovercraft was stored under her bed, just to see if Denise had so little imagination that she'd go looking there. But she decided that she'd pulled Denise's chain enough for now. "It's out in the garage."

Denise looked at Eve's bare feet. "You can't go out there like that."

She could so if she wanted to. But the floor would be cold and there was no point in rebellion just for the sake of bugging Denise. "I'll stand in the doorway and answer questions from there." She noticed that Denise had picked up all the pans in front of the door and stacked them neatly on the counter. Of course. Opening the door, she held it back so Denise could walk through.

"It's *purple.*" Denise said it as if the color were illegal.

"It's designed as a fun toy. It needs to be bright. Besides, I like purple."

"I know." Denise walked around the hovercraft. "I'll never forget the birthday cake you made me. Lavender inside, dark purple frosting outside."

"Yeah, I used grape Kool-Aid." Eve had been proud of that birthday cake, too, one of her first efforts in the kitchen. Her family's horrified reaction had killed any urge to keep experimenting in there. Now she ate mostly salads, anyway, where all you had to do was slice and dice. Tough to louse up a salad. But she usually put beets and purple cabbage on the salad, to give it visual zip.

"How does it work?"

"There are magnets underneath, which are what make it hover—like those hoverboards in *Back to the Future Part II*. Remember those?"

"Vaguely. I thought those movies were kind of silly, but I know you loved them." She looked at the engine mounted on the workbench. "So you're going to put this in there?"

No, I'm going to wear it on my head for a photo shoot next week. "Yes. After I test the new fuel source I brought home last night and make sure the engine runs okay with it."

"What fuel source?"

"Used cooking oil." She pointed to the can sitting beside her workbench. "I need to do some analysis on it, but it might convert much better than the veggie scraps I've been using."

And by explaining these things about the hovercraft, she was handing Denise all the ammunition she needed to sabotage the project. Charlie might think she was being foolish, but what was she supposed to do, refuse to show the hovercraft to Denise? If Denise was guilty, she'd already seen the project, anyway.

Denise made another circuit of the hovercraft. "You talk as if you've done some research on this." She sounded reluctantly impressed.

"I've been researching this kind of thing all my life," Eve said. "I model to make a living, but inventions are what I love. I always have."

"That would be all well and good if you'd stayed in school, but I'm afraid you have just enough knowledge to be dangerous."

Eve crossed her arms, because if she didn't she might run into the garage, bare feet and all, and start a girl fight with her sister. "You know what? It's not your responsibility whether I'm taking unnecessary chances with my safety. I'm an adult now. I'm free to make my own choices." And didn't that sound defensive?

Denise faced her. "How do you expect me to stand by and let you kill yourself?"

"I won't, but if it comes to that, how do you propose to stop me?" That was the crux of the situation. Was Denise prepared to do whatever it took?

"You are impossible, you know that?" Denise's expression darkened. "Don't you ever think of anyone besides yourself? First you dump a guy that the whole family liked, and now this!"

"I was supposed to marry Lyle because everybody *else* liked him?"

"You liked him, too! Or I assume you did. You dated him for a year, so you must have thought he was worth something."

"He definitely was." Eve shifted her weight uncomfortably. She'd stayed with Lyle way too long, and she wasn't happy about that. She'd led him on, in a way, because she been unwilling to face the truth about herself.

"What was wrong with him, anyway? He was cute, made good money, treated you like a queen. Guys like that aren't all that thick on the ground. At least I haven't met that many."

Eve heard the underlying envy in that statement. No doubt Denise would have taken Lyle in a heartbeat, but he wouldn't have dated her. He required a certain amount of physical beauty from his girlfriends, which was another reason Eve hadn't wanted to stick around. She could see him trading her in once her looks started to fade.

"Lyle would never have understood my need to invent things," Eve said. "He wouldn't have wanted to live in a little town like this, either. He was into glitz and glamour."

"Eve, hel-*lo*. You're a model. It doesn't get any glitzier than that."

"I *work* as a model. That's not who I am. Who I am is an inventor." There. That was her manifesto. Maybe she'd make a sign out of that and tack it up on the wall somewhere. The sign would be for herself, because Charlie already believed those things about her. She was the one who sometimes doubted it.

Obviously Denise doubted it, too, because she laughed. "You can call yourself an inventor all day long, but until you've invented something that you've patented and marketed, you're a hobbyist."

Eve tried to tell herself that once again, jealousy was the motive behind Denise's comment. But that was small comfort. Unfortunately, Denise was right. Until Eve had created something that was of use to someone, something that would improve the world in some way, her inventions were only a hobby, not a profession.

"Well, now you've seen the hovercraft," she said. "I'll grab a quick shower, you can change into something clean, and we'll go to the Pastry Parlor."

"I'm not sure that I want to go to—"

"Sure you do." And Eve really wanted to go there and see a couple of women who liked and admired her, two people who believed she was going to succeed. She hadn't realized how nice that felt until confronted with Denise's skeptical negativity. "I'll be back in a flash and we'll go."

"I have a suggestion," Denise called after her.

"We're going to the Pastry Parlor," Eve said as she walked quickly through the kitchen. "No arguments."

"About the hovercraft."

Eve paused. Her sister was nothing if not smart, and maybe she'd actually have something to contribute to the project. "What about it?"

"You should put a rubber bumper all the way around the bottom edge."

"Why?" But Eve had a good idea what the answer would be.

"Because, sure as the world, you're going to crash this thing, and a bumper might just save your ass."

"Right." Gritting her teeth, Eve left to take her shower. She had to move the dry cleaning back to her bed before she could do it.

When she finally stepped under the hot spray with a sigh of relief, all she could think about was that damned bumper suggestion of Denise's. It took her the whole length of her shower to finally admit that it might be a very good idea.

Rick stared across the table at Charlie, his expression one of complete disbelief. "You're shitting me, Charlie."

"Don't I wish. But not this time. Someone is definitely out to steal this hovercraft concept from Eve."

Rick pushed away his empty plate and brought his coffee cup closer. "But this is Middlesex. People don't break into houses and steal things in this town. We have a few speeders, a few more jaywalkers, especially during tourist season. Right before graduation somebody always paints the water tower. That's the crime beat around here."

"I know." Charlie was having a hard time believing it himself. If he hadn't seen Eve's back door and heard that ominous click of the front door closing, he'd have Rick's same reaction to the news. "But considering that Eunice could be the one, I wanted to clue you in."

"Thanks, cuz." Rick gazed down into his coffee cup. "It's a damned shame, though." He glanced up and grinned. "Because she may be crooked, but she's also bent, if you get my drift."

"I could see that for myself when she opened the door wearing black underwear and a set of antennae."

"Was that wild or what? And I don't care if she got her techniques from that Gonaug dude or from *Penthouse*. She knows stuff, man. She knows *lots* of stuff."

"I'm sure." Charlie wondered if she knew how to market a hovercraft design.

"Like for instance, she does this thing with her tits where she coats them with something sweet and gooey. I know because she let me taste it. She claims it's made by a certain kind of beelike insect on Trillium. So she puts it on her tits and then she rubs them all over my—"

"I get the picture." Charlie wasn't in the best of shape to hear Rick's war stories. They only made him think about being in bed with Eve. "Listen, we have to focus on the problem. You can't let yourself get distracted by sex." And neither could Charlie. "It's not only Eve and her invention I'm worried about. You could be a victim, too."

"Me? How?"

"I'm not sure. Was there . . . bondage involved?" That made him think of leather, which reminded him of his chaps.

"Oh, *yeah*. You know how most people do it by tying each other to the bedposts?"

"Um, I guess."

Rick gazed at him. "You don't know squat, do you? I can see it on your face. You've never stuck your toe in the bondage game pool. Am I right?"

"Well, I've . . . no, I've never done that." But he'd bet Eve would like to play. Anybody who wanted to have him wear chaps to bed would definitely be interested.

"Eunice, she doesn't mess around with bedposts. She has eyebolts in her bedroom wall, two at the top and two down by the baseboards. Sort of like a medieval torture chamber, you know?"

"See, this is what I'm talking about. This kind of extreme thing." Charlie wasn't ever getting into eyebolts in the wall. Bedposts would be fine. Except he didn't have any, and Eve certainly didn't, with her round bed. If he designed a trapezium-shaped bed for her, though, he could put bedposts on it. Cool.

"Extreme sex! Exactly. Charlie, you don't know what you're missing. There I was chained to her bedroom wall, and you could have used my dick for a coatrack."

"You were helpless. She could have taken your credit cards, your—"

"Actually, she did hang a few things from my dick." Rick stared off into space, lost in his hot memories. "She played ring-toss with these big hoop earrings she has, and then there were the feathers. She used those to tickle my balls."

"She could have done *anything*, Rick!"

"I *know*." Rick's eyes glazed over. "That's what makes it so damned exciting."

"Especially when you discover she's stolen your identity. That would be very exciting. Rick, will you pay attention? We have a thief among us, and I'm trying to figure out who it is."

"All by yourself?"

"No. Eve's thinking about it, too. And I was hoping you'd be some help." But after this lunch discussion, Charlie had serious doubts.

"What about the cops?"

"No cops. First of all, Eve doesn't want to answer questions about the hovercraft. When she tests it, she'll be flying it without any kind of license, and she'd rather do that quietly."

Rick nodded. "Smart. Okay, let me get the players straight. You think it might be either Eunice or the sister, Denise. And there's the off chance that it's the gay guys out at the Christmas tree farm. How am I doing so far?"

"Better." Charlie decided he had to level with Rick. "Don't take this wrong, but Eve's suspicious of Manny and Kyle, too."

Rick laughed. "That's a good one."

"You can't blame her. They were there Monday night when we were talking about this as being a potential gold mine. I don't know how much you're paying them, but they might see this as a shortcut to some fast money."

Rick smiled and picked up his coffee cup. "You don't have to worry about Manny and Kyle."

"How can you be so sure?"

"They have their eyes on the big picture. They want advancement in their field. They wouldn't louse that up with something like this. It would be professional suicide." He took a sip of his coffee.

"I hope you're right."

"Cuz, you can take that to the bank. Kyle and Manny aren't suspects. But I have a plan."

"Yeah?" Charlie was hesitant, but ready to listen. Right now he could use a plan, and sometimes as kids Rick would surprise him with a halfway decent idea. "It doesn't involve explosives, though, does it?"

"Hey, will you ever let me forget that? Sheesh."

"Not likely. When your cousin and best friend decides it would be cool to build a bomb, and he's thinking *cool idea* and you're thinking *juvie,* not to mention the end of all hope for a scholarship to MIT—let's just say that sticks in my mind."

"I wasn't really going to build it," Rick said. "I only said I was to give you a mental wedgie. Worked, too."

Charlie didn't want to concede that point. "I didn't think you'd really build it."

"Did, too. And you thought I'd drag you into it, somehow."

"Yeah, yeah. So what's this idea of yours?"

"I go undercover."

Charlie didn't get it. "I thought undercover was when nobody knew who you were. You're as well-known in this town as I am."

"Yeah, but they don't know I'm a spy, now, do they?"

"A spy?" Charlie groaned. "I'm afraid to hear the rest of this."

"It's simple, but elegant. I seduce *both* Eunice and the sister. What's her name again?"

"Denise, but I think this plan has huge flaws. For one thing, Eunice seems to do the major part of the seducing when you two get together."

"Only because I let that be the case." Rick waggled his eyebrows. "I can take charge if I want. Those eyebolts work both ways."

"Dear God. Forget I asked for help. This is a disaster in the making. And as for Eve's sister, she—"

"Leave her to me. I'll get her to reveal her secrets. Eunice, too. I'll handle both of those suspects for you. But as for Ed and Darrell, you're on your own. I'm not seducing them. I have my limits."

Chapter Twenty-two

Rick decided he was in the wrong damned profession. He should have taken up acting. Charlie had completely bought his fixation on sex, although it wasn't totally an act. Whenever he focused on sex, he forgot about Peterson for a while. So he was willing to take on the challenge of seducing Eve's sister, just for the distraction factor.

But he'd promised Peterson he'd report in, so he finished his coffee and excused himself. "Gotta take a leak," he said.

"Sure. I'm getting some pie and coffee. Want some?"

"Pie would be great, but I'll skip the extra coffee." Rick had the shakes as it was. After going into the single-stall bathroom, he locked the door, pulled out his cell, and dialed Peterson's number. "It's me."

"Does he suspect you of anything?"

"No." Rick swallowed. "But you took a chance last night, staying to watch. They heard you leave."

"That was my reward." Peterson's tone was smooth and unhurried. "God knows if you'll make this spaceship pay off. I need to take whatever benefit I can from this sorry situation, because I doubt you'll come up with the money. I'll get some consolation from watching you die, but not enough."

Rick clenched his jaw to keep his teeth from chattering. "The hovercraft will pay off. I have an appointment in New York on Monday." He tried to calm himself by looking at the framed *Playboy* centerfolds covering the bathroom walls.

"Yes, well, before you go rushing off to that appointment, you have some business to take care of."

"What's that?" Rick's heart beat so fast he wondered if he could be having a stroke. Even staring at Miss July's 36DDs wasn't helping.

"You have to destroy that prototype in the garage, of course. Make it look like she blew it up by accident."

"I don't . . . I don't think that's a good idea." Rick dragged in a breath. "Somebody could get hurt."

Peterson sighed. "That's not your concern, is it? Your concern is to destroy the evidence that someone else created this concept you're selling."

Rick tried frantically to think of an alternative, but Peterson was right about getting rid of the hovercraft. Maybe he could steal the whole thing and then torch it. Except he didn't know how to do that. Somebody would be sure to notice him leaving Eve's garage with that big purple saucer.

"Either you promise to destroy it or I'll have it done," Peterson said.

"No, no. I'll do it." Rick didn't dare turn Peterson loose on something like that. Only a smoking, gaping hole in the ground would be left after Peterson blew up the garage and probably the house right along with it.

"And soon," Peterson said. "They're obviously close to finishing it."

"Soon," Rick said.

"Let me know when it's destroyed."

"I will," Rick said, but Peterson had already disconnected. Rick struggled to breathe. For several seconds the display of centerfolds wouldn't snap into focus. He stood there until all those tits were perfectly clear again. Then he left to rejoin Charlie.

Eve was desperately in need of a carb fix by the time she and Denise arrived at the Pastry Parlor. Denise had acted as if she didn't want to go, but Eve could tell her sister was curious. Eve had always wondered if Denise was a wild child underneath all that bossy, controlling behavior.

When they walked in, Myrtle was behind the counter, looking very chipper considering the fact she'd been up late the night before baking cookies. Eve admired the spunk of these two women, who weren't letting their senior-citizen status keep them from building a business.

The shop was bustling, so Eve and Denise had to stand in line. Denise was trying to look as if she walked into a bakery like this every day of the week, but her glance kept darting toward the cases marked BOOBY BUNS and BAWDY BREADSTICKS. Her cheeks were very pink.

Then Eve noticed that the usual tray of doughnuts had been relabeled. Now they were called COCK RINGS. And a marble cake with a condom packet sitting on top was advertised as SAFE SEX SWIRL. The ladies had decided to go for it.

As Denise stood beside Eve, she ducked her head, lowered her voice, and mumbled a question that sounded like *loco*.

Eve leaned close to her sister and talked out of the side of her mouth. "Not even slightly crazy. Rose and Myrtle are two of the sanest women I know."

Denise frowned and shook her head. Putting her mouth closer to Eve's ear, she said softly. "No. Are these *locals*?"

"*Oh.*" Eve took inventory of the people in front of her. There was Agnes Heath, who ran a dress shop on Main Street. And behind her stood Betty Magnum, who worked in the post office. And there was Jeremy Nagle, bank president, looking dapper in his yellow polka-dot bow tie.

Eve looked at Denise. "All locals," she murmured.

"Amazing." Denise adjusted her purse strap over her shoulder and scanned the bakery cases again. "I'm thinking of switching some things around in my portfolio."

"Huh?" Eve couldn't imagine how being surrounded by Bawdy Breadsticks, Booby Buns, and Cock Rings would make her sister start reevaluating her investments.

"I thought the mood of the country was more conservative than this," Denise said. "So I've been putting my money into sectors that support that mind-set. Home and hearth stuff. But now I'm wondering if I shouldn't diversify into some adult entertainment stocks."

"They have stocks?"

"Sure. You just have to know where to look. I didn't realize that it was a growth market, but it makes sense—two sides of the same coin. Let me know if the Pastry Parlor decides to franchise. I might be interested in being a silent partner."

Eve was in awe of that kind of thinking. The extent of her investment skills included buying a house in Middlesex, buying some savings bonds, and opening an IRA. She could have asked Denise about managing her income, but she hadn't wanted to. Maybe her pride was costing her money.

Jeremy Nagle turned. "Oh, hi, Eve. I heard someone talking about investments, so naturally my ears perked up."

And Jeremy had quite the ears to perk up, too. Eve had always thought they looked like elf ears. "Hi, Mr. Nagle. This is—"

"Please call me Jeremy."

"Okay." Eve thought *Mr. Nagle* fit him a lot better, considering his bow tie. "Jeremy, this is my sister Denise. She's an economics professor at Yale."

"*Is* she now?" Jeremy shook Denise's hand enthusiastically. "I've spent many happy hours at Yale."

"You went to school there?" Denise asked.

"No, no. I just drive over and wander around." He giggled. "I don't normally tell people about this, but we're all here in the Pastry Parlor together, so I guess I'm among friends." He winked broadly at Denise and Eve.

Eve didn't get it. "I don't see anything strange about wandering around Yale," she said. "It's a pretty campus."

"That's not *all* that's pretty." Mr. Nagle winked again. "You know that old song about standing on the corner and watching all the girls go by?"

By now Denise was staring at the banker as if she might be considering calling the guys with the butterfly nets. "I don't believe I know that song."

"I heard it once on an oldies station." Eve was getting the drift of this confession, and it was cracking her up.

Mr. Nagle gave them a nasal, off-key rendition of the first few bars of the song. "And so on," he said, smiling. "That's me at Yale. Standing on the corner watching all the pretty girls. I don't whistle at them anymore like I used to, though. It's not PC to do that now."

Eve worked so hard at not laughing that she choked, causing both Denise and Mr. Nagle to pound her on the back. Or rather, Denise pounded and Mr. Nagle patted. Eve had forgotten how hard Denise could thump a person's back.

Shortly, thanks to Denise's energetic pounding, Eve managed to breathe again. She coughed and cleared her throat. "Thanks. I must have swallowed wrong."

Mr. Nagle took his turn at the counter and ordered a dozen Booby Buns. Eve glanced over at Denise. Ever since Denise was little, when she tried not to laugh, she got very red in the face. At the moment, she was scarlet from holding her breath.

Looking at Denise set Eve off again, and she had to hold her hand over her mouth and stare at the black and white tiles on the bakery floor to get herself under control. It might have been one of the best sisterly moments she'd had with Denise in ten years.

After Mr. Nagle left with his Booby Buns, Eve and Denise took their turn at the counter.

"And this is your sister!" Myrtle said immediately. "I saw you come in and I knew it had to be her. Definitely a family resemblance, there."

Eve smiled. "Myrtle Bannister, I'd like you to meet Denise." Maybe having a sister wasn't so bad, after all. It was nice to be connected to someone.

"Nice to meet you, Denise. Eve tells me you're a professor." Myrtle said it with just the right amount of reverence.

"Yes, I am," Denise said. "And speaking from a marketing standpoint, this is a great concept you're developing."

Eve was liking this more and more. Good vibes all the way around.

"Thank you." Myrtle beamed.

"But you would improve traffic flow and encourage more browsing by giving out numbers instead of having people stand in line."

Eve winced. For a while there she'd actually had warm feelings toward her sister, but apparently Denise couldn't help being Denise.

"I'll take that under advisement." Some of the warmth had left Myrtle's smile. "Until recently, we haven't been this busy."

"And the name of the shop should change. You might consider—"

"Myrtle, we're in kind of a hurry." Eve decided to cut off this discussion before Denise embarrassed her completely. "We'll just take four Cock Rings and two Booby Buns, please."

"Coming up." Myrtle snapped open a paper bag and started loading it with Eve's order.

Denise cleared her throat. "As I was saying, the—"

"Is Manny in the back, by any chance?" Eve asked, desperate to sidetrack her sister.

"That boy is still frosting," Myrtle said. "What a worker. Kyle's home sleeping, but Manny came in with us this morning. I think Rose is trying to make a baker out of him."

"I hate to interrupt that," Eve said. "But I know he wanted to meet Denise."

"I'll go get him." Myrtle put down the bag and pushed through a swinging door that led to the back.

"Who's Manny?"

Eve turned toward her sister and threw out what she hoped was irresistible bait. "He works for Charlie's cousin, Rick. He wants some investment advice."

"Really?" Denise brightened. "Do you know about his holdings?"

"Not my area."

"The market is volatile right now, so I can understand him seeking advice."

Eve heard the unmistakable sound of Denise licking her chops. Then Manny came through the swinging door and Eve heard another, more surprising sound from her sister—a quick intake of breath. Uh-oh. Denise thought

Manny was hot. This was a complication Eve didn't need, but it was too late, now.

"Hey, Eve." Manny stripped off his clear plastic gloves as he came around the counter.

"Hi, there. This is my sister, Denise. Denise, this is Manny Flores, full-time photographer's assistant and part-time cookie froster."

"I'm really getting into this bakery thing." Manny shook hands with Denise. "Nice to meet you. I don't know if Eve told you that I'm looking for some invest-ment advice."

"She mentioned that." Denise's expression softened. "I'd be happy to be of some help."

Eve realized it had been years since she'd seen Denise in the grip of infatuation. She'd forgotten the transforma-tion that took place. Gone was the drill sergeant, replaced by a girly girl who spoke in dulcet tones.

"That's good, because I need all the help I can get," Manny said.

Denise shifted her position so she partially blocked Eve out of the conversation. "Well, Manny, I don't pre-tend to have all the answers, but—"

A snort of laughter came out of Eve before she could censor herself. Manny glanced at her in surprise, but Denise's glare brought back memories of being the little sister hiding behind the couch on a Saturday night.

" 'Scuse me," Eve said. "I had a flashback to our Je-remy Nagle experience. You two continue talking. I'll just step over here and pay for our order." She moved to the counter and left Denise to impress Manny with her Wall Street smarts.

Eve thought she deserved a medal for coming up with such a brilliant excuse for laughing at the wrong moment. But Denise pretending that she might not have all the an-swers was too rich. Eve was also proud of herself for resisting the impulse to remind Denise that they had a washing machine repairman coming to the house soon. Was she a sensitive sister, or what?

No matter how fiercely Charlie argued against it, Rick was determined to follow through with his plan. He was sure that if he put the moves on both female suspects, separately, of course, he'd coax the truth out of each of them during a hot, unguarded moment. As Rick and Charlie polished off large pieces of apple pie à la mode, Charlie tried to convince his cousin that the idea was not only sleazy, it was doomed to failure.

"For one thing," Charlie said, "these two women will be in proximity to each other. You can't seduce one without the other knowing."

"Sure I can." Rick cracked his knuckles. "You're going over there this afternoon to work on the hovercraft, right?"

"Yeah."

"Then I'll tag along and meet Denise, see how far I can get before Eunice comes home from the office."

Charlie was beginning to regret his impulse to fill Rick in on the situation. "Don't you have location scouting to do?"

Rick waved away that objection. "Kyle and Manny are handling that. Well, Kyle is. Manny's spending all his time down at the Pastry Parlor. The guy seems to love bakery work. Who knew?"

"But isn't Manny on your payroll?"

"Ah, it doesn't matter. Mom and Aunt Rose can use the extra help. I can spare Manny, considering that I didn't anticipate spending much time on the scouting end of the trip. It was mostly a good excuse to see the family."

Charlie had been looking for an opening like this. The

closer he got to leaving town, the more he'd begun to think it would be great if Rick would relocate to the East Coast, just so one of them was closer to the two widows. As successful as Rick was, it wouldn't be that tough for him to establish a New York office.

"Speaking of family," he said, "Aunt Myrtle isn't getting any younger."

"I don't know about that. She seems a lot more cheerful than she did when my dad was alive."

"Well, sure, she's cheerful, but she's getting on in years."

"Are you kidding? She'll outlive us all. If she could survive my dad, she'll survive anything. I'm not worried about her."

Charlie took off his glasses and massaged the bridge of his nose. He would go to Nevada in any case, but lately he'd been thinking that it might be good to have Rick around to keep an eye on things. "Have you ever thought about moving your operation to New York? I'm going to be living in Nevada soon, and—"

"Now I get your point. Listen, they don't need me around. They're making it fine. Look at the way they've built this business."

"I just think it would be nice for one of us to be reasonably close."

"You know what? I've been back here for a few days, now, and I think they could get along just fine if neither of us happened to be here. Sure, they'd miss you as a person and they'd miss the ever-available handyman you've been for them. But they'd be okay. In fact . . ." Rick tapped his finger against his empty coffee mug. "They might be better off, in the long run."

"Better off? How?"

"Think about it. There are a few retired widowers living

in Middlesex. I'll bet some of them know how to fix things. But with you always around, there was no reason to call those guys, was there?"

Charlie groaned. "Are you accusing me of standing between my mother and romance?"

"I'm just trying to get you to look at things from a different angle." Rick consulted his watch. "Hey, if I'm going to make any progress at all with Denise, we need to get going."

"Rick, she is so not your type."

"Every woman on the planet is my type." Rick pushed back his chair and stood. "Prepare to watch a master at work."

"Okay, let's go." Charlie had come to the conclusion that it might be fun to see how Rick dealt with someone like Denise. But even better than that was the distraction Rick could create. Charlie and Eve actually might have some time alone. That was something to get excited about.

"But first I have to take another leak."

"But you just—"

"I know, I know. I have a bladder the size of a thimble, dude."

Chapter Twenty-three

Somehow Eve was able to drag Denise away from the Pastry Parlor and Manny. When it looked as if Denise would never leave, Eve hit her with a double-barreled assault on her sense of responsibility—the washing machine repair she'd scheduled and the navy slacks that were in desperate need of washing.

They ate Cock Rings and Booby Buns on the way home, and Denise was so busy talking about Manny and his assets, both monetary and physical, that she didn't complain about ingesting all those sugary carbs. In fact, she seemed to be enjoying every bite.

"Talk about hot buns!" Denise said as she polished off a Cock Ring. "If those women really wanted to make money, they'd hire Manny, wearing those tight jeans of his, to walk around the shop offering samples on a tray."

Eve smiled. "Cute idea. They should name the bakery Hot Buns."

Denise turned to her, her eyes wide. "Exactly! That's *exactly* what they should call it. Brilliant idea, Eve! I'll tell Manny about it. He and I agreed that the bakery should

franchise, and he said he'd like a piece of the action."
Denise fanned herself. "When he said that, I almost had an
orgasm."

Eve was still savoring the fact that Denise had called
her brilliant. "So aren't you glad we made the trip?"

"You know it, girl. Manny and I, we, um, are getting
together for dinner tonight. To talk about his investment
strategy."

"Really?" Eve saw all kinds of advantages to that program. If Denise left, then she and Charlie could be alone.

Denise glanced sideways at Eve. "Unless that's a
problem."

"No! No problem at all. I'm sure Manny is eager to
make use of your . . . expertise."

"Oh, God, Eve, he's such a stud. I don't know if I can
handle him."

Eve was shocked that Denise would admit that she was
feeling vulnerable about anything. "You'll be fine."

"I don't have anything to wear."

Eve thought quickly. "I can fix you up. I have a soft red
sweater with a low-cut V-neck. It would go with those
slacks you have on. And you can borrow a pair of my
hooker shoes and some jewelry. We can make this work."

"Thank you." Denise licked powdered sugar from her
fingers. "You know about these things. I never paid attention to clothes."

"Leave it to me. You'll look really hot." Eve was delighted with the personality change in Denise. She decided not to mention that Manny would be leaving for
California next week. Maybe a fling was exactly what
Denise needed to feel better about herself.

*And maybe then she'd forget about sabotaging the
hovercraft.* Eve didn't want to believe Denise would do
such a thing, but if she was the guilty party, a hot romance
might be just the thing to sidetrack her efforts.

They made it back minutes ahead of the repairman, whose name turned out to be Gus. Denise shooed Eve away. "Go design a bumper for that hovermobile," she said. "This is what I do best."

"Hovercraft." Eve wasn't about to go away. She'd prepared her response to the inevitable reaction when Gus opened the washing machine. So she pretended that she was going into the garage, but instead she lingered in the kitchen.

Right on schedule, Denise shrieked in horror. "*Eve!* Come *quick*! Someone's vandalized your washing machine!"

Eve hurried down the hall to her bathroom. "My washing machine?" she said, making sure to inject the right amount of surprise and concern. "Why would someone vandalize a washing machine?"

Gus looked up, his Bassett-hound face telegraphing bad news. "In my line of work I see all kinds, but whoever did this is really sick. Personally, I'd say they belong in an institution."

"Brace yourself," Denise said. "It's unbelievably disgusting."

Eve approached and leaned over to look into the washer. The smell of wet newsprint and mildew mingled with the overly sweet smell of cheap chocolate mixed with the soap she'd poured in. The contents of the washer were no longer easily identifiable, and the chocolate had melted and mixed with the water until the entire mess was the color of grayish mud.

Eve made herself gasp in disbelief. "My God! This is the work of a maniac!"

Denise sighed. "I have to agree. I can't imagine what kind of person would dream up something this diabolical." She glanced at Gus. "Can this washer be saved?"

"Hard to say." Gus shook his head. "No telling if this

stuff has any corrosive properties. It could have started eating through the basket. By now it could be in the motor. I won't know until I get in there." He squared his shoulders as if preparing for battle. "I should probably call in the HazMat team."

Eve couldn't have that. She was on the verge of telling him what was in the washer.

"But I won't." A gleam of anticipation shone in his eyes. "I'm going to handle this myself, ladies. Stand back. I need to get more equipment from my truck."

Eve and Denise moved aside to let him walk out of the bathroom.

At the doorway, he turned back. "I'd advise both of you to clear the area. You might want to vacate the house."

"I'm willing to risk staying," Eve said. "I have work to do." As if on cue, her kitchen phone rang. She'd been expecting Charlie to call, and she needed to clue him in so he wouldn't reveal his part in the washing machine mess. "Denise, do you feel okay about keeping an eye on the washer?"

"Sure, but if anything crawls out of there, I'm leaving."

"Right." Eve ran for the phone and caught it before the answering machine clicked on. "Hello?"

"It's me."

"Hi, me." Her heart started thumping rapidly. "Where are you?"

"I'm at the Rack and Balls. Rick and I just finished having lunch. He's in the bathroom, so I grabbed a chance to call and warn you."

"I have to warn you, too. Let me have the first round of warning, okay?"

Charlie laughed. "Go."

"Denise is convinced some maniac put all that stuff in the washer. I didn't deny it."

"That's funny."

"Oh, and she has the hots for Manny. We just got back from the bakery and Manny was there. She thinks he's yummy."

"Huh. Very interesting. Okay, here's my warning. I told Rick that Eunice might be trying to steal your design. And I . . . also told him Denise might be sabotaging you."

"Charlie, I wish you hadn't said that."

"I think we have to consider the possibility."

"I just can't." At least not out loud. The suspicion lurked in the back of her mind and she couldn't completely ignore it. "And besides, even if she is the one, I'm betting she's about to abandon her plan."

"How come?"

"She and Manny are getting together tonight, supposedly to talk about investments, but Denise is hoping for more than that. I'm going to help her with clothes and jewelry so she looks good. I mean, she always looks good, but tonight she wants to look sexy."

"Are you sure you want Manny dating your sister?"

Eve knew what he meant. Manny had been high on her list of suspects. "I've changed my mind about him. He's too nice a guy to break into somebody's house and steal things. He's spending all his free time helping frost cookies for your mom and aunt. That's endearing."

"Eve, you don't want to suspect anybody. I admire that, but logically the culprit is someone you know, someone who's found out about the hovercraft and either wants to sabotage it or steal the idea."

Eve sighed. "I suppose."

"Rick will be out of the bathroom any minute. Before he gets here I need to tell you his bonehead solution is to get friendly with your sister so she'll confess. I tried to talk him out of it, but he—"

"No way." Eve didn't know whether to laugh or to be

outraged. Fortunately she couldn't imagine Rick would succeed with Denise. She'd see right through him.

"I know it won't work," Charlie said. "But then I thought of one advantage. If he keeps her occupied this afternoon, you and I could be alone to . . . um . . . work on the hovercraft."

"Oh." Eve started getting very warm. She could almost feel his lips on hers. "That would be great. I want to get started. And I have some new thoughts I want to run past you."

"Such as?"

She'd meant to tell him about the bumper, but somewhere along the way her mind had jumped the track and was now focused on sex. "Lubrication."

"Mm." His voice grew deeper. "Very important for any moving . . . part."

"Crucial." She figured they had the whole afternoon. They could still work after they'd taken the edge off their sexual urges. "The lubrication needs to be just right. Too much and there's excess slippage. Too little and the resulting friction can cause problems."

Charlie cleared his throat. "I think we need to design a few more experiments for the purposes of quality control."

"Definitely." Heat shot through her veins. "We have to work diligently until we get it right. How soon can you be here?"

"I'm on my way."

Parking was becoming an issue at Eve's house. Denise's Volvo was sitting next to Eve's Civic. Behind Eve's car was a white van with *GALLOPING GUS, YOUR CHEERFUL APPLIANCE REPAIRMAN* lettered on the side. Charlie parked his bike beside the van and Rick was forced to put the Subaru at the curb in front of the house.

Rick had wanted to drive over because his plan was to

invite Denise out for a cup of coffee. Charlie liked the idea of getting Denise out of the house, but it wouldn't do much good if Galloping Gus spent the afternoon working on the washing machine. Charlie knew the guy—he came into the Rack and Balls once in a while.

Now that Charlie knew who was working on the washer, he was glad Eve hadn't told Gus who had helped make the mess. That could ruin Charlie's rep as Mr. Magna Cum Laude, SAT whiz, and all-around bright guy. He might not like having his mother brag about him to bakery customers, but he didn't want to become the town joke, either.

After Charlie climbed off his bike he walked back to have another talk with Rick. "You need to know a few things," he said. "First of all, Eve doesn't think her sister is guilty."

"That makes sense. It's her sister. But you think she might be guilty, right?"

"It's possible, but if she is, she's not a hardened criminal or anything."

"Hey, I didn't think she was!" Rick finger-combed his hair. "Not Eunice, either. I wouldn't be putting the moves on any chick who's dangerous. The really bad ones would as soon chop your dick off as look at you."

"I wouldn't know about that." Charlie wondered what sort of crazy world Rick lived in out there in L.A. that he'd even think of such things. "But the other point I wanted to make is that if it is Denise, she may give up the whole sabotage deal because now she's interested in Manny."

"Manny? Manny Flores, my assistant?"

"Yep. Apparently they met today at the bakery and sparks were flying. They have a date tonight."

"You don't say." Rick rubbed his chin. "That puts a different slant on things. Is Manny interested in her?"

"I don't know. They're seeing each other tonight. That's all I can tell you. You could find out from Manny." Aha. This might be a way to sideline Rick's plan. "Yeah, you should probably call him and get that info before you go inside to meet Denise, so you won't muscle in on his territory."

"Nah. I would do that for you, cuz, but Manny's another story. The way I look at it, I got here first. He can eat my dust."

"Wait a minute, Rick." Charlie's conscience was pricking him. Being alone with Eve for the afternoon might not be worth it. The fallout from Rick's seduction attempt could be nasty, especially if Denise was innocent of any wrongdoing. "You're not planning to get involved with Denise for real, so I think you should forget this whole scheme of yours."

"Who says I'm not?"

"I do! You just spent last night with somebody else!"

"So?" Rick looked genuinely perplexed.

Charlie stared at him, unable to comprehend that kind of thinking. "I guess I'm more of a small-town guy than I like to think," he said. "Jumping from one woman to another in less than twelve hours seems . . ."

"Awesome," Rick said. "You should try it sometime, cuz. And don't think this is strictly a guy thing, either. Girls are into it, too. That's the beauty of living in a big city—more choices. I figured Eunice was my only avenue of expression. I didn't count Eve, because I think something's developing between you two."

Charlie didn't bother to deny it.

"And now I have a second possibility staring me in the face!" Rick grinned. "I realize I haven't met her yet, but she's Eve sister. She has to be decent looking, unless she was adopted. Jeez, I didn't think of that. She could be adopted. She could be a real troll. You've seen her, right? Tell me the truth, now. Is she really ugly?"

Charlie grabbed at what seemed to be the only option left to him. "Yes, she's really ugly."

"She is not." Rick laughed. "You never could lie worth a damn. Come on, let's go in."

As they approached the front door, Gus walked out looking as if he'd come from a funeral parlor. "I couldn't save her," he said.

Charlie panicked. "Who? Who couldn't you save?"

"The washer. She's deader than a doornail."

Air whooshed out of Charlie's lungs. "Damn it, Gus, when you said *she*, I thought—"

"Didn't mean to scare you, son." Gus clapped him on the shoulder. "But I think of the machines I repair as my girls." His smile didn't do much to change his gloomy expression. "When you live alone, you can get a little strange."

Rick gave Charlie a nudge in the ribs. "So, Gus, did your wife pass on? I've been living back in California, so I haven't kept up with all the news in Middlesex."

"Five years ago last month," Gus said. "I try to keep busy, but I still miss her. Good thing I have the repair business or I'd go nuts. Well, see you two boys later." Carrying his toolbox, Gus trudged over to his van.

"See?" Rick said. "Exhibit A. A repairman who is also extremely single."

Charlie watched Gus stow his gear in the back of the van. "I'm not sure I'd want either my mom or your mom to end up with Gus, if that's what you're leading up to. He would depress the hell out of them."

"You don't know that. I'm thinking he used to be cheerful. Look, it says right on his van 'Your Cheerful Appliance Repairman.' That lettering looks more than five years old. I'll bet when Gus was getting some, he was a regular Mr. Sunshine."

Charlie sighed. "No he wasn't. He's looked that way as long as I've known him."

"Well, okay, then. But he could still fix the machinery at the bakery. That's all I'm saying." Rick punched Eve's doorbell. "Was that the washing machine you were working on last night?"

"Yeah. I ran into some glitches."

"Glitches? You?" Rick shook his head. "You must be losing your touch, dude."

"I have a few things on my mind."

Eve came to the door wearing a bright yellow sweat suit.

"And there's one of them," Rick said under his breath.

Charlie had to agree. He broke out in a grin the minute he saw her standing there. "Hey, Eve."

"Hey, Charlie." As she let them in, she smiled back, but when her gaze drifted to Rick, her pleasant expression vanished. "I don't want you causing problems for my sister," she said as she closed the door behind them. "Denise is—"

"Eve, I wondered what you wanted me to do with all of this." Denise appeared from the back of the house, her arms full of Eve's hobby supplies. "Oh, hi, Charlie."

Charlie could see that Denise had been trying to create some order out of the chaos in Eve's house. He wished that he trusted her more with Eve's stuff. Because he didn't, it made him uneasy that she was poking through Eve's possessions.

Nevertheless, he had no absolute proof that Denise was untrustworthy, and he needed to be polite. "Hi, Denise. I'd like you to meet my cousin Rick Bannister."

"Ah, *Rick*. I've heard so much about you."

Charlie shot a glance at Eve, who merely shrugged and looked innocent.

"All good, I hope," Rick said.

"Let's say it was all interesting."

"I'd rather be interesting than boring." Rick took off his jacket and hung it on one of the pegs beside the front door. "You look like you could use some help with that." Before Denise could reply, he'd scooped everything out of her arms. "Where does it go?"

"That's the point." Denise looked at Eve. "I don't know what you want me to do with everything, but we have to put it somewhere so we can get the washer out."

Eve blinked. "We're taking the washer out?"

"I called a scrap metal place. They'll be out to pick it up first thing in the morning."

"Oh." Eve gazed at the pile Rick was now holding. "I'll get some garbage bags. We can give it all to the Salvation Army. I have some things under my bed that can go, too."

"Great." Denise started toward the kitchen. "I'll call for a pickup ASAP."

"Not necessary," Rick said. "Or at least we used to have a drop-off place by the post office. Charlie, is it still there?"

"It's still there." Charlie was impressed. When Rick needed to be weird to match up with Eunice, he showed his twisted side. But for organized Denise, he was ready with practical suggestions. No wonder Rick had such success with women. He could be whatever they needed.

"Then once we have this together," Rick said, "Denise and I can load it into the Subaru and take it down there." He smiled at Denise. "Sound good?"

Denise gave him an assessing look. "I'll also need some help getting the washing machine out to the driveway."

"I'm your guy."

"Rick and I can handle that," Charlie said. The death of the washer was partly his fault. The least he could do was help get the carcass outside.

"Nope." Rick shook his head. "Denise and I can take care of it. You and Eve have things to do in the garage. All we need is a few garbage bags, and we'll be all set."

"I'll get them," Eve said.

By the time Charlie had taken off his jacket and chaps, Eve was back with a box of black trash bags.

She handed them to Denise. "I've shoved a bunch of other hobby projects under my bed. You can get rid of all of them. From now on, I'm focusing on my inventions."

Denise nodded. "Okay. Rick, come with me."

Charlie watched them go down the hall and into Eve's bedroom. "What did you tell your sister about Rick?"

"That he was the kind of guy who prided himself on being able to get any woman he met into bed in a matter of hours." Eve turned to him. "The more I thought about it, the more I was convinced that his whole double-agent deal is an excuse to try and seduce two women in one day."

Charlie nodded. "Probably."

"That said, if he tells you anything you think I should know, please pass it on."

"I will." He looked into her eyes and saw a gleam of determination that hadn't been there before. "Sounds like you're not going to let anyone or anything stand in the way of completing this project."

"That's right." She hooked a finger into the open collar of his shirt. "And I want my chief consultant on the job." Backing toward the kitchen, she pulled him forward with just a feather touch.

He wasn't about to resist. "I'm at your disposal."

Her glance started at the top of his head and traveled

slowly down to his feet, lingering ever so subtly at his crotch. "All of you?"

"Every last molecule."

She laughed. "You sure know how to get a girl hot, Charlie Shepherd."

Chapter Twenty-four

Much as Eve longed to get it on with Charlie, she wanted to wait until the Subaru pulled away from the curb and they were completely alone. So she put him to work checking out the hovercraft's electrical system while she fired up her converter for the cooking oil they'd brought home from the bakery.

She left the kitchen door open because the sun was shining and the house's oil heater hadn't clicked on in some time. With the door open she could glance out once in a while and watch Charlie going over her hovercraft with a fine-tooth comb. She loved how he looked in his prescription safety goggles.

She also loved his thoroughness. She especially loved it when they were having sex. And they would be doing that before too long. She'd tucked a condom in the pocket of her sweat suit.

This arrangement, with Charlie in the garage and her in the kitchen, felt strangely traditional. She might be whipping up some biofuel instead of dinner, and he might be checking out her hovercraft instead of changing the oil in the family station wagon, but even so, Eve had a cozy feeling as the two of them attended to their separate chores.

She wouldn't mind if their chores had been more traditional. If she had Charlie around all the time, she might even learn to cook. He could be the kind of guy who would appreciate a lavender cake with dark purple frosting.

From the other end of the house came the scraping and clunking sounds of Denise and Rick maneuvering the washer down the hall and out the door. Eve hoped they didn't scratch the hardwood floors doing it, but knowing Denise, that wasn't a worry. Once the washer went out the front door with a thud, there was silence for a few minutes.

Then the front door opened and closed as they came back in to package up Eve's discarded hobby supplies. Eve couldn't listen to that front door close without remembering the creepy feeling of hearing it while she was in bed with Charlie. She didn't want that intruder to have been her sister. In point of fact, she would love to have dreamed the whole thing.

"Eve?" Charlie's voice coming from the garage had an uneasy quality to it.

"What?" She walked over to the doorway. "Did I screw something up?" She'd so hoped he'd give her a clean bill of health.

"I wish I could say that, but this doesn't look like something you'd do." He'd taken off the hovercraft's dashboard and was gazing at the wiring behind the panel. "Is this how you set it up?"

She looked at the wiring and felt a chill run through her. "No, I didn't. I'm positive of that."

"Then somebody disconnected everything and reconnected it to the wrong terminals. If you had the motor installed and started it up, you'd have a fire on your hands."

Eve gazed at the wires, then up at Charlie. She was picturing herself getting into the hovercraft, closing the hatch, strapping herself in and turning on the ignition. The cockpit was snug to conserve space. Getting in and out of it took some agility. Would she have been able to climb out before getting burned?

She swallowed. "I thought they were after the invention. I never thought they were after me."

"They might not be, specifically," Charlie said quietly. "My guess is that they don't want this thing to take off before they can sell the concept to the highest bidder."

"Maybe they've already done that."

Charlie shook his head. "I don't think so. Whoever it is wouldn't hang around once they'd clinched the deal. None of our suspects are AWOL."

"We don't know that." Eve could think of one person she hadn't seen since last night. "I'm assuming Eunice went off to work this morning, but we don't know that for a fact. She could be on her way to the Grand Caymans."

Charlie stared at the wiring. His voice was tight. "Call her."

Trembling, Eve hurried into the kitchen and grabbed the Middlesex phone book. She'd never called Patriots Independent Insurance Agency before, and she spent precious time tracking down the number. It wasn't made any easier because adrenaline was raging through her system.

She was furious. She'd worked so hard on this hovercraft. How dare anyone think they could steal the concept and get rich? How dare someone fool with the wiring and risk a fire that could burn her?

Finally she found the number for the agency and dialed it. Charlie came into the kitchen and put his arm around her shoulders. She wondered what she would have done without Charlie.

It was obvious that she'd been far too naïve. Someone

was willing to do whatever it took to keep her from profiting from the hovercraft design, and they didn't care what happened to her in the process. She hated to think someone she knew was that screwed up, but it looked as if they were.

"Patriots Independent Insurance Company. This is Eunice Pivens. How can I help you?"

For a moment Eve wasn't sure what to say. In the time it had taken her to find the number for the insurance agency she'd convinced herself that Eunice had made off with the hovercraft specs and was now headed to the tropics with her ill-gotten gain. "Um, Eunice! Hi! I was just . . . wondering if you were coming over tonight." She rolled her eyes at Charlie.

"Is that stud-on-a-stick going to be there?"

"You mean Rick?"

"Who else? I spent my lunch hour going over my notes from Gonaug. If you happen to see Rick, you can tell him I have a whole new repertoire lined up, if he's interested."

"I'm sure he will be."

Charlie abruptly moved away from her and glanced toward the kitchen doorway. "You guys about ready to leave?"

"We are." Denise stood just outside the kitchen while Rick hovered in the background, a bulging trash bag in each hand.

"Just a second, Eunice." Eve put her hand over the mouthpiece. "Thanks for taking care of that, Denise."

"No problem. Did someone call?"

"My neighbor." Glancing beyond Denise, she could see Rick gazing up at the ceiling. She hoped he was having a massive attack of conscience.

"Oh." Denise eyed the phone book on the kitchen counter. "I think we should cancel the exterminator. I won't be here to supervise, so it'll be a waste of time and money."

Eve wondered what would happen if she recorded

comments like that and played them back to Denise. Would she hear herself? Probably not. "I'll cancel the exterminator," she said.

Looking doubtful, Denise walked into the kitchen, aiming for the phone book. "That's okay. I can call on my cell, since you're using the phone."

Eve took her hand away from the mouthpiece long enough to snatch up the phone book and hand it to Charlie. "Would you please look up the number for Creepy Critters Exterminators?"

That stopped Denise in her tracks. She obviously had respect for Charlie's ability to follow through. "Fine. See you later, then." She backed out of the kitchen.

"Is someone there?" Eunice said. "I heard a woman's voice."

"My sister, Denise."

"Is that right? Well, if she wants a crack at Rick the Wonder Boy, she's going to have to go through me. I saw him first."

"Absolutely, Eunice. Anyway, I'll talk to you tonight, okay?"

Eunice chuckled. "I'll be there with my antennae on."

"You know, you might not want to—"

"Just kidding! I could tell you were freaked when I came to the door like that. You surprised me, that's all. I try to keep the kinkier stuff under wraps. Well, here comes the boss man. See you tonight!"

Eve disconnected the call and turned toward Charlie.

"Creepy Critters Exterminating," he said. "The number is—"

"Forget that." She tossed the phone on the counter and launched herself at him, crushing the phone book between them. "Kiss me. Kiss me right this minute."

He did. They bumped glasses and had to pull them off in the midst of a frantic meeting of mouths. The phone

book plopped to the floor and Charlie kicked it aside so he could pull Eve tight against him.

But that wasn't close enough. She worked at his belt buckle while he jerked down the zipper on her sweat-suit jacket.

"Oh, Lord," he murmured. "The purple bra."

"Just for you."

He took a moment to cup her breasts, bra and all. "Gorgeous. But it has to go." He quickly unfastened it and took her breasts in both hands. His breath ragged, he backed her up against the kitchen counter. "I thought they'd never leave."

"Me, too." Unzipping his jeans, she shoved her hands under the waistband of his briefs and pushed everything down over his hips. There. That was what she was after. She wrapped one hand around his erect penis and cupped his balls with the other.

He groaned. "You'd better have something handy to put on that equipment you're playing around with. I don't think we'll make it to the bathroom cabinet this time."

She stroked him lovingly. "I came prepared." Releasing him, she reached in the pocket of her sweats, pulled out the condom and held it up. "See?"

"When it comes to those little raincoats, I have twenty-twenty vision." His voice roughened. "Put it on me."

She laughed softly. "Is that an order?"

"Yeah." He sounded desperate. "Do it."

Woo-hoo! Her mild engineer had become a wildman! "Yes, *sir*." She had him fixed up in no time, and the process of doing that turned her on more than she could have believed.

"Ah, good." He pushed her sweats and panties down and lifted her up to the counter. The pots and pans still sitting there went flying in one direction, the phone in another.

The cool laminate of the counter caressed her hot bottom as he yanked off her sweats and panties and threw them across the room. No man had ever made love to her on the kitchen counter before. Trust an engineer to figure out how to work it.

Crouching down, he hooked her feet over his shoulders. "Wrap your ankles around my neck."

Bracing her hands on the counter, she shivered in anticipation. "Oh, *Charlie*."

"Hang on." Grasping her hips, he stood slowly until he was looking into her eyes again. "I'm coming in."

"I hope so." She held his gaze as he shifted his hips and thrust forward. She was so open, so wet and ready, that he had no trouble finding his way. In the time it took her to take a quivering breath, he was deep inside.

His pupils dilated. "This is good."

"It has promise." All her bells and whistles were going off. "Are you sure we have the right combination of lubrication and friction to create the maximum deployment of our resources?"

"I'm assessing that data now." He gripped her bottom and sighed. "You have some of the finest test equipment I've ever been able to get my hands on. Firm, yet adaptable."

"With added features." She contracted her muscles to give him an extra jolt of sensation.

His eyes widened and he drew in a quick breath. "That's a . . . valuable extra."

"I agree." She squeezed again, which ratcheted up her response.

He groaned. "Maybe we should continue with the test before we lose control . . . of the experiment."

"A constant risk."

"Testing in progress," he murmured as he eased back and pushed forward again. "It should be noted that the . . .

equipment conforms exactly to the intruding implement."

Her happiness muscles began to contract and she gasped in delight. "I can confirm . . . the efficacy of the intruding implement."

He stroked faster, watching her, looking deep into her eyes. "Then it's . . . producing the . . . desired test results?"

"Yes . . . oh, yes . . . Lubrication to friction ratio is . . . optimal. Resources will be . . . deployed soon." She kept her gaze fixed on his.

"Test nearly complete." His thighs slapped against hers as the room filled with the sound of their rapid breathing.

She whimpered as her climax hovered near. "Test results are . . ." Her orgasm hit. "In!" Crying out, she fought to keep herself steady as the waves of pleasure rolled over her. Through it all, she left her eyes open, her attention focused on Charlie.

"Ah, Eve. *Eve.*" With a massive shudder, he buried himself deep. There was a flash of heat in his eyes, but it was followed by something more, something far greater than physical passion.

She saw it, knew that the same emotion was reflected in her eyes. How could they help it? Like it or not, they were made for each other.

Then he closed his eyes and murmured something she couldn't hear.

"What?" she asked gently.

Opening his eyes, he allowed her to see all the caring there, and the confusion, too. "Too good," he said.

She swallowed. "Yeah," she said, her voice softened by both joy and sadness. "I know what you mean."

Battling a host of conflicting feelings, Charlie was very gentle with Eve as they disentangled themselves and picked up their discarded clothes. "You know I want to forget about the hovercraft and head for your bedroom," he said as they each began getting dressed.

"But you're not going to do that, are you?" Her blue gaze was quietly understanding.

"No."

"I didn't think so." She zipped the jacket of her sweat suit.

Longing tasted bitter on his tongue. "We need to do whatever it takes to get that hovercraft operational."

"And that's not all there is to it." She took a long, slow breath. "We're getting in too deep, aren't we?"

She'd said what he'd been unwilling to. He nodded. "I think the more we do this—"

"The more we have sex, you mean."

"Right." He searched her expression, hoping she would help him deal with the problem. "The more we have sex, the tougher we're going to make it on ourselves."

"So getting wild and crazy while Denise is out with Manny is off the table."

He groaned. "I wish you hadn't mentioned tables."

"You want to do it on the table?"

"I want to do it on the table, on the floor, on top of the hovercraft—"

"Now *there's* a heck of an idea." Her cheeks glowed pink. "Beats smashing a bottle of champagne over it by a country mile."

Charlie clenched his jaw against the rising tide of desire. He'd just had a mind-shattering orgasm, and he wanted more. "I've never felt this out of control. It's scaring the shit out of me."

She looked contrite. "It's my fault for suggesting the chaps. That's probably what started you thinking of unusual sexual experiences."

"I wish I could blame it on you, but I can't, unless you want to take responsibility for your amazing body, your incredible brains, your happy laugh, your sexy mouth, your unbelievably blue eyes, your . . ."

He stopped himself before he strayed into dangerous territory. He was ready to start describing parts of her that were better not put into words. Once he spoke those highly sexual words, he'd inflame himself even more.

"Were you about to mention my testing equipment?"

He gulped. Yes, he had been about to do that, and he would have dispensed with the euphemisms this time around. That was so unlike him to talk like that, but she brought out an earthy, hedonistic side he'd been blissfully unaware of until now.

"God, Eve." He shoved his hands in his pockets to keep himself from reaching for her. "I want you in ways I've never wanted another woman. I want to say things to you, do things with you, that go beyond what I've ever thought of before. I worry that I'm becoming obsessed with you."

She gazed at him, her color high. "I'm flattered. I think."

"I'm not trying to flatter you. I'm just telling you how it is."

"You know I would never ask you to stay in Middlesex because of me."

"I know. Just like I wouldn't ask you to leave this town you love." *Love.* The word felt thick and unwieldy in his mouth. He almost stumbled while saying it, probably because he'd been working so hard not to say it earlier, when he'd looked into her eyes and known it was the only word that described how he felt.

"Well, then." Eve cleared her throat. "If we've made the decision not to go back to the bedroom—"

"I have. Now all I have to do is get my cock to cooperate."

She lifted her eyebrows. "O-*kay*. I see we're no longer mincing words."

"Did I shock you?" He almost hoped he had. That might dilute some of this incredible sexual tension.

Slowly she shook her head. "Sorry. I'm not that easily shocked."

"Too bad."

"But I'm here to help. It's time to get to work on the hovercraft, Charlie. Let's channel some of this energy into the project."

He sighed heavily. "Thank you."

"If you'll change those connections, I'll have the new fuel available in a little while and we can test it in the new engine."

He nodded. "And if that goes well, then I'll help you mount it in the chassis."

A tiny smile lifted the corners of her mouth. "I could do a whole riff on that, but I won't."

"I'm grateful." He looked at her and wondered if he was the biggest fool in the world. He'd never find another woman who could talk like an engineer while she was having sex. He loved the way she did that.

Oh, hell. The truth was he loved *her*. And he wasn't planning on telling her that, because such a conversation was supposed to lead to a whole other conversation that ultimately resulted in rings and vows and happily-ever-afters.

"So, get thee to the garage," she said. "I'll be out with the fuel in a few minutes."

He hesitated, wanting one more kiss, one more chance to hold her and act out his increasingly erotic fantasies. But one more time wouldn't be enough. With every moment he spent in her arms, he was that much closer to giving up his dream, and that would poison ever special thing they shared.

Chapter Twenty-five

Two hours later Charlie added mental frustration to his sexual frustration. No matter how he adjusted the carburetor, the custom rotary engine wouldn't run smoothly. He'd brought the booklet Eve had loaned him and had gone over it a dozen times.

"It's the fuel," Eve said. "My converter isn't doing the job."

"It should work, damn it." At least his complete absorption in making the engine run right had somewhat compartmentalized his lust for Eve. The compartment threatened to break open whenever she hovered over him and her warm breath tickled his neck. But mostly, he could think about the engine and why it was being so stubborn.

Eve seemed to have similar powers of concentration. She kept testing the chemical content of the fuel. She'd brought her laptop out to the garage and was running some data on that as Charlie leaned close to the engine and listened to the sound it was making to see if that would identify the problem.

But it was hard to hear with that pounding going on in the background. Finally he lifted his head. "What *is* that?"

Eve glanced up from her computer screen and frowned. "Um . . ." She turned toward the garage door. "Someone's banging on the door."

"That's ridiculous. Why don't they just ring the doorbell?"

"They might have tried. I'll bet we wouldn't have heard it." She walked over to the garage door button and punched it.

"Wait! Put it down again! You don't know who's out there!"

Eve glanced at him, obviously realized that she'd been about to reveal her hovercraft to whoever was outside the garage, and smacked the button again, bringing the door down with a thud. "Whoops."

Charlie sighed. "We have to get this hovercraft operational and patented so we can forget about all this cloak-and-dagger stuff." He heard himself use the word *we* and winced. There was no *we* in this arena. He was a helper, and once his help was no longer needed, he'd be out of the equation.

The banging on the garage door started up again.

"I'd better see who it is." Eve got up and walked toward the kitchen door.

"I'll come with you."

She glanced over her shoulder. "You can keep working. I doubt if our saboteur would come by and bang on the garage door. That's not what you'd call sneaky."

"Sometimes bold is sneaky." He'd appointed himself her protector and he wasn't going to let some garden-variety intruder get past him just because they seemed too obvious.

She reached the entryway and looked out the peephole. "Nobody's there."

"That's because they're still banging on the garage door. They got encouraged when you started to open it." Charlie reached for the dead bolt. "I'll go out there and see who it is."

"I'm going with you."

As soon as Charlie opened the door, he saw a truck with equipment in the back and figured it out. "It's Creepy Critters Exterminating."

Eve groaned. "We didn't call them and cancel."

"No, and the Subaru just pulled up to the curb."

"Damn it. I hate this. Denise is so sure I can't handle things without her being around to organize me. Now I've just proved her right!"

Charlie came back inside and closed the door. Then he gathered Eve into his arms. He'd promised himself to be careful about doing that, but this was an emergency.

Tilting her chin with his forefinger, he looked into her eyes. "Listen to me. You are a genius."

"I am not! Don't you dare call me that!"

"Eve, embrace it." He held her close. "You don't have the kind of brain Denise has, or the kind of brain I have."

"I know. You don't have to rub it in."

"I'm not. I'd love to have your brain."

She wiggled against him. "I thought you wanted my body."

"That, too. But this is about what you have between your ears. It's exceptional, and you need to celebrate that, not feel inferior."

She took a deep breath. "That's not easy. Right now Denise is out there telling the exterminator that she left the job of canceling to me and I failed."

"She probably needs to do that to protect her ego.

She's only the normal kind of smart, the kind that gets top grades and scholarships. She's like me. We know how to catalog, how to sort and quantify. You're miles beyond that. Screw the call to the exterminator. Your mind is too big for that kind of junk."

She gazed up at him, her expression soft and yielding. "Charlie, don't take this wrong."

"What?"

"I'm in love with you. I can't help it. I don't know how I could help it, with the way you are. I know you don't want to hear that, but I have to say it or bust apart."

His chest grew tight. "Eve, I—"

The door opened and Denise barreled through, followed by Rick. "The exterminator just left." Her irritation was obvious. "You're going to be charged with the service call, because he did make the trip. I should have let him come in and inspect, I suppose, but I didn't want to deal with that right now." She stomped into the den and slammed the door.

Charlie released Eve and glanced at Rick. "That looks like more than exterminator-induced anger."

"Did you upset her?" Eve faced him, her eyes flashing. "So help me, if you forced yourself on my sister, I will see that you never work in fashion photography again."

Rick backed away, hands raised. "So help me, I didn't do anything! I was just trying to be nice!"

"I'll bet." Giving him a scathing look, she turned on her heel. "I'm going to go check on Denise."

The minute she'd disappeared into the den and closed the door, Charlie looked at his cousin. "What gives? I thought you were going to try to seduce her, not make her furious."

Rick seemed bewildered. "I think there's something wrong with that woman."

"What do you mean?"

"I have my routine, and it works like a champ. First we have coffee and maybe something sweet, like a piece of pie. We stopped by the Rack and Balls and did that. I didn't finish mine, on account of it was my second piece of the day, but I wanted to stick with my game plan."

"Okay." Charlie doubted even Rick would try anything funny while Archie was watching from the bar.

"Then afterward I usually find a quiet place to park, preferably with a view. I was a little handicapped, because it's daytime and I couldn't find a good view of city lights. In fact, even at night, Middlesex is short on city lights, but—"

"Rick, get to the point. Please tell me you didn't try to force yourself on her."

"No way, dude! We were sitting there, and I did my opening move of running my finger up and down her arm and telling her how beautiful she is, especially in that light. That line works, regardless. There's always *some* kind of light, unless it's pitch-dark, in which case I turn on the dash lights and say she looks good in the glow from the instrument panel. But I didn't have to do that this time. There was plenty of light."

Charlie ground his back teeth together. "You tried to kiss her, didn't you?"

"Well, yeah. How can you get your hand under her bra if you don't start with a kiss?"

"You tried to put your hand under her bra?"

"Don't get so excited. It's all a smooth transition, cuz. Well, normally. I move in for the kiss and start on the buttons of the blouse at the same time. It usually works great."

"I can't believe this."

"I couldn't, either! She hauled off and whacked me!"

"You don't say." Now that Charlie looked more closely, he could see a bruise forming on Rick's cheek. "Sounds like it was justified."

"She could have just said no." Rick's tone was injured.

"Maybe you didn't give her the chance."

"She had plenty of time between the stroking-her-arm part and the kissing-and-unbuttoning stage. But anyway, that's not the important thing. The important thing is what she said about her sister during the pie and coffee part. I quizzed her about Eve, like I said I would."

"And?" Charlie hated to take information from such a gonzo source, but he was desperate to figure out who was stalking Eve and her project.

"She said Eve was so pretty as a kid that nobody paid any attention to a gifted older sister. She said that was fine with her, because everyone left her alone, but nobody likes being ignored, right?"

"No, they don't." And now Charlie was really worried.

"She might be this big-deal professor, which is getting her a certain amount of attention, but I think she's worried about what kind of attention Eve might get with the hovercraft. I think she'd love to see that whole thing go in the crapper, if you want my opinion."

"Thanks, Rick." Charlie was reluctantly grateful, although he wished his cousin had been more subtle with the seduction routine.

"You're welcome." Rick smiled, then he winced and put a hand to his cheek. "She's one strong chick."

Strong enough to pry open a door with a crowbar? Charlie had seen enough cop shows to know that jealousy could be a powerful motive, but his heart ached for Eve. She would never want to face the fact that her sister would rewire the hovercraft and risk a fire that could cause her serious harm.

"Remember, this operation is only half done," Rick said. "I have to find out what's going on with Eunice. Do you happen to know where she works? I thought I'd drop by and set something up, maybe get her in the mood by taking her to dinner."

Charlie almost laughed. "I think you've mixed up your women. That might have been the way to go with Denise, but I don't think Eunice needs any prompting."

"You know, I would have switched things around if I could, but Denise already had a date with Manny for dinner, so I had to work with what I was given. You're right, though. I can do takeout with Eunice. Hey, maybe she likes food sex."

Charlie shook his head. "You're incorrigible."

"Is that good or bad?"

"Neither. Anyway, Eunice works at Patriots Insurance Agency. It's on the corner of Main and Second."

"Thanks, dude." Rick zipped his jacket. "I'll be back, probably in the morning sometime. It's a tough job, but somebody has to do it. Which reminds me. Did you and Eve have some quality time while we were gone?"

Charlie gazed at his cousin. "I don't think I'll answer that."

Rick grinned. "That's an answer, all by itself." He punched Charlie on the shoulder. "Way to go, stud. See you."

After Rick left, his words echoed in Charlie's head. *Way to go, stud*. Yeah, that's what he'd acted like, some horny bastard who couldn't control himself. He'd spent too much time getting laid and too little time doing what he'd promised, which was to help Eve get her hovercraft off the ground. Way to go, stud.

At first Eve had thought she'd have to comfort Denise after her upsetting experience, but apparently Denise had enjoyed the drama of her stomping-into-the-den routine. She was in a better mood than Eve ever remembered seeing her. Obviously she'd never had two men on the string. Although she made it clear that Rick wasn't her type, he seemed to have given her ego a much-needed boost.

Eve located the red sweater, hooker shoes, and flashy jewelry she'd agreed to loan Denise. Then she promised to come back and do her sister's makeup after Denise had showered and dressed. With Denise safely ensconced in the shower, Eve returned to the garage to check on Charlie.

She found him hunched over the rotary engine, his prescription goggles on as he tinkered and swore softly to himself.

"I didn't mean to abandon you," she said.

He glanced up and pulled the goggles down around his neck. "No problem. You had to see about Denise. Is she okay?"

"More than okay. I've never seen her happier."

Charlie looked surprised. "She wasn't insulted? From what Rick said, he acted like a Neanderthal."

"I think he did, but if you ask me, she thoroughly enjoyed pushing away his unwanted advances. I don't think she gets all that many of those."

"Hmm." Charlie's expression closed down a little.

"What?" But she didn't really have to ask. Charlie was making mental notes beside Denise's name in his list of suspects. "Did Rick say something?"

Charlie's gaze was sympathetic. "She really is upset about the hovercraft, Eve. The modeling career is bad enough, but she doesn't want you getting attention for something like this."

Eve's stomach clenched. "She said that?"

"Not in so many words, but she told Rick that she'd been ignored as a kid, because you were so pretty."

"I've heard that a million times before. She's never tried to hurt me as a result of that complaint."

"You've never tried to build a hovercraft before," he said gently.

"It's not her." Eve couldn't imagine her sister switching wires knowing the pilot of the hovercraft could get burned as a result.

"How can you be sure?"

"Because she suggested a safety modification, that's why. I meant to tell you sooner, but . . ." But she'd been overcome with lust. Then she'd forgotten about it until now.

"I know." Charlie looked into her eyes. "We've let ourselves get way too distracted. I'm not letting it happen again, at least not until we have this baby launched."

Eve nodded, knowing he was right. They had to finish this project. Whoever was trying to steal the idea might not care about using alternative fuel. For Eve, that was the main reason to get the hovercraft on the market.

Of course, once they did and the danger of someone stealing it was gone, Charlie would leave. And she wanted him to follow his dream. But she couldn't hold back her sigh of regret.

"This hovercraft is a fantastic concept, especially using the biofuel." Charlie's voice was soft. "I'd say it's worth a little personal sacrifice."

"So we'll both do our part to promote cleaner air?" She wished she felt more noble and less deprived.

"Yeah. All your hard work needs to amount to something. The invention needs to get out there and you deserve recognition for making that happen."

"Eve, are you available for the makeup session?"

Eve turned to find Denise standing in the doorway to the kitchen. Even without the jewelry and makeup, the transformation was amazing. In the low-cut red sweater, black slacks, and hooker shoes, Denise looked nothing like a professor and quite a bit like date bait.

Eve tried to tell from Denise's expression whether

she'd heard any of the conversation and whether jealousy was eating a hole in her sister's stomach. But Denise had perfected a blank look years ago and she was wearing it now.

"Sure," Eve said. "Let's do it."

"You look great, Denise," Charlie said. "Eve was telling me you had a safety modification suggestion for the hovercraft."

"I guess she didn't consider it very important if she's just now telling you about it."

"I thought it was a great idea." Eve wished she'd mentioned it earlier, just so Charlie would know that Denise was thinking of ways to protect her, not ways to do her in. "But we've been concentrating on the engine, and I temporarily forgot." She glanced at Charlie. "She thinks we should attach a lightweight rubber bumper around the outside rim."

Charlie glanced at the hovercraft and nodded. "Good suggestion. We're hoping not to run into anything, but it wouldn't hurt to have something like that, just in case."

Eve noticed that he was still using *we* when she would be the only person in the hovercraft, at least until after the first flight. But she let that go for now. "Yeah, I think it would be a smart move."

"I'd call it essential," Denise said. "Considering that you have no experience in building something like this, it's bound to crash. I hope you're going to wear a helmet, too."

"I hadn't thought of that." She'd been so intent on getting the thing in the air that she'd given no thought to whether she'd be in danger doing it.

"I have two motorcycle helmets," Charlie said. "We can use those. I probably would have thought of it eventually, but thanks for the suggestion, Denise."

Eve couldn't let him keep talking like that. "You're not going up in it, Charlie. We've already had that discussion."

He smiled at her. "And I'll bet we'll have it again. I'm the one with a pilot's license. You need what I can bring to the table."

Oh, yes, I certainly do. "We'll talk about it later," she said.

"Talk about it now, if you want," Denise said. "I'll go start putting on the foundation. I know enough to do that much. But if you want my advice, whoever takes that purple thing out for a test run will suit up like an astronaut. That hovercraft is a death trap." She walked back into the kitchen, her heels clicking on the tile.

Eve tried not to feel deflated by Denise's comments, but it wasn't easy. Denise had always been able to take the air out of her sails. In any case, Charlie had to see that Denise was concerned about her little sister's safety, which removed her from the list of suspects.

She glanced over at him and lowered her voice. "See what I mean? She wants bumpers and space suits, so I'll be protected. It can't be her."

Charlie didn't jump right in and agree. Instead he was disturbingly silent.

She grew impatient. "Come on, Charlie. Surely after what she just said, you can't still think that she's the one."

He took a deep breath. "Oh, she could definitely be the one. She's just hoping to keep you from being hurt when you crash and burn."

Chapter Twenty-six

Charlie had hated like hell to give Eve his verdict on Denise, but he saw her safety suggestions as a potential attempt to keep her machinations from becoming lethal. She might long to stop her sister, but she didn't necessarily want to kill her in the process. Just her spirit.

In all fairness, he didn't have absolute proof of Denise's guilt. But somebody had taken off the dashboard of the hovercraft and switched those wires around. That might have happened right before he and Eve had come home from the bakery the night before. If they'd arrived later, whoever it was might have done even more damage.

He didn't know for sure who that person was, and for now all he could think to do was get the hovercraft up and running. So while Eve helped her sister prepare for her big date with Manny, he put on his goggles so he could concentrate on figuring out why the rotary engine wasn't running the way it should.

About an hour later, Eve came out to the garage. "She's gone."

Charlie looked up from his work and pulled the goggles

off again. But that's all he intended to pull off. This afternoon they'd been all over each other the minute they'd known they were alone. He wasn't going to give in to that temptation again. Maybe the temptation wouldn't be so great this time, anyway. Eve didn't look in the mood for sex.

Instead she was frowning at him.

"I'm sorry if my opinion about your sister upset you," he said.

"You're entitled to it, but you're wrong."

"I hope I am."

Eve sighed. "We had the best time just now while I was working on her hair and makeup. Then I had her try a bunch of different jewelry. We were *giggling* together. That was the second time today, which is a miracle. We never giggle together."

Charlie didn't know what to say. He'd love to be able to tell her that he'd changed his mind about Denise, but he hadn't. Denise was a complex woman, and having a giggle-fest with her sister didn't mean she wasn't planning to sabotage the hovercraft any way she could.

"I've had a chance to think about this." Eve leaned against the workbench, close enough to talk but not close enough to touch.

Charlie figured that was no accident. "And what do you think?"

"Let's say we give ourselves through the weekend to get the hovercraft operational."

Charlie nodded. "That's reasonable."

"I could take it for a test flight either Saturday or Sunday night, depending on when we think it's ready."

He decided not to argue with her about who would be going up in the hovercraft. "Okay."

"You said you had some ideas about who I should market it to."

"I do."

"Do they have offices in New York?"

"At least two of them. I can check on the others." He sensed a nervous energy arcing between them. This was what they'd talked about, the culmination of her dreams and the end of his participation in her project. Neither of them knew what would happen to their relationship after that. "Want me to call tomorrow and see if I can make a couple of appointments for Monday?"

"Yes. Yes, I do." She was still frowning, but her blue eyes gleamed with determination.

He smiled, wanting to lift the mood. "I think for the hell of it I'll identify myself as your secretary."

"Just so you don't identify yourself as my boy toy." Her frown eased and she smiled back.

"That would be okay with me, too."

"I know it would. Temporarily." She gazed into his eyes. "Ah, Charlie . . ." Then she pushed herself away from the workbench and started pacing. "The appointments are the first thing I wanted to talk to you about. The second thing is—" She turned to face him. "I want to catch whoever's trying to sabotage this project."

He should have seen this coming. She wouldn't be satisfied to foil the person's attempt. She'd want to know who was doing it, especially if it might be her sister. "I assume you've figured out a way to do that."

"Yep." She clasped her hands in front of her.

"Hit me." He tried not to think about the purple bra and panties she was wearing under that yellow sweat suit.

"Tomorrow night, almost everybody in town will be at either the bachelor or the bachelorette party."

"Wow, that's tomorrow night already?" Charlie had lost track of everything but Eve and the hovercraft.

"Yes, and Denise and I are invited, along with all the women in town, including Eunice, I'm sure."

"And all the guys are invited to the bachelor party." Charlie could see what she was getting at. "We'll leave the hovercraft as bait, and each of us monitors who disappears from either party."

"Bingo." She balanced on the balls of her feet, as if she wanted to chase down the perps right this minute. "We'll keep in touch by cell phone. If either of us notices someone's been gone a long time, we call the other one and both of us will head back to the house. We'll catch them red-handed."

"One thing. I'll do the confronting. You'll stay in the car."

She waved that aside. "We're not dealing with some seasoned criminal. I'll have my pepper spray on me, if that would make you happier."

"You have pepper spray?" He'd never pictured her aggressively facing down an attacker, but he could picture it now. She'd decided to take charge of this situation, and damned if he didn't find that sexy.

"I only carry it when I go into the city, but this time I'll make an exception. I wouldn't use it on Denise, though. I can take her."

"So you *do* think it might be Denise."

"I don't. But I'm not sure. And that's why we have to do this. So you're up for it?"

"You do have a way with words." As he gazed at her, he tried to concentrate on the plan. But the image of her yellow jacket unzipped to reveal the purple underwire bra, size 36B, wouldn't go away.

"Stop looking at me like that, Charlie. It makes me want to jump your bones and I know you don't want that."

"Oh, I do want that. I want that very much. But I'm going to be a grown-up and work on the hovercraft tonight, and tomorrow, and the next day—whatever it takes for us to get you ready for your appointments on Monday."

"And I appreciate that," she said. "I really do. I'm impressed with your self-discipline. I want to be you when I grow up."

"No you don't." He thought of all the joyous, spontaneous, and creative facets of her personality, all those things that he loved about her. "Don't ever grow up, Eve. If you do, you'll stop inventing purple hovercrafts."

"But I might be able to work in this garage with you and not want to strip you naked and run another test on the compatibility of our equipment."

He fought the urge to walk over there and let that happen. "I have a short-term solution for that problem."

"You're going to weld the zipper shut on your jeans?"

"No, but almost as good. I'm going to call my mother and Aunt Myrtle and ask if they'll bring us dinner."

Aside from having unlimited sex with Charlie, Eve couldn't have dreamed up a more fun time than eating the wonderful food that Rose and Myrtle brought over and hearing their plans for the bakery.

They ate Yankee pot roast, homemade rosemary bread shaped like a pair of breasts, and a salad better than anything Eve had ever made for herself, and she knew her salads. They sat at Eve's kitchen table and discussed whether the bakery needed repainting to match the new line of items being offered. Or rather, Eve, Rose, and Myrtle discussed. Charlie concentrated on his food.

After the meal, Rose and Myrtle went out to admire the hovercraft and tell Eve what a brilliant young woman she was. By the time they left, she was floating on a cloud of loving acceptance and never wanted to come down.

"Thank you for inviting them," she told Charlie. "They make me feel as if what I'm doing is worth something."

"It is." Charlie watched her from the opposite side of the hovercraft, as if keeping that between them would insure that nothing sexual would happen now that the chaperones were gone. "If my mom and Aunt Myrtle help you believe it, then you should spend more time with them."

"I was thinking about that tonight." She hesitated, unsure if he'd think she was presumptuous in imagining she could in any way fill his shoes. "But if you went out to Nevada, I could . . . sort of . . . stay in touch with them. I couldn't repair things, but Gus could do that. If they needed anything else, I could help out. It wouldn't be the same as if you were here, of course," she added quickly. "I wouldn't want you to think—"

"You're looking for ways to help me leave." He said it wonderingly, as if he couldn't quite believe she'd do that.

"I know how you feel about them. I wondered if you were at all uneasy about leaving. Not that you should be." She hoped she hadn't opened up a can of worms. "They're very resourceful, but I saw an expression on your face tonight that made me wonder if you were a little worried about that."

He sighed. "I tell myself not to be, but . . . yeah, Nevada's quite a distance away, and with Rick out in California, that leaves no relatives close by."

"Well, for what it's worth, I could check on them now and then."

"That's . . . that's quite a gift you're offering, considering how you could just as easily ask me to stay."

She shook her head. "No. No, I couldn't. I know what it's like to feel as if you're not doing what you were meant to do."

"Yeah, I guess you do." He swallowed. "I'm staying over in this part of the garage, because I'm afraid if I walk around this hovercraft, I'll start kissing you and never stop."

She quivered. "I don't know how we're supposed to act like adults, now, Charlie. Unless it's X-rated adults."

"Oh, hell." He started around the hovercraft. "What's another—"

"I'm back!" Denise waltzed into the garage, a dreamy expression softening her sharp features. "Manny's turning his portfolio over to me. Can you imagine?"

"That's serious stuff," Charlie said. He glanced at Eve and winked. "It's not often a woman gets to see a guy's portfolio."

"That is so true!" Denise twirled in place. "Most men would rather get naked than reveal the contents of their portfolio. It indicates *such* a degree of trust."

"So the evening went well?" Eve didn't have to ask. She just liked seeing her sister in this gaga condition and wanted to pump it for all it was worth.

"Let's put it this way. We agreed that the bakery should change its name to Hot Buns and become a franchise. If that happens, we will go into business together." She announced it with the same flourish as if they were engaged to be married.

"Hot Buns?" Charlie cleared his throat. "Have you mentioned that to my mom and Aunt Myrtle?"

"Actually, Manny called them on his cell. They loved the name."

"Wonderful," Charlie said.

"It *is* wonderful." Eve sent a warning glance in Charlie's direction. The name of the bakery was the least of the problems. Eve didn't want her sister to come crashing to earth when she discovered Manny wouldn't leave California. "Assuming the franchise works out, where would you and Manny locate your first bakery?"

Denise's eyes sparkled. "In the nation's breadbasket, of course."

"You'd move to the *Midwest*?" Eve couldn't have been more shocked if Denise had said she was piercing her navel. That could be coming next, for all she knew.

"Heavens, no. I would only visit. And Manny would visit. We'd time our visits to coincide, while we checked on our franchise." She gazed off into space, as if imagining those visits as becoming exceedingly conjugal.

"Oh." Eve was trying to picture this arrangement, with Denise managing from the East Coast and Manny from the West Coast, with periodic "meetings" in the middle. Denise obviously had high hopes for these meetings.

"If an X-rated bakery does so well in a town like Middlesex," Denise continued, "then it should make money hand over fist in a small town where the most exciting thing is a potluck at the Grange Hall and bingo in the church basement. Manny and I will introduce them to Booby Buns and Bawdy Breadsticks. The money will pour in."

"Sounds like a plan." Eve wondered what the folks at Yale would think about this little sideline. Yikes.

"It could work," Charlie said grudgingly. "I'm no marketing whiz, but you may be onto something."

"Oh, we are." Denise stretched her arms over her head. "And I *am* a marketing whiz. We have a bright future. Well, it's been a long day. I'm off to bed."

Charlie watched her go. "That might take care of everything."

"What do you mean?"

He glanced at her. "Now she has her own exciting new project. She might not be so jealous of yours."

"That's assuming she's the saboteur." Eve still wanted it to be someone else, preferably someone she didn't know. Although it was illogical, a bushy-haired stranger would work fine with her.

"In any event, I need to get this damned engine to work right." He moved toward the workbench and put on his goggles.

"Charlie, you sound tired." Exhaustion was creeping

up on her, too. Neither of them had gotten much sleep last night, and they'd been going full throttle all day. "Why don't you go home and get some rest?"

Charlie turned toward her. "You have to be as tired as I am."

"So, I'll get some sleep, too. We'll tackle this first thing in the morning."

He glanced around the garage. "That's not going to work."

"Why not?"

"Because while I'm gone and you're asleep, someone could booby-trap the hovercraft."

She must be *really* tired, because she'd forgotten that the house wasn't secure. Not only that, if Denise happened to be the culprit, she was already in residence and could sabotage at her leisure.

"I'll sleep out here tonight," Charlie said.

"Alone?"

"Yeah." He didn't look happy about it. "I don't know who we're dealing with, or how desperate they might be."

"Then I'm definitely staying out here with you! We've already established that you're no Chuck Norris."

"And you are?" He smiled at her.

"No, but it would be two against one."

"Unless there are two of them. Seriously, I'd be a nervous wreck if I thought I had to protect both you and the hovercraft. I wouldn't be able to sleep at all."

That was the only argument that made sense to her. "Okay, I'll take the cushions off the couch and get you fixed up. Because you need sleep now. Your eyes are half-closed."

"Does that mean I have bedroom eyes? I always wanted bedroom eyes."

"Charlie, you most certainly have bedroom eyes. You're all about the bedroom. When you kiss me, you have bedroom lips. When you touch me, you have bedroom hands. Everything about you screams bedroom, especially your very sizable—" The sound of the doorbell prevented her from mentioning the most bedroom thing about him, the part that she'd be dreaming about tonight while she slept all alone in her round bed.

"Let me get that," she said. "Then I'll bring your cushions and some bedding out to you. You just relax."

"Sorry, but we're getting that together." Charlie followed her into the kitchen. "Although I have to say I'm encouraged whenever someone rings the doorbell instead of using a key."

Eve groaned as a piece of logic hit her between the eyes. "Charlie, why didn't we just have the locks changed today?" She couldn't believe she hadn't thought of it.

"Because we're exhausted and not thinking straight. Don't feel bad. We couldn't even manage to cancel the exterminator appointment, let alone think about changing the locks. No wonder I can't break the combination on that rotary engine. My brain is fried."

Then she thought of something even more damning. "Why didn't Denise suggest it?" She turned and looked at Charlie, her chest tight with fear. "Denise thinks of *everything*."

"Maybe not everything," he said gently.

She blew out a breath. "Well, at least we can still set the trap." Now she absolutely *had* to catch the intruder. If they didn't find out who was doing this, she'd always suspect her sister, which would affect their relationship forever.

When she got to the door she checked the peephole. "It's Rick."

"Is he wearing antennae?"

"No, but his hair looks kind of wild and there's a hickey on his neck." Eve opened the door. Because Rick's seduction attempt had actually improved Denise's mood,

Eve felt more kindly toward him. "Come in," she said. "I thought you'd still be with Eunice."

This time Rick was trying to imitate an alien although he sounded more like a chipmunk. "Greetings, earthlings! I am visiting your quaint dwelling to inquire if you have any extra C batteries! Ours seem to be deceased!"

"Bummer." Charlie coughed and cleared his throat, as if he'd been about to laugh. "Take my advice. Use alkaline next time."

"Dude, I don't care what kind they are, just so they keep the vibrator going. We are in desperate circumstances over there. Eunice tore her place apart looking for spare batteries. Man, was she fuming. She was *this close* when the thing up and died."

"TMI, Rick." Eve grinned as she walked back toward the garage. "I'll see what I can find. I think the ones in my flashlight work."

"I hope so," Rick said. "I offered to go down on her, but she said the vibrator would make her climax more intense."

Charlie shook his head. "Modern science is ruining us for the simple things of life."

Eve wanted to say that it hadn't ruined her, but she wasn't quite as willing to share the details of her sex life as Rick seemed to be. She found the flashlight under the workbench and switched it on. "Works fine."

"That's great," Rick said. "The point is, we can't do the actual thing yet, because she has some plans for me. I think they involve that vibrator, so the batteries are critical to the operation. And you know, everything shuts down at nine in this town except the Rack and Balls, which doesn't carry batteries. I called to check."

This time Charlie did laugh. "I'll bet Archie got a kick out of that."

"Yeah, he thought it was pretty funny. It took him a

while to answer, because he couldn't catch his breath from laughing so hard."

Eve emptied the batteries out of the flashlight and handed them to Rick. "Bon appétit."

"Thanks." Rick hesitated. "Um, is it okay if I talk about . . . the investigation?"

Eve's good humor vanished as she remembered what Rick had said to Charlie earlier today. "I understand you think my sister might be guilty."

"She might be," Rick said, "but to be fair, Eunice could be, too."

"What makes you think so?" As much as Eve didn't enjoy the conversation, she had to admit that Rick might get information from Eunice that no one else would.

"She doesn't think it's fair that you got to be so tall."

Eve stared at him. "So what, she's going to cut me down to size?" She was so sick of all the jealousy apparently aimed at her. "Sheesh. I can't help that I'm tall! I can't help that I seem to be what the fashion designers want!"

"I know that," Rick said. "It's not your fault, and Eunice was doing okay with it, but now you might make a bunch more money with the hovercraft. She wasn't worried about that before, but after Charlie said it was a good thing, she . . . well, she just thinks you have it all, and it's not fair."

"Damn it." Eve began to pace. "Why can't people be happy for others? Why can't they be grateful for who they are instead of wishing they could be somebody else? And besides, my life isn't perfect. I can't seem to find the right person to share my—" She stopped abruptly as she realized with horror what she'd been about to say. Exhaustion was a dangerous thing.

She didn't dare look at Charlie. "Anyway, it doesn't matter, I guess. I'm going ahead with this project no matter who gets bent about it."

"Yes, you sure are," Charlie said quietly.

"Okay, then." Rick cleared his throat. "I'll bid you two kids good night. Thanks for the batteries."

After he left, Eve went into the living room and started pulling cushions off the couch. She was using more force than necessary because she was tired, frustrated, and disillusioned.

"Let me help." Charlie started to pick up a cushion.

"Never mind. I've got it." Her jaw was clenched and her whole body vibrated with pent-up emotion as she scooped up all three seat cushions and carried them, balanced precariously, into the garage.

"I wish I could be the man you need," he said gently.

"Well, you can't." She let the cushions fall to the garage floor.

"Wait. Don't you want to put something down first? They'll get all dirty."

"It doesn't matter." She stomped back to the living room and down the hall, where she opened a cupboard and pulled out sheets and a couple of spare blankets. Then she snagged a pillow from her bedroom and started back toward the garage.

"It does matter. There could be motor oil on the floor of that garage."

"So what? Pretty soon I'll be even richer, so I can buy everything new. Didn't you hear the news? In no time, I'll have it all."

"Eve . . ." His voice was pleading as he followed her through the kitchen.

"Don't get me wrong." She kicked the cushions into line and crouched down to tuck the sheet around them. "I'm grateful for everything you're doing. I'll be happy to give you a percentage. I should have mentioned that earlier. What's fair? Fifty percent?"

"I don't want anything."

She laid both blankets on top of the makeshift bed and placed the pillow at the head of it. "I know." She stood, gazing at him, her heart breaking. He wanted nothing from her and she wanted everything from him. "Sleep tight." She walked out of the garage, closing the door after her.

Chapter Twenty-seven

Charlie didn't sleep great, but he slept. Throughout the night he kept waking up. First he'd wonder where he was. Then he'd remember and start dealing with the problems inherent in the sofa cushions. The total length of them turned out to be about ten and a half inches shorter than he was, plus they kept separating whenever he moved. He was also concerned about how dirty they were getting lying on the garage floor.

Once he'd worried about the sofa cushions for a while, he'd lie awake thinking about the chance of an intruder trying to get into the garage. They'd have some trouble, because he'd decided to bring his bike inside and park it next to the door. If the bike fell over, then Charlie would know he had trouble. In case that trouble arrived, he'd laid a twelve-inch crescent wrench on the floor within reach.

After he'd thought about the odds of someone trying to come through that door, he'd get around to thinking about the most troubling subject of all—Eve. He'd remember how sad she'd looked standing there beside the bed she'd

made for him. He'd relive the time they'd spent together—
the pool-playing, the hovercraft work, the sex, especially
the sex.

Then he'd try to talk himself into staying in Middlesex
for the rest of his life so he could be with Eve. When that
didn't feel like the right solution, he'd rehearse speeches
in which he asked her to come with him to Vegas. Then
he'd give up on that option as unworkable, punch the pillow a few times, a pillow that smelled like her perfume,
and finally go back to sleep.

When his bike fell over with an ungodly crash, he
leaped to his feet. A faint strip of light showed under the
garage door, but that could be headlights. He had no idea
what time it was. Heart pounding, he grabbed the wrench
and prepared to defend the hovercraft.

Denise poked her head out the door and a shaft of light
poured through the opening. She looked at the fallen bike.
"What the hell is going on?"

"I decided to stay here through the night. What are you
doing up?" *Planning to sabotage the hovercraft?*

"It's morning, hotshot. Eight already."

Charlie glanced at his watch. So it was. If she was
planning a sabotage move, she was getting a really late
start on it. "Is Eve still asleep?"

"Yeah, she's out cold, so I decided to make some coffee. Then I heard somebody snoring out here, so I thought
I'd better investigate."

"I don't snore." No doubt she was making this up as
she went along, to justify her coming out to the garage to
do . . . something.

"How would you know? You're asleep when it happens."

She had him there. He didn't know if he snored or not.

Denise glanced at the bike. "That's not a very smart
place to park it, you know."

"I meant to park it there."

She met his gaze. "I see. So that you'd know if anybody tried to get in the garage."

"Could be." *And you did.*

"Hey, what's happening?" Eve's voice drifted from inside the kitchen. "Is Charlie okay?"

"Charlie's fine." Denise continued to hold Charlie's gaze, as if looking away would signal a weakness. "I just tripped his booby trap by knocking over his bike, which he'd parked in front of the door."

"Oh." Eve's voice drew nearer. "Why did you open the door?"

Aha. Charlie was delighted that she'd asked.

"I heard him snoring. It startled me. I didn't know he was out there."

"I'm sorry, Denise. I should have left you a note."

"I don't snore," Charlie said again. All he needed was backup on that issue and Denise's excuse for opening the door would be destroyed.

Eve's face appeared over Denise's shoulder. "Um, yes you do."

Shit.

Denise gave him a superior smile. "Coffee?"

"Sure, thanks." So Denise had won that round, but Charlie wasn't going to relax his guard. She was a smart cookie, but so was he. Besides that, he was spoiling for a fight.

Sleep had renewed Eve's optimism about life. She supposed a little jealousy was a natural thing, and she decided not to let it bother her so much. It helped that Denise was in a cheerful mood. Her sister offered to go shopping and be in charge of food during the day so that Eve and Charlie could concentrate on the hovercraft.

Eve suspected the offer to shop was tied in with a desire to visit the bakery and see Manny again. When Denise came home with more Cock Rings and Booby Buns along with eggs, bacon, and lunch meat, Eve's suspicion was confirmed. The trip put Denise in an even better mood.

In contrast, Charlie looked like a thundercloud. He'd made one brief trip home to shower and shave, and she'd hoped that would improve his disposition. It hadn't. On the way back he'd picked up some rubber tubing to use for the hovercraft's bumper, but when she thanked him, he replied in a curt monosyllable. Then he went back to tinkering with the rotary engine and swearing under his breath.

She was tempted to send him home and forget having him help on the hovercraft. As for the phone calls he planned to make, she could do that if he'd give her the info. But she definitely needed him tonight in order to try and catch the saboteur. Or maybe not.

Maybe she could rig up some sort of physical trap that would detain anyone who came through the garage door. Creating such a thing would take time away from the hovercraft, but it would mean she wouldn't have to depend on Charlie, who was currently a royal pain in the butt.

At last she confronted him. "It's obvious you don't want to be doing this," she said. "So if you'll give me the names and numbers of the people you were going to contact in New York, I'll take it from here."

He pulled off his goggles and stared at her, his jaw tight. "I don't think you can accomplish everything all by yourself."

That hurt. "So now you're doubting me, too? Well, I most certainly can do it by myself! In fact, that's exactly what I will do, and show you all!"

He looked as if she'd slapped him. "That isn't what I meant."

She stood there, quivering. "Then what did you mean?"

"I meant that you're under a tight deadline to finish

this project, you have somebody trying to sabotage you, and now you're trying to lay a trap for them. That's a hell of a lot to expect of one person, any person. If anyone could pull it off, you could, but . . . I want to help."

"You do? You aren't acting like it."

He groaned. "I know, damn it! But I can't get the engine to run the way it should, and I can't figure out who the devil is after you. But the worst thing is that every time I look at you I want to rip off your clothes, and yet I know sex isn't going to solve any of our problems and will probably create more." He sighed in obvious frustration. "I'm not reacting well to all that, and I'm sorry."

"You really want to rip my clothes off every time you look at me?" That perked her up considerably.

"Every time. I picture that sexy underwear and go nuts. But then I have to stop myself. We have work to do, and your sister's here, and . . . well, we have some problems that aren't exactly worked out."

She smiled. "So you get grouchy when you don't have regular sex?"

"I didn't think so." He looked sheepish. "But it looks that way, doesn't it? At least when it comes to you."

"Then I guess I can take your grouchiness as a compliment."

"I'll try to be more pleasant, I promise."

"Don't worry about it." Her heart felt considerably lighter now that she knew the primary source of his dark mood. She put on her goggles. "Let's get to work. We have lots to do."

Late in the afternoon Charlie decided he would never get the engine to run as smoothly as he wanted it to. Perfection wasn't achievable, much as he wanted that. So he and Eve mounted the engine in the hovercraft. By the time they wound the rubber tubing around the chassis and got that attached, they were out of time.

Both parties would start in thirty minutes. Denise was already dressed and waiting in the living room.

Because Charlie wasn't sure if Denise would make a sudden appearance in the garage, he kept his voice low. "Let's double-check the plan. If any of our suspects are gone from either party for more than ten minutes, we speed-dial each other, but we also head immediately for the house."

"Right. And make sure your cell is on vibrate. The parties will be loud."

Charlie had a moment of anxiety. Maybe this wasn't such a good idea. It could put her in danger. "Eve, promise me something. If you get there ahead of me, wait for me."

"Only if you promise the same thing."

"I don't have to promise." He wondered if this was an oversight on his part. "I don't have a key to get in."

"And I don't have a spare."

"Of course not." He laughed softly. "You gave them all away. There are probably keys to your house for sale on eBay."

"Very funny."

"Yeah, I'm a regular David Letterman. Listen, please be careful. Don't go charging into the garage if someone's there. I should arrive ahead of you, but in case I don't, just wait."

"Okay." She looked up at him. "How about a kiss for luck?"

"We can spare about one minute. Can we keep it to that?"

"I doubt it." She wound her arms around his neck. "Kiss me anyway."

He didn't need to be asked again. He'd been aching to

kiss her for hours. His lips meeting hers felt like homecoming, like the first right thing he'd done all day. He'd never been sure what his place in life was supposed to be, but holding her seemed to be part of the puzzle.

She tasted so damned good. He knew the minute was up, but she'd pressed her body close to his and opened her mouth to let him explore with his tongue. He could do that all night. She had the most—

"Do you think you could wrap it up? We're going to be late. I don't like being late."

Charlie opened one eye, and Denise was leaning in the doorway to the kitchen. She wore another one of Eve's slinky sweaters, silver this time, and she'd borrowed a few pieces of jewelry to go with it. He thought it was a good sign that Eve hadn't immediately leaped away from him the minute she'd heard her sister's voice.

She did, however, slowly pull back. "We do need to go."

"I know."

"You two don't *have* to go," Denise said. "If you want to stay here and, uh . . . work, it's no skin off my nose."

"No, I want to go." Eve stepped out of Charlie's arms and walked toward her sister. "I like Jill, and I'm happy for her and David. Besides, I want to get the reaction to those cookies we worked so hard on. I'll be ready in no time. We won't be late."

"If you say so." Denise sent Charlie a parting glance. "See you later, Charlie."

"Bye, Denise." He wondered if he would see her later, in this very garage. Then he had a sudden thought. "Are you two riding over there together?" If so, and Denise took the car to come back and do mischief, Eve would be stuck at the party.

"Actually, no," Denise said. "I'm supposed to meet Manny later on, so we're going separately. I was just going to follow Eve to make sure I found the right place."

And so you'll have wheels to get back here during the party? The setup was too perfect, the motive too strong. She'd suggested that Eve and Charlie skip the party while knowing full well that her sister wouldn't give up a chance to bond with the women of the town she'd adopted. He felt sorry for Eve, but he thought he'd found the culprit.

An hour later, Charlie was watching a belly dancer Archie had imported from New York and wondering why Eve hadn't called yet. He felt sure Denise would have slipped out of the bachelorette party by now. And if not Denise, then Eunice. This was their golden opportunity.

He'd been keeping an eye on Manny, Kyle, Darrell, and Ed, but he didn't really think any of them were guilty. Finally he slipped over to a dark corner and called Eve.

She answered immediately. "Got something?" Music with a heavy bass thumped in the background, along with a chorus of feminine laughter.

"Not me. Are you sure you're watching?"

"You betcha. Right now both my sister and Eunice are very involved with one of the three male strippers."

"Three? We've only got one belly dancer over here."

"Too bad for you."

"You're not watching the strippers, are you? You have to concentrate."

"I can watch the strippers while I concentrate."

He fought down that stupid green monster. She'd had enough jealousy in her life without him adding to the mix. "Well, I guess I'd better—" Someone tapped him on the shoulder. "Just a minute," he said to Eve. "Don't hang up." He found that he liked talking to her. He missed her.

He turned to find David, the eager groom, standing beside him. Charlie envied the guy having all his matrimonial ducks in a row. And he had a great fiancée. Jill was blond and gorgeous, almost as pretty as Eve. She was also a terrific person. She was the hairdresser for both his mother and Aunt Myrtle, and Jill was responsible for giving them their red hair every couple of months.

"Have you seen Rick around?" David was several drinks into his evening and had gotten to the happy and congenial stage. "The guy's so generous that I hate to bug him, but he offered to take a few pictures, and I'd love to get some with the groomsmen and the belly dancer."

"I'm sure he's here somewhere. I'll check the bathroom." Charlie walked in that direction and put the phone back to his ear. "Eve, I'll call you back in a minute. I have to get Rick to do his photographer thing."

Rick wasn't in the bathroom, though. In fact, he wasn't anywhere in the Rack and Balls. When Charlie finally put on his coat and went out to the parking lot, he discovered the Subaru was no longer there.

Of course there was an explanation. Of course. Except a sick kind of certainty was settling into Charlie's gut. He speed-dialed Eve.

"Hi, there. Listen, nobody's moving here."

"Well, someone did here. I'm heading over to your house."

"Who? Kyle? Ed and Darrell? I can't believe that Manny—"

"Rick." Then he hung up and hopped on his bike. Maybe nobody would be at Eve's house. Maybe Rick had a very good explanation for leaving the party. Charlie should call his cell, in fact.

Driving one-handed, he punched in Rick's number. And got Rick's voice mail. Well, that didn't mean anything. Rick could have . . . what? Charlie couldn't imagine what would make his cousin leave a party, especially one where there was a seminaked woman dancing.

But stealing the hovercraft design made no sense at all.

The guy was a successful photographer with big-deal clients. Wasn't he?

When Charlie pulled up in front of the garage, everything looked perfectly normal. There was no garage light on, no Subaru parked at the curb—nothing out of the ordinary. But he had no idea how long Rick had been AWOL from the party. He hadn't been watching Rick. Rick had not been a suspect, damn it! He was his rich cousin!

Now he had a better appreciation for how Eve had felt every time he'd mentioned that her sister might be doing this. People you'd grown up with weren't supposed to engage in criminal behavior. They were supposed to operate under the same value system you did.

Eve swung into the driveway and the garage door rolled up, activating the light inside. She hopped out of her car. "Everything looks fine! Nobody's here. How long was Rick gone, anyway?"

"I don't know." Charlie hated like hell to admit that. "I had no idea that it might be him."

"It might not be." Eve walked into the garage and started looking around. "He might have another reason for leaving the party. Let's not jump to conclusions."

Charlie followed her into the garage. She made him feel lower than a mealybug. He'd been all set to blame her sister, but she was trying to keep Rick from being a suspect. He could learn a lot from Eve, if he allowed himself to forget his plan to leave Middlesex. And he could have a damn good life, too. And plenty of hot sex.

"Charlie!"

His heart lurched into high gear. She'd found something.

"Is this what I think it is?" She crouched down and peered under the workbench.

Charlie knelt down beside her and looked up. "Holy

shit." He was staring at a small homemade bomb. Worse yet, he recognized the design. It was the same one Rick had joked about building when they were kids.

"Can you stop it?"

His mouth went dry. "I don't think so. It's a cheesy bomb, and if I mess with it, it could go off in my hand." Rick had moved the tank of hydrogen right next to it. The bomb was small, but the hydrogen would amplify the blast and take out the garage, including the hovercraft. Charlie quickly moved the tank a distance away.

"Charlie." Her voice was tense. "It's showing one minute, forty-six seconds."

"Yeah." In red digital numbers. Rick would have chosen red numbers for dramatic value. "A minute forty-three, now. Let's go. We'll call the police once we're out of here."

"No. We can't leave the hovercraft."

"I care more about you than the damned hovercraft!"

But she was already beside it and lifting the canopy. "I'm flying it out of here."

"Damn!" Charlie knew it was no use arguing with her. She'd already climbed in the cockpit. By the time he dragged her out and hauled her down the driveway, the bomb would explode.

As she started to close the canopy over her, he grabbed it and climbed in.

"No, Charlie! Get out! Run!"

"No way." He latched the canopy. "Go."

The engine didn't catch. Charlie stopped breathing. Then it did catch. It was rough, but it was running. The hovercraft lifted off the cement. In spite of the fear pumping through him, Charlie felt the wonder of that. "Punch it!" he yelled.

Eve pulled back on the throttle and the hovercraft shot out of the garage so fast Charlie's head snapped back.

She miraculously sailed over his bike, but they were headed straight for the house across the street. "Pull up, pull up!"

She brought up the front of the disk so sharply he saw nothing but the starry sky. "Level it out!" When this was over, he was so giving her flying lessons.

"Charlie, it *works*." She was laughing as they skimmed over the top of the house. "It—"

Her garage exploded, rocking the hovercraft so that it tipped sideways.

"Use your rudder!" Charlie cried out as the hovercraft began to veer toward a leafless oak tree. "We're going to hit that—"

With a snap, crackle, and pop, they flew into the tree. Eve killed the motor and the hovercraft balanced there, cradled by the branches like some futuristic tree house.

Charlie took a deep breath. "I think it might be time to call 911."

Chapter Twenty-eight

"No, wait." Eve pointed down the street. "Here comes the Subaru."

"That son of a bitch. Returning to the scene of the crime."

Eve had to admit the evidence was damning, but she hated to think Charlie's cousin, who was also Myrtle's son, would do such a thing. "Are you sure?"

"I'm sure. That bomb was exactly like one he talked about building when we were kids." Charlie unlatched the canopy. "And he almost got us both killed. I don't want him getting away."

"Me, either, but I'd rather you didn't fall out of the tree and bash those valuable brains of yours. We need a fire truck."

"Yeah, and that will scare him off." Charlie eased out of the cockpit. "You wedged us in here pretty good. I should be able to climb out without dumping you."

"That would be nice." Eve was already assessing the branches on her side of the hovercraft. If Charlie could climb out, so could she.

"Just sit tight." He gripped a limb of the tree. "If you see him drive away, call 911. Otherwise, assume I've got him under control."

"Okay." She said it as convincingly as possible, so he wouldn't get suspicious that she was following him down this tree.

"I mean it. Don't try getting out of this tree."

"Okay."

He gave her one last glance. "Seriously."

"Right."

He swung down, suspended from the branch. Eve leaned over to watch. With his long arms and legs, he wasn't more than three or four feet above a snowbank. Once he dropped with a soft thud, she pushed herself out of the cockpit onto the smooth surface of the hovercraft.

As she did that, she noticed that the rubber bumper had been a huge factor in keeping the hovercraft snugly tucked into the tree. Without that, the hovercraft might have tilted and fallen to the ground below. Denise, far from being the villain of the piece, might have helped save the day.

On Eve's side of the hovercraft the branches formed more of a ladder effect, so she didn't have much trouble dropping down to the snowy ground. Once she was on the ground she glanced toward her house and gasped. The blast had destroyed the garage, blowing off the roof and sending debris everywhere. Little tongues of flame consumed whatever flammable things were left in the garage.

But that wasn't the only casualty. The blast had lifted Charlie's bike and tossed it on top of her car, where it had crashed through the roof. Both car and bike seemed totaled.

Rick stood looking at the destruction, his body completely still. He was probably in shock. Eve had to believe he hadn't known that she and Charlie would be anywhere near the blast, and for all Rick knew they were both dead as a result of his actions.

Charlie took advantage of that moment when Rick was riveted by the horror of what he'd done. Creeping up behind him, he had him in a choke hold before Rick knew what was happening. The funny thing was, Charlie apparently had wasted all that force, because once Rick realized who had grabbed him, he dropped to his knees, sobbing.

Charlie released him and walked around to face his cousin. He flexed his fingers as if he'd love to pound on Rick for a while, except Rick wasn't giving him a good opportunity to do it.

"You're alive." Tears streaming down his face, Rick gazed up at Charlie. "Is Eve . . . ?"

"She's fine." Charlie's tone was clipped, his expression filled with rage. "No thanks to you, asshole." Unzipping his jacket, he pulled out his cell phone and punched in 911.

"Where . . . where is she?"

"Sitting in her hovercraft across the street. That's in fine shape, too, by the way." Then he spoke into the phone. "Yes, we have an explosion." Charlie gave Eve's address and hung up.

"Actually, I'm not across the street." Eve walked over to stand beside Charlie. "I'm right here."

Charlie glanced at her and sighed. "I knew you wouldn't stay there. I knew it."

"Then why did you tell me to?"

"It's what guys do."

Rick looked from one to the other. "You're both alive. Thank God! I was so afraid you were both . . ."

"So what's your story, Rick?" Charlie stood there tapping his cell phone against his palm. "You'll have to give it to the cops in a minute, but I want to hear it now. You owe us that much."

"Good Lord!" Manny came loping up the street, followed closely by Kyle. "What happened here?"

"Your boss blew up Eve's garage," Charlie said. "He's been trying to steal the hovercraft project for some unknown reason. In any case, he'll soon be going to jail, so you may need a new job."

"The hell he's going to jail." Manny came striding forward. "He owes too much money."

Rick let out a wail. "Peterson. Dear God, Peterson. I'm a dead man."

"What?" Eve glanced quickly at Manny. "What's he talking about?"

Manny cleared his throat. "We only have time for the short version. Ricky likes to bet on the ponies, but he's not all that lucky. He's into our boss Peterson for a sizable chunk of money. He either pays up by next week or . . . let's just say that Peterson isn't a forgiving kind of guy."

Charlie looked from his cousin to Manny. "So you two work for this Peterson?"

"Yep."

"I can get the money!" Rick staggered to his feet. "The hovercraft didn't work out, but I can get it from my mom. She didn't want to give it to me before, because she didn't know I was in trouble. But if she knows that I'm history if I don't get the cash, she'll come up with it. She can use the bakery as collateral."

"That's nuts," Eve said. "You're not going to put the bakery at risk."

"Damn straight," Manny said. "The bakery is my future. I've been wanting to get out of this business for the past year, anyway. Denise and me, we've got plans."

Sirens sounded in the distance. Eve wasn't sure she

had all the particulars, but she needed to have a strategy in place before the police and the fire trucks arrived. She faced Rick. "I can get you out of this. I can say that I left a welding torch on and it was too close to the hydrogen tank."

Rick stared at her. "Why would you?"

"Yeah," Charlie said. "Why? This idiot almost blew us to kingdom come."

"I know that, but he didn't mean to." Eve gazed at Rick. "And you're Charlie's cousin and Myrtle's son. I happen to be very fond of both people and hate to bring them pain."

"It won't bring me pain," Charlie said. "I'd love to see him wearing stripes, or orange, or whatever they put on them these days."

Kyle edged his way into the conversation. "I hate to say this, but he wouldn't last long in jail. Peterson has connections. But if Manny and me let him get picked up by the cops, we'll get whacked for losing him."

Eve began to wonder who her sister had hooked up with. "Are you two hired killers?"

"Nah," Kyle said. "We're glorified babysitters. Our job is to make sure nobody has to be killed."

"Oh." Eve still didn't like the connection, but Manny had said he was quitting. And she was running out of time. She turned back to Rick. "Here's my offer. I won't press charges and I will help you get the money out of my hovercraft project, which is obviously what you need to do."

"*Eve.*" Charlie sounded beyond upset. "This clown deserves nothing!"

She glanced at him. "Are you prepared to have him killed? And Manny and Kyle along with him?"

"No, but there has to be another answer."

A squad car pulled up at the curb, followed by a fire truck, lights flashing.

Eve grabbed Rick by the lapels of his coat. "If I let you off, you have to promise that you'll move back to Middlesex and watch out for your mother and aunt. And you have to do a good job, or I'll expose what you did here. I might not be able to prosecute by then, but I can ruin your photography career."

Charlie groaned. "I hate this."

"Promise me!" She looked into Rick's eyes.

"I promise." Rick heaved a sigh. "Thanks, Eve."

Eve looked over at Charlie. He was gazing at her and shaking his head. But the way she looked at it, she had no choice. And as long as she was giving away her hovercraft, she might as well get something back, something that might help the man she loved.

Two hours later Charlie joined the crowd that had gathered in Eunice's living room. Eunice had arrived home from the bachelorette party to discover the catastrophe next door. She'd immediately invited Rick, Eve, Charlie, Manny, and Kyle to hang out at her house. Manny had called Denise and told her where he was, so she'd joined the group soon afterward.

Charlie was determined to stop Eve from giving away her invention. He'd found out exactly how much Rick owed and figured if he cashed out his retirement account, sold all his electronic equipment, and floated a loan, he might be able to scrape together most of it. He wasn't planning to let Eve do this thing, especially when he'd decided to stay in Middlesex to be with her.

It might have been the moment they'd lifted off the garage floor that had brought him to that decision. He wanted to be with somebody who generated that kind of excitement. He wanted to be with her forever. If that meant staying here and working for the ML&P, he'd do that.

So it was settled. He'd pay Rick's debt and Eve could

get the money she deserved from the hovercraft. Rick could go wherever the hell he wanted. Charlie didn't think he'd ever be able to trust the guy again.

But he needed to talk to Eve alone, and that didn't seem likely right now. She was huddled with her sister, Denise, having some deep sisterly discussion. At least one good thing had come out of this. Eve had already thanked Denise profusely for suggesting the rubber bumper, which even now was keeping the hovercraft stable up in the tree. In the morning they'd get a crane to haul it out.

Between Eve's gratitude and Manny's admiration, Denise was blossoming. Even the sharp angles of her face seemed softer. Charlie thought he might be able to tolerate her as a sister-in-law, after all, assuming Eve said yes.

In another corner of the room, Rick was pouring out his heart to Eunice. Her initial shock at hearing what he'd done had apparently turned to sympathy. Better Eunice than him, Charlie thought. Once he'd heard the whole story—how Rick had broken down the back door while Eve was gone and then swiped Eunice's key and made a copy so he had access after that—Charlie had been ready to land into his cousin.

Rick swore he hadn't watched while Charlie and Eve had sex, but Charlie wouldn't take bets on it. And the moron had mixed up the wires by accident. He'd set up his camera on a tripod so he could take pictures of himself "working" on the hovercraft, and in his rush, he'd reattached them to the wrong terminals.

Charlie's cousin was a big screwup who had almost gotten two people killed. For Aunt Myrtle's sake Charlie was glad Rick wouldn't end up in prison or worse. Someday Charlie might even find it in his heart to forgive the guy, but not tonight, not when Eve had almost died because of what his cousin had done.

"Okay, everybody." Eve stood. "Denise and I have come up with a game plan for Monday morning. She and I will go into the city with Rick to market the hovercraft concept. I'm going to be billed as the talent, Rick will be identified as my manager, and Denise will be our deal negotiator. I—"

A cell phone rang. Rick turned pale. As everyone stopped talking, he reluctantly reached for the phone clipped to his pants pocket.

"That would be Peterson," Manny said in a low voice.

Charlie left his chair and moved toward Rick. In spite of his anger, he didn't want his cousin to die at the hands of a mobster.

Rick's hand shook as he flipped open the phone. "H-hello?"

Eunice wrapped her arm around his shoulder and held on tight as the room went completely quiet. No one even seemed to be breathing.

Rick listened for a moment. "Uh, thank you. Yeah, it was a little bomb I made." He licked his lips as he held the phone to his ear. "Well, thanks. Thanks so much. Okay. Have a good flight." Then he closed the phone and looked around the room in dazed wonder.

Eunice shook him gently. "What did he say?"

"I can't believe it." Rick swallowed. "He congratulated me. He thinks I blew up the hovercraft. He drove by the garage and thought—"

"What do you mean, he drove by the garage?" Charlie grew rigid. "He's here?"

"I'm afraid so," Manny said. "Flew in Wednesday night. Had some business in New York so he decided to come up here and check on his investment."

Charlie thought about Rick's statement that he hadn't stayed to watch Eve and Charlie make love. *Maybe it was*

Peterson. He hoped Eve wouldn't think of that, but one glance at her face told him she had. Shit.

"He's on his way back to JFK." Rick's voice was a little steadier. "Seeing the garage blown up renewed his faith in me."

"So he didn't notice the hovercraft up in the tree?" Charlie couldn't imagine anyone missing that.

"It's not all that easy to see," Kyle said. "With it being dark out and the hovercraft painted purple. Besides, Peterson was looking at the messed-up garage. He wouldn't have any reason to look in the other direction. As a hiding place, that tree isn't bad."

Eve gazed at Kyle. "Either you or Manny could tell him the hovercraft still exists. After all, you work for him."

"I don't think we'll be telling him, right, Manny?"

"Right. In fact, this is my last job for Peterson."

Kyle nodded. "Mine, too. I'm ready for a change."

"Well!" Eve clasped her hands in front of her. "Then let's move on, shall we? As I was saying, that's the plan for the trip to New York on Monday. I guess Manny and Kyle need to be there."

"We have to stick around until Peterson gets his money," Manny said. "We can't give our notice until this job's done." He smiled at Denise. "Besides, I want to see how my prospective business partner negotiates this deal."

"Then we'll call you business consultants," Eve said. "I imagine Eunice has to work, and Charlie, you probably do, too. But either of you can come along, if you want to."

Charlie moved toward her. It was now or never. "Eve, before this gets set in concrete, can I talk to you alone for a minute?"

Rick winced. "I wish you'd used a different expression, cuz."

"Aw, they don't do the cement overshoes anymore," Kyle said. "That's so last century."

"Nothing's going to happen to Rick," Eunice said. "Right, Eve?"

"That's right." She glanced at Charlie, a question in her eyes.

"It's important," he said.

"Okay, but where—"

"Go on back to my bedroom," Eunice said. "Last door on the left. If you don't come out in an hour or so, we'll know the discussion got really serious. Oh, and feel free to use anything you find in there." She winked at Charlie.

Charlie had no answer for that. He cleared his throat and gestured for Eve to go ahead of him down the hall. "This feels like girl-boy parties in eighth grade," he muttered.

"Seven Minutes in Heaven," Eve said over her shoulder.

"Yeah." And he'd been good at it, too. He'd always liked kissing girls. Now he had one in particular he wanted to kiss . . . for the rest of his life.

He followed Eve into the bedroom. It was dark in there, so Eve flipped the light switch on the wall next to the door, which activated the blue lights they'd seen the night they'd come over here looking for Rick. The sound system came on at the same time, playing the theme from *X-Files*.

Charlie couldn't help glancing around. Anybody would have, after Rick's description. Sure enough, there were the eyebolts fastened to the far wall, with velvet ropes dangling from each one. The quilt on the king-sized bed featured Mulder and Scully from *X-Files*.

Next to the bed sat a machine with a probe thing attached, which Charlie decided was the muscle stimulator. A serious-looking vibrator lay on the nightstand. And then there were the feather dusters, the pots of fluorescent paint, and various bottles of oil that glowed different colors.

"Maybe she actually was abducted by aliens," Eve said.

"You know, I don't really care." Charlie closed the door. "Come here, you." He took off his glasses and tucked them in his pocket. "I need to hold you. We've just been through a hell of an experience."

"I would agree." She snuggled against him and gazed up into his eyes. "Do you think Peterson was the one who watched us?"

"I think we need to forget about it. He's gone, and that's all that matters."

She sighed. "You're right." Then she smiled. "The blue light makes you look like an alien."

"You, too." He pushed her glasses to the top of her head and framed her face in both hands. "But I recognize you. I'd recognize you anywhere."

"Same here."

He looked into her adorable face. How he loved doing that. "I'm not leaving Middlesex."

"What?" She backed out of his arms. "Charlie!"

"I'm staying. And I can get the money to pay my worthless cousin's debt, so I don't want you turning over a dime of your money from the hovercraft. And that's all there is to it. Come over here and kiss me. I really need a kiss right now."

She stayed where she was. "Are you staying in Middlesex because of me?"

"Um, sort of."

"That's dumb. You'd be miserable."

He shook his head. "Not with you around. When we lifted off in the hovercraft, it hit me. This is all I need, to be with you. Everything I needed was inside that hovercraft."

"Isn't that interesting?" She began to smile, and her lips were a deep shade of purplish-blue. "I had the same thought."

He wanted to kiss her so much he had trouble absorbing what she'd said. "What do you mean?"

"When we were both in that hovercraft, I realized all I wanted in the world was right there with me."

"No, that's not right. You love this little town. You want to make your home here, and I want to help you do that. We'll buy Ed and Darrell's Christmas tree farm and put a house there. We'll put a pool table in the basement. We'll—"

"Charlie, you're not listening."

He had to admit he had a tough time listening when he wanted to kiss the breath out of her. "Eve, we'll stay here and raise a family. You needed a home base, and this is it."

"I thought I needed to live here, but I figured out that all I really need is a place to come home to."

He tried to understand. He really did. But he wasn't getting it. "I'm confused."

"So was I, until we took off in the hovercraft. I loved flying away with you, knowing we'd come back. It doesn't matter if we take off for Vegas, or anywhere you want to explore. We'll come back here for visits to see your mom and Myrtle. We'll stop at Hot Buns and the Rack and Balls. We'll bring the kids, although we'll have a little explaining to do about grandma's pastries."

"Eve, I—"

"Don't you get it? We'll have a place we both know and love, a place to come home to."

"Oh." He was beginning to see, and the possibilities glittered in his mind.

"You always had that, which was why you wanted to leave. I didn't have that before, but I do, now. We'll get married here, of course, but then we'll leave, knowing Middlesex is here when we need a hometown fix."

"Oh, God. Are you sure?" He was afraid he'd misunderstood, and he really wanted to make sure that they had this straight. "You'll go with me to Hoover Dam?"

"I'll go with you to the moon." She stepped closer.

"Space travel's still too experimental. I have no plans to do that."

"Oh, no?" She moved in close and ran a finger up and down the buttons of his shirt. "I was thinking if we went back to your apartment, we could get to the moon in no time at all."

With a moan of happiness, he gathered her close. "I love you."

"That's convenient." She wound her arms around his neck. "Because I love you, too. What do you say we get out of here and run our equipment through another testing session?"

Just the suggestion of that was all he needed to fire up his intruding device. "We have a small problem. My bike is stuck in the roof of your car."

"I've already discussed that with Denise. Typical for my sister, she has it all figured out. Rick's staying here with Eunice. Manny and Denise are dropping Kyle off at your mom's house on their way to a little B and B Denise knows about. Which leaves Denise's car conveniently for us."

"I'm growing fonder of your sister by the minute."

"She likes you better too now that you don't consider her a criminal."

"I'll try to make that up to her."

She stroked his cheek. "Just think, you'll have years to do that."

"Years. I like the way that sounds."

"Me, too. And it starts now. Ready to leave?" She glanced at the eyebolts in the wall. "Unless you think we should—"

"Who needs that?" He let himself taste her lips, just a little. "I'm going to build us a trapezium-shaped bed. With big bedposts."

"Tonight?"

"Soon." Releasing her, he took her by the hand and led her to the door. "In the meantime . . . we have chaps."

Where Are They Now?

Eve Dupree Shepherd is a multimillionaire as a result of her many inventions, including the now-famous Skimmer hovercraft and the more recent Rocket Girl personal propulsion system. She is the spokesperson for her inventions, which are marketed through Techno-Thrills, a New York–based company. Eve's also polishing her pool game and plans to try the professional circuit in the next six months.

Charlie Shepherd is a systems consultant for many large hydroelectric plants in the western U.S. His expertise also is solicited by new hydroelectric installations in developing nations all over the world. Charlie and Eve return to Middlesex every April to celebrate their wedding anniversary and every December for little Rosie's birthday. Rosie was Eve's special Christmas present to Charlie nine months after they said "I do."

Rosie Myrtle Shepherd, age three, is an experienced traveler who already speaks several languages and has constructed a working Skimmer for her Barbie.

Denise Dupree Flores divides her time between her classes at Yale and her numerous Hot Bun franchises, which she co-owns with her husband, Manny Flores. Their twins, Kyle and Kyla, age three, are already working simple algebraic formulas which astound their nanny and namesake, Kyle Harrington.

Rose Shepherd and Myrtle Bannister have turned the Hot Buns operation over to Denise and Manny Flores so that they can concentrate on their new venture, Naughty Knits. Business is booming. Myrtle has given up smoking. Again. Rose recently turned down an offer of marriage from Galloping Gus Tedder, appliance repairman. But Gus is not giving up.

Rick Bannister and Eunice Piven Bannister have opened a glamour photography studio in Middlesex, Connecticut. Business is sporadic, but during lulls Rick and Eunice take remote-control nude photos of themselves in the midst of uninhibited behavior. They've decided against having children, wisely realizing that rugrats would interfere with their spontaneous sexual activities.